For Chris Wallis

**Susanna Gregory** was a police officer in Leeds before taking up an academic career. She has served as an environmental consultant, worked seventeen field seasons in the polar regions, and has taught comparative anatomy and biological anthropology.

She is the creator of the Matthew Bartholomew series of mysteries set in medieval Cambridge and the Thomas Chaloner adventures in Restoration London, and now lives in Wales with her husband, who is also a writer.

Also by Susanna Gregory

# SUSANNA GREGORY

# THE HABIT OF MURDER

THE TWENTY-THIRD CHRONICLE OF
**MATTHEW BARTHOLOMEW**

sphere

SPHERE

First published in Great Britain in 2017 by Sphere

1 3 5 7 9 10 8 6 4 2

A CIP catalogue record for this book
is available from the British Library.

ISBN 978-0-7515-6263-7

Typeset in ITC New Baskerville by Palimpsest Book Production Ltd,
Falkirk, Stirlingshire
Printed and bound in Great Britain by Clays Ltd, St Ives plc

Papers used by Sphere are from well-managed forests
and other responsible sources.

Sphere
An imprint of
Little, Brown Book Group
Carmelite House
50 Victoria Embankment
London
EC4Y 0DZ

An Hachette UK Company
www.hachette.co.uk

www.littlebrown.co.uk

# Clare in the 1300s

Sheepgate Lane

◄ To Cambridge

Hawe Ditch

Chilton Ditch

Water Meadows

Vicarage

Rutten Row

Church

Bell Inn

Grym's House

Churchyard

Swan

Heigh Row

Hermitage

Outer Bailey

Gardens

Nethergate

Inner Bailey

Cistern Tower

Austin Priory

River Stour

Approximate Scale

| 0 | 500 | 1000 | 1320 Feet = ¼ Mile |
|---|-----|------|---------------------|
| 0 | | 1 | 2 Furlongs |

# PROLOGUE

*Cambridge, 28 March 1346*

It was the worst day of Richard de Badew's life. Two decades before, he had founded a new College, which he had proudly named University Hall. It had started out as two cottages, but he had worked tirelessly on its behalf, and it now owned several large houses and a sizeable tract of land. Its membership had grown, too, from three Fellows to eighteen, and Badew ensured they were always paid on time even when it meant hardship for himself. University Hall had flourished under his watchful eye. Or so he had thought. Unfortunately, its Fellows disagreed.

He looked at them as they stood like peacocks in their ceremonial finery. All were young, greedy and ambitious, and thought they deserved the best of everything – a larger salary, a bigger library, newer rooms and smarter robes. Badew had done his best to oblige, but he was not a very rich man, and he had been forced to refuse some of their more outlandish demands. So what had they done? Gone behind his back to the wealthy Elizabeth de Burgh, known as the Lady of Clare, and asked *her* to take over the role of major benefactor instead.

It was an act of treachery that had wounded Badew to the core.

His first instinct had been to wash his hands of the lot of them and have no more to do with the place ever again, but then he had reconsidered. Why should he make things easy for the damned ingrates? So, in an act of defiant retaliation, he had deployed the only weapon

1

he had left to him: refusing to sign the quit-claim – the deed whereby all rights and claims to the property would pass from him to the Lady. He had become quite an expert at devising reasons as to why he could not do it – the scribe's writing was illegible, the wording was wrong, an important clause had been omitted, he had lost his seal.

He had managed to stall and dissemble for ten long, gratifying years, but even he had run out of excuses eventually, and the exasperated Fellows of University Hall, sensing victory at last, had arranged for him to put his name to the quit-claim that very day.

Because he had caused them so much aggravation, they had spitefully invited a crowd to witness his final defeat. They included not only the Lady and several members of her household, but a host of scholars and townsfolk as well. Glancing around, Badew saw there were only two he could count as friends among the entire throng – Saer de Roos and Henry Harweden, who stood behind him, each with a hand on his shoulder as a gesture of solidarity.

The 'ceremony' was taking place in University Hall's lecture room, a handsome chamber with tapestries on the walls and a huge fire snapping in the hearth. It was uncomfortably hot, and Badew was not the only one who mopped sweat from his brow as young Master Donwich made a gushing, sycophantic speech about the Lady's largesse. His mind wandered back to the day when he had founded the place – a whole new College born with a single stroke of his pen. He had been the University's Chancellor at the time, a man at the height of his powers.

And then Donwich stopped talking and everyone looked expectantly at Badew: it was time to sign. Truculent to the last, Badew picked up the document and began to study it, aware of Donwich exchanging anxious glances with his cronies. Good! Once they had his signature, they would be rid of him for ever, so it was his last chance to be irksome.

As he pretended to read, he was pleased to note that it was not only the Fellows who were becoming riled by his antics – so was the Lady of Clare, who considered herself far too important to be kept waiting by the likes of him. Widowed three times before she was thirty, she had inherited a vast fortune, which had given her an inflated sense of her own worth. Well, it would do her good to learn that money could not buy everything, because he would *not* be rushed.

Another person made uneasy by the delay was the Lady's steward, Robert Marishal. Rashly, Marishal had brought his children to Cambridge with him – twins, nine years old. Thomas and Ella looked like angels with their golden locks and blue eyes, but within an hour of their arrival, they had broken three valuable plates, torn a book, and let a pig into the parish church. And now some new delinquency was in the making, because they were nowhere to be seen. Their apprehensive father was desperate for the signing to be over, so that he could find the brats before there was yet more trouble.

'You have had an entire decade to ponder this quitclaim, Master Badew,' barked the Lady eventually. 'Do you really need to go through it again?'

'I am a lawyer, My Lady,' Badew replied with haughty dignity. 'And the law and haste make for poor bedfellows. None of us want to be subjected to this disagreeable rigmarole a second time, just because some facet of the transfer is badly worded.'

'We both know that is unlikely, given the number of times it has been redrafted,' the Lady retorted drily. 'Or would you rather I took my patronage to another foundation?'

'There is no need for that,' blurted Donwich in alarm

3

before Badew could tell her to do it. 'We are all delighted by your offer to save us from financial ruin.'

'Financial ruin?' echoed Badew indignantly. 'I have been more than generous, and—'

'It takes *sixty* pounds a year to run a College properly,' interrupted Donwich acidly. 'Not the twenty you provide. So unless you can give us what we need, it is time for you to step aside and let someone else help us.'

'Sixty pounds?' cried Badew, shocked. 'That is outrageous! Greedy, even! But regardless, I refuse to be bullied, so either shut up while I read this thing, or I shall go home.'

Everyone immediately fell silent, knowing he meant it. Only when the audience was completely still did Badew bend to the quit-claim again, carefully weighing the implications of each word until he reached the end. And then there was no more he could do – the last battle was over and the war was lost. With a sense of bitter regret, he picked up his pen, acutely aware of the tension that filled the room. He gave the nib a good dunk in the inkpot and started to write . . . then flung the pen away with an exclamation of disgust. It was not ink in the pot, but thick red blood.

'You put that in there yourself, Badew,' snarled Donwich accusingly. 'You cannot bear to admit defeat, so you resort to low tricks instead. You will do anything to postpone—'

'How dare you!' bellowed Badew, affronted. 'What do you take me for?'

'I shall offer my purse to Michaelhouse if this business is not resolved today,' warned the Lady before Donwich could tell him. 'I have had enough of Badew's juvenile capers.'

'*Juvenile* capers,' mused Roos, and pointed to a bulge in a tapestry; the cloth trembled as the two small culprits laughed helplessly behind it. 'I think an apology is in order, Donwich.'

4

'I saw the twins at the slaughterhouses this morning,' put in Harweden with a moue of disgust. 'I wondered what they were doing there, and now we know. They have been planning this nastiness for hours.'

Mortified, Marishal hauled the guilty pair out of their hiding place, although neither child was contrite.

'But surely important documents *should* be signed in blood?' declared Ella, her cherubic face the picture of bemused innocence, although mischief sparkled in her eyes. 'It will make them more binding.'

'And red is a nicer colour than black anyway,' piped her brother. 'Black is boring.'

Marishal marched them out in disgrace, while the onlookers exchanged disapproving glances, all thinking that such ill-behaved imps should have been left at home. Then Donwich produced a pot of proper ink, and everyone waited in taut silence again while Badew reread the document. But the prank had unsettled the older man and he was suddenly keen for the whole affair to be over, so it was not long before he leaned forward and wrote his name. When he sat back, the relief among the Fellows was palpable. It was done – they were free of him at last.

'Now we have something to give you, My Lady,' announced Donwich grandly. 'From this day forth, University Hall will be known as *Clare* Hall, in recognition of your generosity.'

'*What?*' Badew was stunned. He had always assumed the College would be named Badew Hall after his death, in recognition of his vision in founding it, as was the custom in such situations. However, it was clear that the Lady had prior knowledge of the Fellows' intentions, because she was not surprised at all by Donwich's proclamation. She merely inclined her head in gracious acceptance of the honour. 'But you cannot—'

'Under your patronage, we shall become a centre for

academic excellence,' Donwich went on, rudely cutting across Badew and addressing the Lady directly. 'University Hall was mediocre, but *Clare* Hall will attract the greatest scholars from all over the civilised world.'

'No!' objected Badew, aghast. '*I* am your founder. She is just—'

'Your association with us is over, Badew,' interrupted Donwich curtly, eyeing him with dislike. 'You may see yourself out.'

While Badew sat in open-mouthed shock, the young Fellow swept out of the chamber with the Lady on his arm. The guests followed, chattering excitedly, and it was not long before only Badew and his two friends were left. Silence reigned, the only sound being the crackle of the fire.

'I cannot believe it,' breathed Badew eventually, his voice unsteady with dismay. 'They *must* name the College after me. I created it – all the Lady will do is throw money at a venture that is already up and running. I did all the hard work.'

'You did,' agreed Harweden kindly. 'And you shall have your reward in Heaven, while the Lady and her newly acquired Fellows are destined for another place altogether. Leave justice to God, and forget about them.'

'Forget about them?' cried Badew incredulously. 'I most certainly shall not! They will not get away with this outrage.'

He was barely aware of his friends escorting him home, so intent was he on devising ways to avenge himself. Unfortunately, none of the schemes that blazed into his fevered mind were very practical. He brooded on the matter for the rest of the day, and then went to bed, hoping a better plan would occur to him in the morning, when he would not be quite so incandescent with rage. None did, but that did not mean he was ready to concede defeat – not when he knew things about the Lady that would tear away the façade of pious respectability she had so carefully built around herself. He went to his church, knelt before the altar and made a solemn vow.

'I will not rest until University Hall is mine again,' he whispered fiercely. 'I will do anything to bring it about – steal, beg or even kill. It *will* be Badew Hall, even if it is the last thing I ever do. I swear it on my immortal soul.'

## Clare, Suffolk, February 1360

The parish church of Clare had a unique claim to fame: it was the only one in the country with a fan-vaulted ceiling. Its vicar, Nicholas, gazed admiringly at it – or rather, he gazed at the parts he could see through the scaffolding. Fan vaulting – an architectural style where clusters of 'ribs' sprang from the supporting columns to form a fan-shape – was an entirely new invention. It was the brainchild of Thomas de Cambrug, who had first tried it in Gloucester Abbey. But Clare's roof was better, because Cambrug had still been experimenting in Gloucester, whereas he had known what he was doing by the time he arrived in Suffolk.

It had been expensive, of course, but Clare was wealthy, and its inhabitants had leapt at the chance to transform their rather dull church into something remarkable. Donations had poured in, and work had started at once – removing the old, low roof and replacing it with a tier of elegant clerestory windows and the magnificent ceiling above.

Unfortunately, there was a downside. The Lady of Clare had been complaining for some time that her castle chapel was too small, especially when she had guests, but when she saw Cambrug's innovations, she realised that a solution to her problem was at hand – the church was not only large enough to accommodate her entire household, but the rebuilding meant that it was now suitably grand as well. However, she was not about to subject herself to the unsavoury company of commoners while she attended her devotions, so she gave Cambrug some money and told him to design a new south aisle. The parishioners could have that, she declared, while she took the nave.

The townsfolk were outraged. It was *their* church and they resented her gall extremely. They marched to the castle as one, where they objected in the strongest possible terms to her projected south aisle. The Lady refused to listen. She ordered Cambrug to begin work, not caring that every stone laid destroyed more of the harmony that had existed between her castle and their town for the last three hundred years.

As soon as the aisle was completed, Cambrug took a new commission in Hereford Cathedral, relieved to be away from the bitterness and hostility that festered in Clare. He left his deputy Roger to finish the roof, but promised to return and check that all was in order before the church was rededicated the following April.

Unfortunately, Roger was entirely the wrong man to have put in charge. First, he was a rigid traditionalist who hated anything new, so the fan vaulting horrified him. And second, he was a malcontent, only happy when he was grumbling, which was irritating to his employers and downright exasperating for his workforce.

'I will not answer for it,' he said, coming to stand at Nicholas's side and shaking his head as he peered upwards. 'You should have stuck with a nice groin vault, like I told you. This fan lark is dangerous, and will come to a bad end.'

Nicholas fought for patience. 'Nonsense! Cambrug's ceiling will be the talk of the country, and we shall be celebrated as men of imagination and courage for having built it.'

Roger sniffed. 'Oh, it looks pretty enough, but it should have taken twenty years to raise. We tossed it up in a few months.'

'Yes, because we had so much money,' argued Nicholas, although he did not know why he was bothering; he and Roger had been through this countless times already. 'We were able to hire a huge army of masons and use high-quality stone.'

'The stone is acceptable, I suppose,' conceded Roger reluctantly. 'But the men . . . well, most are strangers, so their work is shoddy.'

'Not so, because you dismissed all those you deemed to be unsatisfactory. Of course, the same is not true for the south aisle. The Lady's donation was niggardly, so corners have certainly been cut there.'

He glared at it, resentful that such an ugly, functional appendage should have been planted on the side of his glorious church, but then his eyes were drawn upwards to the ceiling again. The artists were at work now, painting it with geometrical patterns designed to complement the intricate stonework. It would be a riot of blue, red, gold and green, made all the more impressive for stretching unbroken across both nave and chancel. In Nicholas's view, this would render it far more imposing than the one in Gloucester.

As the new work made the older parts look shabby, Nicholas had arranged for the whole building to be re-decorated, and Clare's wealth was such that the murals commissioned were the best that money could buy. He could not resist a grin of pride. Here he was, a one-time soldier in the King's army, now in charge of a church as fine as any cathedral. How fortune had smiled on him since he had taken holy orders!

'*She* does not like the fan vaulting,' grumbled Roger. 'She told me so herself.'

'She' was Clare's anchoress, a woman who was walled

up in a cell attached to the north wall. Her little room had two windows – the squint, which opened into the chancel and allowed her to receive Holy Communion; and a slit opposite that was used for passing in food and other essentials. Anne de Lexham had entered her 'anchorhold' two months before the renovations had started, so her life of religious contemplation had not been exactly peaceful.

'She will change her mind once she sees it with the scaffolding down,' said Nicholas confidently. 'Besides, she has benefited hugely from Cambrug's presence here – her poky wooden cell exchanged for a nice new stone one, all designed to her own specifications.'

'The church will not be ready for the rededication in April,' declared Roger, who had an annoying habit of never acknowledging that someone else might be right, and always conceded defeat by segueing to a different gripe. 'The artists are behind schedule, and so are the glaziers.'

'Only by a few days, and they will make up for lost time when they hear the news I had this morning – namely that the Queen herself plans to be here for the occasion. They will not want to disappoint her.'

'It is you who will be disappointed,' warned Roger, looking upwards with a disparaging eye. 'Because it will take longer than a few weeks to finish this lot, you mark my words.'

Nicholas was glad when the mason went to moan at someone else. He continued to watch the artists swarm over the scaffolding high above, but jumped in alarm when there was a sickening thud, followed by a babble of horror. It came from the chancel, so he hurried there at once. A number of workmen had clustered around someone who lay unmoving on the floor. Nicholas elbowed through them to find out what had happened – there had been surprisingly few mishaps so far, and he had been worried for some time that their luck would eventually run out.

Roger was dead, his skull crushed. A piece of wood lay on the floor next to him, and blood seeped across the paving stones.

'It is part of the scaffolding,' said Nicholas, squinting up at the mass of planking, ropes and ladders overhead. 'It must have come loose somehow.'

'Our scaffolding does not "come loose",' objected one of the carpenters indignantly. 'I assure you, that plank did not fall of its own accord.'

'Of course it did,' countered Nicholas, startled. 'What else could have happened?'

The workman shrugged. 'Someone could have picked it up and belted him with it.'

'You mean one of you?' asked Nicholas, looking at each one in turn. 'Because you are tired of his sour tongue?'

'No, of course not,' gulped the carpenter. He managed a feeble grin. 'Ignore me, vicar. You are right – it was an accident. Let us say no more about it, eh?'

# CHAPTER 1

*April 1360*

The acrimony between the scholars began while they were still in Cambridge. The plan had been for all three foundations to leave at dawn, so that the journey to Clare – a distance of roughly twenty-five miles – could be completed in a day. This was particularly important to Michaelhouse, which was short of cash, so a night in an inn was a luxury its members were keen to avoid.

The first trouble came when the Michaelhouse men arrived at the town gate at the appointed hour, mounted and ready to ride out, but those from Clare Hall and Swinescroft Hostel did not.

'Where are they?' demanded Master Ralph de Langelee, looking around angrily as time ticked past and there was still no sign of them. 'They promised not to be late.'

He was a bluff, stocky man, who had been henchman to an archbishop before deciding to try his hand at academia. He was no scholar, but he ran his College fairly and efficiently, while his military bearing and famed skill with weapons meant that tradesmen were disinclined to cheat him.

'They did,' agreed Brother Michael, who was not only a Benedictine theologian of some repute, but also the Senior Proctor – a post that had been lowly when he had first taken it, but that he had adjusted to the point where he now ran the entire University. He possessed a very princely figure – tall as well as fat – which he maintained by inveigling plenty of invitations to dine out.

'I am not surprised, though,' said Matthew Bartholomew,

Doctor of Medicine and the last of the three Michaelhouse men who were to travel that day. He had black hair, dark eyes and was considerably slimmer than his companions. 'Clare Hall men always rise late, while Swinescroft . . . well, Roos is the youngest of them, and he is well past sixty.'

'Swinescroft,' said Michael with a smirk. 'You know that is not its real name, do you not? It is officially St Thomas's Hall, but so many vile characters enrol there that it has been Swinescroft ever since it opened its doors fourteen years ago.'

'Really?' asked Bartholomew. 'I always thought it was because it stands on Swinescroft Row.'

Michael waved an airy hand. 'I am sure that is what its members believe, but they would be wrong. Of course, with Richard de Badew as its Principal, how could it attract anything other than a lot of disagreeable ancients?'

'Badew,' mused Bartholomew. 'When I first met him, he was a good man – generous, kind and dedicated. But when his Fellows changed the name of his foundation from University Hall to Clare Hall, he became bitter, angry and vengeful, virtually overnight.'

'Who can blame him?' shrugged Langelee. 'It was a disagreeable business, and revealed them to be ungrateful, dishonourable and sly.'

'It is a pity he let it turn him sour,' said Michael, 'because he makes for unpalatable company these days. And yet he is an angel compared to Saer de Roos, who is quite possibly the least likeable person I have ever met – and that includes all the killers and thieves we have confronted over the years.'

'Gracious!' murmured Langelee. 'And he will be travelling to Clare with us today?'

Michael nodded. 'Along with Badew himself and their friend Henry Harweden, who is another surly rogue. None are known for congenial conversation.'

'They had better not be uncongenial with me,' growled Langelee, patting his sword. 'Because I will not put up with it. However, their characters – whether sullen or charming – will be irrelevant if they fail to turn up.'

'Yes – where *are* they?' Michael looked around crossly, aware that it was now fully light, and well past the time when they should have left. 'Perhaps you are right, Matt: they are too old for such an excursion, so they decided to stay in bed. They are not like us – men in our prime.'

Bartholomew was not so sure about the last part. There were several grey hairs among his black ones, while Michael had to use a special glass for reading, and Langelee had recently been forced to retire from his favourite sport – camp-ball – because he could no longer run fast enough to avoid being pummelled by the opposition.

'We cannot afford to dally,' determined Langelee. 'If they do not come soon, we shall have to leave without them. We will be safer in a large group, I know, but a lot is at stake here – Michaelhouse's coffers are empty, and unless we get our bequest from the Lady of Clare in the next few days, we shall have to declare ourselves bankrupt and close down.'

'I will not allow that to happen,' vowed Michael. 'Not after all we have been through over the past decade to keep the place going.'

'Then let us hope the Lady has been generous,' said Langelee, 'because we will not last another month without a substantial donation. Thank God she died when she did!'

Bartholomew winced, still uncomfortable with the true purpose of their mission – not to attend the Lady's funeral, as Michael and Langelee told anyone who asked, but to collect what they hoped she had left them in her will.

'Are you *sure* we will be among her beneficiaries?' he asked uneasily. 'I had no idea she had promised us anything until you mentioned it last night. Did she tell you privately?'

'Not in so many words,' hedged Langelee. 'But she liked us, and I often had the impression that she wished she had taken Michaelhouse under her wing, rather than Clare Hall. She loved being generous to scholars, so I am sure she will have remembered us.'

'Which is why we must reach Clare in time to pay our respects to her body,' said Michael. 'It will look grubby if we just appear for the reading of the will – as if we only want her money.'

'But we *do* only want her money,' Bartholomew pointed out. 'As does Clare Hall. I fail to understand why Swinescroft wants to come, though – they and the Lady hated each other.'

'Probably to dance on her grave,' shrugged Michael. 'I told you: they are despicable characters, and gloating over the death of an enemy is exactly the sort of thing they will enjoy.'

For the next hour or so, they watched the little Fen-edge settlement come to life. Scholars and priests hurried to their daily devotions, while townsfolk emerged yawning and scratching for a day of honest – or dishonest – toil. Carts of all shapes and sizes poured through the gates from the surrounding villages, bringing wares to sell at the market – vegetables, sacks of peas and beans, woven baskets, pottery, wooden cages filled with agitated birds. It was hectic, noisy, and over it all came the sound of bells from at least twenty churches and chapels, ranging from the bass boom of St Mary the Great to the tinny clang of nearby St Botolph's.

'Here they are,' said Langelee eventually, as two horsemen rode towards them with insulting insouciance. 'Or Clare Hall, at least. Damn! They have sent Donwich and Pulham as their emissaries. I cannot abide that pair.

15

I am the Master of a respectable College, but they still make me feel like a grubby serf.'

It was true that Donwich and Pulham considered themselves to be very superior individuals. Both were in their late thirties, and were smug, conceited and pompous, with reputations built on their contribution to University politics rather than their intellectual achievements. They hailed from noble families, and their travelling clothes were cut from the very finest cloth.

'We overslept,' explained Pulham breezily, careless or oblivious of the inconvenience this had caused. 'But we are here now. Shall we go?'

'We cannot,' replied Langelee sourly, 'because we are still missing Badew, Roos and Harweden. Stay here and do not move. I will find out what is keeping them.'

'Do not bother,' drawled Donwich. 'They will have hired nags from some inn, which will never match ours for speed. We shall make better time without them.'

He smirked, because he and Pulham rode young stallions with glossy coats and bright eyes, whereas Langelee, Michael and Bartholomew had elderly ponies with shaggy manes and lazy natures. To emphasise the point, he performed a series of fancy manoeuvres designed to show off his mount's pedigree. Michael and Langelee watched with grudging admiration, but Bartholomew, who was not remotely interested in horsemanship, wished Donwich would stop fooling around, because their departure would be delayed even further if he was thrown.

'So why wait for Swinescroft?' Donwich went on, to prove he could talk and control his horse at the same time. 'We should leave now.'

'There is safety in numbers, and the Clare road has been plagued by robbers of late,' explained Langelee. 'Simon Freburn and his sons, who have a penchant for cutting off their victims' ears.'

'If we are attacked, *we* shall just gallop away,' declared

16

Pulham smugly. 'No thief will ever catch us or our ears. I only hope that you will be able to follow.'

'Galloping away is *exactly* what they want you to do,' retorted Langelee disdainfully. 'You will ride directly into an ambush, where two men will be much easier to manage than eight. If you want to reach Clare in one piece, I strongly suggest you remain in the pack.'

The Clare Hall men blanched, as well they might, because it was clear from their clothes that they were worth robbing, and neither carried a weapon. By contrast, Michael had a stout staff, Bartholomew had a selection of surgical blades, while Langelee toted a sword, a crossbow, several very sharp daggers and a cudgel. Donwich gave a short, uneasy laugh.

'My colleague jests,' he blustered. 'Of course we will not abandon you, and you can count on us to be at your side in the event of trouble.'

'Behind us, more like,' muttered Langelee venomously. 'Cowering.'

It was some time later that the door to a nearby tavern opened, and the three scholars from Swinescroft emerged, brushing crumbs from their tabards as they did so. The scent of smoked pork and fried eggs wafted out after them. They strolled unhurriedly to the adjoining yard, where they heaved themselves on to three nags that looked older than their riders.

'Do not rush,' called Donwich acidly. 'We are quite happy to sit here, twiddling our thumbs.'

'We have no intention of rushing,' shot back grey-haired Badew, the oldest of the trio. There was ice in his voice. 'Not on your account.'

He had once been a formidable figure in the University – a chancellor, no less – but that had been before his treacherous Fellows had inflicted the wound from which he had never recovered, and that had turned him sour and twisted with hate. His favourite pastime now was suing other scholars, so that barely a month went by when he was not engaged in one lawsuit or another, ranging from disputes over books and money to accusations of theft, assault and damages.

'Have you been waiting?' asked Saer de Roos, the youngest, sweetly. 'Oh, we *do* apologise.'

He was still a handsome man, with blue eyes and fair hair, who continued to win admiring glances from women – although the attraction tended to wane once he engaged them in conversation and they discovered that he was sly, lecherous and cruel. That day, he had donned a peculiar brown woollen hat with flaps that came down over his ears. Donwich regarded it askance.

'I hope you do not intend to wear *that* to the funeral,' he remarked. 'It would be an insult to the Lady.'

Roos smirked. 'Would it? Good! However, I was not thinking of her when I put it on this morning. I did it because I have earache.'

'Would you like a tincture?' asked Bartholomew sympathetically. 'I have one in my bag.'

'I do not want your rubbish, thank you very much,' retorted Roos unpleasantly. 'I would sooner endure the pain than be treated by a man who deals with filthy paupers.'

'As you wish,' said Bartholomew mildly. 'But let me know if it becomes worse. Earache is caused by flesh-eating worms, and you do not want those boring into your brain.'

He was ashamed of the lie when he saw the glance of horror exchanged between Badew and Harweden, although Roos was unconcerned, and merely gave Bartholomew a look of such disdain that the physician felt himself bristle.

'I trust you had a good breakfast, Doctor,' he said tauntingly, 'because only fools embark on long and dangerous journeys on empty stomachs. Does Michaelhouse run to providing real food these days, or are you still subsisting on sawdust and grit?'

Bartholomew opened his mouth to defend his College, but Langelee, ever a man of action, was unwilling to waste time trading insults with colleagues. He nodded to Michael and the two of them began to trot forward. Unfortunately, Donwich thought it was Clare Hall's prerogative to be first, and tried to over- take, which resulted in his horse stumbling in a pothole, after which it began to limp. Dismayed, Donwich dismounted to fret over the damage. Michael and Langelee watched in contempt, disgusted that Donwich's self-serving antics should have resulted in harm to such a fine animal.

'He will have to rest that for at least a week,' said Michael, regarding the afflicted leg with the eye of a man who knew. 'You will have to hire one instead.'

Another delay followed, as Donwich declared himself to have high standards where horseflesh was concerned and rejected a dozen animals before accepting one that he considered to be of sufficient quality. By the time he was satisfied, the three Swinescroft men had repaired to the tavern for more food, obliging everyone to wait until they had finished a second time.

Then, just as the party was about to ride through the gate, a panting student arrived from Clare Hall to report that water was dripping through the library ceiling. Horrified, Donwich and Pulham raced home, and refused to go anywhere until they were sure their precious collec- tion was safe. It was noon by the time the travellers assembled again.

'You go first, Donwich,' said Langelee acidly. 'We cannot have you ruining a second horse by attempting to shove past me. We are late enough as it is.'

'We will make up the lost time,' shrugged Donwich

carelessly. 'Once we are on the open road, the miles will just melt away. You wait and see.'

'They will not,' growled Langelee to his Fellows. 'Not with our poor nags and the three old men from Swinescroft. We shall be lucky to arrive by midnight.'

As it happened, they did not reach Clare at all that day, because they were plagued by a series of mishaps, all of which resulted in spats that held them up even further. First, Donwich's new horse threw a shoe, which Michael and Langelee claimed was down to poor handling. Donwich naturally took exception to their remarks, and a furious quarrel ensued.

Then Badew was taken ill with indigestion – no surprise there, thought Bartholomew, as he prepared a soothing remedy – forcing everyone to wait until the pain had subsided. A muttered remark about gluttony by Pulham sparked yet another ill-tempered tiff, this time between Clare Hall and Swinescroft.

And finally, there was a fractious debate when a pack of farmers demanded a substantial and illegal fee for the privilege of riding through their village. Donwich wanted to pay it, on the grounds that a detour would take them too far out of their way, but Langelee refused. He claimed it was on principle, although Bartholomew and Michael knew it was to conserve their scant funds. He capitulated only when an exasperated Donwich offered to pay the whole amount himself.

They rode on, the three Michaelhouse men watching anxiously as daylight began to fade. Dark clouds massed overhead, promising an early dusk and rain before morning. Langelee urged his pony into a trot, but although the others matched his pace, nightfall came when they still had at least another five miles to go. Then they saw lights gleaming in the gloom ahead.

'That is Kedyngton,' said Donwich. 'It would be folly

to press on tonight, so we shall stay there and continue in the morning.'

'But the funeral,' argued Langelee worriedly. 'It will—'

'I cannot see it starting before midday,' interrupted Roos, 'so we shall arrive in plenty of time. The White Horse here will accommodate us. I have stayed there before, and it is a lovely place.'

The White Horse was an upmarket establishment that cost considerably more than Langelee was willing to spend. It was busy, and there were only two rooms left, which Clare Hall and Swinescroft quickly bagged for themselves. The landlord was acutely embarrassed that he was unable to accommodate all the scholars from the famous University, and declared himself much relieved when Langelee graciously agreed to accept three straw pallets in the hayloft free of charge.

'I wish we had come alone,' said Michael, eyeing the makeshift beds in distaste before choosing the one he thought would be the most comfortable. 'We would have been there by now.'

'Perhaps,' said Langelee, watching a servant bring water, so they could rinse away the dust of travel; it was cold, so Bartholomew was the only one who bothered. 'Or maybe we would be lying in a ditch without our ears. I sensed eyes on us a mile back – Simon Freburn's, no doubt. He would have chanced his hand if we had been three rather than eight.'

Bartholomew was astonished to hear it. 'You think it was our companions who struck fear into the hearts of these hardened robbers? Three elderly men and two prancing monkeys?'

'Swinescroft and Clare Hall are no warriors,' agreed Langelee. 'But neither is Freburn, and he was loath to risk a skirmish in which he would be quite so heavily outnumbered.'

Michael murmured a prayer of thanks for their

deliverance. 'I wish Cynric could have come,' he said, referring to Bartholomew's book-bearer, who was almost as formidable a fighter as the Master. 'It is a pity he is away visiting kin in Wales.'

'We shall be safe enough if the eight of us stick together,' averred Langelee. 'But I shall be glad to be home again, even so.'

'Yes, we shall attend the funeral, collect our inheritance, and hurry home with it as soon as we can,' determined Michael. 'Fortunately, none of our party can dally in Clare, given that term starts next week. We all need to be back.'

'But we three have the strongest reasons not to linger,' sighed Langelee. 'You left our University in the dubious hands of Chancellor Suttone, while I had to appoint Father William as Acting Master. Neither can be trusted alone for long.' He glanced at Bartholomew. 'And you have a wedding to arrange.'

Bartholomew experienced a familiar stab of unease as he contemplated the changes that were about to occur in his life. The University did not allow scholars to marry, so he would have to resign from Michaelhouse and move into the little house that his betrothed, Matilde, had bought. He would no longer be able to teach, and he knew he would miss the intellectual stimulation of the debating chamber. To take his mind off it, he turned the discussion to Clare.

'I still do not understand why you think the Lady left us something in her will. Perhaps she did like us, but she also liked other foundations, including several nunneries, her local community of Austin friars and Clare Hall – the place that named itself after her. They are far more likely to be remembered than us.'

'We should have left him behind,' said Langelee to Michael. 'His attitude is entirely wrong. We must give the impression that she *definitely* promised us a legacy, so if it transpires that she did not, we can claim it was an oversight and demand one anyway.'

'There is no need to explain it to me,' said Michael irritably. 'I have been browbeating awkward executors for years. Matt is the one who needs priming.'

'We must approach—' began Langelee.

'I know what to do,' interrupted Bartholomew impatiently. 'And I shall do my best, although you should have brought someone else. I am not very good at this sort of thing.'

'Unfortunately, we had no choice,' replied Langelee. 'The other Fellows either had duties that kept them in Cambridge, or they would have been even worse at it than you. And do not say Michael and I could have come alone – we *had* to send a bigger deputation than Clare Hall, so it will look as though we care more about honouring her.'

A series of unwise investments and poor financial decisions meant that Michaelhouse had been teetering on the brink of fiscal ruin for years, but every time the Master and his Fellows managed to remedy the situation, something happened to put them back to square one again. For example, a handsome donation from York had been eaten up by urgent repairs to the roof, while the generous gift of a pier, which should have brought in a steady income, had been lost to fire – not once but twice. The second inferno had been especially disheartening, and Bartholomew was not the only one who was beginning to wonder if they were cursed.

'We should sleep,' said Langelee, and snuffed out the candle before his Fellows could demur. 'All that quarrelling was very tiring, and I am exhausted.'

'I hope we *are* mentioned in the will,' muttered Michael, groping about in the dark for a blanket. 'It will be much easier than persuading her executors that we should have been.'

'If only she had chosen to finance *us* fourteen years ago,' sighed Langelee. 'Donwich and Pulham do not have to fret about how much Clare Hall has been left.'

'Do not be so sure,' countered Michael. 'Relations between them have been strained these past few years, because she insisted on meddling in their affairs. She wanted to control every aspect of their lives – who should have which room, how much ale they drink, what entertainment should be provided at Christmas . . .'

'Then they are petulant fools,' declared Langelee. '*I* would have swallowed however much ale she stipulated in return for sixty pounds a year.'

'Why do you think Swinescroft really wanted to come?' asked Bartholomew, after a while. 'I do not believe it is to gloat over her death. Not even they are that spiteful.'

'Never underestimate the power of malice, Matt,' warned Michael. 'Especially from that trio. I recommend that we watch them very closely while we are in Clare, because we do not want their vindictiveness to turn the executors against *all* scholarly foundations.'

'No,' agreed Langelee drowsily. 'So let us hope they behave themselves, because I am loath to use my sword on such elderly colleagues.'

Bartholomew hoped the Master was speaking metaphorically; Michael knew he was not.

Bartholomew had wanted to visit Clare ever since he had heard a description of it several years earlier, so he had been pleased when Langelee had ordered him to accompany him and Michael, despite his misgivings about hoodwinking the Lady's executors. But he had not imagined that the journey would be plagued by such a gamut of emotions.

When he had first become intrigued by the place, it was because he had liked the sound of its setting on the River Stour and its wealth of handsome houses. However, he had since learned that Matilde had lived there after the misunderstanding that had caused her to leave him – he had been slow in asking her to be his wife, which she had interpreted as a disinclination to give up teaching for a life of wedded bliss. He had hunted for her for months afterwards, travelling as far afield as France, and had later been stunned to discover that she had been in Clare – virtually on his doorstep – the whole time.

Once she had learned that a future with him was still possible, Matilde had set about earning a fortune in venture capital, aware that Bartholomew would not be able to keep her in the style to which she was accustomed – most of his patients were paupers, who were not only unable to pay for his services, but who needed him to buy their medicines into the bargain. When she felt she had accumulated enough, she had returned to Cambridge and waited for him to renew his courtship.

It had not been easy to accept her back into his life again. Both had changed in the years they had been apart, and while he still loved her deeply, all was not harmonious perfection. They argued more than they had, and neither remembered the other as being quite so stubborn. Or was it simply that they were now thrust together a lot more? One of the reasons Bartholomew had been glad to visit Clare was that it provided them both with an opportunity to step back and reflect on their relationship and decision to marry.

'I hate Suffolk,' grumbled Michael, breaking into his thoughts, as they rode along side by side the following morning. 'Every time I step over its borders, it rains. It was sunny in Cambridge.'

The weather had indeed taken a turn for the worse overnight. There was a persistent and drenching down-pour that looked set to continue for the rest of the day, the sky was a solid, unbroken grey, and everything dripped. There was new growth in the hedgerows they passed, and celandines and primroses dappled the banks, but their bright colours were dulled by the sullen light.

The rain soon turned the track slick with mud, so progress was both slow and uncomfortable. Thus no one minded very much when Badew declared himself to be too tired to continue, and demanded that they stop at a wayside inn for refreshments. Clare Hall and Swinescroft then proceeded to order themselves handsome repasts of roasted meat and bread, but Langelee shook his head in alarm when Michael started to do the same. The monk, however, was not a man to let a small thing like money stand between him and his stomach.

'My colleague can cure that painful knee of yours,' he informed the landlord confidently. 'Of course, you could never afford the fees of a famous University physician, but I am in a generous mood, so we shall allow you to provide us with a meal instead.'

'I wish you would not do that, Brother,' whispered Bartholomew crossly, once the grateful patient had hobbled away clutching a pot of salve. 'What would have happened if he had been suffering from something I could not help him with? Would you have returned his food?'

'I doubt he would want it now,' retorted Michael, wiping grease from his chin. 'But you *did* heal him, so where lies the problem?'

Bartholomew knew there was no point in arguing. He glanced to the other side of the room, where Donwich, Badew and Roos had embarked on an ill-natured debate over whether Clare was a large village or a small town. It should not have been a subject that provoked high passions, but it was not long before they were screeching at each other. Wincing at the racket, Harweden came to join the Michaelhouse men, and without a by-your-leave, began to pick at their food. Michael and Langelee were naturally indignant, so soon a second spat was under way.

Unwilling to be dragged into it, Bartholomew went to

sit with Pulham, who was reading by the fire. To be civil, he politely asked if the book was from Clare Hall's library, brought on the journey lest the ceiling leaked again.

'No, it belongs to me,' Pulham replied, laying an affectionate hand on its exquisitely crafted cover – soft red leather with letters picked out in gold. 'It is my most cherished possession, and far too valuable to leave in a place where some grubby undergraduate might get hold of it.'

Bartholomew blinked his incomprehension at the sentiment. He was always delighted when a student expressed an interest in reading one of *his* books, as it meant the lad wanted to know what was inside – and education was the reason they were all there, after all.

'What is it?' he asked. 'A legal text?'

'A Book of Hours. It was crafted by John de Weste, who is cofferer at Clare Priory and also one of the country's finest illustrators. I am sure you have heard of him.'

Bartholomew shook his head apologetically. Books of Hours were devotional tracts, filled with prayers and psalms. He barely had time to study the medical tomes he was obliged to teach, so religious books were a luxury with which he was wholly unfamiliar.

'It cost a fortune,' Pulham went on. 'But the moment I saw it, I knew I had to make it my own. Just look at the pictures – each one is a work of art.'

Bartholomew leaned forward to see an intricate pastoral scene, showing a blue-frocked shepherd tending his flock in attractively rolling countryside. Birds fluttered overhead and the sun shone. Yet darkness lurked, because Satan was watching from behind a tree. The Devil was depicted peculiarly – he had a tail and cloven hoofs, but his head was that of a man with a mane of white hair and snowy whiskers. Something about the face was vaguely familiar, although Bartholomew could not have said why.

'It is beautiful,' he acknowledged. 'But surely you could

27

have left it with a trusted colleague? What happens if it gets rained on? Or lost?'

'I brought it with me because I have discovered a flaw,' explained Pulham. 'In that picture, as a matter of fact. I want Weste to put it right.'

'What flaw?' asked Bartholomew, studying the page again. 'The fact that lambs tend not to be born in high summer, which is what seems to be happening in the left-hand corner?'

'Is it?' Pulham peered at it. 'Lord, so it is! I had not noticed, but I am not a farmer, so it does not matter. No, I refer to Satan, who is far too human-looking for my liking. He should—'

He stopped abruptly when the tome was ripped from his hand by Roos, who peered at the picture briefly, then flung the whole thing into the fire. Pulham gave a shriek of dismay and leapt to rescue it, but Roos grabbed his belt and held him back. Equally appalled – he had never approved of book-burning – Bartholomew darted forward and managed to pluck the volume from the flames. The pastoral illustration was gone, but the other pages were mostly unscathed.

'What is wrong with you?' Pulham howled at Roos, snatching the book from Bartholomew and cradling it to his breast. 'Are you mad?'

'It is a vile piece of heresy,' snarled Roos, lunging for it again, 'and the fire is the only place for it. Give it to me, or I shall tell everyone that you are a warlock.'

'Roos, stop,' ordered Bartholomew sharply, thinking this was unacceptable behaviour even by Swinescroft standards. 'It is a Book of Hours – it contains prayers and psalms. There is nothing untoward about it. Show him, Pulham.'

'Yes, look at it!' screeched Pulham, waving the damaged bit at Roos as tears started from his eyes. 'Look at what you have done to an exquisite piece of art, you damned lunatic!'

Roos peered briefly at it, then turned and stalked away.

'Just keep it away from me,' he snapped over his shoulder as he went.

Bartholomew could only suppose that breaking off the altercation so abruptly was Roos's way of acknowledging that he had made a mistake. Clearly, an apology was not going to be forthcoming.

'The man is insane,' sobbed Pulham, hugging the book to him again. 'I feel like clouting him over the head with it, and continue bashing until his brains fall out.'

Bartholomew started to reply, but was distracted by raised voices from the other side of the room. Badew was ill again, which was small wonder given the amount of food he had just managed to pack away. Unfortunately, he was more inclined to blame his discomfort on someone else rather than admit his greed, and had accused Donwich of poisoning him.

'You do not want me to go to Clare,' the old man was declaring, eyes flashing hotly, 'because you are afraid of what I might tell people there.'

'I assure you,' drawled Donwich, with the kind of arrogance that was sure to rankle, 'nothing you say could matter less to me. You are an irrelevance.'

'Is that so?' snarled Badew. 'Well, you can think again, because I know things – secrets that will put the Lady's executors in a flutter.'

'What secrets?' asked Michael curiously.

Badew smirked tauntingly. 'You will have to wait and see. Come, Roos, Harweden. The company here has begun to stink, and I can stand it no longer.'

'Thank God we are nearly there,' muttered Langelee, as they stepped into the teeming rain for the last leg of their journey. 'I do not think I can take much more of this bickering – they are worse than fractious children.'

As soon as he saw it, Bartholomew understood exactly why Elizabeth de Burgh had chosen to make Clare her seat of power. It was a jewel of a place, even in the rain with water sluicing down its roofs and tumbling along its gutters. It was dominated by the castle, a vast fortress that occupied a sizeable tract of land, all protected by curtain walls, ditches, ramparts and towers. However, the inner bailey buildings had plenty of large windows, suggesting it was as much a palace as a military garrison. Outside the walls, but still within the encircling moat, were gardens, orchards and vineyards.

The town itself was just as splendid, and Bartholomew looked around with interest as he rode, admiring the decorative plasterwork on the houses of those who had grown rich from Clare's strategic position on the River Stour and the great castle on its doorstep. There was an atmosphere of conceited well-being among the people he passed, but no indication that the Lady's death was cause for sorrow. Perhaps they were glad to see the back of her, he thought, recalling her as a domineering woman with firmly held opinions.

They crossed a bridge and had their first glimpse of the parish church. It was unusually large and had been the subject of a recent renovation, as parts of it were still swathed in scaffolding. The top half of the building was new, and so was the south aisle, while the lower half was ancient, dating from the time of the Conqueror.

'It looks odd,' declared Langelee, reining in to regard it critically. 'As if some giant has come along and sliced off one roof in order to replace it with another. The two parts do not fit together properly – they are different colours, for a start.'

'That will not be so noticeable once the new parts have weathered a bit,' said Bartholomew, and smiled appreciatively. 'The nave and chancel are an impressive height, though, so the ceiling must look splendid from within.'

'Maybe,' conceded Langelee. 'But I am unimpressed

by that south aisle – it is crafted from cheaper materials than the rest, and is not nearly as handsome.'

'We should go in,' declared Michael. Their arrival had attracted attention, and he was keen for his piety to be reported to people who mattered. 'To give thanks for our safe arrival.'

No one liked to argue, so they dismounted and trooped into the porch. Hoods were pushed back and hats removed, although Roos declined to part with his vile woollen cap.

'Do you still have earache?' asked Bartholomew sympathetically, wondering if discomfort had been responsible for the unedifying incident with the book in the tavern earlier.

Roos nodded and raised one hand to the side of his head. 'It throbs like the Devil, and I shall be glad to lie down. Your fat friend knows it, of course, which is why he suggested a prayer – to cause me additional pain by dallying.'

Bartholomew opened his mouth to deny it, but Roos had already stamped away. Pushing the surly old man from his mind, he walked into the nave, aware of the clean scents of wet plaster and fresh paint. Then he gazed upwards in astonishment.

The clerestory windows high above allowed light to flood in, even on that dull day, and it illuminated something he had never seen before – a ceiling that soared, so high and delicate that it seemed impossible that it should stay up. At the top of each pillar, stone ribs had been carved in a fan pattern, to intertwine like lace with the ones adjacent to it. Each fan had been given a unique geometric design, executed in a blaze of bright colour. Much was hidden by scaffolding, but enough could be seen through the gaps to show that it was a remarkable achievement.

'Well,' said Donwich eventually, the first to find his

voice. 'I knew they had been working to improve the place, but I was not expecting anything so . . .'

'Tasteless,' finished Badew, sniffing his disdain. 'It is ugly.'

'It is stunning,' countered Donwich. 'As any fool can see. What a pity that the Lady did not live to enjoy it. I imagine it was her money that paid for the project.'

'Not too much of it, I hope,' murmured Langelee to his Fellows. 'I should not like to think she spent so recklessly that there is none left for us.'

Still braying their admiration, Donwich and Pulham went to inspect the murals that covered every wall, prayers forgotten. The Swinescroft men pretended to be indifferent as they perched on a convenient tomb to rest their legs, although even they could not resist surreptitious glances at the glories around them. Michael, Bartholomew and Langelee went to the chancel, where they knelt to say their prayers. As a professional, the monk had more to say to his Maker than the other two, so when they had finished, they withdrew to give him some privacy.

'I have never seen anything like it,' whispered Bartholomew, gazing upwards at the ceiling with renewed awe. 'Not even in France.'

'It is called "fan vaulting",' came a voice from behind them. 'The only other place you will see it is in Gloucester Abbey, but ours is better.'

They turned to see a vicar. He was an Austin friar of middle years, whose fine robes indicated that he earned a good living from his parish. He had a shock of yellow hair and a physique that was almost as impressive as Langelee's. He introduced himself as Father Nicholas de Lydgate.

'Who designed it?' asked Bartholomew, sensing that the priest wanted to brag.

'An architect named Thomas de Cambrug. If you are

in Clare next Tuesday, you will meet him, because he is coming for the rededication ceremony. He is working on Hereford Cathedral at the moment, but has promised to return for the unveiling.'

'Tuesday?' asked Bartholomew, looking around doubtfully. The scaffolding would take a while to dismantle, and artists were still working feverishly on several bare patches of stone. 'That is in six days. Will you be ready by then?'

'We had better be, because the time and date have been set for months,' replied Nicholas. 'It will start at seven o'clock in the evening, and will be conducted by torchlight. I made the arrangements myself, and it will be the most beautiful service that anyone has ever seen.'

'I am sure it will be impressive,' said Bartholomew. 'But Hereford is a long way away. Are you sure Cambrug will make the trek?'

Nicholas smiled serenely. 'Yes, because the Queen is coming, and no ambitious man wants to miss his work being praised by royalty. He will be here, of that I am certain.'

'All this beautification must have been expensive,' fished Langelee. 'Did the Lady fund it?'

Nicholas pursed his lips. 'You have hit upon a bitter bone of contention. It was to have been the town's project, as it is our parish church, but when the Lady saw what was happening, she wanted to be part of it – which caused a lot of bad feeling.'

'Did it?' asked Bartholomew, surprised. 'In Cambridge, the town would be delighted if the castle offered to pay for something.'

'She funded the south aisle,' explained Nicholas, waving at the section in question, 'which sounded generous until we learned that the townsfolk were expected to stand in it, out of the way, while she and her cronies took over the nave.'

33

'The castle does not have a chapel of its own?' asked Bartholomew.

'Yes, but it is too small to accommodate everyone, so they have to attend Mass in shifts. This place, however, can hold them all, so they aim to steal it from us. They have already started meddling in parish affairs. For example, they want me to leave my current house and move into a smaller one. But where I live is none of their damned business!'

He continued to rail until the latch clanked and two men entered. The older of the pair reclined on a litter carried by a couple of moon-faced boys; all three were clad entirely in purple. The other was so plump that he barely managed to squeeze through the door. Nicholas broke off from his grumbles to say they were Mayor Godeston and Barber Grym.

'They will tell you about the Lady's gall,' he confided, 'because they were obliged to deal with most of her infractions – I confined myself to the religious issues that arise from this sort of undertaking. It is never wise for a priest to take sides, although it is hard to remain impartial sometimes.'

'What religious issues?' asked Langelee, while Bartholomew thought that Nicholas had not remained impartial at all, and clearly sided with his parishioners.

'Tending our anchoress while her cell was being refurbished, praying for the work to be finished on time, burying our Master Mason, who was tragically killed a few weeks ago – your three friends over there are sitting on him.'

'You have an anchoress?' asked Bartholomew quickly, preferring to discuss a holy woman than the fact that his Swinescroft colleagues had made themselves very comfortable on the final resting place of someone who was so recently dead.

Nicholas smiled. 'Her name is Anne de Lexham, and she is very religious. I shall introduce you to her after you have spoken to Godeston and Grym. Here they come now.'

The Mayor cut a very stately figure in his litter. His lavender robes were made of unusually fine cloth, and there was silver embroidery on his sleeves. His bearers' clothes were coarser, but they were obviously proud of the way they looked, because they kept glancing at their reflections in the windows.

'Robbers,' Godeston said without preamble, staring up at Bartholomew and Langelee through sharp mauve eyes. 'Did you encounter any on your way here?'

'Specifically Simon Freburn and his sons,' elaborated Grym, identifiable as a barber because his enormous girth was encircled by a belt from which dangled implements to cut hair, shave faces and extract teeth. He had twinkling eyes and a ready smile, and was not 'grim' at all.

'No, we were too large a party to tackle,' replied Langelee. 'Although I sensed them watching us as we passed. If we had been fewer, I am sure they would have attacked.'

'Scum!' spat Godeston. 'I would give my right arm to see Freburn and his sons hang.'

Grym changed the subject with a smile. 'We do not see many scholars these days. Why—'

'We do not see them because of Freburn,' interrupted Godeston bitterly. 'People are loath to use the road as long as he haunts it.' He scowled at Bartholomew and Langelee. 'Or have you kept your distance these last few years because the College named after our town is tired of us?'

'I thought Clare Hall was named after the Lady,' said Langelee, puzzled.

'I am sure that is what its Fellows told her,' sniffed Godeston, 'but *everyone* knows the real truth, which is that one of them travelled here fourteen years ago, and thought our town so fabulous that he decided to honour us.'

'And who can blame him?' shrugged Grym. 'It is the nicest place in Suffolk. No, let us be honest about this – in the *whole world*!'

'I was telling them how the castle insisted on providing us with a new aisle,' said Nicholas grumpily. 'Even though we did not want one.'

Godeston's face hardened. 'Especially as they think they will shove us in there, out of sight, while they worship in the nave. Well, we are not going anywhere.' He folded his arms defiantly.

'But the nave is huge,' said Bartholomew. 'Surely there is enough room for everyone?'

'Not at the front,' explained Godeston. 'Which is where we all like to be. We refuse to give way to them, so they bring their weapons and give us a poke.'

'It is only a matter of time before someone is hurt,' put in Grym, shaking his head disapprovingly. 'And do not say that should please a man who stitches wounds – it is not the way I like to win new business.'

'There was talk of a *north* aisle as well,' growled Godeston, 'but we scuppered that plan by making sure the south one cost the Lady a fortune. There is gold leaf in all its murals, and its floor came from Naples. Of course, the stone in the walls is *very* inferior . . .'

'Well, she is dead now, so you are safe from her unwelcome meddling,' said Langelee.

'Dead?' echoed Nicholas, startled. 'What are you talking about? The Lady is not dead.'

'More is the pity,' put in Godeston acidly.

'Of course she is,' countered Langelee. 'A messenger rode all the way to Cambridge with a letter. Her funeral is today.'

'Then I am afraid you have been the subject of a practical joke,' said Grym. 'Because the Lady is no more dead than I am. I saw her myself, not an hour ago.'

'And there is no funeral today,' added Nicholas. 'There is one tomorrow, but not hers. Grym is right – someone is playing games with you.'

36

# CHAPTER 2

When he emerged from his devotions, Michael was deeply unimpressed to learn that he had had a wasted journey, although Bartholomew was happy to pass a day or two exploring the glories of Clare. Personally, he felt the visit had been worthwhile for the fan vaulting alone.

'Are you sure?' the monk asked for at least the third time. He, Bartholomew and Langelee were in a chapel dedicated to the patronal saints – Peter and Paul. It was in a part of the church that had not been revamped, so it was dark, old and rather plain. 'You did not misunderstand what the vicar and the others told you?'

'Of course we did not misunderstand,' snapped Langelee, disappointment turning him testy. 'The Lady is in fine fettle and has no intention of being buried today.'

'Then who sent the letter telling us about her funeral?' demanded Michael. 'And hired a messenger to take it all the way to Cambridge?'

'Lord knows,' replied Langelee, disgusted. 'But he had better not come to gloat about it, not unless he wants a blade in his gizzard. This jaunt cost us money we can ill afford. The bastard has no idea of the damage he has done.'

Michael was silent for a while. Then his expression turned from irked to calculating, and his green eyes gleamed with the prospect of a challenge.

'Yet what is to stop us from turning the situation to our advantage? The Lady may appreciate three busy scholars coming here to pay their respects, and it is our chance to ensure that when she does die, Michaelhouse is mentioned in her will for certain.'

'But I do not like Clare,' objected Langelee sulkily. 'There is a nasty dispute between the town and the castle about who has the right to stand where in the church. Oh, you can smile, Brother, but passions are running very high over it.'

'Probably because so much money has been spent on its refurbishment,' surmised Bartholomew. 'Mayor Godeston and Barber Grym mentioned a couple of the sums involved, and even the smallest would keep Michaelhouse afloat for a decade.'

'In that case, we shall certainly stay,' determined Michael. 'If Clare folk have so much spare cash, then we must persuade them to put some of it our way. I do not care if they hail from the town or the castle. Merchants, knights, tradesmen, nobles . . . their gold is all the same colour.'

'I suppose we can try,' conceded Langelee. 'Everyone here is very well dressed, even the paupers. Indeed, I feel like a beggar in my shabby academic attire.'

'You *are* a beggar,' Michael reminded him. 'But not one who will go home empty-handed if I have anything to say about it. We shall stay for this rededication service next Tuesday – that will be our excuse for lingering. And in the interim, we shall tout for benefactors and court the Lady.'

Langelee regarded him in alarm. 'But that is six days hence – we cannot afford to dally here that long! And what about the beginning of term? We dare not leave William and Suttone to manage on their own. William will drive off all our new students with his fanatical bigotry, while Suttone is lazy and incompetent.'

'Term starts on Thursday, so we shall leave first thing Wednesday morning,' determined Michael. 'And do not worry about lodgings. We shall find somewhere cheap.'

Langelee frowned unhappily. 'Very well, if you are sure. I admit that I am loath to return home with an empty purse.'

Bartholomew left them plotting tactics and went to admire more of the church. Yet again, his eyes were drawn to the roof. He could hear rain drumming on it, and marvelled that there were no leaks, as there would be at home. Personally, he was delighted that Michael and Langelee had agreed to stay, as he wanted to see the ceiling without the scaffolding. And, of course, he was interested in meeting Cambrug, as only a genius could have invented fan vaulting.

It seemed that Nicholas had driven the Swinescroft men off the mason's tomb, because they were now sitting in the porch. Badew was laughing, which made Bartholomew suspect he did not yet know that the Lady was still in the land of the living. He considered breaking the news, but then decided against it: they would be livid, and he had no wish to bear the brunt of their disappointment. He was about to go and admire more murals, when he was intercepted by Donwich and Pulham.

'Look at Roos,' said Donwich disapprovingly. 'The man is a disgrace.'

Bartholomew could see what he meant. While Badew and Harweden chatted to each other, Roos's eyes were fixed on a young woman who was sweeping the floor. His leer was brazen, and Bartholomew did not like to imagine how she would react if she looked up and saw it.

'He shames us with his open lust,' said Pulham, repelled. 'Someone should tell him to desist before there is trouble.'

'Well, I am not doing it,' said Donwich firmly. 'Indeed, I think I shall adjourn to the Swan for the rest of the day. It is the best inn in Clare, and I much prefer it to the castle. The Lady always insisted that I stayed with her whenever I visited in the past, but now she is dead . . .'

'What about the funeral?' asked Pulham, startled.

'It is not until tomorrow,' replied Donwich. 'The vicar just told me. Where will you stay tonight, Bartholomew? With us in the Swan? Oh, I forgot! Michaelhouse cannot afford it.'

He smirked, which meant that Bartholomew, who had been about to report that the Lady was still alive, decided to let him find out for himself. At that point, Badew and Harweden approached, although Roos did not join them, and continued to ogle the woman.

'The Swan!' spat Badew in distaste, overhearing. 'I would not demean myself by using a garish place like that. The Bell is more to my liking – staid, decent and respectable.'

'He means dull,' said Pulham to Donwich, and turned back to Badew. 'We shall leave you to enjoy it, then. However, you had better hope that the husband of that young lady does not work there, or you may find yourselves stabbed during the night.'

He nodded towards Roos, who was creeping towards his quarry with one hand extended for a grope. With a hiss of alarm his friends hurried over to stop him. Wanting nothing to do with any of them, Bartholomew beat a hasty retreat and returned to Michael and Langelee.

'They do not know about the Lady,' he said. 'And I am disinclined to tell them.'

'So am I,' said Michael, 'but I imagine they will hear the news when they book into their respective inns. And if not . . . well, it is hardly our problem.'

Worried about the expense that six nights in Clare would incur, Langelee disappeared to locate the cheapest available tavern, leaving his Fellows with strict instructions to stay in the church until he returned. Bartholomew did

40

not mind, content to examine the paintings in more detail. He roamed the nave, while Michael chatted to Nicholas about the Lady.

'She was unwell a couple of weeks ago,' the vicar obliged, 'but Master Lichet put her right. Or so he claimed. Personally, I think it was Grym's posset that finally settled her stomach.'

'Who is Lichet?' asked Michael. 'A physician?'

'A learned man,' replied Nicholas. 'At least, that is how he describes himself. To me, he is the Red Devil and an ignoramus. When he arrived here a few months ago, he did not even know that we have an anchoress *and* a hermit.'

'Good gracious,' said Michael mildly, unwilling to confess that neither had he. 'I have not met an anchorite since I was last in Norwich. Where is she?'

'In her anchorhold, of course,' said Nicholas. 'Where else would she be? Like all her ilk, she is walled inside it, and the only way to extricate her would be to smash a hole in the stonework.'

'I know how anchorites live,' said Michael impatiently. 'What I meant was: where is her cell? Here in the church, or has she chosen a more remote place for her life of saintly contemplation?'

'She is near the chancel,' said Nicholas. 'Our hermit is the one who lives in the wilds. Well, at the back of the castle, actually, although he can always be seen at the market of a Wednesday, as it is when he likes to buy his groceries.'

'A hermit who goes shopping once a week,' drawled Michael, amused. 'And who has chosen a busy fortress for his retreat. Singular!'

'We are lucky to have him,' said Nicholas sharply, sensing an insult. 'Pilgrims will flock here to see him once the word spreads. And Anne the anchoress will draw crowds, of course, not to mention the hordes who will come to see the fan vaulting. We shall be inundated with visitors. But speaking of Anne, when would you like to meet her? Now or later?'

'Neither,' replied Michael. 'I imagine she would rather be left to her devotions.'

Nicholas smiled indulgently. 'She loves company, and there will be hell to pay if I do not introduce her to scholars from the University at Cambridge. Come.'

Bartholomew tagged along, too, as the vicar led the way to the chancel, where the anchoress' cell abutted the church's north wall. It was unusually well constructed – most anchorholds tended to be rough lean-to structures built by the occupants themselves, but Clare's was made of stone and possessed a tiled roof. The cell was spacious, with a screen across one end, which allowed the inmate to do some things without an interested audience.

Bartholomew had visited such places before, and braced himself for an unpleasant smell – personal hygiene tended not to feature very high on anchorites' lists of priorities. Anne's abode, however, was fragrant with the scent of fresh straw, and he peered through the squint to see a pile of clean clothes, water for washing and a broom for keeping the cell tidy. Like everything else about Clare, its holy woman was rather more superior than average.

'I shall leave you to it,' murmured Nicholas. 'But do not take up too much of her time. She usually has a nap about now.'

'A nap?' blurted Michael in astonishment, but the vicar had gone.

The anchoress sat on a stool, humming over some sewing, although she put it aside when she saw strangers at her squint. She was of indeterminate age, and wore a fine blue gown with a bright white wimple. Bartholomew blinked his surprise – not just at her handsome attire, but at the fact that she should be indulging in needle-work. Most people who allowed themselves to be walled up inside churches tended to reject earthly pursuits in favour of the spiritual.

'You are like no anchoress that I have ever met before,' he remarked, unable to help himself.

Anne chuckled. 'You mean I am not some smelly old fanatic who would rather babble nonsense at the Almighty than wash?'

'Well, yes,' acknowledged Bartholomew. 'And they are not usually so well dressed.'

Anne smiled as she smoothed out a couple of wrinkles in her elegant kirtle. 'I tried wearing sackcloth, but it is difficult to pray when all you want to do is scratch, so I begged some more comfortable apparel from those who come to ask for my blessings.'

'What about food?' asked Michael, cutting to what would matter to him. 'Do you have enough? Itchy clothes are unpleasant, of course, but being hungry would be worse.'

'Most folk are generous,' she replied, 'and those who fall short can expect a piece of my mind. I am not in here being holy for nothing, so if they want me to petition God on their behalf, they can damn well provide me with proper victuals. And they do, generally speaking. Indeed, I usually get so much that I have plenty left over to sell.'

'Sell?' echoed Bartholomew warily, while Michael stepped smartly away from the squint so that Anne would not see him smile. 'You mean for money?'

'Of course for money! What else? Then I can buy nice things for myself, like scented water, hairpins and silk thread for sewing.'

'Lord!' muttered Bartholomew, recalling the grim little cells he had seen in France, where the occupants were so absorbed in matters of the soul that they had to be reminded to eat.

'Perhaps I should become an anchorite,' mused

43

Michael, struggling to keep the humour from his voice. 'Then I could lounge about all day, doing nothing but gorge.'

'And being holy,' Anne reminded him earnestly. 'Not everyone can manage it. But I have a reputation for sanctity, and people from the castle *and* the town come to me for religious guidance.'

'What prompted you to take this particular path?' asked Bartholomew, not sure that 'sanctity' was the word *he* would have used to describe what she had to offer visitors.

'I was called by God, of course. He asked if I would mind sitting in here, dispensing wisdom on His behalf, and He phrased it so nicely that I decided to oblige.'

'I am sure He is grateful,' said Bartholomew, aware of Michael's large frame quaking with silent laughter next to him.

'Oh, He is. And it is not a bad life. I got that architect – Cambrug – to put a fireplace in here, so I am very snug of an evening. And once pilgrims come en masse to admire the fan vaulting, they will pay me handsomely to solve their personal problems. Which is why I am here, of course.'

'Is it? I thought it was to lead a life of quiet communion with God.'

Anne waved a dismissive hand. 'Giving advice is a lot more fun. Now, do you need my guidance on anything? All it will cost you is a flask of Rhenish wine.'

'I do not have wine of any description. Does that mean you will withhold your help?'

'It means we can negotiate,' she replied smoothly. 'But do not think you can cheat me, because I am very well versed in the sly ways of men.'

Michael guffawed aloud the moment they were out of earshot, amused by the concept of a recluse with such a worldly outlook on life.

'She has carved a very comfortable niche for herself here,' he remarked when he had his mirth under control, 'and she lives in greater luxury than most monastics.'

'She is a fraud,' declared Bartholomew, less inclined to see the funny side of the situation. The poor and desperate would buy her services, but would be cheated of their money's worth. 'The Bishop should oust her.'

'I shall write to him once we are back in Cambridge,' promised Michael. 'You are right – something should be done. But not yet. We cannot afford to annoy anyone here until we have secured Michaelhouse's future. It is all very well for you – you will be living with Matilde in a few weeks' time – but the rest of us would like a College to call home.'

Despite Langelee's injunction to remain in the church, Bartholomew and Michael stepped out into the graveyard. The rain had stopped, and both felt the need for some fresh air. Neither spoke, Bartholomew reflecting again on the changes that would occur in his life when he exchanged wedding vows with Matilde, while Michael pondered the anchoress and her lack of spirituality. He noticed that a queue had formed outside her outer window, of people waiting to talk to her.

'You are thinking about Anne,' came a squeaky voice near the monk's elbow. 'You have that look about you – the one visitors always get after their first audience with her.'

The speaker was a thin, scrawny man with wiry hair somewhere between red and grey. He was dirty and stank of animals, although his cloak was fur and his boots sturdy, both far better than the scholars'. Over his arm was a basket full of fresh produce.

'You are the hermit, I suppose,' surmised Michael. 'Come from your remote refuge behind the castle to shop for victuals.'

'Yes, I am Jan,' replied the man, blithely oblivious of

45

the monk's sarcasm. 'I always lay in supplies on a Wednesday, as it is the best time for butter and smoked pork.'

'A worldly anchorite and a hermit who likes busy markets,' remarked Michael, raising his eyebrows. 'Clare is certainly full of surprises.'

'Oh, yes,' said Jan earnestly. 'No other town can match us for them. Do you have any spare change, by the way? If you do, I shall pray for you this evening.'

'And if we do not?' asked Michael.

Jan raised his bushy eyebrows. 'Then I shall "forget" to include you on the list of names I give to God each night, and you do not want that. So come on. Give.' He waggled his fingers.

'I am afraid Master Langelee has all our money,' lied Michael. 'So you are out of luck.'

'I suppose you can bring it to the hermitage later,' said Jan grudgingly. 'Although do not leave it too long – my list does not remain open indefinitely.'

'The hermitage,' mused Michael. 'Is it as elaborate as the anchorhold?'

Jan made a moue of disdain. 'It is the abode of a spiritual man, not of some wench who likes sitting around braying her opinions. My home is a cave, with nothing in it but the bare essentials – furniture, bedding, pots, pans, a goat, ten chickens, two pairs of shoes, four baskets of—'

'A cave?' asked Bartholomew, interrupting because he suspected that the list might go on for some time otherwise. 'In this sort of countryside?'

'A cottage, then,' conceded Jan. 'Although I do not see that it matters what I call it. Would you like some advice on credit? Because I have three things to say to you.'

'No, it is all right,' said Michael quickly, unwilling to run up debts that they might be unable to pay. 'We are not—'

'First, do not trust that Anne,' said Jan, cutting across him. 'Not as far as you can spit, as she is a liar and a cheat. Second, do not join the war between castle and town, because it is deadly. And third, if the Austin friars invite you to stay in their priory, wear armour.'

'Why?' asked Michael, startled. 'Are they the kind of priests to stab guests, then?'

'No, but they have sworn oaths,' replied Jan, and lowered his voice to add darkly, 'Oaths to help each other in time of need. It is all wrong, if you ask me.'

Bartholomew wanted to know why, but the hermit was already hurrying away, moving with a curious sideways scuttle that was redolent of a crab. Jan had no sooner disappeared into the leafy darkness of the churchyard when someone else strode towards them. It was an Austin with a neat grey beard, a scarred face and a black eyepatch. Bartholomew could only suppose that Jan had seen the friar coming, and it was this that had prompted the curious warning.

'Is Nicholas in there?' the priest asked. He nodded towards the church, then went on without giving them time to answer. 'He probably is – he has a lot to do if he wants the place ready in time for the ceremony next week. So, who are you? Scholars from Clare Hall? We do not see you very often these days, not since you started objecting to the Lady telling you how to run your College.'

'We are from Michaelhouse,' replied Michael. 'A far superior foundation.'

'Never heard of it,' declared the friar, but listened with interest as Michael introduced himself and Bartholomew. He gave a military-style salute. 'And I am John de Weste, the priory's cofferer.'

'The artist?' asked Bartholomew. 'I saw some of your work yesterday – a Book of Hours.'

Which had almost been incinerated by the surly Roos,

he recalled, although it did not seem prudent to mention that to its creator.

Weste beamed with genuine pleasure. 'My work is at the University in Cambridge? Then perhaps I shall be famous yet! You must visit me in the priory and tell me all about it. But I had better find Nicholas before any more of the day is lost. Good day to you.'

He bowed and hurried away. Bartholomew watched him go.

'I wonder what Jan has against the Austins. It cannot just be that they have sworn vows to help each other – there is nothing wrong with being loyal to friends.'

'No,' agreed Michael. 'There is not.'


It was some time before Langelee returned, dejected because he had visited every tavern he could find, only to learn that there was no such thing as cheap accommodation in Clare. Even the lowest place charged top rates, and they would run out of money within two days if they accepted the terms on offer. Lines of strain showed around his eyes. It was never easy being Master, but Langelee's tenure had been harder than most. The College had been plagued with problems from the moment he had taken office, virtually none of his own making. He had done his best, but worry was taking its toll, draining even his ebullient spirits.

'But if we disappear to sleep under a hedge, it will raise eyebrows,' he said glumly. 'And no one will give money to a foundation that cannot pay its envoys' basic expenses.'

Bartholomew frowned. 'But surely they will want to give us more, on the grounds that their help will be especially appreciated?'

'That is not how it works,' explained Michael impatiently. 'Rich folk invest in foundations that are thriving, not ones that teeter on the edge of collapse, where their

48

money might be wasted. We must look as though we are awash with cash.'

'How?' asked Bartholomew. 'By staying at the Swan?'

'I will think of something,' promised Michael, and glanced up at the sky, aware that the rain had started again. 'Because I am not sleeping under hedges in this weather.'

'I met that anchoress,' said Langelee disapprovingly. 'She hailed me through her window – in a voice like a fanfare – and demanded to know my business.'

'What did you tell her?' asked Bartholomew.

'The truth,' replied Langelee. 'That we came to pay our respects to the Lady, and that we are a flourishing College which does not need more benefactors, but if anyone here would like to contribute, then we would consider making an exception in their case.'

'That is the truth, is it?' said Bartholomew, amused.

'Then I asked her about the town's worthies, so as to know who to target first – I thought I could trust her to give me an honest answer, being holy and all – but she told me to keep my thieving fingers to myself. What sort of saint comes up with that kind of response?'

'The kind of saint who comes from Clare,' replied Michael. 'You should meet their hermit – a "recluse" who lives near a busy castle and likes shopping.'

'Perhaps we should stay with him then,' suggested Langelee. 'He probably has guest quarters we can use, and we will be better fed than at home.'

'I do not think so,' said Michael in distaste. 'He smelled of goat and I do not want to share my bed with a menagerie. Perhaps the Austins will put us up. I know for a fact that they are wealthy.'

'They are unlikely to extend their hospitality to a Benedictine,' predicted Langelee gloomily. 'Maybe we should visit the castle, and hope the Lady offers to house us in return for the pleasure of our company.

She likes scholars, and we *are* charming fellows. Especially me.'

'How about Nicholas?' suggested Bartholomew. 'He might find us a corner, and we can tell everyone that we accepted his offer because we want to be near the church.'

'That is a good idea,' said Langelee, brightening. 'It will make us look pious, which is not a bad thing, and he has the look of an old soldier about him. He will not turn a fellow warrior away.'

The three scholars entered the church to see Nicholas and Weste talking near the anchorhold. Unwilling to beg in front of an audience, Langelee made a show of removing a stone from his boot, murmuring that they would make their move once the friar had gone. Unfortunately, the moment Weste walked away, Nicholas was approached by Badew, Roos and Harweden, all demanding to know about the following day's funeral. Again, Langelee held back, although he, Bartholomew and Michael were close enough to hear the conversation that followed.

'It was to have been today, but I delayed it because of the rain,' said Nicholas. 'And Anne thought it would be better tomorrow, as no one likes standing around open graves in a downpour.'

'I do not mind,' declared Badew with a vindictive smirk. 'Especially if it is to bury someone I hate. What time will it be?'

'Mid-morning,' replied the vicar, eyeing him askance. 'Anne said that is the best hour for burials, as it leaves plenty of time for a drink afterwards, to remember the deceased's virtues.'

'Anne thought, Anne said,' scoffed Harweden nastily, although the three Michaelhouse men were thinking much the same. 'Do you make no decisions for yourself?'

'It is not a crime to confer with a holy woman,' retorted

50

Nicholas stiffly. 'Indeed, it would be foolish not to. She is a very wise lady.'

'Is she?' sneered Roos. 'She seems rather worldly to me.'

Nicholas regarded him coldly. 'You are an experienced traveller, are you?'

Roos frowned suspiciously. 'Not especially. Why?'

'To ascertain how many other anchorites you have met, because if Anne is the only one, then your opinion is worthless.'

'He is very well travelled,' declared Harweden, indignant on his friend's behalf. 'He has kin in Peterborough, whom he visits every three months. Is that not so, Roos?'

'Hah!' exclaimed Nicholas triumphantly. 'I hail from Peterborough, and there are no future saints living anywhere near the place. Thus Anne is the only one he has—'

'Come, Harweden,' said Roos, plucking his crony's sleeve. 'We have better things to do than converse with this ignoramus. Like wiping horse muck from our boots.'

The three old men sailed away, although their haughty departure was spoiled when Badew skidded in mud, almost pulling his friends to the ground with him. They walked more carefully after that. When they had gone, Langelee, Michael and Bartholomew approached the vicar.

'You do realise that they were asking about the Lady's funeral, do you not?' said Michael. 'The one that will not happen tomorrow, because she is still alive?'

Nicholas smiled smugly. 'Then they should have made themselves more clear. I assumed they were asking after Robert Skynere, who was killed by someone from the castle four days ago.'

'How do you know the culprit is from the castle?' asked Bartholomew warily.

'Because who else would dispatch a townsman?'

Nicholas shot back. 'Moreover, he was poisoned, and sly toxins are difficult to acquire – townsfolk do not know where to buy them, but some of the castle residents have been to London.' He pursed his lips, as if this was all the proof that was needed.

'How can you be sure that Skynere was poisoned?' pressed Bartholomew. 'Death by such means is notoriously difficult to diagnose.'

'Because Grym says so,' replied Nicholas. 'And as he is a barber-surgeon, he is familiar with such matters. The culprit is doubtless one of those nasty squires. Or that knight Albon, who is so stupid that he probably does not even know what he has done.'

'I am beginning to feel quite at home here,' murmured Michael to Bartholomew. 'Murders, feuds, unfounded accusations. It is just like Cambridge.'

'Yes, except that it is not our responsibility to investigate anything,' warned Bartholomew, afraid that the monk would see it as a challenge worthy of his talents. 'Thank God.'

While the two of them spoke, Langelee started to work on Nicholas, casually mentioning his own military background. The vicar beamed his delight, and clapped a burly arm around the Master's broad shoulders.

'I once knew the garrison in York *very* well,' he declared. 'Indeed, I still have friends in the Austin Priory there.'

'I did not mix with clerics,' said Langelee, making it sound like a very undesirable thing to have attempted. 'But there are several soldiers who you might have met.'

He began to list them, and the vicar chortled with pleasure when several names were familiar to him. And then, while Bartholomew and Michael watched in silent admiration, Langelee secured not only three beds for the night, but an invitation to dine as well.

'Unfortunately, it cannot be for longer,' said Nicholas apologetically. 'Do you remember what I told you earlier about the castle meddling in town affairs? Well, the Lady decided that the Queen's priests will lodge with me when Her Majesty comes for the rededication service, and tomorrow is when everything will be made ready for them.'

'We have other plans for the rest of our stay,' lied Langelee, affecting insouciance to conceal his disappointment. 'We shall not trouble you after tonight.'

When Nicholas showed the three scholars around his home, Bartholomew thought it was small wonder that the Lady aimed to commandeer it. Most vicars occupied modest houses, but Nicholas's, located a few convenient steps across the graveyard, was palatial. It comprised a large chamber on the ground floor, three bedrooms on the one above, and five little attics on the top.

'Perhaps I should become a priest,' said Langelee, looking around enviously. 'You have ten times as much space as me, and I am Master of a College!'

They deposited their bags, saw their horses settled in the adjoining stable, then used the rest of the day getting to know the town and its residents. Bartholomew was more interested in the architecture, but Michael and Langelee made the acquaintance of several wealthy locals, who they decided could later be targeted for donations.

When the last of the daylight had faded, they returned to the vicarage, pleased to discover that Nicholas had a fire going and a stew warming over it. Outside, a spiteful wind hurled rain against the window shutters, and Bartholomew was glad they did not have to spend the night in the open. So was Langelee, who began to unwind, especially after his third cup of mulled wine. The lines of worry eased from his face, and he reverted to his old ebullient self – the man he had been before College troubles had dragged him down. He perked up even further when the stew transpired to comprise meat and no vegetables, which was the kind of manly fare he loved.

'So you were old Archbishop Zouche's henchman,' said Nicholas admiringly. 'I heard a lot of good things about him.'

'He was a fine leader,' averred Langelee, already firm friends with the worldly vicar. It was not surprising, as they had a great deal in common – a fondness for drink, flexible views on religion, and a penchant for revelling in their warlike pasts.

'He brooked no nonsense and knew how to deal with awkward customers,' nodded Nicholas. 'I respect that in a man.'

'In a man, perhaps,' put in Michael disapprovingly. 'But in a prelate?'

'*Especially* in a prelate,' countered Nicholas. 'Or sly seculars will run circles around him. Have a bit of this pork fat, Bartholomew. You look as if you need feeding up.'

'He is all skin and bones,' agreed Michael, while Bartholomew regarded the glistening lump in revulsion. 'It comes of eating too much greenery, which is a very unhealthy habit. He should know better, being a physician.'

'He should,' nodded Nicholas, regarding Bartholomew as if he had just sprouted horns. Then he turned back to Langelee. 'But why did you really come to Clare? If you thought the Lady was dead, was it to find out what she left you in her will?'

'Of course not,' lied Langelee, managing to sound genuinely indignant. 'Michaelhouse is awash with money, and her legacy, while nice, will make scant difference to our bulging coffers. But on the subject of wills, who are her executors?'

Nicholas scratched his chin. 'Let me think. Her steward, Robert Marishal, is one. He is her right-hand man, and she does not so much as cough without consulting him first. Then there is Sir William Albon, her favourite knight, although a duller-witted fellow does not exist.'

'Why did she choose him then?' asked Langelee.

'Because she likes him, and he does cut a dashing figure at ceremonies. And finally, there is the Red Devil – Master Lichet. I cannot abide him. He has a sly tongue, and it is a pity she likes to hear him wag it, because even castle folk are leery of the rogue. So there you are: those are the three you will have to petition for your bequest when the time comes.'

'Tell us a bit more about the townsman who was killed,' said Langelee. 'I heard a few snippets when I was in the taverns earlier, looking for a cheap place to . . . to buy a drink.'

Nicholas was happy to gossip. 'His name was Burgess Skynere, and he was fed hemlock by someone from the castle. His body was found by Mayor Godeston and Barber Grym, who were worried when he failed to appear at an important meeting.'

'How do you know it was hemlock?' asked Bartholomew. 'Because Grym told you?'

Nicholas nodded. 'Godeston ordered Grym to investigate, but the culprit was cunning – he left no witnesses and no clues. Ergo, Grym's hunt quickly ground to a halt.'

'So the feud between town and castle has turned murderous?' mused Michael, wondering if it was such a good idea to stay in Clare after all.

'It turned murderous long before Skynere,' averred Nicholas. 'Three of the Lady's men have also died over the last two months – killed by the town, according to the castle. Sir William Talmach was on her council, Charer was her coachman, and Wisbech was her chaplain. Wisbech was an Austin, like me, and will be missed. Charer will not, though – he was a drunken sot.'

Nicholas expressed his disapproval of such behaviour by draining his own goblet and pouring himself another so full that there was a meniscus over the top.

'How did *they* die?' asked Bartholomew, thinking it was hardly surprising that the castle had attacked Skynere if the town had already dispatched three of their number.

'Talmach fell off his horse, Charer drowned and Wisbech swallowed poison – hemlock, just like Skynere.'

Bartholomew frowned. 'But if one victim of hemlock was from the town and the other was from the castle, perhaps you are wrong to accuse each other of foul play. Maybe there is just a single killer – one who does not belong to either faction.'

'Unfortunately, we will never know,' sighed Nicholas, 'because, as I told you, Grym's enquiries are at a complete standstill.'

'Is he a skilled investigator, then?'

'He is the only one I have ever seen in action, so I am not really qualified to judge. However, I can tell you that he spent a long time with the bodies, and asked lots of questions of the victims' friends and relations. He certainly did his best.'

'Hemlock is not a good poison for sly murder,' said Bartholomew. 'It is slow-acting, so its victims take ages to die – which gives them plenty of time to raise the alarm.'

Nicholas raised his hands in a shrug. 'They may have tried, but they lived alone and they died at night. Their cries would have gone unheard. Of course, the castle accused Grym himself of the deaths, but we all know that was just them being spiteful.'

'Why would they accuse Grym?'

'Because he keeps a supply of hemlock himself – he feeds it to patients who need bits sawing off.'

'Does he?' asked Bartholomew, thinking *he* would never use it for such a purpose. The herb could relieve pain and promote healing sleep, but dosage was critical, and it was frighteningly easy to give too much, condemning a patient to paralysis and eventual death. He deployed it rarely – usually only on those who were dying or in such agony that the risk was acceptable.

'What do your fellow Austins say about losing one of their own?' probed Michael. 'And where do they stand in this dispute?'

'They refuse to join in, on the grounds that they would rather have peace. There is also the fact that they have friars in both places – me in the town and Father Heselbech as castle chaplain. And do not suggest that Wisbech was killed to *force* them to pick a side, because Prior John is not so easily manipulated, and will remain neutral no matter what.'

'Well, it is a sorry state of affairs,' said Michael. 'And it is not—'

'God's blood!' exclaimed Nicholas, his eyes fixed on Langelee, who was playing idly with one of his smaller weapons. 'That is a handsome piece. Where did you get it?'

'He gave it to me,' replied Langelee, nodding at Bartholomew as he handed the little blade over for closer inspection. 'It is a letter-opener.'

It had been a letter-opener originally – a small, knife-like device with a blade that could be slipped under a seal to break it cleanly. Bartholomew had bought it in France, as a gift for Langelee, and had expected him to toss it into a chest and forget about it. But Langelee had been delighted, and the physician had watched an innocent little implement become something else entirely in the Master's warlike hands. The blade had been honed to a wicked sharpness, and the pretty mother-of-pearl handle was wrapped in leather for better purchase. Langelee was inordinately fond of it.

'*Very* nice,' said Nicholas, turning it over apprecia-tively. 'I might get myself one of these – it is small enough to fit up a sleeve, but large enough to do what is needed.'

'What do you mean by that?' demanded Bartholomew uneasily.

'Defending myself. A parish priest is a tempting target in these uncertain times, and while I cannot arm myself brazenly, something like this would be ideal.'

'It works for me,' agreed Langelee. 'We scholars are also supposed to forswear arms, but only a fool would do it. I always have my letter-opener to hand, and it often comes in useful.'

'Will you sell it to me?' asked Nicholas, taking a piece of gristle from his bowl and testing the blade for sharpness. His eyes widened in appreciation at the result.

Langelee took it back from him with an apologetic smile. 'I shall never part with it – it is like an extension of my own arm. Besides, I need it for opening letters.'

Bartholomew knew he did not, because the Master was not a man for neatly slitting seals when it was quicker to break them with his fingers.

'Come on,' wheedled Nicholas. 'You can hide all manner of weapons under an academic tabard, but a habit is much more difficult. I need it more than you do.'

'I will send you one from Cambridge,' promised Langelee, putting it away before there was a spat and they ended up being evicted. 'One that is smaller and sharper.'

'All right,' said Nicholas, although with ill grace. 'As long as you do not forget.'

'I will not,' vowed Langelee, and offered a large, callused hand to seal the deal. 'As one old soldier to another. Now, shall we have another drink?'

# CHAPTER 3

It was still raining the next morning, although not as hard as it had done during the night. Drizzle swept down in gauzy sheets and wreathed the top of the church tower in white. The three scholars rose before dawn, as was their custom, and went with Nicholas to celebrate Mass, where Michael assisted at the altar, and Bartholomew and Langelee gazed contemplatively at the ceiling, although for different reasons. The physician was admiring the fan vaulting again, while the Master of Michaelhouse was pondering ways to win new benefactors.

The rite was well attended, although it quickly became apparent that the congregants were more interested in staking a claim on 'their' piece of the nave than in what was happening in the chancel. Within moments, there was a scuffle near the rood screen – a handsome affair of stone with soaring pinnacles along the top – between a troupe of squires and some young merchants. The squires wore the silly pointed shoes and flowing sleeves currently popular at Court, and strutted about with the arrogance of entitlement. The merchants' robes were more practical, although every bit as gorgeous, and the supercilious glances they shot their rivals were calculated to provoke.

They might have come to blows had Michael not gone to see what was happening. As Senior Proctor, he was used to dealing with fractious youths, and stilled the brewing spat with a gimlet-eyed glower. None of them knew him, so it said much for the power of his personality that he was able to restore peace with a single scowl.

'Yes, you behave yourselves,' came an admonishing

voice from the anchorhold. 'It makes us look bad when you squabble in front of visitors. Do it again and you will answer to me.'

There was no further trouble, and when the ceremony was over, Bartholomew went to pay his respects to Anne. She was wearing a different gown to the one she had donned the previous day, and people had already presented her with gifts of food, as six or seven sweet-smelling parcels sat on a shelf by the window. He was surprised to note that a pie had several bites taken out of it, while one plate contained nothing but crumbs.

'You do not wait until after Mass before breaking your fast?' he asked, astonished.

Anne shrugged. 'Being holy is hungry work. Besides, I worked at the castle for thirty-seven years before taking up a life of religious contemplation, so I think I have earned the right to ignore the rules when I feel like it.' She sniffed resentfully. 'I gave my all to that place, although my efforts were never truly appreciated.'

'What did you do there?' asked Bartholomew, sensing her need to talk.

'I was a nurse,' she replied grandly. 'I raised a host of children – the sons and daughters of lords and their senior servants – and saw them all safely through to adult-hood. My charges include Master Marishal's twins and the naughty squires you saw just now. But then God called me, so I came here instead.'

'Was it very difficult to make the transition?'

She waved an airy hand. 'There were one or two trying weeks at the beginning, but I soon had people trained to bring me what I need. I have been in here for a year and a half now.'

'You must find it very noisy, with all these builders and artists.'

'That work began just two months after I took my holy vows. Of course, it was because of me that it happened at all. I told Clare to provide a church worthy of my presence, and the town responded by funding the new roof, while the castle added the south aisle. I am looking forward to the rededication ceremony next week – the culmination of all my labours.'

Bartholomew smothered a smile that she should claim so much credit for the project. 'It must have been disruptive, though.'

'At times, but I do not mind. Sitting in here all alone can be tedious, so watching the masons and painters gives me something to do. Of course, I do not like the fan vaulting very much. It is too fussy for my taste, and I would rather have had something simpler. It is a—'

She broke off abruptly and hurried to her other window, where the squires had appeared. Their company was evidently more appealing than Bartholomew's, as she was soon laughing and joking with them. She demanded the latest gossip, so they obliged by telling her of a scandal involving the baker's mother. Bartholomew moved away, disinclined to listen, and taking the charitable view that she wanted the information so as to know who to include in her prayers.

He met Nicholas and Langelee by the door. The vicar was begging again for Langelee to sell him the letter-opener, and Langelee was becoming irked by his persistence.

'I have just been talking to your anchoress,' interjected Bartholomew before the Master said or did something that would offend, which would be unfortunate after they had just enjoyed Nicholas's hospitality. 'She tells me she was a nurse before coming here.'

'A very good one,' said Nicholas, accepting the change of subject with obvious regret. 'And it is a pity that the Lady decided to dispense with her services.'

'Anne was dismissed?' asked Bartholomew. 'She told me that she was called by God.'

Nicholas became flustered. 'It was both. She was invited to leave the castle, but when God saw she was available, He decided to claim her for Himself.' Then it was his turn to change the subject. 'I cannot wait for Tuesday. In just five days, my church will host the Queen of England *and* the greatest architect in the world.'

'I am looking forward to seeing it in its full glory,' said Bartholomew keenly. 'But are you *sure* all the scaffolding will be down by then?'

'Positive,' replied Nicholas confidently. 'Would you like to see the ceiling from the roof space? It is just as impressive, although for a different reason. Come.'

The door to the stairs that led to the roof was in the new south aisle. Nicholas opened it to reveal a spiral staircase built inside one of the thicker piers. It was dark and narrow, lit only by the occasional slit in the stonework. The climb seemed to go on for ever, until Nicholas reached a second door, which he unlocked with a key that he wore around his neck.

He flung it open and stepped aside to reveal the roof space – the area between the ceiling and the outside slates. It was indeed impressive, and comprised an intricate system of horizontal beams and vertical struts with the roof arching overhead. The fan vaulting was apparent in the stone domes that bubbled up through the floor. Interspersed between the domes was more scaffolding, a complex mess of planks and ropes that were larger and stronger than the ones in the church below. Nicholas indicated it proudly.

'Cambrug installed all that to prevent the fans from collapsing while they were being assembled,' he explained. 'Now they are finished, except for the paintwork, the supports are no longer needed. But we shall leave them where they are for now.'

'Because no one will see them up here anyway,'

surmised Langelee. 'And you can dismantle them at your leisure, once the Queen and her retinue have gone.'

'Precisely! It is cheating, I suppose, but needs must. Yet the supports have a beauty of their own, and I shall be sorry to see them go. In some ways, they demonstrate Cambrug's genius more than the fan vaulting, as there are not many who could have devised so clever a system of braces.'

'They are clever,' acknowledged Bartholomew, surveying them with the eye of a man who understood loads and angles. He pointed. 'I assume those two central posts took most of the weight until the vaults were self-supporting?'

'Exactly! And what is even more amazing is that we can see everything quite clearly, even though none of us has a lantern. Cambrug left ingenious little gaps, so that the light can filter up from below. Do you know why? So that no one will ever be obliged to come up here with a lamp, thus reducing the risk of fire. He thought of everything.'

'Is that one of his "ingenious little gaps"?' asked Bartholomew, pointing again. 'Only it looks like a crack to me. A rather large one.'

'Oh, that *is* a crack,' acknowledged Nicholas. 'It happened early on, but Cambrug said it was just the stone settling into its final position, which is quite normal. We shall fill it with glue once the ceremony is over.'

'Anne said she has been here for a year and a half, and building began some eight weeks after she arrived. That means you have done all this in sixteen months. It is a remarkable achievement.'

'Yes, it is,' agreed Nicholas, pleased by the praise. Then he grimaced. 'Of course, our success is no thanks to Roger the mason, who was a dreadful grumbler. I cannot imagine why Cambrug appointed him as his deputy. I am sorry he is dead, of course, but he was such a malcontent.'

'He did not die in suspicious circumstances, did he?' asked Bartholomew warily. 'Like the others you told us about last night?'

'There are some who will tell you so, but the truth is that he was struck by falling scaffolding – an accident. Do you want to see his tomb? It was only finished last week. Go down the stairs and wait at the bottom. I shall join you there as soon as I have locked up here.'

'Why do you need to keep the roof secure?' asked Langelee, beginning to do as he was told.

'Lest the castle folk come up here for mischief. I would not have invited you, given that you are strangers, but . . . well, if I cannot rely on two old soldiers to behave, then who *can* I trust?'

Bartholomew winced. When he had been in France, searching for Matilde, bad timing had put him near the little town of Poitiers, where a small English force had defeated a much larger French one. He disliked remembering the carnage, but Langelee had run out of stories about his own military achievements the previous night, so had started to invent ones about the physician's instead, determined to repay the vicar's hospitality with plenty of gory tales. Now Nicholas laboured under the misapprehension that Bartholomew was a seasoned warrior.

When the vicar joined them at the bottom of the stairs, he led the way to the tomb that the Swinescroft men had used as a seat the previous day. It comprised a plain chest with a marble top, and its location and height meant it was not only a convenient resting place for elderly legs, but also a handy workbench – the artists were currently using it to mix paint.

'Was Roger unpopular?' asked Bartholomew, wondering if there was a reason why Cambrug's second-in-command had been buried below such a functional piece of furniture.

'Very,' replied Nicholas. 'He thought the roof should

64

have taken years to build, and refused to admit that he was wrong, right up until the day he died. And he hated the fan vaulting – he considered it too modern.'

'Why did Cambrug choose such a person as his deputy?'

'Because he was local, I suppose,' shrugged Nicholas. 'The diplomatic option. Yet I wish Roger was alive. It would have been a delight to watch his resentful face as I officiate at the ceremony that will mark the work's completion.'

Nicholas went to speak to Anne at that point, leaving Bartholomew to recall what Michael had said the night before: that Clare had even more suspicious deaths than Cambridge. Then the monk himself arrived, grumbling about the disgraceful spat during Mass.

'If they cannot control themselves, they should not have come,' he said, tight-lipped with righteous indignation. 'And if they do it during the ceremony next Tuesday they will be sorry – the royals levy fines for that sort of behaviour.'

'There is Grym,' said Bartholomew, nodding to where the enormous barber-surgeon was standing with the Mayor, both of them gazing up at the ceiling. 'I want to ask him about using hemlock for amputations.'

'Not in an accusing way, I hope,' said Langelee pointedly. 'He is one of Clare's richest residents, and thus on my list of potential benefactors.'

'In a medical way,' Bartholomew assured him. 'I am always keen to learn new things.'

'Well, just watch your tongue,' warned Langelee. 'And remember, even if you do find out that he made an end of the folk who Nicholas claimed were poisoned – Wisbech and Skynere, was it? – we do not have the authority to do anything about it.'

Bartholomew did not bother to say that he had no intention of delving into the unsavoury business of

65

murder, and went to the rood screen, where Mayor Godeston and Grym peered up at a part of the ceiling that was relatively free of scaffolding. Michael and Langelee followed, although all three held back politely until the two townsmen had finished their discussion.

'It is not a crack,' Grym was saying. He wore a dark green tunic with frills that, combined with his rotund shape, made him look like a cabbage with legs. 'It is just a smear of paint.'

'Then someone must go up there and scrub it off,' declared Godeston irritably, 'because it spoils the effect. I would do it myself, but I do not think my couch will fit up the steps.'

He was in his litter as he spoke, lying back to squint upwards. He was again clad entirely in purple, although this time it was gold embroidery, rather than silver, that adorned his sleeves. His bearers wore the same clothes as they had the previous day, including their hats, which they had neglected to remove. Bartholomew suspected it was because their hands were full of their employer's litter, but they were still the subject of scowls from three castle knights, who evidently considered it disrespectful.

'I do not think I would fit up them either,' Grym was saying unhappily. 'So perhaps one of your lads would go instead.'

'And what happens to me while he messes about up there?' demanded Godeston testily. 'Am I to sit on the floor until he comes back?'

'Am I to sit on the floor until he comes back?' mimicked Langelee, in a disconcertingly accurate imitation of the Mayor's high-pitched and rather prissy voice that made Bartholomew and Michael regard him askance. He shrugged. 'I do not like him. He was rude to me yesterday when I mentioned that Michaelhouse is looking for new benefactors.'

'Then we must work to win his good opinion,' determined Michael, 'because we cannot have him speaking against us to his wealthy cronies. However, we will not succeed if you make fun of him, so you might want to control your parodying urges.'

'Although you did do it rather well,' said Bartholomew, winning himself a conspiratorial grin.

'Good morning, good morning,' said Grym cheerfully, turning to smile as the three scholars approached. 'How are you this fine day?'

'It is not a fine day,' countered Langelee. 'It is raining.'

'Every day is a fine day in Clare,' averred Grym. 'How could it be otherwise?'

'True,' acknowledged Godeston. 'There is no better place in the whole wide world.'

'Nicholas told me that you use hemlock when you amputate,' said Bartholomew to Grym, launching into a medical debate with an abruptness that made his colleagues wince. 'Does it work?'

'It depends what you mean by "work",' replied the barber cautiously. 'It certainly stops the patient from thrashing around, especially when combined with a good dose of poppy juice. Unfortunately, they are usually dead by the time I finish.'

'I see,' said Bartholomew, not sure *he* would be so flippant about what sounded to be a rather high failure rate. 'How long do these procedures normally take you?'

'Oh, not long at all. I do not maintain my princely size for my own benefit, you know – I learned years ago that a surgeon needs a bit of meat on his bones for amputations, or he is forced to saw and hack for ever, which patients tend to dislike. Perhaps you would care for a race later?'

'I do not think so,' said Bartholomew primly, startled by the offer, not to mention the problem of acquiring suitable subjects. 'Speed is not everything.'

'It is as far as the victim is concerned,' countered Grym, not unreasonably.

'I understand you are the town's investigator,' said Michael, before he could hear something he might wish he had not – he knew from past experience that Bartholomew could be grisly when conversing with fellow *medici*. 'And you have explored several suspicious deaths recently.'

'He is not an investigator,' interposed Mayor Godeston. 'He just offered to inspect the bodies and give us an official cause of death for our records.'

'Because no one else is qualified,' explained Grym, and smiled amiably. 'Although I have something of an aptitude for it, if you want the truth.' He gestured to the mason's tomb. 'Roger was my first. I was able to ascertain that he was killed by a falling plank, but that it was all his own fault for standing in a dangerous place without a proper hat.'

'So it was an accident?' probed Michael.

Grym nodded. 'Next was Talmach from the castle. He was old and frail, but insisted on riding with the hunt to impress his pretty young wife. It was a wet day, so no one was surprised when his horse skidded in mud and threw him. However, it was I who pointed out that he was unlikely to have landed square on his dagger.'

'In other words, he was murdered,' said the Mayor. 'Probably by one of his castle cronies.'

'Then Charer the coachman drowned,' Grym went on. 'He was a sot, who should not have been walking by the river alone and in the dark, but I am fairly sure he should have been able to pull himself out – which means that someone prevented him from doing so.'

'And Skynere and Wisbech died from swallowing hemlock,' prompted Bartholomew.

Grym inclined his head. 'Wisbech was found dead in the castle chapel—'

'The Lady thinks the town killed him,' put in Godeston, 'but she is wrong. One of her minions did, in the hope that the Austins would join their side in the quarrel.'

'I ascertained that there was hemlock in the meal he had eaten in his vestry the previous evening,' Grym went on. 'He died during the night, and was discovered the next day. The same thing happened to Skynere – the poison was in his dinner, and Godeston and I found him the following morning, stone dead and still sitting at his table.'

'It was horrible.' Godeston shuddered and his bearers did likewise, forcing him to grip the litter to avoid being pitched out. 'He was just sitting there, as if he had fallen asleep. Personally, I suspect the squires did it. They are a wild horde.'

'Hemlock takes time to kill its victims,' said Bartholomew. 'So why did Skynere – or Wisbech, for that matter – not summon help?'

'Perhaps they tried, but it was night and they were alone,' replied Grym, essentially repeating what Nicholas had claimed. He turned to Godeston. 'Yet I do not think the squires were responsible, as poison seems too artful a *modus operandi* for brutal fellows like them. My money is on Philip de Jevan. I have never liked him.'

'Who is Philip de Jevan?' asked Michael.

'A member of the Lady's council, who comes from London four times a year to give her the benefit of his wisdom.' Grym pulled a disagreeable face. 'He is a terrible man.'

But the Mayor was shaking his head. 'If it is not the squires, then it will be Stephen Bonde, the Lady's favourite henchman. Now *there* is a killer if ever I saw one.'

'A killer, yes, but not a poisoner,' argued Grym. 'He is more the kind to use his bare hands. Jevan would use hemlock, though – a sly weapon for a sly man. He reminds me of a rat, slinking about and never stopping to exchange pleasantries.'

'Jevan is all right,' said Godeston. 'I asked him to bring me some nice cloth when he next came up from London, and he gave me this.' He reached into his scrip and produced a length of purple silk so fine that it seemed to float in the air. 'I have left instructions that it is to be draped over my coffin, should the unlikely day ever come when I might need one.'

'Very pretty,' said Michael, who was also of the opinion that his own death was optional. 'Although Jevan did not need to go to London for it. Matt's sister sells that in Cambridge.'

'Of course, *Lichet* will be familiar with hemlock,' mused Godeston, putting the silk away. 'He calls himself a learned man, but he has the look of the warlock about him. Nicholas calls him the Red Devil, which suits him very well – we all know that red is Lucifer's favourite colour.'

'I always understood it was black,' said Michael.

Godeston raised his eyebrows. 'Do you really believe that St Benedict would insist on his monks wearing black if it made them attractive to Satan? Of course not! Satan loves crimson, which is why you will never see any habits of that colour.'

'Cardinals wear scarlet,' Bartholomew pointed out.

'Quite, and what does that tell you?' retorted Godeston. 'However, I know for a fact that Satan loves red, because it is the colour of Christ's blood – something in which he rejoices.'

'I am sure he does not, theologically speaking,' argued Michael. 'Because it symbolises eternal salvation and the forgiveness of—'

'Rubbish,' interrupted Godeston. 'Lichet is the Devil's familiar, and if you have any sense, you will stay well away from him and trust nothing he says.'

'We shall bear it in mind,' said Michael.

\* \* \*

70

Clare Castle boasted two huge baileys, both protected by walls, wet ditches and earthworks. The outer one was filled with wooden service buildings – stables, storehouses and quarters for retainers. The inner was marked by four squat towers and a motte with a massive central keep. However, the building that really commanded attention was the handsome palace that stood at the heart of the complex. It had been designed for comfort rather than security, and had large windows to fill it with light and a plethora of fireplaces to keep it warm.

'Oxford, Maiden, Auditor and Constable,' said Langelee, gazing approvingly at the fortifications – the living quarters did not interest him. He became aware of the bemused glances of his Fellows. 'Those are the names of the four towers.'

'How do you know?' asked Bartholomew.

'Nicholas told me last night, after you two had retired. After all, only a fool ventures into enemy territory without first learning the lie of the land.'

'We have come to inveigle money, not lay siege to the place,' said Michael.

'It amounts to much the same,' shrugged Langelee. 'Both will involve tactics and strategies.'

The castle had several entrances, but the main one was at the end of the road called Nethergate. Bartholomew, Michael and Langelee were about to pass through it when they were hailed. They turned to see their University colleagues hurrying towards them. The Clare Hall Fellows wore academic gowns of exquisite quality, while Pulham had his Book of Hours tucked under one arm, and Donwich carried the regalia used for writing. Clearly, they aimed to present themselves as men of learning and refinement.

By contrast, the Swinescroft trio were scruffy. They had not shaved, their clothes were spattered with mud, and they had not bothered to clean their boots. Roos looked

71

the most disreputable of the three, because he still wore his horrible woollen hat, tugged down so low that Bartholomew wondered how he could see where he was going.

'You should have waited for us, Langelee,' said Donwich coldly. 'Or do you aim to impress the Lady's executors by arriving first? What time is her funeral, by the way?'

It was Badew who replied, eyes agleam with malice. 'Mid-morning. Do not worry, Donwich – we have plenty of time before the old witch is dispatched on her journey to Hell.'

'They still do not know,' whispered Michael in astonishment, as their colleagues hastened to enter the castle before them. 'They consider themselves too grand to chat with local folk, so no one has had the chance to enlighten them. That will teach them to be aloof!'

Langelee chuckled. 'It will be hilarious to watch what happens when they see her alive.'

'I hardly think—' began Bartholomew uneasily.

'All is fair in war,' interrupted Langelee. 'And the future of Michaelhouse depends on the next few days, so we cannot afford to be gentlemanly. Now shut up and follow my lead.'

Donwich and Pulham had contrived to be first up the ramp to the gatehouse, with the three Swinescroft men hot on their heels. They were about to pass under the portcullis when they met some people on their way out. They were the squires who had caused such a rumpus at the church earlier, along with a golden-haired couple in their mid-twenties. At a glance, the pair – who were so alike that they had to be the Marishal twins – appeared angelic, but a closer inspection revealed mischief sparking in the blue eyes. Both were sniggering, and Bartholomew suspected he knew why when he looked at their companions.

Since Mass, the squires had been at their toilet. Their beards had been slicked into two sharp points below their chins, kept in place by a waxy gel. It was an odd fashion, and in combination with their long-toed shoes and flowing sleeves, made them look like travelling magicians.

Bartholomew wanted to laugh, too, but prudently resisted the urge – the clothes were effete, but their wearers were not. All carried swords and had the arrogantly swaggering gait that suggested they would like nothing more than a brawl. Moreover, they were on Mayor Godeston's list of suspects for killing Skynere, so needed to be approached with care.

'Scholars!' exclaimed the male twin. His clothes were fine but sensible, and although Bartholomew could not have said why, he knew that the oiling of the others' beards had been his idea – a practical joke to make them look silly. 'Welcome! To what do we owe this honour?'

'We are not here to talk to the likes of you,' declared Badew rudely, regarding him with open disdain. 'We want Marishal the steward.'

'I am his son, Thomas,' said the twin pleasantly, although his cronies bristled at Badew's manners. 'And this is my sister Elizabeth, although we call her Ella. Perhaps we can help you.'

'Leave them, Tom – we have better things to do than wait on scholars,' growled the largest of the squires, a beefy fellow with a big, heavy face. A scar on one cheek suggested he was no stranger to fighting, and his fancy clothes looked more ridiculous on him than the others – akin to a bull wearing lace.

'There is always time to help men of learning, Nuport,' said Thomas, although the sly cant in his eyes suggested that any assistance offered should be accepted with caution.

'Thomas and Ella,' mused Badew, regarding them

73

closely. 'You came to University Hall and made a nuisance of yourselves on the day that I was forced to sign that quit-claim.'

Ella inclined her head. 'But I am afraid I do not recall you, sir. It must be thirteen years ago now, and we were just children at the time.'

'Fourteen years, one month and eighteen days,' corrected Badew briskly. 'It is not an event I shall ever forget.'

'I remember it, Ella,' said Thomas. His face was sombre but there was laughter in his eyes. 'The quit-claim was very nearly signed in blood. Surely that cannot have slipped your mind?'

Badew seemed to inflate with rage at the reminder, and his face turned a worrying shade of puce, but Ella spoke before he could begin a tirade.

'Perhaps it will come to me later. Meanwhile, we shall call a servant to conduct these men to our father. It is—'

'Universities are a waste of time,' interrupted Nuport, and gave a grin that was all bared teeth and menace. 'Learning to kill is much more fun. We are going to France next week with Sir William Albon, to join the Prince of Wales. The war will be as good as won once *we* arrive.'

'It is as good as won now,' said Michael. 'I have it on good authority that peace will be declared within the month.'

'What are you talking about?' demanded Nuport, while his friends regarded each other in dismay. 'How can there be peace when our King does not yet wear the French crown?'

Michael shrugged. 'His Majesty has gained as much as he can realistically expect from the campaign, and he knows when it is time to stop. There will be no more battles, so your task will be to guard the territories he has gained these last few years.'

'I am not going then,' declared Nuport sulkily. 'What would be the point? I want to kill Frenchmen, not defend a lot of fields and hovels.'

'Oh, come now,' chided Pulham. 'It will be an interesting experience regardless, and I am sure your kin will be delighted to know that you are in no danger over there.'

'I am not so sure about that,' murmured Donwich, glancing around at the stricken faces of those who had heard the monk's announcement. 'I have the sense that folk were looking forward to being rid of this lot, and your news has just ruined their day.'

In the end, it was Ella herself who conducted the scholars to her father, while Thomas trailed along behind. The squires retreated to a nearby guardroom to discuss Michael's alarming news over jugs of ale. They remained blissfully unaware of the amusement their appearance was affording the people of Clare – castle and townsmen alike. However, the grins faded as word spread that the squires might not be going to France after all – Donwich was right to predict that most folk had been looking forward to seeing the back of them.

As they walked, Ella homed in on Michael, regarding him in a way that suggested she liked what she saw. Women were often attracted to the monk, although Bartholomew failed to understand why, given that he was fat, unfit and not especially handsome. Michael claimed his dynamic personality made him more appealing than ordinary men, and it seemed he was right, as Ella clung to his arm and chatted brightly.

'We do not see many Benedictines in Clare,' she gushed. 'There is a whole priory of them a few miles away, but they rarely come here.'

'No?' asked Michael curiously. 'And why is that?'

'Because they do not like the Lady very much, as she

refuses to give them donations. But why should she? She already funds several other foundations.'

'Such as Clare Hall,' mused Michael. 'Although they are seculars, and she would do better to invest in a College filled with priests and monks instead. A College such as Michaelhouse. The Masses *we* recite will lessen her time in Purgatory.'

'Oh, she will not go to Purgatory,' laughed Ella. 'She will fly straight to Heaven. She told me so herself – when she also said that my brother and I would go directly to Hell.'

'What did you do to earn that sort of censure?'

Ella giggled. 'We sewed up the sleeves on her ladies' kirtles. You should have seen them struggling to get dressed while she screeched with increasing impatience for them to hurry.'

'Very droll,' said Michael. 'It is the kind of thing I might have done when I was eight.'

'You were eight, Brother?' asked Ella impishly. 'Good Lord! Did you know Moses?'

She flounced ahead at that point, treating him to a fine view of her jauntily swaying hips.

'She aims to seduce me, Matt,' he murmured. He nodded to where Thomas chatted to a girl with raven hair. 'And there is another man who is irresistible to women. She was scowling a moment ago, but now she simpers like a lovesick calf. It is a gift some of us have.'

But Thomas's real attention was on his sister, and it was obvious from the sly glances that were exchanged between the pair that more mischief was in the offing. Sure enough, Thomas eased the dark-haired girl into the centre of the path that led across the outer bailey, forcing Badew to step off it to go around her. The old scholar howled his alarm when he disappeared up to his knees in mud.

'You did that on purpose!' he screeched, batting away

Thomas's outstretched hand – probably wisely, as it would almost certainly be withdrawn at a critical moment. 'You vicious little bastard! If I were twenty years younger, I would thrash you.'

'If you were *forty* years younger, you could try,' retorted Thomas. 'But do not blame me for your clumsiness. You should have watched where you were going.'

Bartholomew and Langelee hurried forward to extricate the furious Badew, although at the expense of getting smeared with muck themselves. Fighting down her amusement, Ella returned to take Michael's arm again, and began to point out features of interest as they went.

'That is the Oxford Tower,' she said, gesturing to the smallest and oldest of the four squat turrets. She wrinkled her nose. 'It is not very nice inside, and no one wants to live there. When the Queen arrives, we shall put her conceited clerks in it, just for the delight of seeing their horror.'

'The name alone would render it undesirable,' drawled Michael.

'Of course, we are not always so strapped for space when the royals come to visit,' Ella went on. 'The problem is that Sir William Albon arrived with his entire retinue two weeks ago. He is one of the Lady's councillors, and he came to take my brother and the squires to France. He had intended to leave the day after the rededication ceremony, although if peace really is declared . . .'

Michael was puzzled. 'If he is one of the Lady's councillors – not to mention an executor of her will – what will happen to her affairs while he is away?'

Ella lowered her voice. 'He is not a very useful administrator, to be frank, and my father makes all the important decisions anyway.' She went back to her tour of the castle. 'There is the Constable Tower, where I live with my parents and Thomas. It is the steward's prerogative to have better quarters than anyone else, so we have all five storeys to ourselves.'

'Impressive,' said Michael. 'Will *you* be obliged to share when the Queen arrives?'

'Yes, we shall host *her* steward and his retinue. Over there is the Maiden Tower, where Lichet lives. But we call it the *Cistern* Tower, because it is as deep as it is tall. Below ground, it forms a great cylindrical well, where we store all our fresh water. As you can imagine, it is full to overflowing at the moment, with all this rain.'

Bartholomew was intrigued, and wondered if there would be time to inspect it, while Langelee murmured approvingly about the value of such a device in the event of a siege.

'And Lichet lives above it?' Michael was asking.

'He has the whole tower to himself – for now, at least; he will have to share it when the Queen comes. Personally, I cannot imagine why he likes it there. I know for a fact that it is damp.'

'How many people live in the castle?'

'We are about three hundred souls at the moment, although that will double when the Queen arrives. I am looking forward to it.'

'I am sure you are,' murmured Michael. 'It will provide you and your brother with more victims for your japes. I only hope you are wise enough not to target Her Majesty.'

Ella took the eight scholars to a reception room in the Constable Tower, where she presented them to a black-haired man and a fair-headed woman. Robert Marishal was tending to stoutness, although there was strength and determination in his stern features. He wore the kind of clothes that suggested he was about to go hawking, an activity usually confined to the gentry, indicating that he considered himself a cut above a mere retainer.

78

His wife Margery had one of the loveliest faces Bartholomew had ever seen, not just for its even features, clear skin and blue eyes, but for its expression of astonishing sweetness. She was simply dressed in a rose-coloured kirtle, and her only items of jewellery were a string of pink pearls and a small onyx ring bearing a tiny carving of a bird.

'Clare Hall,' said Marishal in surprise when he saw Donwich and Pulham. 'This is an unexpected surprise.'

Donwich bowed. 'May I take the opportunity to offer my condolences?'

'If you like,' replied Marishal cautiously. 'Although it is not a death that touches us very deeply, you understand. I shall attend the funeral, of course, but I hope it will not take too long, as I want to go hawking with Albon.'

Michael and Langelee exchanged a smirk when the other scholars blinked their astonishment at the confidence – all except Roos, who was leering at Margery. She blushed uncomfortably, and edged behind her husband, but Roos simply changed positions and ogled her afresh. Unwilling to stand by while a woman was harassed, Bartholomew stepped into his line of sight, causing Roos to scowl his annoyance.

'I did not expect to find anyone out gallivanting today of all days, Marishal,' said Donwich with rank disapproval. 'Do you not consider it disrespectful?'

'I am not "gallivanting" – I am entertaining a guest.' Marishal was obviously nettled by the censure, and would have added more, but a servant hurried up. 'Yes, Quintone? What is it?'

Quintone was a sly-faced man in brown clothes. He strutted with more arrogance than was appropriate for a minion, and there was nothing deferential in his manner.

'Sir William Albon is about to leave his quarters,' he reported. 'You asked me to tell you when he was ready.'

'Wait here with Ella,' Marishal instructed the scholars. 'I shall return as soon as I can, but my Lady's most important guests must take priority over you. I am sure you understand.'

He strode away without waiting to hear whether they understood or not, leaving his wife to provide a more sincere apology. But she did not linger long either, perhaps because Roos had managed to inch towards her and was standing offensively close. She ordered Ella to fetch wine from the kitchen, before hurrying after her husband.

'I know why Marishal toadies to Albon,' said Michael, once the scholars were alone. 'He is afraid that Albon will refuse to take Thomas and the loutish squires off his hands. Having them at large must interfere with the smooth running of his castle.'

Langelee agreed. 'There is nothing more dangerous than bored young men who know how to fight, and I should know, because I was one, once upon a time. France is the best place for them. They may be too late to fight enemies, but at least they will not be here.'

'This is all very peculiar,' said Pulham, frowning worriedly. 'The castle goes about its normal business while its Lady lies dead, then her steward reveals that he would rather go hawking than attend her funeral. What are they thinking?'

Bartholomew waited for them to surmise that there had been a misunderstanding, but none of them did, and instead they began a sniping argument about what was suitable behaviour for such an occasion. Acutely uncomfortable with the deception, he went to the window and looked out.

There was a flurry of activity in the yard below as Sir William Albon emerged from the Auditor Tower with his retinue at his heels. He was a glorious man in glorious clothes, and stood for a moment looking around imperiously. He had a head of golden hair, shot through with noble streaks of grey, a fine beard and an imposing physique. He wore a scarlet gipon with a gold cloak, and anyone looking at him might be forgiven for thinking that he was royalty.

Head held high, he raised his hands. No orders were given, but Nuport pressed a cup of wine into the left one, while Thomas slapped a pair of hawking gauntlets into the right. The great man took a sip from the cup, savoured it for a moment, then nodded to say it was of acceptable quality. He passed it back to Nuport and snapped his fingers, which was the signal for Quintone to hurry forward with a horse. Unfortunately, something was wrong with the way it had been saddled, because Nuport kicked the servant, who yelped and hobbled away. It was probably fortunate that no one other than Margery saw the murderous look Quintone shot the belligerent squire, or he might have been kicked a second time. Margery took Quintone's arm and whispered in his ear; whatever she said coaxed a reluctant smile.

Then all was bustle and shouting as more horses were led from the stables, and Albon and his followers mounted up. They were a bright crowd, all sporting the latest court fashions, although ones that were far less extreme than those favoured by the squires. Dogs scampered everywhere, men arrived with hawks, and servants rushed about with equipment and refreshments.

Michael, Langelee and Bartholomew watched the noisy chaos with interest, although the men from Clare Hall and Swinescroft retreated to the furthest corner of the chamber, where they continued to bicker among themselves. Then Ella returned, bringing goblets of wine on a tray.

'Perhaps you will tell us who all these people are,' suggested Langelee, aiming to find out which ones might be suitable to approach for a donation.

Ella was happy to oblige. 'The tall, ginger-headed person is Philip Lichet, who the Lady keeps for intelligent conversation. I think he is a warlock, although he denies it, of course.'

Bartholomew could see why Nicholas had dubbed Lichet the Red Devil. The man wore his auburn hair long, tumbling well past his shoulders, although he did not take good care of it, so it was greasy and unattractive, like his beard. He wore a scarlet cloak, and his great height made him a striking figure, albeit one that was a trifle shabby.

'And the dangerous-looking man who lounges by the stable?' asked Michael. 'Does he have half a nose, or do my eyes deceive me?'

He referred to a man clad completely in black, who seemed to belong to the shadows. Even from a distance, it was possible to see that his eyes were cold, hard and calculating.

'That is Stephen Bonde,' replied Ella. 'And yes, he is missing part of his nose. He lost it to Grisel, whom it is never wise to annoy.'

'Who is Grisel?' asked Bartholomew.

'Someone who does not put up with nonsense, and who will have the rest of it if Bonde goes near him again. Bonde is the Lady's chief henchman. He loves her more than his own mother, and will do anything for her.'

'Including murder?' asked Michael, recalling that Bonde was on Godeston's list of killers, along with the squires and Lichet.

'Oh, yes. He killed one of our neighbours and should have been hanged, but the Lady is as loyal to him as he is to her – she bribed the judges and got him acquitted.'

'So we have yet another mysterious death in Clare,' mused Michael. 'To go with Roger, Talmach, Charer, Skynere and Wisbech.'

'It was not in Clare,' replied Ella. 'It happened miles

away in Wixoe. And there is nothing mysterious about it – Bonde knifed Master Knowl in front of several horrified witnesses.'

And with that, she turned on her heel and flounced away.

It was some time before the hawkers were finally ready to leave. Albon led them out, mounted on a prancing white stallion that was draped with a silver blanket – which seemed inappropriate tackle for what promised to be a muddy excursion. His retinue clattered after him, followed by the dogs and men with birds. When they had gone, the silence seemed deafening. Marishal gazed after them wistfully, clearly wishing he could go too, then began to issue instructions to the castle servants, so that a hot meal would be ready for when the party returned.

Meanwhile, the quarrel between Clare Hall and Swinescroft had escalated, and the participants were on the verge of coming to blows.

'You came to gloat over her death,' Donwich was declaring hotly. 'It is disgusting, and you should be ashamed of yourselves. Thank God you are no longer part of our College, because I should be mortified to be associated with you.'

'Oh, we are not here to gloat,' countered Badew, eyes flashing. 'We came to reveal a secret. We have kept it for years, but now the she-devil is dead, it is time to share it with the world.'

'Tell them she is alive,' whispered Bartholomew to Michael and Langelee, alarmed. 'Or he may say something to harm the whole University.'

Michael started to step forward, but the Clare Hall men were too intent on Badew to notice.

'If you damage our chances of an inheritance,' Donwich was snarling, 'I will kill you with my bare hands. I swear to God I will!'

'The secret has nothing to do with you,' sneered Badew. 'It is to do with *her*. And while we are speaking the truth, I have something to tell Marishal about his brats as well.'

Pulham's expression was murderous. 'If you say or do anything untoward, we will make it known that you falsified the accounts when you ran "University Hall".'

Badew blinked his shock. 'But I never did!'

'Perhaps not,' acknowledged Pulham, 'but can you prove it? No? Then who do you think folk will believe? Two distinguished members of Clare Hall, or a man no one likes? You may have been respected – even loved – once, but your bitterness and rage these last fourteen years mean that no one will baulk at thinking ill of you.'

Badew spluttered his outrage, but the spat was cut short by the return of Marishal.

'I shall escort you to the Lady now,' he said. 'She is in the hall.'

'Is she?' blurted Donwich, startled. 'Good gracious! Is that not a little . . . public?'

Marishal frowned his bemusement at the question, but he was keen to be finished with business so he could join the hawking. Thus he did not ask for clarification, and instead led the way at a brisk trot to the palace, where he opened the door to the ground-floor hall.

It was a beautiful room. Tapestries adorned the walls, while the ceiling was hung with banners from the Lady's knights. The floor was made of stone and very clean, and the whole place smelled of herbs and fresh food, as opposed to sweat and wet dog, like the hall in Cambridge Castle. There was a throne-like chair on the dais at the far end, and the men from Clare Hall and Swinescroft stopped abruptly when they saw the Lady sitting in it, slumped with her head lolling to one side. Michael and Langelee chuckled at their shocked expressions, especially when she sat up, and fixed them with bright, beady eyes.

'My Lady of Clare,' gulped Donwich, the first to regain

his composure. 'May I congratulate you on your radiant good health? We expected to find you . . . rather less ambulatory.'

# CHAPTER 4

A short while later, seven of the eight scholars waited in a pleasant antechamber, where the Lady had agreed to grant them a private audience, away from the hundred or so courtiers who clustered around her. Roos had disappeared, which annoyed Badew and Harweden, who muttered darkly about needing his support in the light of the recent unwelcome developments. Both were trembling with anger and disappointment.

'So what of your secret, Badew?' asked Michael curiously. 'Will you still reveal it today?'

Badew scowled. 'It will have to keep for a little longer. However, I still have something to say to Steward Marishal. I shall never forget the vile behaviour of his brats when I was forced to sign that quit-claim, and it is time for revenge.'

'Badew, please,' said Michael quietly. 'It was a long time ago and they were children—'

'It feels like yesterday to me,' flashed Badew. 'And fourteen years is *not* a long time ago. Not when you are my age.'

Donwich and Pulham did not care about Badew and his secrets. They were more concerned about their benefactress finding out that they had travelled to Clare in the expectation of attending her funeral.

'It must be kept from her at all costs,' Pulham said worriedly. 'We cannot afford to annoy her – she is old, and there may not be enough time to regain her good graces before she really does die. Our College will not survive without the handsome legacy she promised.'

'Do not fret – I have a plan,' said Donwich soothingly.

'No one will accuse you and me of circling like vultures, Pulham, I promise. What about you, Langelee? Do you have a convincing excuse to explain your presence here?'

'*I* shall tell her the truth,' hissed Badew, before the Master could reply. 'And that will be the end of so-called *Clare* Hall.'

'Then it will be the end of you as well,' countered Pulham warningly. 'Because if you hurt us, I shall ensure that you are forever remembered as a thief. Your contributions as Chancellor will be forgotten, and when you die, scholars will spit on your grave.'

'You would not dare,' snarled Badew, although his eyes were uneasy. 'It would be a lie.'

'I *would* dare,' Pulham flashed back, 'so think very carefully before you open your mouth. In fact, why not cut your losses and leave now, before the Lady sees you? You will not be dancing on her grave today, so there is no reason for you to linger.'

'We cannot go home on our own,' said Harweden indignantly. 'Not with ear-loving robbers at large. Much as your company sickens us, we have no choice but to wait for you.'

'Besides, I still have things to say to Marishal,' said Badew, so venomously that Bartholomew was repelled by the malice that blazed from the old man's face. Clearly, the passage of time had inflamed rather than soothed the wound that Clare Hall had inflicted when its Master and Fellows had invited the Lady to take his place.

'Here she comes,' whispered Langelee, cocking his head at the clatter of approaching footsteps. 'Best behaviour now, everyone. We do not want her to denounce us *all* as greedy opportunists with long-standing grudges.'

The Lady had visited Cambridge fairly regularly when she had first agreed to finance Clare Hall, but her appearances had decreased over the past two or three years.

Bartholomew understood why when she entered the ante-chamber. She had aged since he had last seen her – her gait was stiff, her skin was papery, and there was a pallor about her that was indicative of a recent illness.

She was followed in by Marishal and Lichet, with Bonde bringing up the rear, toting enough weapons to supply a small army and looking as though he would dearly love to try them out. Donwich and Pulham swept forward to make a gushing obeisance, effecting courtly bows and remarking again on their benefactress's radiant good health.

'Then you are not very observant,' the Lady retorted, 'because I have been unwell. However, I am better now, thanks to Master Lichet. He tended me day and night until I recovered.'

'He is a medical man?' asked Donwich with polite interest.

'A *learned* man,' corrected Lichet in a voice that had a peculiarly booming quality. He stroked his red beard importantly. 'Which means my knowledge extends far beyond a single discipline. I have studied medicine, of course, but I also know philosophy, theology, geometry, music, the law and art.'

'But not modesty,' murmured Michael to Bartholomew, who struggled not to laugh.

'It is always interesting to meet a fellow intellectual,' said Pulham, inclining his head courteously. 'Where did you earn your degrees? Oxford? Perhaps we have mutual acquaintances.'

'I did not insult myself by studying in England,' declared Lichet, his voice dripping contempt at the very notion of it. '*I* attended the great university at Bordeaux.'

'Bordeaux?' echoed Michael suspiciously. 'I did not know it had one.'

'Then you are an ignoramus,' stated Lichet. 'Because it is by far the best *studium generale* in the world. Of course, only the top minds are accepted to study there – the rest have to make do with Paris, Oxford and Cambridge. We shall have no mutual friends, Pulham, of that I am sure.'

'So am I,' muttered Michael in distaste, 'because he is a charlatan. Maybe he *is* a warlock who has bewitched his host – the Lady is no fool, and should be able to see through such transparent mendacity.'

'Then let us hope he does not bewitch us as well,' Langelee whispered back, 'or we might find that he has inveigled us into making him a Fellow, and we do not want a man like *him* offering to teach medicine when Bartholomew leaves.'

Michael raised his voice. 'Perhaps you will show us dim-witted Cambridge men how to debate properly, Master Lichet,' he said, a wicked glint in his eye. 'So how about a public disputation? I am sure the Lady will agree, as there is no entertainment quite like it. Then you can demonstrate Bordeaux's superiority to us dullards.'

'I do not have time for that sort of nonsense,' declared Lichet pompously, although not before alarm had flared in his eyes. 'I am too busy with the paroquets.'

'Paroquets?' queried Michael. 'What are those?'

'Exotic birds,' explained Lichet, and smirked. 'Perhaps you can debate with *them* instead. Then you might stand a chance of winning.'

The Lady chuckled, so Marishal and Bonde did like-wise. Bartholomew held his breath – scholars were sensitive to insults about their intelligence – but Michaelhouse and Clare Hall needed the Lady's money, and dared not risk offending her by exposing Lichet as a dolt, while Swinescroft was under threat of blackmail. There were pained smiles or glares, but no reckless rejoinders.

'So to what do I owe the pleasure of your company?' asked the Lady eventually. 'I am sure it can have nothing

89

to do with money, as I am already generous to Clare Hall, while Michaelhouse must wait until I die to learn if it features in my will. And I have nothing to say to Swinescroft.'

Donwich effected another of his fancy bows, at the same time snatching the Book of Hours from Pulham's hands.

'Your grateful Fellows bring you a gift, My Lady,' he announced grandly, while his colleague's face filled with horror. 'This lovely tome was illustrated by John de Weste, the cofferer from Clare Priory. As it is so valuable, Pulham and I decided to deliver it directly to your hands.'

'Of course, you may not want it, given that you have so many books already,' added Pulham in a strangled voice. 'We shall not be offended – we will just put it in our own library.'

'He jests,' said Donwich smoothly, shooting him a warning glare. 'It was commissioned especially for you, My Lady, and we hope that you will derive much pleasure from it.'

He handed it over before Pulham could stop him. The Lady accepted it without much enthusiasm, and leafed through it in a desultory manner. But not for long.

'It is damaged!' she declared indignantly. 'One page is burned beyond all recognition, while several others are badly singed.'

'We have Roos to thank for that,' said Pulham tightly. 'But I am sure Weste can repair it.'

Bartholomew glanced around for Roos, thinking it would be unfortunate if the curmudgeonly old scholar ripped it from the Lady's hands and tossed it in the fire. But he was still nowhere to be seen, so Bartholomew supposed he was making a nuisance of himself with some hapless female.

'Well, the rest of it is very nice,' conceded the Lady, and passed it to Marishal to put away. Pulham watched it disappear with open dismay. 'Now tell me what you want in return.'

'Nothing,' replied Donwich greasily. 'It is enough to know that we have pleased you.'

The Lady raised her eyebrows. 'Truly? You are not here to demand some boon?'

'We merely wish to express our appreciation for your past generosity, and to offer our assistance in your preparations for this royal visit.'

'Then you may report to the kitchens,' said the Lady. 'There are pots that need scouring.'

'Oh,' said Donwich, taken aback. 'I see. Well . . .'

'I jest,' said the Lady with a smile that was rather malicious. 'Go and wait in my steward's quarters. He will find some task that is commensurate with your status.'

'Then we shall go with them,' determined Badew. 'Our business is with Marishal, not you.'

'No,' countered the Lady, her harsh tone stopping the old man dead in his tracks. 'You will state your purpose here and now, Badew. What do you want with my steward?'

'It concerns information that came to me via Roos,' replied Badew haughtily. 'And Marishal will want to hear the news in private, as it is of a personal nature.'

'Roos?' asked Marishal, looking around. 'I saw him talking to my wife earlier. Where is he? Why does he not give us this "information" himself?'

'Perhaps he could not bring himself to be in the same room as you,' sniffed Badew. 'And my news concerns your offspring, who are just as sly now as they were when they were children.'

'Thomas and Ella are not for you to—' began Marishal uncomfortably.

'What news?' demanded the Lady. She sighed crossly when Badew pursed his lips and indicated that Marishal was to precede him through the door. 'No! You will tell us what you have heard now, or I shall direct Bonde to

91

throw you out of my castle by the scruff of your neck. Well? Why do you hesitate still?'

Badew turned to the uneasy steward. 'Very well, then. You forced Ella to marry Sir William Talmach – an old man, but a rich one. Yes?'

Michael, Bartholomew and Langelee blinked their surprise – no one had mentioned this before. Warily, Marishal inclined his head to acknowledge it was true. Harweden took up the tale.

'She was desperately unhappy with the arrangement, and who can blame her? To avoid years of suffering his unwelcome advances, she and her brother conspired to dispatch him.'

'He did not fall off his horse and on to his dagger by accident that fatal day,' said Badew, eyes bright with malice. 'He fell because *they* sawed through one of his saddle straps.'

'You claim Roos told you all this,' said the Lady contemptuously, although it was clear from Marishal's stricken face that his heirs' involvement in the knight's death was a possibility he had already considered. 'How would he know? Did he witness it personally?'

'No, but one of your grooms visited Cambridge a couple of weeks ago and he gossiped about it to him,' replied Badew triumphantly. 'In other words, the twins *murdered* Talmach and the whole castle knows it.'

'Leave,' ordered the Lady, pointing an imperious finger at the door. 'I will hear no more slanderous lies from you. Go on, get out!'

'With pleasure,' declared Badew. 'Come, Harweden. We sully ourselves in this filthy place.'

They stalked out, heads held high. Several servants stood near the door, hovering lest their mistress should need them. None seemed surprised by the allegations, and Bartholomew even saw one or two nod agreement as the surly pair pushed past. He was thoughtful. He had seen for himself that the twins loved practical jokes – perhaps they had hacked through the strap for fun, not appreciating that the consequences might be serious. Or had they guessed exactly what would happen when an elderly husband went riding on an unstable perch in the wet?

'Ignore him, Robert,' instructed the Lady, when Badew and Harweden had gone. 'He is a snake, who will say or do anything to hurt me. Besides, he heard the gossip from Roos, who had it from a groom, who happened to be in Cambridge. How likely is that? It is malicious nonsense and any fool can see it. Now – Michaelhouse.' She turned to Langelee, Michael and Bartholomew. 'Do you come bearing gifts, too?'

'We heard you were ill,' lied Michael, and indicated Bartholomew, 'so we brought the University's Senior Physician to tend you. However, we are delighted to learn that his services will not now be required.'

'A physician,' mused the Lady, eyeing Bartholomew appraisingly before turning to Lichet. 'You have been itching to resume your travels for weeks now. If this man agrees to replace you, you will be free to leave.'

Bartholomew regarded her in alarm. He had wanted to visit Clare, not live there permanently!

'I shall only allow it if he is worthy of filling my shoes,' said Lichet quickly, and Bartholomew was greatly relieved to see that the Red Devil had no intention of abandoning the comfortable niche he had carved for himself in Clare, and that the threat to depart had almost certainly been made to secure himself a better deal. 'I could not, in all conscience, leave you in the hands of an inferior practitioner.'

'Then let us hope he continues to judge himself to be the better man,' murmured Langelee under his breath. 'Because Matilde will never forgive me if I arrive home without her husband-to-be. That was a reckless offer,

Brother – even if it did have the desired effect of making us look solicitous without costing any money.'

'You are kind, Lichet,' smiled the Lady, patting the Red Devil's hand. 'So let us put our visiting *medicus*'s skills to another use instead – he can cure my paroquets. But first, he and his Michaelhouse friends must dine with me, and tell me all the latest news from Cambridge.'

Bartholomew was irked that Michael should have made free with his services yet again, and none too pleased about being ordered to cure birds either, about which he knew very little. Nor did he want to join the Lady for what might transpire to be a lengthy meal when there was a whole new town to discover. He trailed after her resentfully, noting that she leaned heavily on Marishal's arm, and was not as hale and hearty as she would have everyone believe.

With a train of servants in their wake, they processed through a series of rooms, each one grander than the last. He was startled to see Roos and Margery sitting in one, talking in low voices. They shot to their feet when the Lady and her retinue trooped past, although neither she nor Marishal appeared to notice them, absorbed as they were in their own private discussion.

'Where have you been, Roos?' asked Langelee, pausing to chat, so that everyone behind him had to stop, too; oblivious, the Lady and Marishal continued alone. 'Badew is vexed with you for disappearing. And what are you doing in the Lady's private apartments anyway?'

'Badew is always vexed about something,' said Roos sourly. 'And if you must know, Mistress Marishal and I were discussing the recent rains. Not that it is any of your business.'

'I was telling him how our cistern is nearly full for the first time in months,' elaborated Margery, raising one hand to the pink pearls at her throat; they went perfectly with her rose-coloured kirtle. 'And how I am worried that it might overflow and flood the bailey.'

'It will not flood,' declared Lichet confidently. 'The improvements I made to the original design will prevent it. And a good water supply is essential for any fortress – it will stand us in good stead if we ever come under siege.'

'Under siege?' echoed Bonde. He had a deep, gravelly voice, which dripped hostility. His mangled nose had healed badly, accentuating his coarse, battle-scarred demeanour. 'What nonsense you speak! Who would want to attack the Lady?'

'You have obviously not been in the town of late,' Lichet flashed back. 'They hate her for foisting the new south aisle on their church.' His thin, sharp face turned vicious as he jabbed an accusing finger. 'They hate you as well, because *you* are a killer.'

'They hate you more, Red Devil.' Bonde fingered his dagger in a way that made all the hair stand up on the back of Bartholomew's neck. 'They think you are a warlock, who has bewitched her.'

'Please, gentlemen,' said Margery softly, coming to lay a soothing hand on the arm of each. 'No sparring, I beg you. There is no need for enmity, as I have told you both before.'

Surprisingly, much of the bristling menace promptly drained out of Bonde, and he mumbled a sheepish apology. Lichet was less easily appeased – he effected a stiff bow, then turned to hurry after the Lady and Marishal.

'I am sorry, mistress,' mumbled Bonde. He sounded sincere. 'But he aggravated me. He knows exactly how to do it, and it works every time.'

'I know, Stephen,' said Margery gently. 'But you must learn to resist or it will see you in trouble. Now, will you do something for me?'

'Anything,' declared Bonde, and gave a shy smile that

transformed his cold, brutal features into something almost pleasant.

'Good,' said Margery, patting his hand affectionately. 'Then take Anne a basket of food with my compliments. I have put it ready in the kitchen.'

Bonde nodded, clearly desperate to win her approval. He even attempted a bit of genial chatter, although it sounded forced and he was obviously uncomfortable with small talk.

'I am astonished that there is anything left, given what those greedy paroquets put away. They ate all the march-panes again yesterday. It is a wonder they can still fly.'

'I do not think Anne needs supplies,' put in Michael. 'From what I can gather, she receives so many gifts that she is obliged to hawk most of them, making herself a fortune in the process.'

'She sells it to the poor – at a much lower price than they can get at the market,' explained Margery. 'Go now, Stephen. Ask Quintone to help if the basket is too heavy for you.'

Bartholomew instinctively liked Margery Marishal, both for her compassion and for her sensitive intervention in the burgeoning row. He hoped there would be an opportunity to talk to her later, as she was by far the nicest person he had met in Clare so far.

A short while later, the three Michaelhouse scholars were seated at a table with the Lady, Marishal, Margery and Lichet. Bonde stood guard at the door, one hand on the hilt of his sword, and Bartholomew could not help but notice that the courtiers who hovered sycophantically in the adjoining chamber were careful to go nowhere near him.

Michael's eyes gleamed as the food arrived. There was soft white bread, dried fruit, wine imported from Spain, a variety of meats and cheeses, and pats of yellow butter.

The Lady asked him to say grace, then indicated that her guests should eat. Michael did not need to be told twice.

'I am ravenous,' he declared, helping himself to a generous portion of roasted venison and then placing the platter so it would be difficult for anyone else to reach. 'The quality of the fare on our journey was very poor.'

'Probably because of Simon Freburn,' said the Lady. 'No one wants to trade with remote villages as long as he is at large, waiting to pounce. Bonde is doing his best to hunt him down, but the fellow is tiresomely elusive.'

'Bonde!' spat Lichet, although not so loudly that his voice would carry to the man in question. 'He is an imbecile, and I do not know why you keep him. He should be dismissed, and someone more efficient – and more personable – appointed in his place.'

'He has a good heart,' countered Margery. 'He just needs a little patience and understanding.'

Lichet sniffed in a way that suggested Bonde would not be getting them from him. 'When will Jevan next come to Clare? Soon?'

'For the next Quarter Day council meeting, I imagine,' replied Margery, frowning her puzzlement at the abrupt change of subject. 'Which will be eight weeks hence. Why?'

'Because he brought Godeston a lovely piece of purple silk from London the last time he came, and I want him to do the same for me – only in scarlet,' explained Lichet. 'Although it will be galling to beg a favour from such a person. I cannot abide the man.'

'He has his virtues, too,' said Margery, evidently one of those people who saw the good in even the most undeserving of specimens. Then it was her turn to skip to a different topic of conversation. 'I had the strangest dream last night, Master Lichet. Perhaps you can tell me what it means. I dreamt that Anne and Vicar Nicholas were strolling arm in arm across the bailey.'

Lichet stroked his beard, delighted by the invitation to pontificate. 'It means you had a holy vision, as anchoresses and priests are God's chosen. Clearly, their wandering souls came to this castle because it is blessed by the presence of one of the Almighty's *favourite* people.'

He inclined his head to the Lady, lest she had not understood that he was paying her a compliment. Bartholomew winced at the clumsy flattery.

'I disagree,' said Michael, reaching for the roasted pork. 'It means that Anne is on your mind because you care for her welfare, while Nicholas must figure large in the arrangements for the royal visit. You merely dreamed of events that occupied you during the day.'

Lichet shot him a furious glance, and before the monk could say more, began to hold forth on a variety of subjects, although when anyone challenged him on one, he deftly segued to another. So when Michael questioned his understanding of Apostolic Poverty, Lichet simply moved to camp-ball, assuming himself to be on safer ground. He was wrong.

'That would be an illegal move,' declared Langelee, who loved that particular game more than life itself. 'You would be disqualified.'

'Nonsense,' countered Lichet, and turned to Bartholomew. 'I am an expert at curing unsightly rashes. I order them smeared with honey and—'

'You cannot do it,' interrupted Langelee, not about to let such an important matter go. 'And if you did, then you won this fabled victory by cheating. Camp-ball does not have many rules, but not moving the goal lines once the game has started is certainly one of them.'

'Well, I did,' stated Lichet shortly. 'It was—'

'Then you are a scoundrel of the first order,' interrupted Langelee sharply. 'And I hope you never try to play in Cambridge, because you will not be welcome.'

'I am sure an accommodation could be reached,' said Margery hastily, and began to talk about the weather with such sweet charm that even Langelee felt compelled to let the burning issue of goal-moving drop.

She contrived to chat amiably about nothing until the Lady, whose attention until then had been focused on her victuals, pushed her empty plate away and leaned back in her chair.

'So you are a physician,' she said to Bartholomew. 'I think I recall you from my visits to Cambridge, although my memory is not what it was. I remember you, though, Brother. Such a princely figure is difficult to forget. Your remit is to keep the peace in that rough little town.'

'It is not as rough as Clare,' countered Langelee indignantly. 'Ever since we arrived, we have been regaled with tales of murder, and there is a bitter feud between the castle and the town.'

'The feud is a passing phase, sparked by the church's restoration,' said the Lady dismissively. 'It will soon blow over. And as for the murders, well, these things happen from time to time.'

'They were accidents, not murder,' announced Lichet with authority. 'Our townsfolk live dull lives, and love to excite themselves by pretending that perfectly natural deaths are examples of unlawful killing. However, this is not a suitable discussion for the table of a great lady, so instead, would you like to hear about the time when I saved an entire town from the plague?'

That did not sound like a very genteel topic of conversation either, but Lichet forged on before anyone could stop him. The Lady appeared to hang on his every word, making Bartholomew wonder if Lichet *had* bewitched her, because the tale was poorly told and patently self-serving. While it was going on, he happened to glance at Marishal. The steward's expression was distant, and Bartholomew was under the impression that he was mulling over the accusation that Badew had levelled against his unruly offspring.

It felt like an age before the Lady stood to leave for her post-prandial nap, and Bartholomew was dismayed when she indicated that she wanted him to assist her to her chambers. He had hoped to escape – to explore Clare before any more of the day was lost, or even to help Langelee and Michael recruit wealthy benefactors. Anything other than wasting more time indoors.

'Have you visited the church yet?' she asked, as he helped her to lie on a bed that was heaped with furs. She indicated that he was to remove her shoes, while Margery hovered solicitously, ready to intervene if he proved unequal to the task. 'Those improvements cost a fortune.'

Bartholomew nodded. 'But worth the expense – the fan vaulting is astounding.'

'Our anchorite would disagree – poor Anne does not like it at all. She worked here once, you know, nurse to the children of my servants and knights. She tended Margery's pair.'

'They are still as meek as lambs with her,' said Margery ruefully. 'Far better behaved than they ever were with me.'

The Lady rolled her eyes. 'Because you are too gentle. We are lucky that Anne knew how to handle the rascals, or their mischief would have been the end of us. She even cowed Nuport, who rarely listens to anyone. Well, other than Albon, of course.'

'Albon,' said Margery with a fond smile. 'He is a fine man, and I am delighted that he will soon take my son away to France. Thomas will flourish under his manly guidance.'

'I imagine Anne told you that she was called to her

cell by God,' said the Lady, turning back to Bartholomew. 'But the truth is that I dismissed her. She tried to rid Suzanne de Nekton of an unwanted child, you see, and the process almost killed the girl. So she was offered a choice: trial by her peers or a life dedicated to God. She picked the latter.'

'She does not seem suited to such an existence,' said Bartholomew carefully, thinking that the Lady's tale explained a lot. 'She is too worldly by half.'

'Perhaps the sentence can be commuted in time,' said Margery, glancing hopefully at her mistress. 'I would not mind buying her a cottage somewhere, so she can live out her days in quiet contentment. It would be the least we could do for such a faithful servant.'

'She is not going anywhere until she expresses some remorse,' said the Lady coolly. 'As things stand, she believes we are wrong to condemn what she did.'

'What do *you* do when desperate and frightened girls say they are with child, Doctor Bartholomew?' asked Margery conversationally. 'How do *you* deal with unwanted pregnancies?'

Bartholomew was not about to share his views on such a contentious matter with two people he did not know. 'I live in a community of male scholars,' he hedged. 'It is not a problem I encounter very often.'

'You will encounter it if you stay here,' sighed Margery. 'The squires are relentless in their pursuit of pretty lasses, who are so eager to win rich and handsome husbands that they will do anything to get one. Mishaps are distressingly frequent.'

Even more reason to go home quickly then, thought Bartholomew.

The physician was glad to leave the Lady in Margery's solicitous hands. He hurried out of the palace, and began to hunt for Michael and Langelee. He tracked them

101

down to the outer bailey, where they were talking to Marishal.

'Normally, we would be happy to accommodate you,' the steward was saying. 'But Albon brought a sizeable retinue with him, while whole swathes of the castle have been put ready for the Queen, so are currently off limits to guests. We have no room for unexpected visitors.'

'It does not matter,' lied Michael. 'We have had several other offers, all from folk who are frantic to win an association with Michaelhouse – for the fabulous benefits it will bring them.'

'Then you will be far more comfortable than your friends from Clare Hall,' said Marishal slyly. 'When they saw how cramped we are, they wanted to room at the Swan, but how can I put them to work for the Lady if they are away in the town? I insisted that they stay in the Oxford Tower instead. Unfortunately, no one likes it there, as the paroquets occupy the top floor, and they can be very noisy.'

As if on cue, there was a raucous screech that made the three scholars jump.

'The ones I am expected to cure,' mused Bartholomew. 'What is wrong with them?'

'Who knows,' shrugged Marishal. 'However, I would keep your distance if I were you, for two reasons. First, they can be dangerous. And second, Lichet considers them to be his responsibility, and you do not want to make an enemy of the Red Devil.'

'Then that is too bad, because Bartholomew will see them today,' determined Langelee, who cared nothing for danger, so tended to assume that others did not either. 'The Lady told him to cure them, and we cannot afford . . . I mean we have no wish to annoy her by ignoring a direct order.'

Marishal's expression turned crafty. 'Then ask Lichet's permission. He will refuse, and when the Lady asks why Bartholomew has disobeyed her, you can report that

102

Lichet declined to accommodate him. It is high time she was irked with the rogue.'

'Perhaps it is,' said Michael. 'But I do not see why we should be the agents of it – not if he is the kind of man we do not want as an enemy.'

Marishal smiled thinly. 'It would be worth your while. He is unpopular here, and any number of courtiers would love to see him fall from grace. Indeed, they might be so pleased that they would make generous donations to your College.'

'Then we shall do as you suggest,' said Langelee, capitulating promptly. 'There he is now. Hey, you! Red Devil! Come over here.'

Langelee possessed a voice that carried, and it was clear that Lichet was indeed disliked, as several courtiers broke into delighted grins at the disrespectful summons. Lichet scowled indignantly and started to walk pointedly in the opposite direction, but quickly reconsidered this strategy when Langelee bellowed at him a second time, louder than the first, so even more people heard and exchanged looks of amusement.

'What do you want?' he demanded testily, stamping up to the Master. 'I am busy.'

'So are we,' retorted Langelee. 'However, we have been asked to cure the Lady's paroquets of a malady – one that is beyond your meagre skills. So take us to them at once.'

Bartholomew was impressed by the Master's uncharacteristic guile: Lichet could not possibly accede to such a 'request' without losing face, so a refusal was inevitable.

The Red Devil spoke between gritted teeth. 'She entrusted them to me, and I do not let amateurs anywhere near them. And for future reference, you will address me as Master Lichet.'

'Will I indeed?' said Langelee softly, fingering his enormous sword.

Lichet took a nervous step away. 'Just stay away from my birds,' he ordered, before turning on his heel and stalking away, head held high.

He was so keen to escape that he walked too fast, and almost fell when he skidded in mud. There was a gale of laughter from the watching courtiers – louder and longer than was really warranted. Then one came to clap Langelee appreciatively on the shoulder. He was a short but elegant man with a huge moustache, who introduced himself as Peter de Ereswell.

'For that display, I shall give you a pig,' he promised. 'I cannot abide Lichet.'

'We prefer money,' said Langelee bluntly. 'It is easier to transport than livestock.'

'Then I shall give you the equivalent amount in cash,' said Ereswell, eyes twinkling with amusement, 'just for being audacious enough to demand it. Will you see what else you can do to annoy the Red Devil? You will find that baiting the bastard can be very lucrative.'

'You see?' asked Marishal, smiling. 'You could leave here wealthy men.'

But the moment he and Ereswell had gone, Langelee's bullishness faded. 'I wish we had never come,' he said gloomily. 'The venture has been a disaster from the start. The Lady dead indeed! She is fitter than the rest of us put together.'

'She is not,' argued Bartholomew. 'Her health is fragile, and she feels old and tired. But look over by the gate. Is that the messenger who delivered the letter about her so-called demise?'

'It is,' said Michael, eyes narrowing. 'And he has some explaining to do.'

The messenger was named Justin, a pimply youth with an eager smile and a bloody bandage wrapped around his head. He raised his hands defensively when he saw the Michaelhouse men bearing down on him, and began to gabble an explanation.

'It is not my fault! I knew nothing of what was in that letter until it was opened and read in Cambridge. I am as stunned as you are to learn it was a lie. *Please* do not tell anyone it was me who took you the news. Marishal will never use me again, and I love riding.'

Langelee nodded to the stained dressing. 'But are you any good at it? Or did you fall off your horse, and that explains why we seem to have reached Clare before you, even though we dallied for a day before setting out?'

Justin was indignant. 'Of course I did not fall off! I was almost home when Freburn appeared out of nowhere and tried to lay hold of me. I was able to escape, but it meant a lengthy detour. I only arrived back an hour ago – to learn that someone has used me to play tricks on you.' He raised one hand to his head and winced. 'The Red Devil insisted on binding me up, but now it hurts.'

Bartholomew was not surprised that Justin was in pain when he saw how tightly the filthy, stinking bandage had been tied. He unwrapped it to discover a bruise but no broken skin, which meant the blood belonged to someone else – Lichet had reused the material without washing it first. It was shoddy practice, and one Bartholomew deplored.

'Who gave you the letter?' asked Michael. 'Someone who does not like you, and wants to see you fall prey to Freburn? Or in trouble with Marishal?'

'*Everyone* likes me,' declared Justin confidently. 'And the letter was just waiting for me on Sunday morning – four days ago now – with a note saying that I was to take it to Water Lane in Cambridge with all possible haste. I rode like the wind, but when I got there, I was not sure which house to knock at . . .'

'Whose name was on this missive?' asked Langelee.

'No one's.' Justin looked sheepish. 'Unfortunately, it

and the accompanying note had been left in a place that my horse can reach, and he loves the taste of parchment. We were lucky that there was anything left for me to deliver at all.'

'Not really,' sighed Michael. 'It would have been better for everyone concerned if he had scoffed the lot with no one any the wiser.'

'True,' acknowledged Justin ruefully, and resumed his tale. 'Anyway, as I was not sure where in Water Lane to go, I waylaid that bad-tempered scholar – Roos. He said it was for him, so I handed it over.' He shrugged defensively. 'I had no reason to think he was lying.'

'Chancellor Tynkell used to live on Water Lane,' mused Michael. 'Perhaps whoever sent the letter does not know that he is dead and his successor now resides in Michaelhouse. Still, these details do not matter, because the prank worked – the lie about the Lady has spread all over Cambridge.'

'Even so, I am astonished that Roos had the audacity to open it,' said Bartholomew. 'It must have been obvious that the intended recipient was the current Chancellor.'

'Of course it was obvious,' said Michael tightly. 'But how could he resist? A message from the lair of an ancient enemy to the University's highest-ranking scholar? Of course he would seize the opportunity to pry.'

'He never hesitated for a moment,' put in Justin. 'He just broke the seal and read what was written. Then he laughed.'

'I bet he did,' muttered Langelee.

Michael became businesslike. 'There is a way you can make amends for this debacle, Justin. You can ride straight back to Cambridge and inform Chancellor Suttone that we have been the victims of a cruel hoax. Then you can take the news to Clare Hall, who will pay you for your trouble. Go now – unless you want to confess what you did to Marishal.'

Justin hurried to do as he was told, and was galloping through the gate in record time.

'Roos has no right to open messages intended for the Chancellor – *any* Chancellor,' said Langelee indignantly, when the lad had gone. 'What a rogue!'

'I quite agree,' said Michael crossly. 'And I shall fine him when we get home. But first, he will hand it over so that we can identify the jester who sent it. We shall confront him as soon as we are settled into our new lodgings.'

'What new lodgings?' asked Langelee sourly. 'We do not have any.'

'We shall stay in the Austin Priory for the rest of our visit,' determined Michael. 'It is one of the wealthiest foundations in the county and can afford to keep us for a few days.'

'But the hermit advised us against it,' objected Bartholomew. 'Besides, they will also be preparing for the royal invasion, and I cannot see them inconveniencing themselves for you – a man from a rival Order.'

'We shall see,' said Michael serenely.

The Austins had chosen an idyllic spot for their community. It was just south-west of the castle, on what was effectively an island with two arms of the River Stour sweeping around it. It boasted a range of impressive new buildings, along with gardens, fishponds and an orchard, although it was its church that most caught the eye. This was a lovely creation of soft grey stone, with tiers of large windows to let in the light.

The priory was centred around its cloisters, which allowed the friars to move between church, dormitory and refectory without being subject to the vagaries of the weather. Stone seats were provided for restful repose during summer, while a tinkling fountain offered not only clean water for washing, but an attractive centrepiece.

Its founders were aware that relations between it and the town would not always be peaceful, so there was only one way to reach it: over a small bridge that had its own gatehouse. One of the brothers stood sentry there, ready to repel unwanted visitors.

'A Benedictine,' he said, eyeing Michael's black habit. 'We do not allow those in here.'

He looked like another old soldier – he carried himself ramrod straight, there was a large knife in his belt, and he wore his habit like a uniform. It was not uncommon for military men to become nervous about the amount of killing they had done in their lives, and large numbers did elect to make amends by taking holy orders in their autumn years, but it seemed to Bartholomew that Clare possessed an unusually high percentage of them.

'We have important business with your Prior,' declared Michael, all haughty dignity. 'He will want to see us, I assure you, so step aside at once.'

At that moment, a bell chimed to announce a meal in the refectory, and friars began to emerge from the surrounding buildings. When they saw their sentry preparing to repel invaders, several came to see if he needed help. Bartholomew was disconcerted to note that all carried daggers, while a few stopped en route to grab pikes and cudgels from what were evidently caches of arms.

'Is this a convent or a refuge for retired warriors?' he asked the guard.

'Or both,' muttered Langelee. 'I wager every one has been in France or the Holy Land.'

'You have a keen eye,' said the guard approvingly. 'Prior John was once a captain in the King's army, and most of his former comrades have asked to serve under him here. Hah! He is coming towards us now – to ask why a Benedictine is trying to infiltrate our sacred confines.'

'I was a soldier once, too,' said Langelee, rather more

wistfully than was appropriate for a man who was supposed to be dedicated to scholarship. 'In York and its environs.'

'So was Prior John,' said the guard, pleased. 'Perhaps you will know each other.'

Prior John was a stocky man with a savage scar on one side of his shaven head. He walked with brisk precision, and carried his Bible in a way that made it look like a weapon. His friars were cast in the same mould, and sported an impressive array of battle wounds. Among them was Cofferer Weste, who was snapping his black eyepatch into place over an empty socket.

'Do not worry about these three fellows,' Weste informed the guard amiably. 'They are just some of the scholars from Cambridge. I told you about them last night.'

'Do they include the one who has your Book of Hours?' asked the guard. 'If so, we should buy it back. It is a lovely piece – far too good for academics, who always have inky fingers.'

He tried to see if that was true of the ones whose way he still barred. Bartholomew, by far the cleanest member of Michaelhouse, presented his own for inspection. The guard nodded approval at what he saw, although Michael and Langelee wisely kept theirs tucked inside their sleeves.

'My word!' breathed Prior John as he approached. 'If it is not Ralph de Langelee! What are you doing here, old friend? I thought we had seen the last of each other when I left York.'

Langelee blinked. 'John? I did not recognise you! Where are all your fine yellow locks? And what happened to that handsome beard you were so proud of?'

'The years stole my hair,' replied John ruefully, then rubbed his bare chin. 'And the whiskers had to go when I took holy orders – my Prior General said they made me look like a pirate.'

109

'*You* took holy orders?' blurted Langelee. 'God's blood! That must have annoyed the Devil – yours was a soul he must have felt was his for certain. When did this happen?'

'A decade ago, although I have only been Prior here for the last twelve months. Coming to Clare was a good decision, because it is a lovely place. Would you like to join us? There is always room for another old warrior, and it is never too soon to consider one's immortal soul. You have more atoning to do than most, so I would not leave it too long if I were you. I say this as a friend.'

Bartholomew and Michael exchanged a glance. They had always known that Langelee had done some disreputable things before he had decided to pursue a career in academia, but it was never comfortable to be reminded of it.

'It is a tempting offer,' lied Langelee, 'but I am Master of Michaelhouse now, which is a very prestigious post. At the University in Cambridge.'

'Really?' blurted John. 'How in God's name did you convince them to take you?'

'Easy – I impressed them with my intellect,' explained Langelee. 'I am a philosopher.'

Neither claim was true. None of Langelee's colleagues would ever consider him a thinker, and while he did run a basic course in his chosen subject, all he did was read aloud the set texts that his students were obliged to hear.

'Are you? Goodness! Who would have thought it? Ralph de Langelee, a famous academic!'

'And you a priest,' said Langelee, clapping him on the back with genuine affection. 'When we were lads, you always dismissed friars as a lot of—'

'That was a long time ago,' interrupted John quickly, while his brethren exchanged amused glances behind his back. 'When death felt like something that happened to other people. Now Judgement Day looms, and I find myself wanting to make amends. You are younger, but it will come sooner than you think. I urge you again – do not leave it too late.'

'I will not,' promised Langelee, but with the kind of airy insouciance that suggested he set scant store by such concerns. 'You must have impressed someone important, John, because such appointments are not handed out to just anybody. Brother Michael here has been angling for an abbacy or a bishopric for years, and *he* is very talented.'

'No one else wanted it,' explained John, who apparently knew Langelee well enough not to be offended by the insult implicit in the remark. 'There is trouble brewing, you see. The last Prior saw it coming and resigned as soon as he could put pen to parchment. I was the only one willing to take his place.'

'What trouble?' asked Langelee warily.

'Unrest – which started when the town began to rebuild its church, and the castle insisted on interfering. My remit is to keep the peace, while simultaneously ensuring that we Austins are not drawn into the spat.'

'Is that why you are armed to the teeth?' asked Langelee, gesturing to the listening flock.

John grinned impishly. 'You will know when we are "armed to the teeth", believe me. What you see is us relaxing. Taking up arms is not something we expected to do again, but our Prior General gave us permission to defend ourselves as we execute our duties. We are obedient men, ready to obey his commands to the letter.'

Langelee beamed back. 'You and I have much to talk about, old comrade, so we shall stay with you for the next week. I am sure you can find us a corner somewhere.'

'If it were anyone else, I would refuse, given that we shall be overrun with royal retainers in a few days. But seeing as it is you . . .'

A short while later, Langelee, Bartholomew and Michael sat in the Prior's House, each holding a cup of unusually

111

fine claret. They were being entertained by John and three other Austins. One was Weste, whose post as cofferer meant he was entitled to be there; one was Nicholas, who had come to borrow a Psalter but had decided to linger when he saw a party in the making; and the last was John de Heselbech, the castle's current chaplain, appointed after Wisbech's death. All four were much of an ilk – brawny men with missing teeth, although each had one feature that made him distinctive: John was bald, Nicholas was huge, Weste had his eyepatch and Heselbech's teeth had been filed into points, which made him seem an odd choice to serve a high-ranking noblewoman.

'The Lady does not find your sharpened fangs alarming?' asked Langelee, more inclined to speak his mind than Bartholomew and Michael, although both were thinking the same thing.

Heselbech grinned, revealing his imposing incisors in all their glory. 'If she does, she is too polite to mention it.'

'I was worried about appointing a second friar to the castle after what happened to Wisbech,' confided John. 'But the town has Nicholas, and I did not want to be accused of favouritism . . .'

'And I am much better at looking after myself than poor old Wisbech was,' put in Heselbech. 'You will not catch *me* swallowing hemlock.'

'Good,' said John fervently. 'You should be especially wary of anything that comes from the squires. They have grown wild of late – terrorising servants, bullying towns-folk and generally acting like despots. Thank God Albon will soon take them to France.'

'If you think they poisoned a priest, you should inform the Bishop,' declared Michael. 'We cannot let that sort of thing pass unremarked. It sets a bad precedent.'

'And how would we prove such an accusation?' asked

John quietly. 'There were no witnesses, and no clues left to lead us to the perpetrators.'

'How do you know there were no clues?' pressed Michael. 'Did you investigate Wisbech's death yourselves? Or did you rely on Grym? I understand he is Clare's official investigator.'

John winced. 'Poor Grym! He knows nothing of such matters, but dares not refuse Godeston – not if he wants to be Mayor when the old man retires. But of course I did not entrust such an important matter to a barber. Obviously, I examined the scene of the crime myself.'

'You are qualified to do such a thing?'

'More qualified than Grym. But there was nothing to find. Wisbech was in the chapel, lying on his side. To be frank, I thought he had suffered an apoplexy brought on by strain – night offices can be hard on older folk – until Grym mooted the possibility of hemlock in his supper. I saw no evidence of it, but I am willing to accept his professional opinion on that at least.'

'And we *did* inform the Bishop,' put in Heselbech. 'But letters take a long time to reach Avignon, which is where he has lived ever since falling out with the King. We discussed it with the Lady, too, but she merely informed us that her squires would never stoop to poison.'

'Having met them, I am inclined to agree,' said Langelee. 'They strike me as lads who would opt for a sword or a dagger. Hemlock is too subtle a mode of killing for them.'

'Nuport is a dimwit, but do not tar the others with the same brush,' warned John. 'Thomas is very clever – and sly. But their days with us are numbered, thank the good Lord, and if they survive their experiences in France, they may return as better men.'

'Oh, they will survive,' predicted Langelee. 'Michael says peace is about to break out.'

'Even with a truce, there will still be skirmishes,' said

113

John with certainty. 'His Majesty will not disband his army just yet. Of course, Albon will be of scant use over there. He may be an excellent jouster, but he has never seen real warfare, and *I* would not trust him with my back.'

'True,' agreed Langelee. 'You can tell just by looking that he is all fuss and feathers.'

'So have you two known each other long?' asked Nicholas, taking a huge gulp of wine and settling down in the way old soldiers do when a good tale is in the offing.

'Years,' replied John. 'Not only were we warriors together as boys and men, but we both helped the Archbishop of York with some of his more delicate problems. Of course, it was those that compelled me to take the cowl, so I cannot look back on them with pleasure.'

'I can,' countered Langelee with a grin. 'They were the best days of my life, and I was much happier doing his work than battling debt at Michaelhouse. Being Master is fraught with petty worries, and I have considered resigning more than once of late.'

Bartholomew was sorry to hear it. Langelee might be lacking in academic skills, but he was a good Master – conscientious, fair and able to keep the peace among a large, disparate and argumentative body of men.

'You will always have a place here,' said John quietly. 'We have sworn oaths to help each other make our peace with God, and we will happily include you.'

'The hermit mentioned those vows,' said Langelee. 'Although he made them sound sinister.'

'Because he does not understand the depth of our desire to save each other's souls,' explained Nicholas earnestly. 'And he is jealous of a camaraderie that he will never share.'

The subject was a dull one as far as Langelee was concerned – he was not an overtly religious man – so he began to entertain Nicholas, Weste and Heselbech with tales of his military past. While he did so, Michael and Bartholomew took the opportunity to chat to Prior John. After all, if they were to be in Clare for the next few days, it was wise to learn more about the feud between the town and the castle, so they would know how to avoid being drawn into it.

'One of the scholars from Swinescroft has accused Ella and Thomas of murdering Sir William Talmach,' began the monk. 'Is it possible? Or was he just prompted by malicious gossip?'

John ran a hand across his shiny pate. 'One of Talmach's saddle straps *was* badly frayed, but there was nothing to say it was done deliberately. And a belt is a very silly place to carry a blade. It sliced through the great vein in his groin, and he bled to death before anyone could help him.'

'And *was* Ella pleased to be rid of an unwanted elderly husband?' asked Michael.

John shrugged. 'All I can say is that I urged her to think of her immortal soul when she next attended Confession. Perhaps she did, but as her priest was Wisbech, we shall never know.'

'Was she nearby when Talmach fell?' asked Bartholomew. 'Or was Thomas?'

John nodded. 'Both were very quickly on the scene once the alarm was raised, but there is nothing suspicious about that. They were his kin, and families often hunt together.'

'But what do *you* think?' pressed Michael.

'It is not for me to speculate, Brother. All I hope is that if they did harm Talmach, they do penance for it before their sins are weighed on Judgement Day.'

'I cannot say I took to Thomas,' mused Michael. 'He struck me as arrogant, calculating and untrustworthy.'

'Most women would disagree,' said John. 'They are always giving him presents. It must be his golden curls.

I had a mop just like it as a youth, and it did bring the lasses flocking.'

'What about the others who died?' asked Bartholomew. 'Roger, Charer and Skynere?'

'Roger's death was an accident: he was brained by falling scaffolding. At first, we thought Charer was an accident as well – he was a drunkard, so we assumed that he had lost his footing in the dark. However, he had been weaving his way home along that stretch of river for years, so why would he suddenly fall in? And Grym suggested hemlock for Skynere.'

'Did you see Skynere's body, as well as Wisbech's?' asked Bartholomew.

John nodded. 'He died at his dinner table. I think he had swallowed too much wine with his last meal, so when the poison struck, he was incapable of saving himself. However, that is a guess on my part, and I cannot prove it. No one can – not now.'

Bartholomew did not want to listen to a lot of ex-warriors recounting deeds of bloody glory – he had heard enough of those from Nicholas the previous night – but Langelee hissed angrily that if the physician wanted a free bed, then the least he could do was feign an interest in his hosts' exploits.

Time passed slowly, and the tales were still in full flood when the bell rang for vespers. The three scholars joined the Austins in their beautiful church for the ceremony, and as they were hungry afterwards, accepted an invitation to dine in the refectory. Mercifully, John imposed a rule of silence at meals, so Bible readings took the place of grisly stories. Unfortunately, the cantor had selected the Book of Joshua, and the subject was the Battle of Jericho.

By the time they emerged, the sun had set. The cool air smelled of wet soil and spring blossom, and was damp from a recent shower. A blackbird trilled a final song from the roof of the church, clear and sweet, while one of the cooks sang lustily in the kitchens. Other than that, the evening was still, and Bartholomew was aware of a growing sense of peace. Unwilling to lose it, he begged to be excused a return to the Prior's House for another session of entertainment.

'Very well,' said Langelee, although it was clear from his bemused expression that he failed to understand why anyone should choose to opt out of what promised to be a rollicking good time. 'But have an early night, because I want you and Michael to start recruiting new benefactors first thing in the morning. I shall spend tonight devising a list of who to target.'

But when Bartholomew saw the barrels of ale that were being hefted into the Prior's House by the bulky Nicholas, he knew Langelee would do no such thing. The Master was about to indulge in the kind of occasion he loved – one in which the tales of his and others' victories flowed freely, and the drink flowed more freely still. He might make a stab at working on Michaelhouse's behalf, but it would not be long before the College and its fiscal problems were forgotten.

'Come on, Langelee,' bellowed Nicholas cheerfully. 'The ale will turn sour if you stand there gossiping much longer.'

With a grin, Langelee loped towards him, stopping en route to fling comradely arms around the shoulders of Prior John and Heselbech. Other friars were already inside the house – they could be heard bawling the songs that soldiers sang while on campaign.

'Lord!' muttered Bartholomew. 'I am glad we are to be spared more of that, Brother.'

'Let me show you to your quarters,' came Weste's voice from the darkness behind them. It made them jump, as neither had heard him approach. For such a stocky man, the cofferer possessed a very stealthy tread. 'And when you children are tucked up in bed, we men can make merry.'

'I am sure you will,' said Michael primly. 'But do not forget your calling – priests are not supposed to carouse all night, revelling in the violence they committed in the past.'

'It will do us good,' countered Weste. 'We have been in a state of high alert for months while the feud between castle and town has escalated. It is high time we relaxed for a few hours.'

The sounds of manly laughter faded as Bartholomew and Michael followed him across the precinct towards the room that had been readied for them. Bartholomew breathed in deeply, enjoying the sweet scents of the fading day. The friars were not the only ones who had been busy of late – he himself had worked frantically during the last term, struggling to make enough time for Matilde in his busy schedule. It felt good to retire with the sun, secure in the knowledge that his sleep would not be disturbed by patients, students or a demanding fiancée.

'You think you will rest easy, do you?' murmured Michael, reading his mind. 'When there have been at least five suspicious deaths since Roger was felled by scaffolding in February, and the town is on the verge of some serious civil disorder?'

Bartholomew shrugged. 'We should be safe here – the place is full of soldiers.'

'The hermit does not consider it safe. He told us to wear armour.'

Having met the friars, Bartholomew was inclined to think that Jan was wrong to malign them. Yes, they were warlike, but their desire to atone for the blood they had spilled seemed genuine to him, and meant they would be loath to kill anyone else.

'It was your idea to ignore his warning and come here anyway,' he retorted.

'Only because you and Langelee failed to come up with an alternative. Lord! All that talk of slaughter! I shall have nightmares tonight.'

As Langelee was a friend of the Prior, they had been allocated a very handsome chamber in the guesthouse, although resentful glares from three men carrying hastily packed bags told them that it had not been standing vacant.

'Albon's people,' explained Weste. 'Billeted here because the castle is full. They claim to be soldiers, but they do not have a single battle scar among them. I cannot see the enemy being overly alarmed when *they* land on French soil. Not like they were when I arrived with John and the lads all those years ago.'

'Is that where you lost your eye?' asked Bartholomew, while Michael shot him an agitated glance for encouraging the telling of yet another bloody tale.

'In a skirmish near Paris.' Weste flipped up the patch to reveal the empty socket beneath. Bartholomew examined it with polite interest, while Michael studiously looked in the opposite direction. 'Would you like to hear about it?'

'Perhaps tomorrow,' said Michael hastily before he could oblige. 'But does being single-eyed interfere with your work as an illustrator?'

'It does not help, certainly. Did you see my Book of Hours? Some careless rogue set it alight, so Marishal brought it to me for repairs. I was horrified. How could anyone have treated a book so badly? Especially that page, which was the best in the whole tome.'

'The one with the shepherd?' asked Bartholomew. 'And the white-whiskered demon peering out from behind a tree?'

Weste nodded. 'It was meant to serve as a reminder

119

that Satan is always present. I gave him a human face to underline the point – if I had made him a serpent, it would be patently obvious that we should steer clear of him. But Lucifer looks like us, which is what makes him so dangerous.'

'Too true,' agreed Michael, and glanced around uneasily.

The guesthouse was supremely comfortable. The beds were soft and smelled of clean straw, the blankets were freshly laundered, and someone had set a bowl of spring flowers on the windowsill, which released a delicate scent. Michael retreated primly behind a screen to perform his ablutions. He was particular about his privacy, and hated anyone seeing him in a state of undress.

Bartholomew enjoyed a vigorous wash, glad to sluice away the dirt of travel, then rinsed his shirt and hose, and set them to dry in front of the fire. By the time he had finished, Michael had bagged the best bed, and was lying in it with the blanket pulled up to his chin. Bartholomew took the one by the window, which he opened the moment the monk had doused the lamp and could not see what he was doing – he hated stuffy rooms. He closed his eyes, and was just dropping off when Michael began to speak.

'Roger was the first victim in this turbulent town. He died eight weeks or so ago, killed by a piece of scaffolding. It was deemed an accident, but there were no witnesses and he was unpopular. I suspect he was brained deliberately.'

Bartholomew was barely listening. 'By whom?' he asked drowsily. 'Town or castle?'

'Who knows? Next was Talmach, who fell off his horse and on to his dagger. He was elderly and the track was slick, but his saddle strap was later discovered to be defective. Again there were no witnesses, but his young widow and her twin were quickly on the scene.'

120

Bartholomew tried to concentrate. 'The Lady's servants were not surprised when Badew bawled his accusation. I saw them nodding agreement. And Marishal was not surprised either, although the Lady seems sure they are innocent. At least, she gave that impression . . .'

'After Talmach came Wisbech, poisoned by hemlock, then Charer the coachman, who drowned while staggering home along a familiar path. And finally Skynere, also fed hemlock. So what do they have in common? Three hailed from the castle, one came from the town – and we are not sure about Roger . . . What do you think, Matt?'

'That I am glad it is not our responsibility to investigate. Goodnight, Brother.'

Bartholomew was not sure how long he had been asleep before he was jolted awake. It was still dark, but he sensed dawn was not far off. He sat up, and saw Langelee and Michael sitting by the fire they had stoked up. Langelee was rumpled and seedy, and his red-rimmed eyes suggested he had yet to retire. By contrast, Michael was shaved, dressed and ready to go about saving Michaelhouse by recruiting new benefactors.

'Something woke me,' said Bartholomew. 'Did you hear it, too?'

Michael snorted his disbelief. 'I imagine the rumpus is audible in Cambridge! The friars are stampeding about like wild horses, shouting their heads off. Perhaps the French have invaded.'

Bartholomew was an unusually heavy sleeper, and could doze through the most frantic of nocturnal crises. It was not a good trait in a physician, and it was fortunate that his friends knew how to rouse him when there was a medical emergency, or there might have been all manner of tragedies. He climbed out of bed and went to peer through the window.

The sky was dark, although there was a faint glimmer

of light in the east, so it would not be long before sunrise. Lamps blazed in the refectory, dormitory and Prior's House, and pitch torches bobbed by the gate. Shadows flitted everywhere, and hammering footsteps sounded in the night.

'Should we find out what is happening?' he asked.

'Best not,' advised Langelee. 'It is priory business and none of ours.'

Bartholomew glanced at him. 'What time did you get back? I did not hear you come in.'

'I did,' said Michael wryly. 'Less than two hours ago. Good night, was it, Master?'

'I was working,' replied Langelee stiffly. 'Acquiring information about potential donors.'

'Then you must have an enormous list for us,' remarked Michael, smothering a smirk. 'Given that it took you six hours or more.'

'I do – all the names are tucked away up here.' Langelee tapped his temple, which made him wince and told his Fellows that he would probably have trouble accessing most of them. He changed the subject before they could quiz him further. 'Yet perhaps I was over-hasty in saying we should stay out of the priory's affairs. I cannot sleep through this commotion anyway.'

'Maybe there has been another murder,' suggested Michael, then blanched as an unpleasant thought occurred to him. 'Lord! I hope it is not the Lady. People might think *we* killed her, to avoid making a second journey for her funeral.'

'No one knows we came here for that,' said Langelee, and closed his eyes suddenly, one hand pressed to his stomach. Wordlessly, Bartholomew handed him a bucket, thinking the Austins would not appreciate vomit on their nice clean floor.

'I think Marishal has guessed the truth,' countered Michael. 'He is no fool and—'

122

He stopped when there was a rap on their door. It was opened before they could answer, and Prior John strode in. He was bright-eyed and fresh-faced, suggesting that he had either been more abstemious than Langelee, or was better at handling large quantities of ale.

'There has been an unexpected death,' he announced without preamble. 'And I am sorry to say that the victim is one of your scholars.'

'Badew,' predicted Michael grimly. 'Because of the accusations he levelled against Thomas and Ella. It was a reckless thing to have done and—'

'It is Roos,' interrupted John. 'The bad-tempered one.'

'All of the Swinescroft men are bad-tempered,' remarked Langelee. 'But how did Roos die?'

'A dagger, apparently,' replied John. 'In the castle, although no one knows why he was there. The squires think a townsman did it, and Mayor Godeston sent a frantic plea for us to intervene, to prevent them from retaliating in kind. Unfortunately, we were all a bit addled from ale, so we were rather less efficient than usual. You may have noticed the racket as we rallied.'

'Racket?' asked Michael flatly. 'What racket?'

'I am sorry, John,' said Langelee unhappily. 'I should not have kept you up so late.'

John smiled. 'We are grown men: it was our own decision to drink ourselves silly. Besides, we intercepted the squires before any harm was done, so there is no need for recriminations.'

'We had better go to the castle then,' said Michael, standing and reaching for his cloak. 'Roos was a scholar, so his death comes under my jurisdiction. And my Corpse Examiner's.'

Bartholomew held this particular post, and was paid three pennies for every case he judged – money he then spent on medicine for the poor. It was a job he would lose once he resigned his Fellowship, as other University physicians were entitled to a turn. He would miss it, not just for the additional income, but because he felt that studying the dead had taught him much about how to help the living. Yet again, he reflected on all he would lose when he married Matilde.

Langelee and John decided to go too, lest Bartholomew and Michael needed their protection, and the four of them hurried across the precinct towards the bridge.

'Apparently, Roos died in the cistern,' the Prior said, and crossed himself. 'Thank God he was found, or his rotting cadaver might have killed everyone. Do you remember how we used a dead sheep to oust those illegal tenants from the Archbishop's manor, Langelee? It worked like a charm, although I was sorry that some of the culprits died.'

'I had forgotten.' Langelee was as white as a ghost in the light of John's torch, and Bartholomew hoped they would not have to wait for him to throw up again. 'Lord! Does this mean the folk at the castle will sicken from bad water? I cannot say I should want to drink from a well where a corpse has been floating.'

Before Bartholomew could reply, they met Heselbech, who was reeling along in the opposite direction. The chaplain seemed much more the worse for wear than his fellows, and in the dim light looked vaguely demonic with his curiously pointed teeth.

'You should be at Mass,' admonished John sternly. 'Not even murder should distract you from your religious duties, and there will be Hell to pay if the Lady decides to attend and discovers that you are not there.'

'I bring more bad news,' slurred Heselbech. 'Namely that there was a second body in the cistern with Roos, also stabbed. By all accounts, it belongs to Margery Marishal.'

# CHAPTER 5

The castle was in turmoil. Servants scurried in every direction, although to no apparent purpose, while their masters stood in huddles and whispered in low, frightened voices. The atmosphere was thick with fear and confusion. Marishal should have taken charge, but he stood in shocked immobility, clutching Ella's arm. It would have been a good opportunity for Thomas to prove his worth, given that the post of steward was hereditary, but he only lounged by the stables, watching events unfold with a peculiarly blank expression.

'He does not seem overly distressed about his dam,' remarked Michael.

'Then shame on him,' said Prior John, lips pursed in disapproval. 'She was gentle, kind and loving, and the world will be a sadder place without her. She will be missed more than anyone else in Clare – and that includes all us priests.'

'The artists in the church certainly admired her,' said Michael. 'When painting their murals, it was her face they used to depict the Blessed Virgin. She is carved in the rood screen, too.'

'As they should. She was a saint.'

A number of folk were sobbing, women and men alike. Bartholomew recalled his own reaction when he had met Margery the previous day – how he had been struck by her sweetness and had hoped to talk to her more. He glanced at her family. Marishal had tears streaming unheeded down his face, which was as white as snow. Ella was also pale, but her eyes were dry. Thomas had stepped into the shadows, so was now virtually invisible.

'Who is in charge?' asked Langelee. 'The Lady? Why is she not here, leading her people in their hour of need? Her steward is understandably incapable at the moment.'

'She does not enjoy the best of health, and mornings are difficult for her,' explained John. 'Even so, she should have detailed one of her council to oblige – Albon, Lichet or Jevan.' He grimaced. 'Unfortunately, we cannot expect much of poor Albon, while Jevan is away, and it would be a mistake to appoint the Red Devil – no one will heed any instructions *he* issues.'

'But she has a whole court of retainers,' Langelee pointed out. 'Hundreds of them. Surely one is capable of stepping up and taking control?'

'You give them too much credit,' muttered John. 'But Ereswell is over there – he has a loud voice and is malleable, so I shall stand behind him and murmur advice in his ear. If we do not impose order on this mêlée soon, there will be more trouble with the town.'

He started to stride towards the courtier, but it was too late, as Lichet had emerged from his quarters in the Cistern Tower. The Red Devil had taken considerable trouble with his appearance. His clothes were the best money could buy, his hair was brushed, and his beard had been fluffed out to impressive proportions. Every head turned towards him, so he drew himself up to his full height, and looked around with an imperious gaze. The hubbub gradually faded into silence.

'There has been a great tragedy,' he boomed in a voice that radiated confidence and self-importance. 'Margery Marishal is dead. So is one of the scholars from Cambridge – both stabbed.'

He paused when Marishal whimpered his distress, and there was a flutter of movement as several ladies hastened to murmur words of comfort – Margery's friends, eager to help him for her sake. Only when silence reigned again did Lichet continue.

'The Lady has appointed *me* to run the castle while her steward is . . . indisposed.' He raised his hand to quell the immediate clamour of objections, but it was ignored.

'But you are a stranger,' shouted Ereswell angrily. 'Why should you rule over us?'

'Because it is the Lady's wish,' replied Lichet sharply. 'And besides, who else is able? You? If you were, you would have done it when all this fuss began. Instead, you retreated into a huddle and cooed with your cronies.'

'Go on then, Red Devil,' challenged someone from the back of the crowd. 'Show us your superior leadership skills. What do you want us to do?'

Lichet thought fast. 'Go to the chapel and listen to Heselbech celebrate Mass. That should keep you quiet for a while. Then I will—'

'How?' shouted one of the watchmen. 'The chapel is too small for us all to fit inside.'

'Just the courtiers then,' determined Lichet. He glared angrily when none of the brightly glittering throng moved. 'Now, please, not next week.'

'We do not want—' began Ereswell indignantly, but Lichet swung around to address the servants, cutting across the nobleman in a way that was sure to annoy.

'Cooks and scullions,' he boomed authoritatively, 'return to the kitchens and start baking the bread for our breakfast.'

'We did that hours ago,' called a young baker with floury arms, disbelief thick in his voice. He had a deformity in one leg, which gave him a lopsided gait. 'The loaves are cooked *and* the ovens are raked out ready for tomorrow – as they always are by this time in the morning.'

'Then peel some vegetables instead,' Lichet snapped, and before the lad could argue, he whipped around to scowl at the squires, who were sniggering because Nuport had just aped the baker's limp. 'And you lot can exercise the horses and polish the saddles.'

'Us?' asked Nuport, grin disappearing. 'But that is what the grooms do. We are squires—'

'Do as I say or face the consequences,' snarled Lichet, obviously irritated that his authority should be questioned at every turn. 'Everyone else will wait in the hall, where breakfast will be served in one hour.'

'One hour?' cried the castle cook. 'Do you have any idea how long it takes to prepare a meal for three hundred people? Not to mention those greedy paroquets, which requisition all my best—'

'It will be ready or else!' roared Lichet. 'And when you have finished, you can wash all the pots until they gleam. I shall inspect them later, and if I see so much as a speck of black, I shall want them all done again.'

'But some are *meant* to be black,' objected the cook. 'They are—'

'Enough!' screeched Lichet. 'The next person to defy me will answer to the Lady. Now, do as you are told – all of you. Well, what are you waiting for?'

Despite the threat, it was still some time before the onlookers deigned to obey. Servants dragged their feet, and the courtiers took a deliberately long time to file into the chapel. Then Lichet saw the scholars with John.

'You can go home,' he told the Prior. 'You are not needed, because we have Heselbech. The rest of you can collect your colleague from the cistern and put him in the chapel when Mass is over. But do not lay a finger on Margery. I shall make the arrangements for her myself.'

Obediently, Michael, Bartholomew and Langelee walked to the Cistern Tower. The door was closed, and Bonde was standing guard outside. The henchman was pale and there was a moistness around his eyes that suggested tears – Margery's death had upset even that warlike ruffian.

'Step aside,' ordered Michael, while Bartholomew was grateful for Langelee's reassuring presence, as there was something about Bonde that unnerved him profoundly. 'We are here at Lichet's behest, and he carries the Lady's authority.'

Bonde moved away. 'As you wish.'

Michael reached for the handle, only to find the door locked. 'Do not play games with me, Bonde,' he snapped, holding out his hand for the key. 'It is neither the time nor the place.'

'I am not playing games,' retorted the henchman. 'Marishal took the key with him, as he did not want his wife to become the subject of ghoulish scrutiny. He told me to stay here and stop anyone from entering by force, so that is what I am doing.'

'Very laudable,' said Michael. 'But we only want Roos – we will not disturb Margery, I promise. Now fetch the key, if you please.'

'I cannot abandon my post on your say-so,' argued Bonde. 'But I imagine Lichet will be along in a moment, so he can let you in.'

He looked away, and there was enough light in the bailey for Bartholomew to see a fresh glitter of tears. Michael smiled predatorily.

'Then while we wait for him, you can answer some questions. Start by telling us what happened here from your perspective.'

Bonde struggled to pull himself together. 'I was in the gatehouse when I heard a commotion. I hurried over and watched Marishal, Quintone and a few others go down the cistern to investigate reports of a body – Roos. A short while later, they climbed back up to say that there was not one corpse, but two. The other was Margery Marishal . . .'

129

'I see. So where were you all night? Can someone verify your whereabouts?'

Bonde's eyes narrowed. 'Why should that be necessary? I never harmed Margery or the scholar. And if you must know, I was not even in the castle for most of the time. I was in the town, watching the squires. Albon asked me to do it, because he heard them say they were off to a tavern, and they can be disorderly when they are drunk.'

'Why you?' asked Bartholomew, puzzled. 'Surely he should have done it himself? They are supposed to be under his command, after all.'

Bonde regarded him insolently. 'He delegated the matter to someone he trusts instead. He is a very busy man.'

'I am sure he is,' muttered Langelee. 'It takes time to look that gorgeous.'

'So you can give the squires alibis?' pressed Michael 'And vice versa?'

'I am afraid not. I kept myself hidden, so they did not know I was there. And there are eight of them, so one was always off at the latrine or frolicking with a lass. I could not possibly monitor them all on my own.'

'Then what was the point of you being there?' asked Bartholomew.

'To prevent fighting. And I did – the moment a spat looked set to erupt with some merchant boys, I hurried forward and ordered our lads home.'

Michael regarded him coolly. 'I hear nothing in your testimony to convince me of your innocence.'

Bonde sneered. 'I suppose you have been listening to gossip about the man I killed in Wixoe. Well, the Lady got me off that particular charge, so I am free of all blame for it.'

'We heard she bribed the judge,' countered Michael, 'which rather suggests that you *were* guilty and she interfered with the course of justice. The Wixoe victim was

130

stabbed, and now we hear that the same has happened to Roos . . .'

'Anne warned me that the Wixoe affair would result in me being accused every time there is a suspicious death,' muttered Bonde bitterly. 'She is a clever lady, and I wish I had wed her. I should have done it when she was a nurse here – then she could not have been forced into an anchorhold, and I would have been in bed with her last night, not out doing Albon's dirty work.'

Bartholomew tried to envisage the sullen killer and the opinionated woman living in married bliss. He could not do it – they were entirely unsuited to each other, and the match would almost certainly have ended in tears. Or worse.

'So tell me why we should not accuse you,' suggested Michael.

Bonde shrugged. 'Well, for a start, when the squires and I came home at about midnight, Margery was still alive. I saw her chatting to some of her friends outside the hall. Then the lads staggered away to their quarters, while Thomas went off alone. I followed the squires, and saw them fall into their beds.'

'Then what?'

'I went to the main gate and stood watch for the rest of the night with the other guards. I saw Margery again a bit later, tiptoeing along with a lamp. I assumed she was aiming for the Constable Tower, where she lives. Lived.'

'When was this?' demanded Michael. 'Exactly?'

'I cannot say for certain. Two o'clock perhaps, or a little before.'

'Did you see Roos?'

'No, but I spotted the hermit. Jan often comes here of a night, when it is quiet.'

'For a recluse, Jan is remarkably mobile,' said Michael disapprovingly. 'Hermits are supposed to stay away from worldly distractions, not wait for cover of darkness to sample them.'

'Even holy men need to stretch their legs, Brother, and the castle is lovely at night – silent, still and interesting. It is when I like it best.'

'It was not silent and still last night,' remarked Michael drily. 'Although I concede that it was interesting. You, eight squires, Roos, Margery and Jan were busily wandering around it – and those are just the ones that we know about.'

Bonde smirked challengingly. 'True, so this crime will not be easy to solve. Perhaps you should give up and go home before you embarrass yourself with defeat.'

Michael smiled back, coldly. 'I have never failed a murder victim yet, and I do not intend to start now. I *will* find Roos's killer.'

'But all your other cases were in Cambridge,' countered Bonde. 'And this is Clare. Things are different here, and you have no authority. But I had better fetch the key, given that so much time is passing and Lichet is nowhere to be seen. We cannot keep you waiting for ever, can we?'

'He is your culprit,' growled Langelee, as the henchman strode away. 'I know a killer when I see one, and he is callous enough to dispatch two victims, then stand guard over their corpses.'

Unfortunately, Marishal was in no state to hand the key to Bonde or anyone else. He stood slack-mouthed and stunned, oblivious to the concerned fussing of his wife's friends. Bonde glanced at Michael, and indicated that the monk would have to wait for someone else to ask for it, because *he* was not about to oblige. Michael was not overly concerned by the delay, content to pass the time by monitoring the reactions of those who might become suspects.

Ella was talking to Thomas near the palace, although the other squires had made themselves scarce, no doubt to avoid being seen by Lichet, who strutted around like a peacock, issuing orders to anyone he met. His instructions were superfluous in most cases, and downright ridiculous in others, but the contemptuous glances he received did nothing to deter him, and he was clearly relishing the power he had been given.

'What an ass,' muttered Michael. 'I am surprised at the Lady. Surely he cannot be the best she has to offer? I suspect even Albon would be better – at least he looks the part. Or another member of her council, perhaps. Let us hope that someone has had the sense to send for Jevan.'

'Give Marishal a potion, Bartholomew,' begged Langelee, troubled by the steward's anguish. 'You must have something that will ease him.'

'There is no remedy for grief,' replied Bartholomew soberly. 'Other than time.'

'His children should be at his side,' Langelee went on unhappily. 'I am surprised Lichet does not tell them so. Of course, if he does, it will be the first sensible instruction he has given all day.'

While Langelee and Michael discussed the Red Devil's ineffectual leadership, Bartholomew looked around him. Dawn had broken, and it had started to rain. Servants still scurried about to no or little purpose, more intent on gossiping than completing their chores. The courtiers had not stayed long in the chapel, and had gone to the hall, where they stood in small clusters.

The news had encouraged droves of townsfolk to come and see what was happening. Several carts had arrived, ostensibly to make deliveries, although the eyes of their owners were everywhere, and all tried to strike up conversations with those who came to receive their goods. Mayor Godeston was toted in on his purple litter, aiming to

133

convey his sympathies to the bereaved. Grym was at his side, clad in a large yellow robe that made him look like a lemon.

'You are not welcome,' Lichet told them coldly. 'Go away before I have you thrown out.'

'Our business is with Marishal, not you,' Godeston flashed back. 'Tell him we are here.'

In response, Lichet clicked his fingers at the castle guards, and indicated that the pair were to be forcibly removed. Godeston opened his mouth to argue, but his bearers knew when it was wise to beat a retreat. They left at a run, jostling their passenger so violently that he was obliged to cling on for dear life to avoid being spilled out. Unwilling to stay on his own, Grym waddled after them.

'I wonder where Badew and Harweden are,' said Michael worriedly. 'They should be hammering at the gate, demanding an explanation. They were Roos's friends, after all.'

'Donwich and Pulham are here, though,' said Bartholomew, nodding to where Lichet was in the process of ordering the two Clare Hall men to read to everyone in the hall, on the grounds that no one could gossip if they were listening to a story. The Red Devil did not wait to see if they did as they were told – which they did not, of course – and descended on Heselbech instead.

'You want *me* to make Margery a coffin?' asked Heselbech, startled. He still looked shabby from his excesses the previous night, although at least he was no longer reeling or slurring his words. 'But I am a friar, not a carpenter. It is—'

But Lichet had already gone, informing Ereswell in a self-important bawl that the task of securing supplies for the Lady's greedy paroquets was now his responsibility. Ereswell gaped his astonishment at the commission, after which Lichet strode away to pounce on someone else. Heselbech came to speak to the three Michaelhouse men, although he was watching Lichet with an expression that made no secret of his disdain.

'This is a sorry business,' the chaplain began. 'What was Roos doing here with Margery in the first place? I was under the impression that all three Swinescroft men hated the Lady and her people. Of course, I did see Roos and Margery talking together a couple of times yesterday . . .'

'So did I,' said Bartholomew. 'And at another point, he ogled her shamelessly.'

'Perhaps Badew and Harweden killed them both for being on friendly terms with each other.' Heselbech turned to Michael. 'Langelee tells me that you are the University's Senior Proctor. Does that mean you will investigate the crime? If so, be warned – the Lady may not like it, and it could cost your College its legacy.'

'That is a good point,' said Langelee worriedly. 'Perhaps we should let Lichet do it instead.'

'Lichet could not catch a snail, let alone a killer,' declared Michael. 'And I am not a man to shirk my obligations. Besides, it is entirely possible that my skills will encourage the Lady to favour Michaelhouse even further.'

'Then be careful,' said Heselbech. 'Because if you pick up rocks, who knows what manner of vermin may lurk beneath?'

While they continued to wait for the key, Michael watched all the gawpers who contrived to walk past the Cistern Tower, aware that the killer might well be among them – he knew from past experience that some murderers liked to revisit the scene of their crimes, to savour the commotion they had generated.

'There are three hundred people living in the castle at the moment,' Langelee told him. 'Plus God knows how many in the town. All with secrets, alliances and animosities. You may never find the culprit, Brother – not when we are strangers, with no notion of where to start.'

'We shall see,' said Michael, who had rather more faith in his abilities as a solver of mysteries. He nodded towards the tower on the other side of the bailey. 'Here is Albon, emerging from his lair at last. He is still surrounded by admirers, despite the fact that his late appearance suggests he is not a man who can be relied upon in an emergency.'

The knight's train was not as large as it had been the previous day, as many of his retainers were in the hall, gossiping, but it was still impressive and so was he. He was clad in red robes that would not have looked out of place on a monarch and his grey-gold mane had been brushed until it shone. However, there were pouches under his eyes and he seemed subdued.

'Perhaps he drank too much ale last night,' suggested Bartholomew. 'Like Langelee.'

'Or he did away with Margery and Roos, and is stricken by conscience,' countered the Master. 'I have never trusted showy warriors. Some are lions in battle, but most are lambs, and it is impossible to know which they will tran-spire to be until it is too late.'

'He does not look very leonine at the moment,' mused Michael. 'Indeed, he seems troubled. Perhaps he *is* our culprit, and it has taken him until now to muster the courage to show his face.'

'He is watching the squires.' Bartholomew nodded to where the young men were making a show of inspecting a horse with a damaged leg, although the animal was gaining nothing from their ministrations, and clearly itched to be back in its stall with a bag of hay. 'I think he is afraid that one of them is responsible, and he does not want the company of a killer in France.'

'He *should* want the company of a killer in France,' countered Langelee. 'They tend to come in useful when one is fighting a war. Unless he is afraid that he might be the next victim – that the killer may decide he is not worth all the adulation he has been given.'

While they were talking, Lichet strode past again, bawling for Quintone to bring him his lute. Michael caught the Red Devil's arm and jerked him to a standstill.

'We cannot take Roos to the chapel because the cistern is locked,' he said. 'And we are reluctant to press Marishal for the key when he is so obviously distressed. You must do it – preferably before you disappear to enjoy yourself with music.'

'My intention is not to *enjoy myself*,' snapped Lichet, freeing his arm irritably. 'It is to calm everyone down. I shall gather them in the hall, and play until the panic and consternation have eased. Music is the best remedy in these situations. It is a medical fact.'

'Is it indeed?' muttered Bartholomew.

'You can lull everyone to sleep in a moment,' said Michael. 'But first, please fetch the key.'

'Later,' hedged Lichet, glancing at the steward and evidently deciding that *he* did not want to be the one to intrude on his grief either. 'When I am not quite so busy.'

'So what happened down there?' asked Michael before the Red Devil could stride away again. 'We know that Roos and Margery were stabbed, but how did they end up in the cistern?'

Lichet assumed a haughty expression. 'My enquiries are at a very preliminary stage, so I cannot possibly answer questions yet. However, I can tell you one thing: Roos should not have been here. He was ousted from the castle with his two Swinescroft cronies yesterday, and he had no right to return uninvited.'

Michael tried a different tack. 'Then tell us how the bodies came to be discovered. Was it on a routine inspection?'

'We do not include the cistern on our regular patrols. What would be the point? It is just a big well filled with

137

water. However, it supplies the kitchens, but nothing was coming out of the pipe this morning, so Adam the baker was sent to find out why. Quintone! Come here. Is that my lute? Good. Now go and tell Master Marishal that Brother Michael wants the key.'

'Me?' asked the servant uneasily. 'But he looks so . . . why can't *you* do it?'

'Because I told you to,' snapped Lichet. 'Well, go on, man. We do not have all day.'

Quintone slouched away reluctantly, and Michael resumed his attack on Lichet.

'You live above the cistern. Did you see or hear anything suspicious at—'

'No, and now you must excuse me,' interrupted Lichet, pulling his lute from its covers. 'I have important work to do. You may speak to me later, if I have time.'

He turned and flounced away. Michael watched him go through narrowed eyes, wondering if the Red Devil's disinclination to answer perfectly reasonable questions should be regarded as suspicious.

Bartholomew was sorry that his few precious days in Clare were going to be filled with the unsavoury business of murder. If he had wanted that, he could have stayed in Cambridge, where scholars died with distressing regularity. He was not looking forward to meeting the paroquets either – he knew it was only a matter of time before the Lady learned that he had dodged the assignment, and issued a second order for him to cure them. He glanced at Langelee. The Master would be a far better assistant for Michael, leaving him free to . . .

'Do not even think about it, Matt,' warned the monk, reading his thoughts with uncanny precision. 'It will take all three of us to find Roos's killer without ruffling sensitive feathers, so you cannot jaunt off to have fun while Langelee and I struggle on alone.'

'Look on the bright side, Bartholomew,' said Langelee kindly. 'This will be your last case – you cannot be Corpse Examiner once you leave the University.'

'Oh, yes, he can,' countered Michael firmly. 'I amended the statutes when I learned that he planned to get married. He will still be mine when he is joined to Matilde.'

Bartholomew was not sure whether to be pleased or angry. He did not enjoy helping Michael catch killers, but there was no question that the money would come in useful.

'Here is Quintone with the key,' said Langelee. 'Thank God someone had the courage to ask for it, or we might still be waiting here tomorrow.'

'Actually, it is the spare one from the kitchen,' explained the servant, and glanced to where Marishal still stood in mute shock. 'I could not bring myself to bother him.'

He bent to unlock the door. As he did, Bartholomew happened to glance across the bailey. Bonde was there, staring back furiously, which led the physician to wonder why he wanted so badly to keep them out. Was it because he had adored Margery, and had hoped to protect her body from the ghoulish scrutiny of strangers? Regardless, it was clear that his name should be included on any list of suspects they might draw up.

As Ella had told them, the Cistern Tower was one huge cylinder. Its upper half loomed over the bailey, but its lower section had been driven deep into the ground, where it formed a massive stone-lined well. Access to the water was via a very narrow spiral staircase with steep steps, which was in the thickness of the wall. Michael took one look and refused to descend unless he was sure that no one else would be in front of him.

'I shall have to go down backwards,' he explained primly, 'which will allow anyone below to look straight up my habit.'

'We will not be tempted, Brother, believe me,' Langelee assured him fervently.

Quintone led the way, skipping down the treacherous steps with an ease that suggested he had done it many times before. Bartholomew and Langelee followed more cautiously, while Michael waited above until he was sure he could make the journey without risk to his modesty.

There were tiny landings at regular intervals in the stairwell, each with a very thick door that would open directly into the cistern. Quintone passed the first two and opened the third.

'This is the entrance we must use today,' he explained, revelling in the role of guide. He shone his lamp to show that the stairwell further down was flooded. 'It has been raining for days, so the cistern is quite full at the moment. There are another five doors beneath this one – eight in all.'

'God's blood!' breathed Langelee. 'That is impressive. The tank must be vast.'

'It is,' said Quintone proudly. 'Enough to keep us in fresh water for years, should we ever come under siege.'

'So what happens if you open the wrong door?' asked Langelee. 'Would you drown in the inrushing water?'

'No, because the stairs are designed to flood,' said Bartholomew, understanding the mechanics of the system at once. 'There will be no inrushing water here, because it will rise at the same rate as in the cistern itself. Ingenious!'

'So the water could reach as high as the door through which we came in?' asked Langelee. 'I assume that is where the tank's ceiling is located?'

'It is,' replied Quintone. 'And the water has got to that level once or twice, after particularly wet spells, when it spilled out to flood the bailey. However, Lichet has now installed a device that he says will prevent it from happening in the future. Of course, if the cooks did their job properly, there would be no need for the Red Devil's inventions.'

Bartholomew frowned. 'What do you mean?'

'The kitchens are lower than the bottom of the well, so the original builders fitted an array of pipes that run directly to them. Thus the cooks always have a plentiful water supply *and* the water level in here can be controlled by opening or closing the sluices. Ergo, the bailey only floods when the cooks do not run off the excess on a regular basis.'

'Where does the water come from?' asked Bartholomew, intrigued. 'The roof?'

'Yes – there is a big vat, which catches the rain. *It* has valves, too, which can either be opened to fill the cistern, or closed to funnel water away down the outside walls. So we can control the level *that* way as well. Clever, eh?'

'Very,' agreed Bartholomew. 'But you say Lichet has devised an additional fail-safe mechanism?'

'A way of making sure that the bailey door never leaks,' explained Quintone. 'Or so he claims – it has yet to be tested. The townsfolk think he is a warlock, and I suspect they are right. I cannot abide the man.'

'Why not?'

'Because he is sly, stupid, dishonest and greedy,' came the prompt reply. 'And it is possible that *he* killed Roos and Margery. However, if you want my advice, look to the squires first. They are arrogant fools, who do nothing but strut around dressed like lunatics. Let us hope that peace does not prevent Albon from taking them to France.'

Still talking, Quintone led the way through the door he had opened. Once inside, they saw the cistern was essentially a deep and very wide circular well. There was a broad platform in front of the door, which tapered away to form a narrow ledge that ran all the way around the inside, so that workmen could access the walls for routine maintenance. Glancing up, Bartholomew saw that there were identical arrangements for the two doors above, and supposed the same was true of the five below. A gauge showed the water was currently forty feet deep. It appeared black in the light of Quintone's lamp, but a ripple on the surface indicated a current.

'The kitchen sluices also prevent it from stagnating,' explained Quintone.

Bartholomew was all admiration for the engineers who had designed it, although his colleagues did not share his enthusiasm. Langelee was looking around with undisguised revulsion, while Michael, who had arrived with his dignity intact, declared it sinister.

'It is,' agreed Langelee, his face unnaturally white. 'And the sooner we finish here, the happier I shall be. Where are the bodies?'

'You are not going to be sick, are you?' asked Bartholomew sternly. 'Because if so, you should leave. People drink this water.'

Langelee took a deep, shuddering breath. 'No, but please hurry. I do not like this place.'

The bodies lay nearby, both covered by cloaks. Marishal's own was over his wife, while a courtier's had been commandeered for Roos.

'Ereswell's,' confided Quintone. 'But he wants it back – I heard him say so myself. I was one of the first to come down here, see, after the alarm was raised.'

'Who were the others?' asked Bartholomew.

Quintone reflected. 'Well, Lichet was the very first, but he lives upstairs, so he had a head start on everyone else. Then came Marishal and Thomas, and after them about two dozen courtiers. I helped Thomas to pull Roos from the water, but as we struggled, I noticed a *second* body.'

'Margery's,' said Langelee softly.

Quintone nodded. 'Yes, God rest her sainted soul. Marishal was distraught. He ordered everyone away, so

142

that he and Thomas could pay their respects without an audience. It was not long before Thomas brought him out, though. I suspect Marishal was too upset to say many prayers.'

'I see,' said Michael. 'Does anything look different to you now than it did earlier?'

'In other words, did Marishal or Thomas tamper with the evidence?' surmised Quintone astutely, and stepped forward to look. 'Not that I can tell, which is a pity, as it would be nice to see Thomas in trouble. I am sick of his nasty pranks. He is old enough to know better.'

While Michael plied him with more questions, Bartholomew examined Roos, watched by Langelee. The old scholar was on his back, still leaking water. He was cold to the touch, and there was a single stab wound in his chest, made with an average-sized blade. It would not have been instantly fatal, and when Bartholomew pressed on his ribs, froth bubbled from Roos's mouth, suggesting that he had been alive when he had entered the water. Technically, the cause of death was drowning, although the knife wound would have killed him eventually anyway.

There were only three other details of note. First, one of Roos's boots was missing. Second, there were some faint bruises on his chest and arms. And third, his old woollen hat, which was secured very firmly under his chin to prevent it from slipping off, concealed a heavy bandage.

'He had earache,' said Langelee, lest Bartholomew had forgotten.

'Yes,' acknowledged Bartholomew. 'Which explains the hat, but not the bandage – it is not the way such ailments are usually treated.'

He began to unwind it. Then blinked his surprise at what was revealed.

'His ear is missing!' exclaimed Langelee, shocked. 'Did

he fall foul of Simon Freburn, do you think? But Freburn just haunts the area around Clare, and I cannot imagine that Roos has been here before – not when it is the acknowledged stronghold of the Lady.'

'Harweden said Roos regularly visited kin in Peterborough,' shrugged Bartholomew. 'So perhaps Freburn ranges further than we know. Yet I am surprised Roos did not tell me about this injury. I could have repaired it much more neatly, and given him a remedy for the pain.'

'When did it happen? Can you tell?'

'Roughly three to five weeks ago, judging by the degree of healing.'

Langelee was thoughtful. 'Which means that last night was not the first time Roos was involved in a violent incident. We should bear that in mind when we investigate.'

While Quintone and Langelee manoeuvred Roos up the narrow stairway, Michael indicated that Bartholomew was to examine Margery. Lichet had ordered them not to, but her body might hold clues that had been missing from Roos, and the case would be difficult enough to solve without making it harder still by complying with needless strictures.

'Besides, who will ever know?' he whispered conspiratorially.

Bartholomew pulled away the cloak that covered her, sorry when he saw the kindly face stilled by death and blood staining the pretty rose-coloured kirtle. It was unfair, he thought, that a good woman should have come to such an untimely end.

It did not take him long to ascertain that she had also been stabbed, although her wound was clean, deep and would have killed her instantly. When he pressed on her chest, what flowed from her mouth was clear, telling him she had been dead when she had gone into the water.

He was just covering her up again when Langelee arrived back, whispering an urgent warning that someone else was coming. It transpired to be Heselbech, who was an unnerving presence in the eerily dripping chamber with his sinisterly filed teeth.

'Lichet ordered me to collect her,' the chaplain explained, nodding towards Margery. 'Which will be damned difficult on my own. Will you help?'

Michael nodded. 'But first, tell us if you noticed anything unusual last night. The Cistern Tower is not far from your chapel.'

Heselbech indicated Langelee. 'I was in the priory for most of it, drinking with him. The party broke up when John said we should celebrate nocturns, but I could barely walk, so reciting a holy office was out of the question. Langelee helped me into my chapel, where I managed to ring the bell, but that is all. Tell him, Langelee.'

'Oh, Christ!' gulped Langelee, pale again. 'I *did* give you a shoulder to lean on while you staggered home. It had clean slipped my mind.'

'You were so drunk, you cannot recall where you went?' Bartholomew was unimpressed.

Langelee winced. 'We had a *lot* of ale. But I remember now my memory is jogged. Heselbech and I left the priory and lurched to the chapel together. I left him lying on the floor, and returned to the priory alone.'

'So did either of you see anything that might help us?' pressed Michael.

Both men shook their heads. 'But we did not know that a killer was at large at the time,' said Langelee defensively. 'If we had, obviously we would have been more observant.'

'I suppose we should be grateful that he did not dispatch you, too,' said Michael sourly.

'He could have tried,' said Heselbech grimly, 'but he would not have succeeded. No sly killer could dispatch two bold warriors from the north, even ones who were drunk.'

'Close your eyes,' Michael ordered. 'Try to visualise the castle as you saw it. No, do not smirk at each other like errant schoolboys. I am serious.'

Chagrined, they did as they were told. Heselbech shook his head fairly quickly, but Langelee persisted, his face screwed up tight as he struggled with his memory. But eventually he opened his eyes and gave a regretful shrug.

'All I can tell you for certain is that I delivered Heselbech to the chapel, where he rang the bell. But then he fell over and went to sleep on the floor, so I removed his boots, covered him with a blanket, and returned to our quarters in the priory.'

'But that is untrue,' said Michael. 'If you had gone straight back, you would have arrived while *I* was saying nocturns. But you did not appear until at least half an hour after I had finished.'

Langelee blushed and his eyes were furtive. 'If you must know, I had to stop to be sick, but please do not tell anyone – we cannot have the world knowing that Michaelhouse's Master cannot hold his drink. Our recent economies mean I am no longer used to large quantities of ale.'

Michael turned back to Heselbech. 'You know this castle and its people. What do *you* think happened here?'

Heselbech stared at Margery's cloak-covered form. 'I really have no idea. However, I can tell you that she was the sweetest, kindest lady in the world, and whoever killed her will be damned for all eternity. I cannot tell you anything about Roos, because I had never met him before yesterday.'

'There are faint marks on Roos's arms and chest,' said Bartholomew, 'which suggest he may have been involved in some sort of tussle. However, it was not with Margery – her only injury is the single stab wound.'

'Which means what?' asked Michael.

'That she was killed quickly and cleanly, but he was not,' replied Bartholomew. 'It appears that he tried to fight his – or their – attacker off.'

'Did she have any enemies?' asked Michael of Heselbech. 'Anyone who was jealous of her popularity, or who resented her kindly nature?'

'Margery was loved by all,' stated Heselbech firmly. 'So you will find that the motive for this horrible crime lies with Roos, not her. He was a member of Swinescroft Hostel, for a start.'

'What does that have to do with anything?'

'It is full of nasty, bitter old men – the kind who encouraged Badew to delay signing the Clare Hall quit-claim for ten long years. Poor Margery. All I can think is that she was in the wrong place at the wrong time.' Heselbech glanced around him. 'Very wrong. She should not have been down here with him or anyone else. It is dangerous.'

'Is it?' gulped Michael uneasily. 'Why?'

'It can flood suddenly if the valves on the roof are opened,' explained Heselbech. 'Fortunately, people know I am down here now, so we are quite safe.'

Bartholomew was not so sure about that, given what had happened to the Austin's predecessor. He took a step towards the stairs, thinking the cistern would be an awful place to die.

'You say Margery should not have been down here, Heselbech,' said Langelee. 'But she was the steward's wife – she could go where she pleased in his domain. Roos, however, should have been in the Bell tavern, so his presence is more of a mystery.'

'True,' agreed Heselbech. 'However, Roos seemed to know his way around the castle yesterday – I saw him striding along inside the palace at one point – which suggests that he has been here before. But how could he have done? No one would have invited him, which

147

leads me to wonder if he invaded on the sly – not just last night, but on other occasions, too.'

'That is an interesting observation.' Michael turned to Bartholomew. 'Were they killed here or elsewhere?'

'Here,' replied Bartholomew. 'If they had been carried down the steps, there would be bumps and scrapes on their bodies. The culprit dispatched them here, then shoved them in the water, expecting them to sink. Unfortunately, he chose the wrong spot to do it, because there is a sill just below this pavement. Look.'

He took Langelee's sword, and demonstrated that the water was only knee deep for the first two or three feet. Then the shelf ended, and it would be forty feet down to the bottom. It meant that the bodies had not sunk out of sight, as had evidently been intended, and the culprit was no doubt horrified that his crime had been discovered so quickly.

'The boot,' said Langelee in sudden understanding. 'Roos was missing one. Is that what plugged the pipes and caused the alarm to be raised?'

'Probably,' said Bartholomew. 'And thank God it did, or the bodies would have rotted in the water. You know from personal experience what a devastating effect that can have on the health of those who drink it.'

Michael stared hard at Heselbech. 'A killer stalks your town, and his victims now include not only a fellow Austin, but a lady everyone loved. You must have some ideas as to suspects.'

'Several,' shrugged Heselbech. 'But none whose guilt I can prove. The squires, especially Nuport, are vicious louts who need a stronger man than Albon to tame them. Then there are Thomas and Ella, whose pranks often end in tears—'

'They certainly ended in tears for Talmach,' remarked Langelee. 'Her unloved husband.'

Heselbech nodded. 'You might want to look at Bonde

as well – he is an evil fellow, who has committed murder before, while the Red Devil should never have been allowed to gain such a firm foothold at the castle. But accusations are nothing without evidence, which I do not have.'

When Bartholomew and Heselbech manoeuvred Margery up the steps and out into the bailey, it was to find a guard of honour waiting to receive her. Servants and courtiers alike hurried forward to take the body from them and lay it gently on a bier, after which it was borne away in respectful silence. Then the three Michaelhouse men retreated to a quiet spot behind the kitchens to discuss what they had learned and how they should proceed.

'I know you want to catch Roos's killer, Brother,' said Langelee worriedly, 'but can you not forget your respon-sibilities, just this once? An enquiry will damage our chances of winning benefactors, because we cannot recruit them *and* chase murderers. There is not enough time.'

'Then you concentrate on winning new patrons while Matt and I find the killer,' determined Michael. 'I cannot return to Cambridge without at least having tried to see justice done.'

'But what happens if I worm a donation from someone who then transpires to be the culprit?' objected Langelee. 'It would break my heart to give it back.'

'You would have to,' said Bartholomew firmly. 'It would be tainted, and would almost certainly come back to haunt us in the future.'

'I agree,' said Michael. 'Which is another good reason for investigating – so we can lay our hands on our hearts, and say we did our utmost to ensure that any money we take home is clean. So let us begin. What more can you tell us about the bodies, Matt? Start with who was dispatched first.'

'It is impossible to say. However, the stab wounds are identical in size and shape, which suggests the same weapon was used. It is indicative of a single assailant.'

'Anything else?'

'We all saw Roos and Margery talking to each other yesterday. I thought it odd at the time that one of the Lady's most bitter enemies should hobnob with the wife of her steward . . .'

'It looked to me as though they were arguing,' said Langelee. 'Perhaps Roos killed her, then dispatched himself from remorse.'

'Never,' said Michael, shaking his head. 'I knew Roos – he was not a remorseful man.'

'I want to say that they cannot possibly share a connection to each other,' said Bartholomew. 'Not just because they hailed from different sides of a bitter feud between the Lady and Badew, but for their characters – hers as a kindly soul, and his as a nasty old lecher . . .'

'I sense a "but",' said Michael.

Bartholomew nodded. 'But I found something that suggests they knew each other rather well. She wore an onyx ring engraved with a bird. Here it is.'

'You *took* it?' gulped Michael in alarm. 'Lord! I hope we are not accused of theft.'

'I was afraid it would fall off when we carried her up the stairs. You can give it back to Marishal now. However, before you do, look at what I found on a cord around Roos's neck. I removed that for safekeeping, too.'

He held both items in the palm of his hand. Michael and Langelee peered at them.

'But they are the same in every detail,' breathed Langelee. 'Why did you not mention it at once? Why wait until now?'

'Because we were not alone when I made the discovery,' replied Bartholomew soberly, 'and it is difficult to know who to trust in this place.'

150

'You mean Heselbech?' asked Langelee, startled. 'He is all right.'

'I agree with Matt,' said Michael. 'It is wise to be cautious until we know more about what is happening. However, the man who makes *me* uncomfortable is Nicholas. I disliked the way he drooled over your letter-opener the other night. It is inappropriate for a priest to covet a weapon.'

'Of course he admired it,' said Langelee impatiently. 'He is an ex-warrior who knows a good blade when he sees one.'

Michael was disinclined to argue, and returned his attention to the rings. 'So what do these mean? That Roos and Margery were lovers, and these are tokens of their shared affection?'

'That does not sound very likely,' said Bartholomew. 'I seriously doubt she could have been tempted by anything Roos had to offer.'

'I agree,' said Langelee. 'Besides, I know women, and she was not the sort to break her wedding vows.'

'Then maybe she and Roos were kin,' suggested Michael. 'Do not forget what Heselbech said – that Roos seemed to know his way around the castle. If Roos and Margery were related, he may have been a regular visitor here.'

'If so, he would not have told Badew and Harweden,' predicted Langelee. 'Familial ties to the wife of the Lady's steward? They would have denounced him on the spot!'

'They would,' agreed Michael, taking the rings from Bartholomew and slipping them in his scrip. 'So perhaps they found out yesterday, and promptly killed them both.'

'Maybe,' said Bartholomew. 'Although if Roos was a regular visitor, you would think that someone would have mentioned it by now – as far as I can tell, everyone here considers him a stranger. Yet he did slip away from his cronies yesterday, to end up in a quiet room in the palace with Margery . . .'

151

'And Badew and Harweden were irked about it,' recalled Michael thoughtfully. 'So I say we put them at the top of our list of suspects. Right after Nicholas.'

'Just because he likes my knife?' asked Langelee irritably. 'I hardly think that is a reason—'

'I have a nose for these things, and there is something distinctly awry about that vicar,' argued Michael. 'For a start, he is enamoured of his anchoress. I heard him call her "sweetest love" yesterday, which is no way to address a holy woman.'

Bartholomew laughed. 'Even if he is smitten, there is nothing either can do about it, given that she is walled up inside a cell. Unless he owns a sledgehammer.'

Michael eyed him balefully. 'You mock, but I am right. Marishal also goes on the list. He was Margery's husband, and may have objected to her relationship with Roos – whatever that transpires to be – so he killed them both in a fit of rage.'

'Then we should include Thomas and Ella for the same reason,' said Bartholomew. 'Along with the fact that they are no strangers to murder, if the gossip is to be believed.'

'Which it should,' said Langelee. 'A frayed strap, a jaunt in bad weather, a carelessly carried blade . . . It is too good to be true when we have a young woman and an unwanted older husband.'

'I agree,' said Michael. 'I do not suggest we investigate Talmach's peculiar demise, but we shall certainly bear it in mind, along with the four other suspicious deaths that have occurred here since February – Roger, Wisbech, Charer and Skynere.'

'We have been told that the squires might be responsible for some of those,' said Bartholomew. 'It would not surprise me – Albon does not have them under control. So they are next on our list. Perhaps they objected to Roos fraternising with the mother of one of their friends.'

'I say we consider Donwich and Pulham, too,' said Langelee. 'They are frantic to keep the Lady's good graces. Perhaps Roos's relationship with Margery threatened that in some way.'

'The same is true of Lichet,' said Bartholomew. 'He will go to any lengths to safeguard his position here, but it is possible that Roos and Margery knew something to see him ousted. Moreover, he lives in the Cistern Tower, where they died . . .'

'True,' acknowledged Michael. 'And we shall finish the list with Bonde, who should have been hanged for murder, but was saved by the Lady's purse.'

'The list is not finished yet,' said Langelee. 'What about Mayor Godeston and Barber Grym? I did not take to them, and if you can include Nicholas on the grounds of dislike . . .'

'But Godeston is carried everywhere on a litter,' Bartholomew pointed out. 'He could never scale a ladder. And Grym would not fit down the shaft – it was a tight squeeze for Michael, and Grym is much fatter.'

'I am not fat,' objected Michael, offended. 'I just have big bones.'

'What about Albon, then?' asked Langelee. 'He pretends to be a knight, but he is all hot air and glorious finery. Such men think nothing of slaughtering old men and women.'

'Very well,' said Michael, although without conviction. 'So there is our rogues' gallery: Nicholas, Badew and Harweden, Marishal and his brats, the squires, our colleagues from Clare Hall, Lichet, Bonde and Albon. Now we must set about narrowing it down.'

'I suspect we are more likely to expand it,' predicted Langelee glumly. 'This is a nasty little town, inhabited by vicious people. I wish we had never come.'

\* \* \*

153

They began their enquiries in the hall, where Lichet was playing his lute. Many of the women were crying, while their menfolk stood in subdued clusters, talking in low voices. Albon had taken a seat on the dais, looking splendid but preoccupied. Lichet strummed next to him, eyes closed in rapture at the sounds he was producing, although he was an indifferent performer at best. Quintone hovered dutifully nearby, ready to run any errands the Red Devil happened to devise.

Then a door clanked, and the squires – minus Thomas – strutted in. They had used the intervening time to change their clothes, and the scholars were not the only ones who gaped at the result. They had kept their long-toed shoes, flowing sleeves and oiled beards, but had added harlequin hose to the ensemble. They swaggered to the dais, confident in the knowledge that every eye was on them. Lichet stopped playing mid-chord, while Albon was so astounded by their appearance that he almost toppled off his seat. When they had made their obeisance to him, they sat with calculated nonchalance on the bench at his side.

'God's blood!' breathed Langelee. 'Someone should tell them that they are making asses of themselves, as they seem to be incapable of seeing it.'

'I doubt it was their idea,' murmured Bartholomew. 'Look at Thomas and Ella.'

The twins were with their father, who was slumped, ashen-faced and unmoving, in a chair by the hearth. Their faces were sombre, but their eyes gleamed at the shock the squires had generated.

'I would have thought they would desist from japes today,' said Michael disapprovingly. 'Do they have no sense of decorum?'

'Margery seems to have been loved by everyone,' whispered Langelee. 'Even I am sorry she is dead, and I barely knew her. But her children have not shed a

154

single tear that I have seen, and now they amuse themselves by playing jokes on their fellows. It reveals a cold-bloodedness that repels me – and I was once a warrior, used to a bit of ruthlessness.'

'They are wild because they have a father who is too busy and a mother who was too gentle,' said Bartholomew. 'Margery admitted that Anne was the only person who could tame them, but now she is walled inside a church. And poor proud Albon is certainly not up to the challenge.'

'They are not children,' objected Michael. 'They are adults in their twenties, and Ella has been married. It is too late for Albon – or anyone else – to mould them now.'

'I could do it,' bragged Langelee. 'Perhaps I should offer my services to Marishal – to turn his spawn into sensible beings in exchange for a donation. What do you think?'

'That we do not want them in Cambridge, thank you very much.' Michael looked around quickly. 'All our suspects are here, except Badew and Harweden, who we will corner at the Bell later. I suggest we interview everyone else right away.'

'Lichet will stop us,' warned Bartholomew. 'He will view it as an affront to his authority.'

Michael smiled thinly. 'We shall see.'

He strode to the dais. Albon looked up questioningly, but Lichet had resumed his strumming and pretended not to notice the monk. Michael climbed on to the platform, and addressed the whole assembly in a loud, clear voice that drowned out the Red Devil's music.

'On behalf of the Master and Fellows of Michaelhouse, I would like to offer my condolences to you all. Our College has many priests, and Masses will be said for Margery's soul.'

A murmur of appreciation rippled around the hall, although Lichet was indignant.

'How dare you interrupt my playing to make stupid announcements,' he snarled. 'In future, you will apply to me before braying to all and sundry.'

'I hardly think the care of Margery's soul is "stupid",' countered Michael, a remark that drew a universal rumble of agreement. He turned from Lichet and addressed his audience again. 'Her body lies in the chapel, available to anyone who wishes to pay his respects.'

'All of us will go,' said Albon quietly. 'Although the squires must change first.'

'Why?' asked Nuport, startled. 'Mistress Marishal loved bright things, as Thomas reminded us just an hour ago. We donned these colourful hose in her honour.'

'They are colourful,' acknowledged Albon in distaste. 'But they are inappropriate in the black presence of Death. Besides, there is a difference between "bright" and "gaudy", and you have not hit the right note at all. She liked pale, discreet shades, not scarlet, emerald and orange.'

Lichet thrust his lute at Quintone, and stalked towards Michael, aiming to claw back the authority that was draining away with every word that was spoken. Quintone rolled his eyes, which made some folk laugh, although they stopped when the Red Devil glared furiously at them.

'Well, monk?' Lichet demanded coldly. 'What did you learn from visiting the scene of the crime? Do you know the name of the killer?'

'It will take days of painstaking detail-gathering before that becomes clear,' replied Michael. 'So when will you start *your* enquiries, Master Lichet? I am sure a man of your vigour does not need to eat or sleep, and can catch a killer, pay court to the Lady *and* run the castle while Marishal is indisposed.'

Lichet thought fast. 'I have decided to delegate the murders to you. However, you will report to me and *only* to me. I shall then decide what should be done with any solutions you might devise. Is that clear?'

Michael inclined his head in acquiescence, a gleam of amusement in his green eyes that Lichet should be so easy to manipulate. 'You will be the first to know anything of import.'

It was such a vague promise that Bartholomew knew Lichet was unlikely to benefit from it. To prevent Lichet from thinking the same, Michael furnished him with a brief account of his findings to date. When he had finished, Lichet strode to the front of the dais and cleared his throat loudly, to attract everyone's attention.

'Through the careful application of logic and skill,' he announced in his booming voice, 'I have ascertained that Mistress Marishal and Master Roos were stabbed by an unknown assailant, and their bodies tossed into the cistern in the expectation that they would sink and be lost for ever. However, the culprit should know that I have ordered an investigation, and I *will* catch him.'

'No, Lichet,' said Albon, coming to his feet and giving a toss of his glorious mane. '*I* will catch him. I swear it by God and by my honour. This vile deed is an affront to the chivalric code by which I live.'

'But you are leaving for France soon,' Lichet pointed out. 'And the monk has just told me . . . I mean it is my learned opinion that the mystery may take longer to solve.'

Albon smiled thinly. 'I shall go nowhere until the culprit is hanged.'

A groan of dismay went up from nobles and servants alike. Yet there were a few smiles. Two serving girls exchanged pleased grins, and so did several young ladies-in-waiting, after which their eyes turned to Thomas, who winked at them.

'If *my* mother had been stabbed, I would join Albon in vowing to catch her killer,' muttered Langelee to Bartholomew. 'Not simper at my conquests. And look at Ella. I am sure I saw those pink pearls on Margery

157

yesterday – she did not wait long before raiding her dam's jewellery box.'

'Maybe she donned them in tribute,' suggested Bartholomew charitably.

Langelee shot him a disbelieving glance. 'There is no doubting their sire's grief, though, so I think we can eliminate him as a suspect for the murders.'

'It may be grief,' acknowledged Michael. 'But it might also be guilt. It is often difficult to tell.'

# CHAPTER 6

It quickly became apparent that Albon had no idea how to conduct a murder investigation, because if he had, he would not have listened to Lichet. The Red Devil advised him to lock everyone in the hall until they had been questioned, which was a bad strategy on several counts. First, it meant that no one could tend livestock or prepare food. Second, as the interviews were conducted in public, it would give the killer an opportunity to listen to others' replies and adapt his own accordingly. And third, a seemingly random assortment of people were allowed to leave. Donwich, Pulham, three dozen courtiers, ten servants and two squires were among those who contrived to sail out unchallenged.

'I do not know who is the greater fool – Lichet or Albon,' muttered Michael, watching the Red Devil stride away to resume his lute playing, although now to a considerably reduced audience.

'*Is* Lichet a fool?' asked Bartholomew. 'Or is he trying to sabotage your enquiry?'

'Why would he do that?' asked Langelee, frowning. 'He has just appointed Michael as his official investigator, with the obvious aim of stealing any solutions and claiming them as his own.'

'Because he is the culprit,' replied Bartholomew promptly. 'Do not forget that Margery and Roos were killed in the Cistern Tower – where he lives.'

'Yes, we shall certainly ask him where he was all night,' said Michael. 'He raced away before I could press him earlier, but it will not happen again. Lord! What is Albon doing?'

The knight had ordered a throne-like chair set up on the dais. He sat, then beckoned to Quintone and proceeded to stare intently at him, leaning forward until he was so close that their noses almost touched. Uncomfortable, Quintone tried to back away, but Albon gripped his wrist to prevent it. The servant gazed back, nonplussed and wary.

'Quintone,' Albon intoned eventually. 'Did you kill Mistress Marishal?'

'God in Heaven!' breathed Langelee in understanding. 'He thinks he will catch the culprit by reading the guilt in his eyes. The man is deluded!'

'Yes,' agreed Michael. 'But go and monitor him anyway. Someone may admit to being near the cistern last night, and if so, it would be helpful to know who they are. In the interim, Matt and I will corner the suspects on our list.'

'No,' said Langelee firmly. 'I would rather secure us some new benefactors.'

'I would rather you did, too, but Lichet has allowed the richest courtiers to leave, and there is no point in wooing paupers. Listen to Albon – that is the most useful thing you can do for us now.'

Langelee glanced at the people who had gathered to watch Albon at work. Most were servants, who were unlikely to have money to spare for a foundation that none of them had ever heard of. He conceded reluctantly that Michael was right, and made for the dais with an expression of grim determination.

'We have been told that it was the baker who raised the alarm,' said Bartholomew, watching the Master go. 'So we should question him first.'

The baker transpired to be the lad with the floury hands and lame leg who had challenged Lichet's orders earlier. His name was Adam, and he had been cornered by Nuport and two of the other squires. They were amusing themselves by pushing him from one to the other, all the while imitating his ungainly efforts to keep his balance.

'Enough,' ordered Bartholomew sharply; he had never liked bullies. 'I cannot see Albon approving of such low antics. He obviously sets great store by the chivalric code.'

Nuport sneered. 'So do we, but it only applies to fellow nobles – servants and cripples do not count. Now piss off, fool.'

'It is you who are the fool,' flashed back Bartholomew, 'for tormenting the man who bakes your daily bread. Or do you like eating spit and rat droppings?'

The squires exchanged horrified glances, and while they contemplated the possibility that their cruelty might be repaid in ways they had not imagined, Adam took the opportunity to scuttle away. Their bluster promptly returned when Michael began to ask questions, but the Senior Proctor was used to dealing with arrogant youths, and it did not take him long to put them in their place.

'Now, where were you when Margery and Roos were killed?' he demanded, once they were sufficiently subdued.

'In the Bell Inn,' replied Nuport sullenly, picking an invisible speck from his multicoloured hose. 'Celebrating the burial of that rogue Skynere, who went in his grave yesterday.'

'Skynere was a liar,' put in a lad named John Mull, who had freckles and spots in equal measure. 'He went around saying that we killed Roger the mason. But we never did.'

'We have not killed anyone,' declared Nuport, then grinned at his friends. 'Although that will change when we get to France.'

'Roos was staying at the Bell Inn,' said Michael, once a hard glare had wiped the smirk from the squire's heavy face. 'Did you cross swords with him there, perhaps

161

because he accused Thomas and Ella of having a hand in Talmach's death?'

'No, we did not,' replied Nuport sulkily. 'We saw his two cronies – they were in the far corner of the room, muttering about avenging themselves on the Lady for stealing "their" College all those years ago. But he was not with them.'

'Then where was he?' asked Michael.

'How should we know? All I can say is that he was not in the Bell.'

'It was a good night,' said Mull brightly. 'We all got very drunk, and I do not remember walking home at all. But I woke up in my own bed, so I suppose I must have done.'

'*I* remember walking back,' scowled Nuport. 'First, because it was raining. And second, because the whore who accompanied us stole my purse. I will trounce her if I see her again.'

'If you do,' said Michael icily, 'I shall see that you are trounced in return. Leave the townswomen alone. Do you hear?'

He glared until Nuport acknowledged that he did.

Bartholomew and Michael found Adam the baker near the door, where he was begging to be let out, all the while glancing over his shoulder, ready to bolt if the squires reappeared. The guards ignored his pleas, so he was more than happy to take refuge with Michael for a while.

'I hate Nuport and his cronies,' he confided tearfully. 'We were all looking forward to being rid of them, but now Sir William has vowed to catch the killer . . . well, they might never go.'

'Could they be the culprits?' asked Michael.

Adam hesitated, but then shook his head, although with obvious reluctance. 'Unfortunately not. I work at night, see, to get the bread ready for morning. I saw them stagger into their quarters at midnight, after which none of them stirred. Well, Thomas went off alone, but the others stayed put.'

'Where did Thomas go?' asked Bartholomew.

'I did not notice, because it is the rest who are dangerous, as far as I am concerned. Perhaps he went to visit his sister. They are very close.'

'How can you be sure the remaining squires stayed put?' pressed Michael.

'Because unless I watch them like a hawk, they catch me and push me around, like they did just now. I *always* know where they are.'

'And before midnight? Where were you then? And where were they?'

'I was here in the hall, listening to the Clare Hall men sing – they were rather good, actually. And the squires were out in the town, drinking. I know they came back at midnight, because the hour-candle said so, and it was when Master Marishal ordered everyone to bed.'

'I am afraid your testimony does not exonerate the squires,' said Michael, 'as we do not know exactly when Margery and Roos died.'

'Well, I can tell you that they were still alive two hours after midnight,' sniffed Adam, 'because I saw them. And by then, the bullying bastards were snoring in their beds.'

Michael narrowed his eyes. 'How can you be so sure of the time?'

'I heard Heselbech chime the bell for nocturns, which is at two o'clock in the morning at this time of year, as you will know.' Adam sniggered suddenly. 'Our chaplain was very drunk and your Master Langelee had to hold him upright.'

'What were Roos and Margery doing when you spotted them?' asked Michael.

'They were not together. I noticed Roos first, strutting

along like he owned the place. Then Mistress Marishal appeared a few moments later.'

'Did it not occur to you that nocturns is an odd time for anyone – other than priests and those keeping them on their feet – to be abroad?'

'It was odd for Roos certainly, as he was a stranger,' replied Adam. 'But it was not odd for Mistress Marishal. She often rose in the night to tend the Lady.'

'Do you know what Roos was doing here?'

Adam shook his head. 'But I can tell you that he was in a temper. His fists were clenched and he stamped along like an angry duck.'

'How did he get in here? I assume the entrances are guarded?'

'Of course they are, or the townsfolk would invade and create havoc. However, I saw Bonde go to the gate-house after he had finished minding the squires. You can ask *him* why he let Roos inside.'

'We shall,' promised Michael.

Adam's hard little face softened. 'Mistress Marishal was kind to me, and I hope you or Sir William catch whoever killed her. She was an angel.'

'Did you see anyone else out and about last night?'

'Just the two Clare Hall men. When they finished singing in the hall, they went to their room in the Oxford Tower, although they never put the lamps out – they kept them burning all night. You might want to find out why.'

Bartholomew winced, hoping Donwich and Pulham would not transpire to be the culprits, as relations between his College and theirs might never recover.

'So, let us summarise so far,' said Michael. 'Roos and Margery were alive at nocturns, but the only squire who could have killed them was Thomas, who had wandered off alone. Besides him and the victims, no one else was about except you, Bonde and our Clare Hall colleagues.'

Adam nodded. 'But I did not hurt her, and I can prove

it. You see, baking is a precise art, timed to the second: if I had jaunted off to commit murder, my bread would have been late and everyone here would have noticed. But it was not – it was exactly on time, as usual.'

Michael acknowledged the alibi with a nod. 'Now tell me how you came to find the bodies.'

'We have running water in the kitchens, but it was not flowing this morning, so I went to find out why. It is not unusual – dirt, bits of stone and leaves are always getting stuck in the pipes. The cistern door was wide open, which was odd, so I took a lamp and went down the steps . . .'

'And?'

'And I saw the scholar in the water. It was a shock, I can tell you! I turned and raced back up the steps as fast as my legs would take me, yelling for help. Of course, it was not the bodies that stopped the water from flowing, because the pipes are blocked still, even though Mistress Marishal and Roos are now in the chapel.'

'Roos was missing a boot,' said Bartholomew.

Adam snapped his fingers. 'That would do it. Someone will have to go down there and flush it out, although I hope it will not be me. Anyway, I reached the bailey, yelling as loud as I could, and Master Marishal, Thomas, Ereswell, Quintone and several others came running. Lichet appeared from nowhere, like the demon he is.'

'What happened then?'

'Master Marishal ordered me back down the stairs to show him what I had found, and a whole host of folk followed. We pulled Roos from the water, and covered him with a cloak. Father Heselbech had arrived by then, but instead of praying for Roos, he raced off to take the news to his priory. Then Quintone spotted a second body – Mistress Marishal.'

'Did you see anyone else in the bailey when you went to the cistern the first time?'

Adam shook his head. 'And I have been thinking about

165

it ever since. Poor Mistress Marishal. Killing her was a terrible sin, and the culprit will roast in Hell for ever.'

'So, we can cross the squires off our list,' said Michael, as the baker hobbled away to hide under a table. 'Adam would have implicated them if he could – it pained him to provide their alibi. However, Thomas has gone right to the top, along with Marishal and Lichet. I find it suspicious that both were to hand when Adam raised the alarm.'

'I wonder if Albon has interviewed them yet,' said Bartholomew. 'We should ask Langelee before we tackle them ourselves – to avoid covering the same ground.'

'Albon will have learned nothing of use,' predicted Michael disdainfully. 'And I hate to say it, but do not expect much from Langelee either. He is an admirable man in many respects, but he is hopeless at identifying liars.'

'Then why did you charge him with monitoring Albon?'

'Because Roos's killer will only be caught by cunning, and Langelee will be more hindrance than help, if he insists on looming over my shoulder with one hand on his sword. Listening to Albon will keep him busy without doing any harm.'

It was a valid point, as the Master was not known for his tact, patience or subtlety.

'We had better find Bonde next,' said Bartholomew. 'Adam thinks he allowed Roos through the castle gate, so perhaps he let the killer in, too. Maybe it was a townsman, and Roos and Margery are just two more deaths in this vicious feud – the culprit targeted Margery because she was popular, and Roos just happened to be in the way.'

'Or Bonde might have stabbed them himself,' countered Michael. 'We know for a fact that he is a murderer, and he said and did nothing to convince me of his innocence earlier.'

166

'He cried for Margery,' Bartholomew pointed out. 'Although he tried to hide it.'

'That does not mean he did not stab her,' said Michael soberly.

When they hailed Quintone, to ask if he knew where Bonde might be, they were given some interesting news.

'I just saw him through the window – leaving,' replied the servant. 'I called out to ask where he was going, and he said he was off to London on the Lady's business. But that is a lie, because she is still in bed, so how can she have given him new orders?'

'Fleeing the scene of the crime,' mused Michael. 'Perhaps he was willing to brazen it out as long as he thought Lichet or Albon would investigate, but wisely decided to disappear when it was announced that I would be exploring the matter.'

'Possibly,' acknowledged Bartholomew. 'Although he cannot be familiar with your reputation as a solver of crimes.'

'He does not have to be, Matt. It may be enough to know that I am neither Lichet nor Albon – men who can be hoodwinked, predicted and manipulated.'

'Well, we will not forget about him, no matter where he goes,' determined Bartholomew. 'We cannot hare after him on our poor old nags, so if we do uncover evidence of his guilt, it will be the Lady's responsibility to bring him to justice. Of course, she may choose to ignore his crime, which will be easier – and cheaper – than corrupting a second judge.'

'The murder of her steward's wife is not the same as some faceless neighbour. If Bonde *is* the culprit, she will have no choice but to act.'

In Bartholomew's experience, the rich and powerful had a rather flexible attitude regarding what constituted the right thing to do, so he was rather less sanguine about justice being done. He turned back to Quintone.

'I do not suppose Bonde mentioned letting anyone – other than Roos – into the castle last night, did he?'

'He would not have let Roos in,' averred Quintone. 'Roos was a stranger, and Bonde is particular about things like that.'

'But he *did* let Roos in,' Bartholomew pointed out. 'The body in the cistern proves it.'

Quintone shrugged. 'Then Roos grew wings and flew over the walls, because he could not have got past the Lady's favourite henchman. You met Bonde – the man is an animal.'

Next, Michael decided to speak to Marishal. However, when they reached the hearth, the steward had gone. There was no sign of the twins either. Lichet saw their bemusement and came to explain.

'I sent them to bed with a potion to ease their minds. They are grieving, you see.'

'So are we,' said Michael coolly. 'Roos was our colleague, do not forget.'

'Yes, but he is not nearly as important as Margery,' said Lichet dismissively. 'She was the steward's wife, whereas he was just a scholar.'

Michael regarded him coldly. 'Roos's murder is just as grave a crime as hers, and will be treated as such. Now, take us to Marishal at once.'

'I shall not! You may apply to me tomorrow, when I shall decide whether he is equal to an audience. Until then, he and his family are off limits. And do not think you can circumvent me – I put guards on the door to their quarters with orders to skewer anyone trying to sneak past.'

'What kind of potion did you feed the Marishals?' asked Bartholomew, while Michael gave the Red Devil the kind of look that suggested he had just replaced Bonde as prime suspect.

'One that brings healing sleep,' replied Lichet shortly. 'All three will be dead to the world by now, so even if you do manage to slink past my security arrangements, they will not be in a position to answer questions. Ergo, I advise you not to bother.'

'Where is the Lady?' demanded Michael, deciding to see what she had to say about such high-handed tactics, while Bartholomew mused that drugging the steward was one way for Lichet to ensure he was not deprived of his new-found power. However, while it might be acceptable to dose a grieving family with a mild soporific, it was definitely not good practice to give them one that rendered them 'dead to the world'. Again, he wondered if Lichet was deliberately sabotaging Michael's enquiry.

'She was also distraught, so I gave her a draught as well,' Lichet informed Michael loftily. 'They will all feel better in the morning.'

'What was in it?' pressed Bartholomew. 'Exactly.'

'It is a secret recipe, although I can tell you that it includes hemlock and honey. It is not one you will find in any of your medical tomes, though, so do not waste your time trying to look it up.'

'You used *hemlock* to promote natural sleep?' Bartholomew was horrified. 'Is that not akin to using a mallet for cracking nuts?'

'It is perfectly safe for those of us who know what we are doing,' retorted Lichet. 'It is only the inexperienced or stupid who make mistakes in dosage.'

Manfully, Bartholomew ignored the insult. 'Did you ever feed any of this "secret recipe" to Wisbech or Skynere?'

'No, because Skynere was Grym's patient, while Wisbech took his medical problems to the priory.' Lichet gave a superior smile. 'I do not believe those two were poisoned anyway. There is no evidence to say they were – just a lot of unfounded speculation by an uneducated barber.'

'What about the other deaths?' asked Michael, before Bartholomew could indulge in a piece-by-piece demolition of Lichet's own medical skills. It was unnecessary, as they had already surmised that he was a charlatan with no university training. 'Roger, Charer and Talmach. Do you have an opinion about what happened to them?'

'Of course – they were accidents, and anyone who claims otherwise is just trying to encourage trouble between us and the town. Roger was killed by a falling plank, Charer fell in the river, and Talmach tumbled off his horse. There was nothing suspicious about any of them.'

'I see,' said Bartholomew flatly. 'Where were you between nocturns and dawn?'

'Me?' asked Lichet warily. 'Why do you want to know?'

'Because you live above the cistern,' explained Michael, before Bartholomew could say something more accusatory – there was no point in alerting the Red Devil to the fact that he was high on their list of suspects. 'You may have seen or heard something.'

'And I probably would, had I been there,' replied Lichet haughtily. 'Because I am an extremely observant man, and very little escapes my attention. But I was in the palace all night, watching the Lady sleep.'

'Why would you do that?' asked Bartholomew, suspicious all over again.

Lichet smiled superiorly. 'Because I have taken it upon myself to ensure that she has eight hours of undisturbed rest every night. I was with her until daybreak.'

'No, you were not,' countered Bartholomew, disliking the fact that Lichet considered them fools who would swallow his lies without question. 'You were one of the first on the scene when the bodies were found. You "appeared from nowhere" according to one witness.'

'Well, obviously a man must slip to the latrine on occasion,' shrugged Lichet, so smoothly that Bartholomew suspected he had been preparing his defence ever since the bodies had been found. 'I took care of business, and was on my way back when Adam raised the alarm. Naturally, I went to see if I could help.'

'Who else was there?' demanded Bartholomew, with the sole intention of catching him out.

Unfortunately, Lichet was too clever to make such a basic mistake, and his reply was flawless, even down to the detail of Marishal covering Margery with his own cloak.

'So your alibi for the time of the murder is the Lady,' said Bartholomew, unwilling to let him off the hook, 'who was fast asleep at the time, so cannot verify it.'

Lichet smiled serenely. 'Who knows? Perhaps she will remember the guardian angel at the foot of her bed, but perhaps she will not. You may ask her tomorrow, when she wakes, although phrase your question with care. She will not appreciate insinuations made against esteemed members of her household, and may respond by excising you from her will.'

'He is our culprit,' determined Bartholomew, once Lichet had strutted away. 'He cannot prove where he was at the salient time, and he wants us to believe that the other suspicious deaths were accidents. He would probably have insisted that Roos and Margery died of natural causes as well, if no one else had been in a position to examine the bodies.'

'Possibly,' acknowledged Michael. 'But he is right about one thing – the Lady *will* resent her favourites coming under suspicion, so we must proceed with care.'

'It will take a powerful dose of medicine to make someone sleep until tomorrow,' Bartholomew went on in disgust. 'One that not even a dubious practitioner like Lichet would dare use on an old lady in indifferent health. Ergo, there *will* be an opportunity to question her today.

Of course, we all know why he wants us to stay away from her.'

'We do?'

'So that when she wakes, he can convince her that he was watching over her all night.'

'Or perhaps he knows that one of the Marishals is the killer,' mused Michael, 'and aims to use the time coaching them on how to evade justice.'

'Why would he do that? He wants them out of the way, so he can run the castle instead.'

'He can pose as Acting Steward temporarily, but the post is hereditary, so must revert to the family eventually,' explained Michael. 'However, the Lady will not want to lose Marishal, and Marishal will not want to lose his brats. Ergo, Lichet could earn their undying gratitude by making inconvenient accusations go away – gratitude that could be permanent and lucrative.'

Bartholomew glanced at the dais. 'Albon seems to have finished interrogating everyone now, although how he managed to work his way through upwards of two hundred people in so short a space of time is beyond me. Perhaps Langelee can explain.'

As they walked towards the front of the hall, Albon stood and nodded to the guards, who opened the doors, allowing bright daylight to stream in and people to stream out. Langelee was shaking his head in stunned disbelief.

'He pressed no one for details,' he said. 'Mostly, he just asked one question: did you stab Mistress Marishal? Not surprisingly, no one said yes, and then he was beckoning his next "witness" forward. He seems to think that no one will lie to a man of honour.'

Michael laughed. 'So what will he do now?'

'Kneel in the chapel, next to Margery's coffin, and reflect on all he has learned. I told him that would not take long, given that he has uncovered virtually nothing

172

to ponder, but he said he expects to be there for the rest of the day.'

'He is out of his depth and he knows it,' surmised Michael. 'So we shall corner him in a moment, and offer some friendly advice – and ask him a few questions into the bargain.'

'Good,' said Langelee, 'because it is possible that he is going to the chapel in order to reflect on the crimes *he* committed – to devise a way to exonerate himself.'

'We should speak to the hermit when we have finished with Albon,' said Bartholomew. 'Bonde mentioned him prowling around, so we should find out what – if anything – he saw.'

'I will fetch him,' offered Langelee. 'Watching Albon has given me a headache, and I need some fresh air.'

When the Master had gone, Bartholomew and Michael went to the chapel. It was a pretty building, although only large enough to hold about fifty people, so it was no surprise that the Lady aimed to stake a claim on the parish church. The chapel was full of her ancestors' tombs, and was a dark, silent, intimate place.

Heselbech was there, praying in the nave, although his nodding head and bowed shoulders suggested that his sleepless night was beginning to catch up with him. He turned at the sound of footsteps and heaved himself to his feet, yawning hugely as he did so.

'Have you come to examine the bodies again?' he asked. 'Or to pay your respects?'

'Neither,' replied Michael. 'We have come to talk to Albon. Where is he?'

Heselbech led the way past the rood screen to the chancel, where the knight was on his knees before the High Altar, hands clasped reverently in front of him. On one side stood an ornate casket draped in green silk; on the other was a bier with handles, suggesting that Roos would not lie there for much longer. Albon was so still and poised that he might have been a statue, but then he sneezed, and spoiled his attitude of elegant piety by wiping his nose on his gauntlet.

'He has come to pray for guidance, given that his first stab at identifying the culprit was unsuccessful,' explained Heselbech. 'I have been instructed to keep the place quiet, so he can concentrate. Of course, that may prove difficult, given that so many folk want to pay their last respects to Margery.'

Bartholomew and Michael left him to it and approached the kneeling knight. Albon sneezed again, sniffed loudly, and this time it was his sleeve that cleaned his running nose.

'How are your enquiries coming along?' asked Michael, striding up behind him and catching him mid-scrub.

'Slowly,' replied Albon, blushing with mortification at being caught in the act of doing something so unmannerly. 'But that will change once I have spoken to God. He will tell me what to do next.'

'Of course,' said Michael. 'But what are your preliminary conclusions?'

'I do not have any, Brother. I may be a novice in these matters, but I do know that it is unwise to begin with preconceptions.'

'Preconceptions often serve me very well,' countered Michael. 'Along with hunches. Indeed, it is sometimes impossible to proceed very far without them.'

Albon gave a pained smile. 'Then I shall confess to you that one solution does keep coming to mind: that Mistress Marishal and Roos were killed by a townsman. You may have noticed that there is a very nasty feud in Clare.'

'Oh, yes,' said Michael. 'So where were you between nocturns and dawn?'

'Why those particular times?' asked Albon curiously.

174

'Is it when the murders were committed? How did you discover that?'

'The usual way – by asking pertinent questions of relevant witnesses.'

Albon inclined his head. 'Then thank you for sharing your discovery with a rival investigator. But to answer your question, I was here, in the chapel. I am about to embark on a holy quest to France, so I spend a lot of time communing with the Almighty.'

'It is not a holy quest,' argued Bartholomew, offended by the claim. 'It is taking a lot of ruffians to join a war that we had no right starting in the first place.'

Albon regarded him coolly. 'I was called to service personally by the King, and he is God's anointed. Thus it most certainly *is* a holy undertaking, and I am honoured to have been chosen.'

'Did you see or hear anything suspicious at all?' asked Michael, speaking before Bartholomew could inform him that this was a lot of convoluted claptrap. 'This building is not far from the Cistern Tower – just a stone's throw from one door to the other.'

'If I had seen the killer commit his foul deed, I would already have hanged him,' declared Albon, and turned his noble visage back to the altar, closed his eyes and re-clasped his hands. 'Now, if you will excuse me, Brother, I must pray.'

'I have nothing against piety,' said Michael, a short while later, after Langelee had returned to say that the hermit was out and no one knew where he had gone. 'But Albon is blinded by it, and it is not healthy. Let us hope *we* solve these murders, because he never will.'

'Perhaps he does not want the killer caught,' suggested Langelee. 'Because then he can stay here on his knees, instead of leading a host of unruly louts to France. He is a coward, and is frightened now that the day of his departure looms. He wants a way to avoid it.'

'I am glad he was not my commander at the Battle of Poitiers,' said Bartholomew, inclined to think Langelee was right.

'So am I,' said Langelee fervently. 'Because then you would not have survived to bring me back that lovely letter-opener. Albon is an ass, who does not know one end of a hauberk from—'

He stopped speaking abruptly and rifled through his scrip, his face a mask of dismay. Then he pulled off his belt and began to pat himself down with increasing urgency.

'What is the matter?' asked Michael. 'You cannot have lost our money – we do not have any.'

'My letter-opener.' Langelee's voice was edged in panic. 'Did one of you borrow it?'

'Of course not,' replied Bartholomew. 'It is far too dangerous for the likes of us. I have told you countless times not to hone it so sharp.'

'It has gone,' gulped Langelee, tipping the contents of his scrip out and pawing through them frantically. 'Someone has stolen it!'

'Nicholas, probably,' predicted Michael. 'He covets the thing, and I doubt he believed your promise to send him one from Cambridge. These things have a way of being forgotten, no matter how sincere the intention at the time.'

'Nicholas would never steal from me! We are old comrades-in-arms.'

'No – you are both ex-soldiers,' corrected Michael, 'which is not the same thing at all. It would be like me saying that *I* share a bond with him, just because we are both in holy orders. He owes you no allegiance, just as he owes none to me.'

'You lost it, Langelee,' said Bartholomew quickly,

disliking the notion of the Master storming up to the vicar and accusing him of theft. 'Probably last night, when you were too drunk to notice. Retrace your steps – start with our room and the Prior's House.'

'I hope to God no one picks the wretched thing up and maims himself,' said Michael, as Langelee sped away, worry creasing his bluff face. 'You should never have given it to him.'

'He adapted it,' replied Bartholomew defensively. 'It was an innocent little implement when I brought it back from France. Hah! There are Donwich and Pulham. That is convenient – I was about to suggest we speak to them next.'

The scholars from Clare Hall did not look their best. Donwich had dark circles under his eyes, while Pulham kept yawning. They were unshaven, and wore the same clothes as they had the previous day, which were rumpled and spattered with ink. It was unusual for them be dishevelled, as both were fastidious men – and likely to be more so at Clare, where they aimed to impress their benefactress.

'No, we did *not* sleep well,' snapped Donwich in answer to the physician's polite enquiry. 'We rashly offered to help Marishal with preparations for the royal visit, and he ruthlessly exploited our good will. First, he ordered us to provide entertainment for the whole castle – which was not how we envisioned being put to use.'

'You sang,' said Michael, recalling that the baker had mentioned their warbling.

'I felt like a common jongleur,' said Donwich sourly.

'I rather enjoyed it,' countered Pulham. 'I love singing, and we performed for hours, because folk kept clamouring for more. We did not finish until midnight.' He grimaced. 'I was ready for my bed at that point, but Marishal had other ideas.'

177

'He has a mountain of correspondence pertaining to the Queen's visit,' elaborated Donwich, 'and he wanted copies made of everything.'

'Which is work for lowly clerks, not scholars of our standing,' said Pulham sourly. 'But they do not have time, so he asked us to do it instead. We dared not refuse, lest he complained to the Lady. We have only just finished.'

'The baker saw lamps burning in your room all night,' mused Michael. 'He—'

'Look at my fingers,' interrupted Pulham, stretching out his hands. 'Filthy with cheap ink.'

'Can anyone corroborate your tale?' asked Michael.

Donwich eyed him coolly. 'You mean did we slip out and murder Roos in the midst of our labours? Well, I am sorry to disappoint you, Brother, but Marishal posted guards outside our door. He claimed it was so they could fetch him if we had questions about the work, but we know it was really to make sure we did not slack. So, yes, there are witnesses to prove our innocence.'

'That is not why I asked,' lied Michael. 'I was hoping you might be able to help us with Marishal's movements. You will appreciate why we want to know.'

'Because he is a suspect for the murders,' surmised Donwich. 'Well, maybe he *did* make an end of Roos, because he is not very enamoured of scholars, as evidenced by his treatment of us.'

'Yet I cannot see him – or anyone else – hurting Margery,' said Pulham. 'She was a lovely lady. She brought us wine and cakes just before nocturns, as she thought we might need refreshment. It was kindly done, and no one else bothered.'

'Did she come alone?' fished Michael.

Pulham nodded. 'She said she decided to bring us the victuals when she saw the light still shining from our window. Then, not long after she had gone, Marishal poked his head around the door to assess our progress.'

178

He glanced at Donwich. 'Which was when you made the quip about no one in the entire castle bothering with nonsense like sleep.'

Donwich shrugged. 'Marishal, his wife, the guards at the door, us, the castle chaplain hauling on his bell rope – all awake in the dead of night. Marishal retorted that Clare folk work for a living, not like the layabouts in Cambridge.'

'So we have decided to move back to the Swan for the rest of our stay,' sniffed Pulham. 'The Lady and Marishal are unlikely to notice our absence, not now there are murders to snag their attention. We shall pay our respects to the Queen on Tuesday, then travel home with you and the rogues from Swinescroft the following morning. Well, not with Roos obviously . . .'

'When did Marishal visit, exactly?' asked Michael. 'Before or after the bell for nocturns?'

'Before,' replied Pulham promptly. 'But he only stayed for a moment and then he was gone. So the answers to your unspoken questions are yes, Brother – *yes*, he was out and about at the same time as his wife, and *yes*, it is possible that he killed her and Roos.'

'Perhaps she and Roos arranged a lovers' tryst and he killed them in a fit of jealous rage,' suggested Donwich, but then shook his head. 'She would never have chosen Roos when she could have had one of us. Roos was a vile individual, whereas we are handsome, wealthy and charming.'

'And modest,' muttered Bartholomew.

'Personally, I think Badew killed them,' said Pulham. 'He allowed hatred to overwhelm his soul, and would certainly sacrifice a friend to strike at an enemy. Marishal will be weakened by the loss of his wife, and what hurts him, hurts the Lady.'

'You think he is that low?' asked Bartholomew doubtfully.

'I do,' said Pulham firmly. 'He has become a bitter, twisted old man who will do anything to avenge himself on the woman he thinks stole his College. He travelled here with the express purpose of harming her, and if he did kill Margery, he has succeeded in that aim.'

Michael lowered his voice. 'He came because he thought she was dead. We all did.'

Pulham reflected for a moment, then raised a fore-finger triumphantly. 'Then think about who opened the letter that contained the "news" of her demise. Roos! No one else saw it, so how do we know he did not lie about the contents – and Badew killed him for falsely raising his hopes?'

'That is possible,' acknowledged Michael. 'Badew does claim to know some secret that he will only reveal when the Lady is dead, so I imagine his disappointment was great indeed when he learned it would have to wait again.'

'Especially as he is older than her, and might die first,' put in Pulham. 'Of course, it will transpire to be a lot of lies, saved for a time when she can no longer defend herself. He can bray this secret all he likes, but no one will believe it.'

At that point, Lichet began to stride towards them, so he and Donwich beat a hasty retreat before they could be lumbered with more work. Moments later, they emerged from the Oxford Tower, still bundling their belongings into saddlebags. They all but ran to the gate and were gone, although they need not have rushed, as Lichet had been intercepted by Ereswell, who was dem-anding instructions about some aspect of the Queen's visit. The learned man quickly became flustered, especially when Adam approached with a question about supplies.

'He had better hope Marishal does not sleep too much longer,' remarked Michael. 'Because even he must realise by now that the post of steward is beyond him.'

But Bartholomew was thinking about their suspects.

'We can cross Donwich and Pulham off our list. We will check their story with the guards, but I believe they are telling the truth. However, I do not like the suggestion of a romantic tryst between Roos and Margery. Both Donwich and Langelee said she was not that sort of woman, and I agree.'

'But what about the rings?' Michael pulled them from his scrip and stared at them. 'They look like lovers' tokens to me. And Roos did home in on her very quickly after we arrived, while Adam claimed he strutted around as if he owned the place, suggesting that he had been here before . . .'

'Well, there is only one way to find out – by asking Badew and Harweden.'

The rain had passed, and the day had turned pretty, with fluffy white clouds dotting a bright blue sky and a warm sun drawing steam from the wet ground. Bartholomew and Michael left the castle, and walked along Rutten Row to the Bell Inn, an attractive establishment with black timbers and pink plasterwork. The appetising scent of frying eggs wafted from within, which perhaps explained why Badew had chosen it – the Swinescroft men liked their victuals.

Inside, the tavern was busy with traders from the market who had sold all their produce and were rewarding themselves with jugs of frothing ale. Bartholomew could not help but overhear snippets of conversation as he wove through the tables to where Badew and Harweden sat. Most revolved around the double murder at the castle, and there was a general feeling that someone had done it to avenge Skynere.

'The wife of the steward,' crowed one man. 'What a coup!'

'Not a coup, Bailiff Paycock,' said a butcher, a man identifiable by his bloody apron. 'She was the only decent person in the whole place, and anyone who revels in her death is a pig.'

'Then what about the death of the scholar?' asked Paycock archly. 'Can I revel in that? The University will not let *that* crime pass unremarked, and it will bring the Lady a raft of trouble.'

Although the tavern was crowded, Badew and Harweden had a table to themselves, perhaps because they were strangers, but more likely because they positively radiated hostility. They scowled when Michael perched on the bench next to them, an expression that deepened when he began to help himself to their food – bread, cheese, eggs, fried pork and apples. Bartholomew sat as well, but the events of the day had deprived him of his appetite.

'When you have finished gorging yourself, Brother, perhaps you will tell us what happened to Roos,' said Badew acidly. 'Who lured him into that terrible place and slaughtered him? I assume the Senior Proctor has the matter in hand?'

'Our enquiries are at a very early stage,' replied Michael, reaching for more meat. 'So I have no answers for you yet. Rest assured, though, I shall do my utmost to bring his killer to justice. And you can help by answering some questions. When did you last see Roos?'

'At vespers,' replied Badew. 'We went to church together, then returned here. Harweden and I share a room, but he has one to himself, because he snores . . . snored.'

'Did he say he might go out again?' asked Bartholomew.

'Of course not, or we would have stopped him. The Lady has never liked us, and would leap at the chance to do us harm. It was recklessness itself for him to have ventured out alone.'

'Especially to the castle,' added Harweden soberly. 'Her lair.'

'She is the Devil Incarnate,' hissed Badew, looking

rather demonic himself with his narrowed eyes and spiteful mouth, 'skilled in deceit and falsehoods. She will delight in pulling the wool over the eyes of a gullible Senior Proctor, so do not believe a word she says.'

'I am not gullible,' said Michael stiffly. 'I have outwitted more killers than you can count.'

'But she is in a league of her own,' whispered Badew, eyes blazing. 'She is a politician, and we all know they are consummate liars.'

'Right,' said Michael briskly, and brought the discussion back on track. 'Now, we have discovered that Roos and Margery shared a close connection. What can you tell me about it?'

'Do not talk nonsense,' spat Badew. 'Roos met her *once* – fourteen years ago, when she was in the deputation that came to Cambridge to steal my College. That is not a "close connection".'

'Tell the truth, Badew,' said Harweden softly. 'How will they catch Roos's killer if we lie? Roos *did* have an association with Margery. You know he did.'

'I know nothing of the kind,' snarled Badew furiously. 'You are reading too much into what you claim to have noticed.'

'And what was that?' asked Bartholomew.

'Roos chatting in a very familiar manner to Margery the moment we arrived here,' replied Harweden, and regarded Badew archly. 'Exactly as he did fourteen years ago. I told you then that they appeared to be intimate, but you refused to believe me.'

'He was our friend,' argued Badew. 'He would never betray us by forging links with the enemy's household.'

'I beg to differ,' retorted Harweden curtly. 'And, as he clearly knew her well even back then, it is obvious that their association was one of considerable duration.'

'Did you ever ask him about it?' enquired Bartholomew.

'Of course, but he fobbed me off with half answers,

although he did once let something slip. It was not long after we lost University Hall, and he and I were bemoaning it one evening over a jug of ale. He said that blood is thicker than water, and Margery should have done more for him. He blanched when I demanded to know what he meant, and claimed that I had misheard.'

'So they *were* kin,' mused Michael. 'That is—'

'They were not!' exploded Badew. 'He would have told me.'

'Would he?' asked Harweden quietly. 'Or would he have kept it secret, lest you expelled him from Swinescroft? If you had, he would never have found another hostel – he was no great shakes as a scholar. Or as a friend, if you want the truth.'

When Badew made no reply, Michael pulled the onyx rings from his scrip and laid them on the table. The Swinescroft men stared at them in surprise.

'He had two?' asked Badew. 'I only know about the one he kept around his neck.'

'The other belonged to Margery,' explained Michael. 'It was on her finger.'

'Hah!' Harweden turned triumphantly to his friend. 'What more evidence do you need, Badew? They *were* related, and these baubles prove it. The sly rogue deceived us for years! Indeed, perhaps it was he who helped the Lady get her claws into University Hall in the first place. I would put no low deed beneath him – not now we know what kind of man he was.'

'I cannot believe it,' whispered Badew, stunned. 'It is impossible!'

There was a short silence, as both old men pondered the revelation and its unpleasant implications. Then Bartholomew moved to another matter.

'It was Roos who read the letter telling us that the Lady was dead. The messenger was told to deliver it to

Water Lane, so we assumed it was for Chancellor Tynkell – that the sender was unaware that Suttone has been elected to replace him. But your hostel stands at the junction of Water Lane and Swinescroft Row . . .'

'I see where you are going with this, Matt,' said Michael. 'You think *Margery* wrote to Roos, because of the connection they shared. However, there is a problem with that theory: Roos was the only one who saw the letter, so we do not know what it really contained.'

'Yes, we do,' countered Harweden, 'because he showed it to me. It *did* say the Lady was dead, and urged the recipient to attend her burial without delay. However, I should have been suspicious of the fact that it was addressed to no one in particular. Roos was all gloating delight that he had read it before the Chancellor – but it was a lie. And I swallowed it like a fool!'

'We are all fools,' said Bartholomew soberly. 'We should have questioned his willingness to share the news with Clare Hall, which he detested. In other words, why was he prepared to give its scholars the chance to pay their last respects and win the executors' good graces?'

Badew regarded him narrowly. 'I can tell from your knowing expression that you have the answer. So come on – out with it.'

Bartholomew was still struggling to put his tumbling thoughts in order, and spoke slowly to give himself time to think. 'He must have made another journey to Clare recently, one where he lost an ear to Simon Freburn. We saw it was missing when we examined his body.'

'But he told us that he had earache,' cried Badew, incensed all over again. 'Are you saying that he lied about that as well?'

Bartholomew nodded. 'He wanted to attend the Lady's funeral, but not at the risk of a second encounter with robbers. However, he knew the University would send a delegation of mourners if he made the news public – and a delegation meant an escort for him.'

'The sly dog!' exploded Badew. 'He *knew* I would want to go, because I have—'

'A secret?' asked Michael when the old man stopped abruptly. 'The one you came here to reveal. Will you tell us what it entails now?'

'No,' replied Badew shortly. 'It must wait until the Lady is dead.'

'May we examine Roos's room?' Michael spoke gruffly to conceal his disappointment. 'Perhaps we will find something there that will explain why he deceived you all these years.'

Badew led the way to a pleasant chamber overlooking the street. The bed had not been slept in, and the water provided for washing was unused. Roos's saddlebags lay on the bed, still packed.

The letter was on the windowsill. It was written on cheap parchment, and the message was short and to the point – that the Lady was dead and the recipient should make haste if he wanted to see her in her grave. It was in the vernacular, rather than the more usual Latin, and it was unsigned.

'How could you believe that this was intended for the Chancellor?' demanded Badew, waving it angrily in Harweden's face. 'Even the Lady's meanest clerk would have composed a more impressive missive than this. And where is the identifying seal?'

'Peterborough!' exclaimed Bartholomew suddenly. 'You said that Roos visited kin there every three months, but he changed the subject with suspicious haste when Nicholas started to chat about the place. Perhaps he did not go there at all, but came here instead.'

'To visit Margery,' surmised Michael. 'It would explain why he seemed to know his way around the castle.

However, if he really did come here when he should have headed north, why did no one recognise him when he arrived with us? Everyone has dismissed him as a stranger.'

'Perhaps he disguised himself,' suggested Bartholomew. 'As a priest, maybe. The guards would not look twice at an elderly man in a habit.'

'Such laxity on their part would certainly explain how Roos managed to slip into the Lady's stronghold last night,' acknowledged Michael. 'It is—'

'Look at this,' interrupted Bartholomew suddenly, waving a second letter – it had been under one of the saddlebags. 'It is on the same cheap parchment and in the same uneducated hand – a message asking for a rendezvous in the cistern "at the usual time". So now we know why Roos went to the castle in the dark.'

'I imagine it is from Margery,' said Michael, putting both missives in his scrip for safekeeping. 'And "at the usual time" suggests they had regular assignations. Perhaps you are right, Matt – Roos *did* come here when he claimed he was visiting Peterborough, although he must have worn a very convincing disguise to have fooled so many people.'

'Damn him!' hissed Badew bitterly. 'No wonder none of my plans for vengeance have worked – Roos told his paramour, and she warned the Lady. Well, I hope he burns in Hell!'

Harweden glanced out of the window. 'I paid the vicar to bury him this morning. Shall we go to his funeral? Or shall we stay away on principle?'

'Oh, we shall go,' said Badew grimly. 'If I cannot dance on the Lady's grave, then I shall dance on his. However, I am not buying Masses for his soul. The Devil is welcome to it.'

Roos had just been delivered to the parish church from the castle chapel when Bartholomew, Michael and the two old men arrived. He was dumped rather unceremoniously on Roger's tomb, after which the bier-bearers disappeared fast, unwilling to linger in a place where they were so heavily outnumbered by townsfolk – the church was unusually full that day.

'At least he will have some mourners,' remarked Michael, as he and Bartholomew went to see what arrangements had been made for the ceremony. 'I wonder why they are here.'

'To watch the scaffolding come down in the south aisle,' explained Nicholas, when the monk put the question to him. 'So we can all revel in the fact that *its* ceiling is plain and dull, compared to the fan vaulting in the nave and chancel.'

'Yes, I suppose it is,' said Michael, squinting up at it. 'I hope they will not make too much noise while we lay our colleague to rest.'

'If they do, he can tell them to desist,' said Nicholas, nodding at Bartholomew. 'A veteran of Poitiers will have no trouble with rowdy civilians, especially once he draws his sword. And while he keeps the peace, we can concentrate on the rite.'

Bartholomew excused himself hurriedly from such an alarming duty, but he need not have worried, as the townsfolk were perfectly well behaved. None joined the mourners, though, so it was just him, Michael, Badew and Harweden who attended the perfunctory little ceremony. They had to carry the body to the graveyard themselves, as the men who should have done it refused to leave the church, preferring to clamour disparaging remarks about the south aisle instead. Once Roos was in the ground, Badew and Harweden paused just long enough to spit on him, then hurried away, leaving Bartholomew to pick up a spade and back-fill the hole.

'Stamp it down hard,' called Anne, who was watching through her window. 'I did not like the look of that man, and I do not want him rising up and messing about in my church.'

'We should go back to the priory, Matt,' said Michael when they had finished. 'To take a leaf from Albon's book, and ponder all we have learned.'

'I will join you later,' promised Bartholomew. 'But first, I want to explore Clare. As Langelee always says, only a fool does not learn the lie of the land when a killer is at large.'

'I have never heard him say that,' said Michael. 'Matt? Matt, wait! We have work to do!'

# CHAPTER 7

In the event, Michael did not ponder the murders either, because he arrived at the priory to find Langelee in a state of gloom over his lost letter-opener. He helped the Master look again, and by the time they had finished, an invitation to dine with John and his senior friars had arrived. Michael accepted, as it had been some time since he had availed himself of the food at the Bell.

Bartholomew joined them in the Prior's House when he returned from his perambulations. The fare was plain, but well cooked, and comprised the sort of food that was popular with soldiers and portly senior proctors – a lot of red meat, very little in the way of greenery, and plenty of bread to sop up the grease and bloody juices.

The wine was copious as well, and Michael grew merrier as the evening progressed. By contrast, Langelee turned uncharacteristically morose, fretting over his missing weapon, and grumbling about the fact that Roos's murder was preventing them from securing the wealthy benefactors that Michaelhouse so desperately needed. Meanwhile, Bartholomew never drank to excess in Cambridge, lest he was called out on a medical emergency, but he had no patients in Clare, so he allowed John to pour him a second and then a third cup of claret, after which he lost count.

The rest of the evening was a blur, and Bartholomew awoke the next morning with a thundering headache and the uncomfortable sense of having entertained the Austins with songs he had learned while with the English army at Poitiers. He hoped it had been at their request.

'That was quite a night,' remarked Michael, speaking

carefully, because he feared his head might explode if he did not. He was pale, too, his eyes bloodshot and puffy. 'Prior John knows how to entertain, although it is a pity I could not persuade him to discuss Clare's spate of mysterious deaths. Every time I tried, he changed the subject.'

'For two reasons,' said Langelee, annoyingly chipper, because he had exercised untypical restraint, and had retired to bed stone-cold sober. 'First, because you were too drunk to debate anything so serious; and second, because he fears gossip will make matters worse.'

'Analysing what we know is hardly "gossip",' objected Michael. 'And one of the casualties was an Austin. Does John not want the truth about what happened to Wisbech?'

'He is afraid of being drawn into the feud – which would break his Prior General's orders,' explained Langelee. 'Not to mention the fact that taking sides will hinder his ability to act as peace-keeper. Incidentally, I asked Nicholas if he stole my letter-opener, and he said no. The culprit is probably Lichet, who I would not trust as far as I can spit. Or Bonde, perhaps, who will also have an eye for a decent weapon. He *is* a hardened killer, after all.'

'So are you, if Prior John's stories are to be believed,' remarked Bartholomew, recalling with sudden clarity one very violent and distasteful tale involving a band of robbers.

Langelee waved a dismissive hand. 'I did what was necessary to protect the innocent, whereas Bonde acts for the love of blood. Indeed, it is possible that *he* dispatched Roos and Margery, given that he has disappeared and no one knows where he has gone. I hope you bear that in mind as you go about your enquiries today.'

'We will.' Michael winced. 'As far as I can bear anything in mind today. My poor head!'

They had slept through the bell for prime, and had missed breakfast as well, although Weste – his one remaining eye bright with robust good health – brought them bread and honey, along with water from what he claimed was a healing spring. It helped, along with Bartholomew's remedy for overindulgence.

'We are sadly out of practice with riotous evenings,' sighed Michael ruefully. 'We could have taken one in our stride ten years ago, when Michaelhouse was rich and we had feasts every week.'

'I shall use your gluttony last night as the basis for my next Book of Hours,' chuckled Weste, 'just as I used Philip de Jevan as an example of Satan lying in wait for the unwary in the tome that now belongs to the Lady.'

'It was *his* face on the Devil in the trees?' asked Bartholomew. 'I rather thought it was someone we have met, as there was something familiar about him . . .'

'Of course it was familiar,' said Weste darkly. 'Satan is everywhere, and we all know him better than we imagine. It is why I took the cowl – to drive him out of my soul.'

'Why choose Jevan? It is Lichet who is called the Red Devil.'

'I did not know Lichet when I illustrated that book – he has only been in Clare for a few months. But I would not have used him to depict Satan anyway – he is not evil, just dishonest, opinionated and greedy.'

'But Jevan is evil?'

'Oh, yes! I dislike his arrogant demeanour, and who knows what he tells the Lady when they are behind closed doors together. I am surprised Marishal allows it.'

When Weste had gone, the scholars discussed what needed to be done that day.

'We must speak to Marishal, Thomas and Ella first,' said Michael. 'Assuming they are not dead of Lichet's sleeping potion. Then I have a few questions for the

Lady, after which we shall pursue our remaining suspects – rather fewer than this time yesterday, thankfully.'

Bartholomew listed them. 'Nicholas, Lichet, Bonde, Albon, Marishal and the twins. Oh, and Badew and Harweden. They put on a fine display of stunned disbelief when we told them about Roos's perfidy, but they held high rank in the University for years. That alone will make them skilled dissemblers.'

'Thank you, Matt,' said Michael drily. 'Do you want to include me as well?'

'I will follow Albon again,' said Langelee, 'lest he happens to stumble across something vital. I will also see about acquiring a few benefactors.'

'Then go now,' instructed Michael. 'We will join you at the castle as soon as I have attended my private devotions in the priory chapel.'

'If you do that, it will draw attention to the fact that you slept through prime,' warned Langelee. 'Use the parish church instead. But no accusing Nicholas of murder. He is not the culprit, Brother – it will be Lichet or Bonde, you mark my words.'


Bartholomew was more than happy to wait in the church while Michael completed his religious duties, as it provided another opportunity for him to admire the fan vaulting. A section of scaffolding had been removed shortly after dawn, revealing a segment of ceiling that had been invisible during Roos's funeral the previous day.

'The Queen will be impressed,' he said, still gazing up in awe when the monk came to collect him a short while later. 'This place is truly remarkable.'

'Are you sure it is safe?' Michael poked a pile of dust with his toe. 'I am never comfortable with innovation. It nearly always needs refinement, so it is better to wait until a thing is tried and tested before having it installed yourself.'

'Well, the geometric principles are sound. You can see from here that the load of the ceiling is spread between the—'

'You can lecture me on principles all you like, Matt,' interrupted Michael. 'But all I see is a lot of fancy stone-work slathered in paint. And pretty does not equal solid.'

'Perhaps Cambrug will convince you. He is due to arrive soon, and I want to ask—'

Michael cut across him a second time. 'Here is Nicholas. He looks unnaturally spry, given that he drank twice as much as you and me combined last night. He must be a sot, used to such debauched occasions.'

'Have you come to call on our anchoress?' asked the vicar pleasantly. 'She will be pleased. The sad events at the castle mean she was neglected yesterday, and she likes attention.'

'She likes it more than she should,' said Michael admon-ishingly. 'She is supposed to spend her time in prayer, not enjoying the company of visitors. But we came to see you, as it happens.'

'I hope it is not to accuse me of stealing Langelee's letter-opener,' said Nicholas coolly. 'It is a magnificent weapon, but I am no thief. He must have dropped it somewhere.'

'No, we want to ask you about Roos and Margery,' said Bartholomew. 'It seems that—'

'I did not kill them,' said Nicholas, so quickly that it sounded furtive.

'We are not accusing you of it,' lied Michael. 'Although we can eliminate you from our enquiries for certain if you tell us where you were between nocturns and dawn yesterday.'

Nicholas gave him a look that was none too friendly. 'In the friary, with Langelee and my brethren. Ask them.'

'I did – last night. But the celebrations finished at nocturns, when John ordered everyone to go and pray.

194

Most did, while Langelee helped Heselbech to the castle. None mentioned being with you, however. They claim they were too addled to notice. In other words, the vows of loyalty you have all sworn prevented them from telling the truth – that you were nowhere to be seen.'

Nicholas made a show of having a sudden attack of memory. 'Hah! I recall it all now. I left just after Heselbech and Langelee. I was close enough to see them enter the castle, and I heard the chapel bell chime. Then I hurried here to say my own prayers. Ask Anne – she will tell you.'

'It is true – he did,' came the inevitable voice from the squint. It made Bartholomew wonder if the anchoress ever bothered with her devotions, and instead spent her whole life eavesdropping on conversations not intended for her ears.

He walked to the anchorhold, where he saw the screen pulled to one side, revealing a very comfortable bed. A dent in the pillow and rumpled covers suggested she had only just risen, which prompted him to ask himself if she spent every night fast asleep – including the one when she claimed to have seen Nicholas recite nocturns.

The anchoress herself was neat and trim in a fresh blue kirtle, while on her feet were soft calfskin slippers. She had already moved to her other window, where petitioners were waiting to regale her with the latest news.

'Katrina de Haliwell requisitioned another three pounds of almonds last night,' Adam the baker was informing her. 'And that was *after* she scoffed two bowls of stew in the hall. She claims the nuts are for the paroquets, but I think she eats them herself.'

Uninterested in castle gossip, Bartholomew returned to Michael and Nicholas.

'The first time I met Roos was three days ago, when he came here with you,' the vicar was saying. 'If he visited Clare before, I never saw him – either in disguise or as himself. But speaking of unpredictable old men, have you seen Jan the hermit? He seems to have vanished.'

'Yes – just like Bonde,' said Michael. 'If you ask me, it is suspicious, and I am inclined to wonder if one is the rogue who killed Roos and Margery.'

'It is certainly possible of Bonde,' said Nicholas. 'He has always been vicious. However, Jan has never shown any inclination to violence, and he *is* a holy man. I seriously doubt he has done anything untoward.'

'Even if he is innocent,' said Michael, 'we would still like to ask what he saw as he strolled around the castle in the dark.'

'Perhaps he is not so much missing as gone shopping,' suggested Bartholomew. 'Again.'

But Nicholas shook his head. 'He only does that on Wednesdays.'

'Then maybe he has decamped to a quieter town,' said Michael. 'Communing with God must be very difficult in Clare, with murders and mayhem every few days.'

'You make us sound like Cambridge,' said Nicholas coolly. 'Which I am told is the most dangerous town in the country.'

'No, you confuse us with Oxford,' Michael informed him earnestly. 'However, even that vile city has nothing on Clare with its seven suspicious deaths. You must be concerned, because the Queen will not come as long as there is a killer on the loose.'

'She will not be deterred by the kind of worm who stabs women and old men in dark cisterns,' averred Nicholas. 'But if there is nothing else, Brother, I must be off. There is still a lot to do before the ceremony, and time is short. Unless you are willing to wield a duster?'

'I am afraid not,' said Michael quickly, although Bartholomew would not have minded an excuse to linger in the church, as there were several murals he had not yet inspected.

196

'Pity,' sighed Nicholas. 'I could have done with the help.'

'I am not surprised,' said Michael, looking around disparagingly. 'You cannot possibly expect to have the rest of the scaffolding down by Tuesday – and the paint on the ceiling will still be wet.'

Nicholas grinned. 'It might, but who will know? Her Majesty is unlikely to climb up there and stick her fingers in it. But the scaffolding *will* be down, Brother, and Cambrug has promised to be here first thing on Tuesday to disguise any damage that might have occurred in the process.'

When Michael spotted a wealthy merchant who was said to be generous to good causes, he decided to abandon murder for a few moments and work for Michaelhouse instead. Bartholomew left him to it and went to feast his eyes on the handsome rood screen, experiencing a sharp pang of sorrow when he recognised Margery's face on a carving of the Blessed Virgin. His musings put him near the anchorhold again, and he glanced inside it to see Anne plying a broom.

'I cannot tell you how sorry I was to hear about Margery,' she said softly. 'It makes me glad I have retired from the world, because such a terrible thing should not happen to a saint.'

'No,' agreed Bartholomew. 'I heard her tell Bonde to bring you a basket from the kitchen the day she died. She cared about you.'

'It was a big one,' said Anne, a catch in her voice, 'containing all my favourite things. She never forgot her old nurse. I hope the fiend who killed her burns in Hell.'

'I imagine he will.'

'But what was she doing in the cistern with Roos in the first place?' asked Anne, after a brief pause during which he heard a muffled sob and a quick wipe of the nose. 'It is an odd place to go at any time, but especially at night. Or were they forced down there – at knifepoint, perhaps?'

'I think they went willingly, although we have no idea how Roos got past the castle guards. Bonde was on the gate, but we cannot ask him about it, because he has left Clare.'

'Roos probably paid him to look the other way,' said Anne. 'Marishal claims he runs a tight ship, but there are many who jump at the chance to earn easy money. Bonde is one of them. And of course he would not linger here to answer for it. He is not stupid.'

'Do you think he has gone permanently?'

'No – he likes being the Lady's henchman, and she has rescued him from trouble before. He will be back. But you did not answer my question: why did they meet in the cistern? It is a terrible place, especially when it rains. The water gushes down from the roof, and it can flood in a flash.'

'I thought the flow could be controlled by sluices and valves.'

'It can, but how would a person opening taps on the roof know that there was someone in the basement below? It is a very dangerous business.'

Bartholomew moved to another subject. 'You must have known Margery well, given that you were nursemaid to her children. Are you aware that she and Roos were related?'

'Oh, I very much doubt that,' stated Anne dismissively. 'She was lovely, while I am told he was . . . not.'

'Do you recall the ring she wore – the onyx one with the bird? Well, he had one exactly the same. He kept it on a string around his neck.'

Anne came to glare at him through the squint. 'I hope you are not suggesting anything untoward. Perhaps they were kin – although she never mentioned him to me.

198

However, even if you are right, there will have been nothing improper going on. She was an honourable lady. But speaking of lovers, do you have one? Yes, I think you do.'

'What makes you say that?'

Anne smiled. 'I am a wise-woman. I look into the souls of men and read their darkest secrets.'

'Matilde is not a dark secret. We are to be married soon.'

'Why? Is she with child? Do not wed her for that reason – it will lead to bitterness and disappointment, which will poison you both. She will have the worst of the arrangement, of course, saddled with a babe she does not want, as well as a useless husband. It is a pity there are laws forbidding women to decide for themselves what grows inside their bodies.'

'The laws are there to prevent dangerous interventions,' argued Bartholomew, although he was uncomfortable with the turn the discussion had taken, 'which can kill the mother.'

'Not if you know what you are doing. And as far as I am concerned, forcing women to have unwanted brats is yet another way for men to control us. No girl should bear a child if she does not want one – a child that may kill her by tearing her innards or leaving her with a fatal fever.'

'Giving birth is a risky process,' acknowledged Bartholomew soberly, racking his brains for a way to change the subject. 'But—'

'Risks men are not obliged to share, or the laws would be very different. It is brazen ignorance that makes them insist on a woman carrying a baby to full term, even when it is patently obvious that it is the wrong thing to do.'

'Suzanne de Nekton,' blurted Bartholomew, suddenly realising exactly why Anne was so passionate about the matter. 'You tried to rid her of one and the procedure went wrong. How did you do it? With herbs?'

There was a person in Cambridge named Mistress Starre, who was quite open about the fact that she was a witch, and made a good living from her charms and remedies. One of her potions was designed to expel unwanted foetuses. It worked, but not without cost, and Bartholomew had been called out several times when a dose had made a patient very ill.

'I did not have time for all that nonsense,' Anne declared loftily. 'I used a hook instead. I performed more than a hundred "special cleansings" and I was very good at it.'

He blinked: it was an enormous number. 'Were you?'

She nodded, and there was pride in her voice. 'I soaked the hook in holy water overnight, and in the morning I rubbed it with mint and rosemary. Then it was scratch, scratch' – here she made the appropriate motion with her hands – 'and it was all over.'

Bartholomew shuddered. 'What happened with Suzanne? Was there a lot of bleeding?'

'There was no bleeding at all, but she screamed a lot afterwards, which attracted attention.'

'So your scraping hurt her?'

'I do not believe so, but she was the daughter of a wealthy merchant and thus soft. The others I helped bore any pain more stoically. Afterwards, her outraged father sent her to a nunnery. Silly child! Her foolish shrieks destroyed us both.'

'I saw that procedure conducted once by an Arab physician,' recalled Bartholomew, 'but only to save the mother. It did not work.'

'Well, the ones I performed did, and I rescued many a careless girl from disaster. I am not sorry I helped them, but I am sorry it led to me being punished. Yet these things happen, and I am happy here. Come to talk to me again. You are nicer than Grym – he refuses to come anywhere near me.'

'Why is that?'

She smiled again. 'He is afraid he will catch my fondness for unorthodox medicine.'

'What next?' asked Bartholomew, when Michael had finished trying to entice the merchant to support Michaelhouse. 'Back to the castle, to speak to the murderous Marishals?'

Michael nodded. 'Although not with that attitude. It is better to keep an open mind.'

Bartholomew shrugged. 'We know that Thomas slunk off alone when the squires returned to the castle. Perhaps he saw his mother meeting Roos in a peculiar place, assumed the worst and decided to defend the family honour.'

'But Roos might be part of that family.'

Bartholomew shrugged a second time. 'Kinship did not stop Thomas from killing Talmach if the rumours are true – perhaps with Ella's help. And do not forget that Marishal himself was up and about at that time. Perhaps it was he who objected to the assignation.'

'We shall bear it in mind, although we still have other contenders for the crime. For example, Nicholas has not eliminated himself to my satisfaction. He claims he celebrated nocturns here, but his alibi is Anne, who I suspect was in bed – she is not a woman to let religious obligations interfere with a good night's sleep.'

'Lichet is more likely to be the culprit than Nicholas. We only have his word that he was watching over the Lady all night – and that he just happened to be visiting the latrine when Adam found the bodies.'

'But if Nicholas transpires to be innocent,' Michael went on, ignoring him, 'then I think we should look harder at the conveniently absent Bonde. Perhaps he killed Roos and Margery for reasons of his own, then decided to disappear until the fuss has died down.'

'Or perhaps he fled because *he* was responsible for letting the culprit into the castle in the first place. Anne says he is easily bribed. I do not like the fact that the hermit is missing, either – a man who was in the castle alone at the salient time. Perhaps Jan is the killer.'

'True,' agreed Michael. 'So shall we visit his lair before tackling the Marishals? He may have returned and be ready to confess.'

The hermitage had been built against one of the castle's outer walls, in a pleasant spot that boasted nice views across the river. Most men in Jan's profession were happy with very basic amenities, but Clare did nothing by halves, and had provided its holy man with some very sumptuous lodgings. There was a lovely little shrine containing a good supply of devotional candles and a comfortable place to kneel, and a small but cosy cottage with a stone hearth, good furniture and plenty of warm blankets.

'He left in a hurry,' remarked Bartholomew, taking in the unmade bed and the pot of burned stew that was suspended over the dead fire. 'But he took his fur cloak and good boots with him.'

'How do you know?' asked Michael.

'Because they are not here,' replied Bartholomew, 'and I know what they look like, because I remember thinking that they were better than my own. I suspect the stew was for his breakfast, but he never had the opportunity to eat it. Which means one of two things: first, that he is the killer or second, that he witnessed the crime.'

'And if the latter, then he has either fled or he has been dispatched to ensure his silence,' finished Michael. 'We may well find that Clare's body count has risen from seven to eight.'

\*　　\*　　\*

As they walked to the castle, they became aware of a commotion emanating from a nearby house. It was one of the more magnificent ones, stone-built with a tiled roof and elegant plasterwork that must have been very costly to produce. The door was new and painted purple.

'Godeston's colour,' noted Bartholomew. 'And his litter-bearers are doing all the wailing.'

Curious, they joined the crowd that was gathering outside, although they wished they had kept their distance when they found themselves to be the focus of much hostility. This was thanks to Paycock, the bailiff who had been so free with his opinions in the Bell the previous day.

'Look here,' he sneered, speaking loudly enough to make people turn towards him. 'Two toadies, come to Clare in the hope of winning some of the Lady's money. Scholars will take against us in our dispute with the castle, and so should be considered our enemies.'

'Then we should trounce them,' declared one of the litter-bearers. His face was swollen from the tears he had shed, and his eyes were mean. 'Because someone from the castle murdered poor Mayor Godeston, and this pair might have done it to please her.'

'Godeston is dead?' asked Michael, unfazed by the threat, although Bartholomew suddenly felt vulnerable, and his hand dropped to the bag where he kept his surgical knives.

'You know he is,' spat the second litter-bearer, who was even more distraught than his companion. 'Because *you* did it.'

There followed a furious clamour, as the crowd demanded to know why the scholars should want to deprive Clare of its most prestigious citizen. The loudest voice was Paycock's.

'This means war,' he howled. 'The castle has gone too far this time, and we will stand for it no longer. I say we send them a message – they can have these two back in pieces.'

The horde surged forward. Bartholomew whipped out a knife, although it was a puny thing, and would do nothing to make anyone think twice about attacking. Michael, however, was used to hostile mobs. He stepped forward, one hand raised in proctorly authority.

'Stop!' he commanded with such force that the angry charge faltered uncertainly. 'I assure you, we have no reason to harm Mayor Godeston or anyone else in Clare. Now tell us what—'

'Murderers!' screeched Paycock. 'Why pick on poor Godeston, a man who could not walk? Well, let us see how you fare with us, because *we* will not be such easy meat.'

There was another enraged roar, and the assault might have resumed, but suddenly the Austins were there, insinuating themselves firmly but gently between mob and scholars.

'What seems to be the problem?' asked Prior John, his voice full of quiet reason.

'The castle has arranged for Mayor Godeston to be slain,' shrieked Paycock. 'Because he was our leading resident and they knew it would hurt us. His death cannot be allowed to pass unchallenged. We agreed not to avenge Skynere on your recommendation, Father Prior, but all it did was encourage them to slaughter someone else. Well, we will not sit quietly by a second time.'

There was a growl of agreement from those who clustered at his shoulder. Again, Bartholomew braced himself for an onslaught, but the Austins merely reinforced their cordon by standing closer together. No weapons were drawn, but it was clear from the way they stood that they would be more than capable of repelling any would-be attackers with their fists.

'Take a deep breath,' John instructed Paycock. 'And

then tell us what has happened properly. And quietly, if you please. We are not deaf, so there is no need to howl.'

'They found Godeston dead this morning,' replied Paycock, pointing at the litter-bearers with a finger that shook with passion. 'Obviously, he was poisoned. Just like Skynere.'

'Just like Wisbech, too,' put in the larger of the two litter-bearers accusingly. 'Although the priory does not care. Well, *we* will not ignore what has been done. The Mayor was good to me and my brother – gave us work when no one else would look at us.'

'Because dressing up in purple and toting him around is all you are good for,' muttered Paycock unpleasantly. 'Idle buggers.'

'Even if Godeston has been poisoned, why blame the scholars?' asked John. 'And do not say they did it to please the Lady, because she deplores bloodshed. She told me so herself.'

'You stepped inside her filthy lair for a chat?' demanded Paycock, angry all over again. 'And then you come from there to here? How dare you!'

'I dare because it is time this foolish feud was over,' replied John sternly. 'It is dangerous and unnecessary, and it diminishes everyone concerned. And I do not mean just physically – it endangers your souls as well. Now, let us have no more of this nonsense. Go about your business like God-fearing folk, and *I* shall find the truth about Godeston's death.'

'Why should we trust you?' snarled Paycock.

'Because I tell you that you can,' replied John shortly. 'We have never taken sides in this dispute, and nor will we – you *know* we are impartial. Now go away, before God loses His temper with you for breaking His peace.'

Paycock opened his mouth to argue further, but John treated him to a sharp glare, and whatever the bailiff started to say died in his throat. Without another word, he turned and slouched away. Most of the onlookers followed, although the litter-bearers and a smattering of folk with nothing else to do lingered to see what would happen next.

'May we come inside with you, Father Prior?' asked Michael. 'Matt will know how Godeston died, and I mean no disrespect, but I trust his opinion more than anyone else's.'

'By all means,' said John amiably.

Mayor Godeston's fondness for purple extended all the way through his home, and virtually everything in it was of that colour. It dominated the tapestries that covered the walls, the cushions on the benches and the rugs on the floor.

'Perhaps he thought he was a Roman emperor,' murmured Michael, looking around in awe.

'It drove his poor wife to distraction,' confided John. 'She left him in the end, and entered a convent, where she said the nuns' black habits were a blessed relief. Of course, that was forty years ago, and I do not know what she thinks now.'

The Mayor was sitting at a table with his eyes closed and his chin resting on his chest. He looked as though he had fallen asleep over his purple meal, the remains of which lay in front of him: dried plums, pickled beet-root and elderberry wine. The only indications that anything was amiss were his total stillness and the vomit that stained his clothes.

Grym had taken the seat opposite, and tears glittered in his eyes as he contemplated the man who had been his friend.

'I suppose I shall be Mayor of this beautiful town now,' he said in a small voice. 'Although it is rather sooner than I hoped.'

Bartholomew bent to examine the body. Godeston was

still warm to the touch, although the sick on his front had dried, telling him that the Mayor had been taken ill some time before he had finally breathed his last. He glanced up to see that the litter-bearers had followed them inside, and were sobbing again, although more in anger than sorrow. He addressed them quietly, struggling not to make his remarks sound accusatory lest it ignited another spat.

'He could not walk, which means he would have needed your help to get to bed when he had finished eating. So why was he not discovered until now?'

'He could walk short distances,' wept one. 'And his bed is only in the next room. He sent us home early, because Barber Grym was here.'

'I was,' said Grym, a catch in his voice. 'We were discussing the murder of Margery and what it might mean for the town. He said he was hungry, so I fetched him some food from the pantry before I went home . . .'

'But he was well when you left him?'

Grym nodded. 'Although desperately worried that Margery's death would bring violent reprisals down on our heads. I suppose the strain of thinking about it induced a fatal attack. I have seen such things many times during my medical career.'

While the barber spoke, Bartholomew had continued his examination, not just of the body, but of the food and wine as well. The plums and beetroot seemed innocent, but the wine was a strong brew with a pungent smell – almost, but not quite, powerful enough to mask the distinctive aroma of hemlock underneath. He announced his findings to the others.

'So Paycock was right?' said Michael. 'Godeston *was* murdered? By whom?'

Bartholomew raised his hands in a shrug. 'He swallowed poison, Brother, and it was in the wine. I cannot tell you who put it there.'

'No, no, no!' whispered Grym, white-faced. 'Godeston was old and in indifferent health. He died of natural causes. He was *not* murdered. It is impossible.'

Wordlessly, Bartholomew handed him the jug so that he could smell it for himself.

Grym accepted it warily, took a quick sniff, then shook his head stubbornly. 'It is not hemlock. What you can detect is the stink of elderberries past their best. Poor Godeston! He never could tell a good brew from an inferior one.'

'Then *you* drink some,' suggested Bartholomew. 'And prove it is innocent.'

Grym raised his eyebrows. 'I am not in the habit of imbibing bad wine.'

And before anyone could stop him, he stepped to the window and emptied the jug into the rose beds below, moving remarkably swiftly for so large a man. Bartholomew regarded him in astonishment, stunned not only that he should deny what was so patently obvious, but that he should destroy evidence into the bargain.

'Good,' said John briskly. 'It is very sad that poor Mayor Godeston is dead, but better natural causes than murder.'

'I quite agree,' said Grym with a sickly smile. 'So we will bury him today, and I shall assume the role of Mayor until we can hold an election. It is—'

'No!' interrupted one of the litter-bearers sharply. 'You want to hide the truth, so the town will not march against the castle. Well, we will not be party to lies – not when it concerns the man who gave us a job. Mayor Godeston was good to us, and we will not turn our backs on his murder.'

'Then remember who told you about the hemlock,' put in Michael. '*We* did – which we would not have done if we had fed it to him. So kindly inform the likes of Paycock that your master's death had nothing to do with us.'

But the litter-bearer was already thinking about something else. 'His silk,' he gulped, looking around in alarm. 'Where is it?'

'What silk?' asked Grym.

'The gauzy purple piece that Master Jevan brought him from London. Mayor Godeston made us promise to drape it over his coffin when the time came. We cannot fail his last wishes! He made us swear.'

'And he said we would not get anything in his will unless we obliged,' put in his brother.

They embarked on a frantic hunt for it. John ignored them and began to interrogate Grym, gathering information that he hoped would allow him to forestall any rumours that Godeston was the latest casualty in the war between castle and town. The barber was eager to oblige, and Bartholomew grew ever more appalled by the wild answers he gave. Michael pulled the physician aside.

'Are you sure about the hemlock, Matt? You cannot be mistaken?'

'I am sure. I suppose this means Grym fed it to him – he fetched the wine from the pantry at Godeston's request, dosed it with poison, then destroyed the evidence when we homed in on it. Now he is lying to protect himself. I wonder if he killed Wisbech and Skynere as well. He admits quite openly that he uses hemlock on patients. Maybe he gave them too much by mistake.'

'I know John wants to avert trouble,' said Michael soberly. 'But I dislike lies, and I am uncomfortable with the fact that he is willing to overlook the murder of a friar. It is unnatural, even for a man who wants peace.'

'Then perhaps we should add him to our list of murder suspects.'

'Perhaps we should,' agreed Michael unhappily.

# CHAPTER 8

There was no more to be done at Godeston's house, so Bartholomew and Michael left Grym to care for his dead friend, and went outside, where John was already announcing that the verdict was death by natural causes. Unfortunately for him, the litter-bearers had a different story to spread, and began ranting to anyone who would listen. John tried to stop them, but to no avail – men like Paycock knew which version they wanted to believe. The Prior glared at Bartholomew.

'I wish you had kept your suspicions to yourself,' he said crossly. 'Godeston's murder will mean trouble for certain.'

'I wish he had kept his suspicions to himself as well,' agreed Michael, 'because then Grym would not have tossed the tainted wine out of the window, thus preventing us from proving our case. Did you not find that odd?'

'I doubt Grym killed Godeston, if that is what you are suggesting,' said John impatiently. 'They were friends, and Grym will be lost without him. However, I accept that Godeston died from hemlock poisoning. I thought I could smell it the moment I entered the room.'

'Then why did you—' began Bartholomew indignantly.

'Because I wanted to avoid the kind of trouble that is brewing now,' interrupted John shortly, and nodded towards Rutten Row, where several young merchants were listening to the litter-bearers with growing anger. 'Those boys have been itching to fight the squires for weeks – several have lost their sweethearts to the rich braggarts at the castle, and they want revenge.'

At that moment, Weste hurried up to report that Nuport

and his cronies were in the market square, where they had entered the shop of a vintner and removed a cask of wine.

'They say they will pay later, but we all know they will not,' said Weste. 'They have heard that the Mayor is dead, and think the town will be in too much disarray to take issue with them. But the likes of Paycock will not stand by meekly . . .'

'No,' agreed John, his face creased with concern. 'We shall have our hands full today if we are to prevent a bloodbath.'

'I hope our peace-keeping duties will not interfere with our religious obligations,' muttered Weste unhappily. 'I have a lot of atoning to do. I cannot afford to miss offices.'

'I know,' said John kindly, then addressed the scholars. 'So if anyone asks you about Godeston, please keep your suspicions to yourselves. Lives *and* immortal souls depend on it.'

'But someone *did* kill him,' argued Michael. 'An old man who could barely walk. Feeding him the kind of poison that takes hours to work was despicable and cannot go unpunished.'

'Leave vengeance to the Lord,' ordered John. 'He knows what he is doing – more than you.'

'Is that why you chose to ignore what happened to Wisbech?' demanded Michael. 'If so, it was a mistake. It left the killer free to claim other victims, which has made the situation worse. How many more people must die before you act?'

'We *are* acting,' growled Weste, his one eye cold and angry. 'We are busily ensuring that eight deaths do not become eighty.'

John rubbed a gnarled hand over his shiny pate and sighed. 'Yet you have a point about stopping the killer, Brother, so investigate if you must. However, I recommend that you stay away from Godeston's death – first, because the town will not appreciate you meddling, and second, because you may put yourselves in danger.'

'And we may not be on hand to rescue you next time,' added Weste, a little threateningly.

'If you want my opinion about Roos and Margery,' said John, more conciliatory than his cofferer, 'it is that someone from the town killed them. That means the guards let the culprit through the gate, so speak to them about it.'

'Unfortunately, the guard was Bonde,' said Michael harshly, 'who has now disappeared.'

'Bonde did not watch the gate on his own,' said John. 'Others would have been with him, so talk to Richard the watchman. He has a keen eye for detail, which I know because he was once one of my patrolmen. He will answer your questions if you tell him that I sent you.'

Richard the watchman was just finishing work when the scholars arrived, and was enjoying a meal with his friends. He was a solid, dependable man with a neat beard, an ancient but well-maintained leather jerkin, and weapons that were carefully honed. He refused to speak to Michael and Bartholomew at first, but capitulated immediately when they said they had been sent by Prior John. He set down his spoon and took them to a stable, where they could talk in private.

'Good man, John,' he declared. 'I would follow him anywhere. Well, other than into holy orders. A number of my comrades have found solace along that path, but it is not for me. I prefer to take my comfort in the arms of a woman. And do not suggest doing both, because John disapproves of those who break sacred vows. He considers it the worst of all sins.'

Michael changed the subject quickly, as his own views on chastity were rather more fluid than his Order allowed.

'We came to ask who visited the castle on Thursday night. We know money exchanged hands, but we do not care about that. We just want a list of names.'

'The squires and Bonde came in at about midnight,' replied Richard, so promptly that it was obvious that he had already given the matter some serious thought. 'Most trooped off to bed, and Bonde joined us at the gate a bit later. Then there were the two priests. The first was Heselbech, with Langelee holding him up. The second came in a few moments later, on his own.'

'Which priest?' asked Michael. 'Nicholas?'

'He had his hood up, so I never saw his face. It was definitely a friar, though. Not only did he wear an Austin's cloak and cowl, but I could tell he was a priest because of the way he walked. They tend to *glide* when they are on their way to holy offices. You must have noticed.'

'Not really,' said Bartholomew, sure Michael could not 'glide' to save his life. 'Who else?'

'Just Jan the hermit, who likes to prowl the castle after dark. And Philip de Jevan, of course, but you already know that. I wondered how long it would take before you made the connection.'

Michael and Bartholomew exchanged a blank look. 'What connection?' asked the monk.

'The connection between Saer de Roos and Philip de Jevan – that they are one and the same,' replied Richard, then frowned. 'You mean you did not know and I have just blurted it out?'

'Of course we knew,' lied Bartholomew, struggling to mask his surprise as realisation dawned. He turned to Michael. 'Because of Weste and the Devil he painted in his Book of Hours. He told us it was Jevan, but the face was oddly familiar. Of course it was – it was Roos.'

And Roos had prevented him from studying it more closely by throwing it on the fire. Bartholomew had managed to pull the book from the flames, but not before

213

the incriminating page had been burned out. The moment he saw it was safely destroyed, Roos had calmly walked away.

'That cannot be right, Matt,' said Michael doubtfully. 'Someone would have addressed Roos as Jevan or vice versa. But no one did, and everyone here claims he was a stranger.'

'But we have already guessed why no one recognised him,' argued Bartholomew. 'He donned a disguise. White whiskers probably, if Weste's picture was anything to judge by.'

Richard nodded. 'They were total opposites. Jevan was always immaculate, with snowy hair and a nice bushy beard. Roos was scruffy, with a nasty old cap and dirty clothes.'

'But *you* saw through the ruse?' Michael asked, still far from convinced. 'How?'

'I am a watchman – it is my business to see people for what they are. I knew Roos was Jevan because of the eyes. I recognised him when you arrived together on Wednesday, and I recognised him again when he came to the gate the night he died and paid us to let him pass.'

'Who else knew?' asked Bartholomew. 'Bonde?'

Richard nodded. 'And the other guards. The Lady and Marishal are in on the secret as well, of course, as was Mistress Marishal. It has been going on for years – fourteen, in fact. I remember because Jevan . . . I mean Roos joined the council at about the same time as I became a watchman.'

'Roos pretended to be another person for fourteen years?' breathed Michael in disbelief. 'But that is impossible! The truth would have leaked out long ago.'

'Why?' shrugged Richard. 'He was Jevan here and Roos in Cambridge. It was perfectly straightforward – until this week, when Roos arrived in "Jevan's" domain.'

'Do you remember the purple silk that "Jevan" brought for Godeston?' asked Bartholomew of Michael. 'He told

214

him that it came from London, but you pointed out that my sister sells it at home. We shall ask her when we get back, but I wager anything you like that she sold a piece to Roos.'

'But Roos hated Clare and the Lady,' objected Michael. 'And now you expect me to believe that he donned a wig and a false beard and sat on her council? With her connivance?'

Richard shrugged again. 'It is what happened.'

'Do you know if Roos and Margery Marishal were kin?' asked Bartholomew.

Richard considered. 'Well, they shared some bond, because she was always the one who came to greet him when he arrived.'

'Greeted him how?' pressed Bartholomew. 'Warmly?'

'No, not warmly, but *familiarly*. Like I might greet a mother-in-law if I had one.'

'So he came here four times a year?' asked Michael, still sceptical.

'Yes, for council meetings, which are held every Quarter Day. The last one was in March, and he was not due again until June. However, I can tell you for a fact that Mistress Marishal wrote and asked him to come early, because she told me to expect him.' Richard smiled fondly. 'She could write, you know – and she taught me.'

'Did she?' asked Michael, astonished anew. 'Why?'

'Because there is nothing much to do as a watchman during long winter nights, but I love the stars and she offered to lend me books on astronomy, if I learned to read them. She was a sweet woman, too good for this world.'

Michael showed him the letters they had found in Roos's quarters. 'Are these from her?'

Richard took them from him, handling them almost reverently. 'Yes – I would recognise her hand anywhere.

But wait! This one says the Lady is dead! Why would she . . .'

'To make sure Roos would come,' explained Bartholomew. 'Which means she must have had some very urgent reason for the lie. Do you know what it might have been?'

'No, but I saw her go to Roos straight away on Wednesday and start talking. I did not hear what passed between them, but she seemed very upset afterwards, while he was angry.'

'What about the night they died?' asked Bartholomew. 'Was she waiting for him then?'

'Not that I saw.'

'Did you follow him after you let him inside?'

'No, why would I? He was a member of the Lady's council, and Mistress Marishal had asked him to visit. They trusted him, so I felt I could, too.'

Bartholomew and Michael left the castle and aimed for the Bell Inn, to tell Badew and Harweden what they had discovered about their erstwhile friend. The two old men had had a night to reflect on Roos's antics, and the monk was hopeful that hindsight might have shaken loose some new information. It was raining again, although Clare's roads were so well drained and free of potholes that Bartholomew's feet remained quite dry inside his leaky old boots.

'I wish we had guessed this Jevan–Roos connection sooner,' muttered Michael. 'We should have known that there was a reason for his peculiar reaction to Pulham's Book of Hours.'

'We might have done, if we had studied the illustration more closely,' said Bartholomew. 'But now I think about it, Weste's Satan *did* have Roos's eyes. He is a remarkable artist.'

They did not have far to go, because Badew and

Harweden had joined the spectators outside Godeston's house, all waiting to watch the Mayor's body carried to the church. Bartholomew was glad when no one spared him and Michael more than a glance as they eased through the throng, although he was alarmed by the anger directed against the castle.

'I hope Prior John is good at quelling spats,' murmured Michael, looking around uneasily. 'Because there will be one before long. The mood is ugly, and set to grow worse.'

Just as they reached the Swinescroft men, there was a sudden stir and Godeston was toted out. His litter-bearers had evidently decided that he should make his final journey in style, so they had strapped him into a sitting position and draped him with purple blankets – although not the piece of silk that he had stipulated.

He swayed alarmingly as he was borne along, and Bartholomew was not the only one who feared he might topple off. So did Grym, who did his best to steady his old friend, but even the stately pace set by the brothers was too fast for the portly barber, who huffed and panted as he struggled to keep up. A number of town worthies fell into line behind them, including Paycock, who was muttering darkly about another murder of a good man by castle rowdies.

'You should not be out on the streets,' Michael told Badew and Harweden, once the body had gone. 'Matt and I were almost attacked earlier. You will be safer indoors.'

'Then escort us back to the Bell,' instructed Badew curtly. 'And while we walk, you can tell us about your progress regarding the murder of . . . that person.'

'Roos,' said Harweden, willing to spit out the name, even if Badew could not.

Michael obliged, outlining as many details as he could about Roos's double life. Badew and Harweden listened with increasing horror.

'I do not believe you,' breathed Badew when the monk had finished. 'You are making it up.'

'It is too incredible a tale for me to have invented,' said Michael soberly. 'Indeed, I am still coming to terms with it myself. But you knew nothing of it? No inkling at all?'

'No, of course not,' replied Harweden, patently stunned. 'I suspected some affiliation between him and Margery, as you know, but him being a member of the Lady's privy council all these years? It cannot be possible!'

'It feels like a bad dream,' said Badew in a small voice, and for the first time, Bartholomew felt sorry for him. 'I keep hoping that I will wake up.'

'Godeston's litter-bearers hope *he* will wake up, too,' said Harweden grimly, nodding to where both boys wept copiously as they delivered their erstwhile employer to Nicholas. 'I hear that they are good for nothing else, and will avenge his murder if it kills them.'

'Then we shall take the Senior Proctor's advice and remain inside the Bell until it is time for us to leave,' determined Badew. 'With our door locked. We should never have come to this terrible place. Damn Roos for his treachery!'

When they had seen the two old men to their chamber, Bartholomew and Michael turned back to the castle, aiming to interview the Marishal clan. They took a detour through the churchyard to avoid a large throng of townsfolk, which allowed them to be hailed by a familiar voice.

'Poor Godeston,' called Anne, as they passed her window. 'He was a pompous old fool, but he did not deserve to die. Personally, I think the Austins did it. It explains why they are now going around telling everyone that he died of natural causes, when his servants say he was poisoned.'

218

'John has made a serious tactical error,' murmured Michael to Bartholomew. 'He should never have tried to hide the truth with lies.'

'They think more about their oaths of loyalty to each other than they do about justice or truth,' Anne went on resentfully. 'They would certainly kill to protect one another, even if it means war between the town and the castle.'

'I disagree,' said Bartholomew. 'As far as I can see, everything they have done is to one end: to avert trouble.'

Including, he thought but did not say, declining to avenge the death of one of their own – a man who certainly would have been included in their controversial vows of solidarity.

Anne sniffed huffily. 'Dismiss my opinions if you will, but you will see.'

'Do you believe her, Matt?' asked Michael, as he and Bartholomew left the churchyard. 'That the killer may be a friar?'

Bartholomew was not sure what to think. 'It is possible, I suppose. Richard the watchman did say that he let two of them through the gate at the salient time – Heselbech, which Langelee can confirm, and one other.'

'Well, there are John and Heselbech now,' said Michael, nodding across the street. 'We shall ask them which of their brethren went out. Of course, we know one who was abroad, and who probably did not say nocturns in his church as he claims – Nicholas.'

'Yet anyone can don a cloak with a hood, and pretend to be an Austin,' mused Bartholomew. 'Perhaps it was an imposter, and the friars are innocent.'

But Michael shook his head. 'Richard thought it was a priest, and I trust his testimony. He is an observant man.'

The two Austins looked very much like former soldiers as they marched along. Both were armed with knives, which was unusual for men in holy orders, although

Bartholomew understood why they were loath to go about unprotected.

'I have already told you,' said Heselbech impatiently, when Michael put his question. 'I went to the castle chapel to say nocturns, but I was too drunk – as Langelee will attest. I rang the bell, but then decided it would be better to sleep than recite the sacred words in a stupor.'

'Quite right,' agreed John piously. 'There is little worse than insincerity. It damages the soul, and should be avoided at all costs.'

'So who was the second friar?' asked Bartholomew.

Heselbech raised his hands in a shrug. 'There was no second friar. I am the castle's only chaplain, and everyone else stayed at home. Is that not so, Father Prior?'

John nodded. 'Other than Nicholas, who went to his church, but we know he arrived without making a detour, because Anne heard him. Heselbech is right, Brother: there was no second friar.'

'Yes, there was,' insisted Michael firmly. 'My witness is positive.'

Then I shall ask my people,' said John, 'but I am sure your witness is mistaken. He mistook a common cloak for a religious one in the dark.'

'Yes, it was probably a servant sneaking home late after a night with friends,' said Heselbech. 'Despite the current trouble, there are plenty of castle folk with connections to the town – Adam the baker and Quintone, to name but two.'

When Bartholomew and Michael reached the castle, they found that Albon had moved to the next stage of his investigation, which entailed him sitting outside the chapel and announcing that he was available for the culprit to confess. Unsurprisingly, the killer had not taken him up on the offer, so Albon remained in splendid isolation. The knight had chosen another throne-like chair to lounge in, and had dressed with considerable care, so he looked like a king holding court.

'Does he really think that will work?' asked Bartholomew wonderingly, when Langelee came to explain what was going on. 'Surely he cannot be that naive?'

'Oh, I think he can,' said Langelee sourly. 'Shall we wager how long he stays there before he realises that he is wasting his time? I think he will persist until the end of tomorrow – it will be Sunday, and he will foolishly expect the culprit's conscience to prick on that most holy of days.'

'He will give up tonight,' predicted Bartholomew. 'It looks like rain, and he will not want to get his pretty hair wet.'

Michael laughed. 'I agree with Matt. Shall we speak to Thomas and Ella now? They are by the kitchen, whispering to each other as usual. I wonder what prank is in the offing this time.'

He started towards them, but had not covered half the distance before there was a shriek, and Adam hurtled out of the kitchen, trailing fire. Quick as a flash, Bartholomew whipped off his own cloak and knocked the screeching baker to the ground so that he could smother the flames. Adam continued to howl, although Bartholomew's speedy reaction had saved him from serious harm.

As he applied a soothing balm to one or two patches of reddened skin, Bartholomew glanced at Thomas and Ella. They were struggling to keep straight faces. The squires did not bother with such niceties, and brayed their mirth openly. Servants and nobles alike eyed them in distaste, which served to make them guffaw all the harder – until Albon put an end to it. He stood with all the dignity at his disposal and strode towards the sobbing baker. The laughter faded away, and only when there was silence did the great man speak.

'You are a brave boy, Adam,' he said, gazing down with kindly compassion. 'Here is a groat for new clothes and another groat for your wounds. Go now, and thank God for your deliverance.'

Adam snatched the coins and fled. He hobbled through the gate and disappeared into the town – the twins' prank had clearly ended any loyalty *he* might have felt towards his castle employers, and had turned a friend into an enemy.

'Your mantle, Doctor,' said Albon, stooping to pluck the garment from the ground. He held it between thumb and forefinger, so as not to soil his soft white hands.

Bartholomew took it resignedly. It was caked in mud, and holes had been burned in several places, which meant some serious needlework would be required before it was functional again. The journey home would be miserable if the rain continued. Then Albon made a second munificent gesture. With a courtly flourish, he removed his own cloak and held it out.

'Take this,' he said, more command than invitation. 'A *medicus* must be properly clad when he visits his patients.'

Bartholomew did not want to accept it. It was a beautiful garment of scarlet wool, with fur around the hem and black silk lining. He was notoriously careless with clothes and would ruin it in a week.

'You are generous,' he said politely. 'But you will need it in France.'

Albon stood taller and straighter. 'Zeal for my God, my King and my country keep *me* warm in the most inclement of weather,' he announced grandly, then lowered his voice so that only Bartholomew could hear. 'Besides, I have five more equally nice ones in my travelling chest, so I shall not miss it.'

A murmur of admiration for his gallantry rippled through the onlookers, and Bartholomew knew that refusing the cloak would not only appear ungracious, but might be construed as offensive. He took it, astonished by its weight and quality, and wondered what Matilde would say when he arrived home in it. He suspected he would be in for a good deal of teasing.

'Then thank you,' he said sincerely.

'You saved an innocent boy from serious harm,' said Albon, loudly enough for his voice to carry across the whole bailey. He treated the twins to a reproachful glance, and both had the grace to look away. 'He might have been maimed for life.'

'It was only a bit of fun,' objected Nuport, too dim-witted to know when he should have kept quiet. His cronies eased away, unwilling to be associated with him if he was going to challenge their hero. 'Can no one take a joke?'

'It was not a joke,' declared Albon angrily. 'It was a despicable act – one devised by cowards and fools. Such antics will be punished, although not by me. By *God*.'

And with that, he turned on his heel and strode back to his throne, where he made a show of sitting in it without the comfort of a nice warm cloak. His sacrifice earned the twins more critical scowls, including from some of the squires. Thomas hid his chagrin with sullen indifference, although Ella was notably subdued. Bartholomew walked over to them, Michael following.

'I hope you will not do that again,' he said curtly. 'Albon is right – it was cruel and stupid.'

Thomas was unrepentant. 'It was Adam's own fault for laying dishonest hands on a silver box that he had no right to touch.'

'It is true,' agreed Ella. 'He is a thief and everyone is sick of his pilfering. We expected him to drop the box when he realised that it was full of hot embers – we did not anticipate that he would slyly shove the thing inside his tunic.'

'Regardless,' said Michael in distaste, 'should you really be playing tricks on servants while your mother lies dead? It is hardly appropriate.'

'We did it for her,' argued Ella. 'She worked hard to turn Adam honest, but the moment she died, he reverted to form. It was disrespectful to her memory.'

'She was an angel,' said Thomas. 'Or so everyone tells us. Unfortunately, she was so engrossed in her good works that she never had time for her own children. Anne was far more mother to us than she ever was. More father, too, given that ours was also too busy to bother.'

'So you are irked with your parents for failing to dote on you,' sighed Michael heavily. 'Is that why you killed her?'

Thomas and Ella blinked their astonishment at the accusation, and Bartholomew thought their shock was genuine. Of course, that was not to say they were innocent – only that they considered themselves to be above suspicion.

'We never did!' cried Ella, the first to find her tongue. 'What a terrible thing to say! We were not close, but we never wished her harm. Besides, Anne was a lot of fun, and we would not have enjoyed ourselves nearly as much if our parents *had* raised us. It all worked out for the best.'

'So what have you done to find the killer?' asked Michael archly. 'Even if you were not fond of Margery, you still must want her murder avenged.'

'We did discuss hunting the bastard ourselves,' said Thomas, eyeing the monk with dislike. 'But Albon told us to let him do it instead. Ella and I do not want to cross the man who will take us to France, so we reluctantly acceded to his request.'

'*You* will go to France,' Michael pointed out. '*She* will stay here, ready to marry another wealthy or powerful suitor.'

Ella regarded him haughtily. 'No, I will not, because I have decided to follow the Lady's example and take a vow of chastity – which means no more weddings for me. I *am* going to France, although not to join the army, naturally. I shall visit religious houses.'

'Of course you will,' said Michael flatly. 'But to return to more important matters, do you have any idea who meant your mother harm?'

'No,' replied Thomas sourly. 'Because she really was loved by all, and I cannot believe this has happened to her. She honestly did not have an enemy in the whole world.'

'What about Roos?' asked Bartholomew. 'He was unpopular in Cambridge, so I cannot imagine his reception was any different here. Did he have enemies in the castle?'

'Roos!' spat Thomas. 'Otherwise known as Philip de Jevan, although we had no idea he was a scholar until Richard the watchman told us just now. We are stunned – we thought he was a merchant from London, which is what he always claimed.'

'We did not recognise him when he arrived on Wednesday,' put in Ella. 'Because we are used to seeing him with white hair and beard.'

'We believe "Jevan" was your mother's kinsman,' said Bartholomew. 'What was their relationship, exactly?'

'Distant cousins,' replied Ella, and looked around quickly to ensure no one could hear before adding, 'but I think they might have been lovers once. I overheard several discussions between them that suggested it, and he was always trying to corner her alone. He was a dreadful lecher.'

'She tried to send him packing countless times,' said Thomas, 'but her rejections were too gentle, and he never did get the message.'

'What did your father think of Roos's behaviour?' asked Michael.

Thomas gave a mirthless bark of laughter. 'Him? I doubt he noticed anything amiss, and if he did, he would have been too busy to do anything about it. Running the Lady's estates is more important to him than anything else in the world.'

'It was your mother who summoned Roos here,' said Michael. 'Why would she do such a thing if all he did was harass her?'

'She doubtless had her reasons,' replied Thomas, while Ella looked away and bit her lip. 'But not ones she confided to us. I wish we could help, but we knew nothing of her business.'

'Then tell us what you were doing the night she died.'

Thomas sighed with exaggerated patience. 'I was in the Bell Inn with the squires for the first part of it, and I came back here at midnight. I went directly to Ella's room, where we played board games until Adam raised the alarm with his screeching.'

'The Bell is where Roos was staying,' said Michael. 'Did you see him there?'

'Not that I recall,' shrugged Thomas, 'but I was looking at the lasses, not old men in nasty hats. I did not know then that your Roos was our Jevan, so why would I have paid him any heed? Have you finished with us? Our mother will be buried tomorrow, and we have to make all the arrangements ourselves, because our father does nothing but sleep.'

'It is Master Lichet's medicine,' explained Ella. 'It is very strong. We only had a sip and it made our heads spin. Father swallowed the whole cup.'

'He will wake up when we visit,' vowed Michael. 'We have questions for him as well.'

Thomas smiled malevolently. 'Not today, Brother. And not tomorrow either, if Lichet has any say in the matter. His potions are nothing if not effective.'

'That pair said nothing to make me think them innocent,' said Michael, once the twins had gone. 'They are irredeemably selfish, and think they have been ill-used by having parents with lives of their own. They might well have dispatched Margery out of bitterness and spite.'

'And Roos for being in the way,' agreed Bartholomew. 'But we should request an audience with the Lady now. Lichet cited her as his alibi, so we should see if he is telling the truth – assuming that he has not dosed *her* with another powerful soporific, of course.'

Lichet was in the Lady's apartments, reciting an ode of his own composition. It was several pages long, and comprised a lot of convoluted rhymes, which perhaps explained why she had dozed off. Lichet had not noticed and read with gusto. The poem was about a dog that seduced women under cover of darkness, which did not seem an entirely suitable subject for an elderly patron, so perhaps it was just as well she was not awake to hear it.

'No wonder folk call him the Red Devil,' murmured Michael. 'Poor Clare! I would not be happy with such a man assuming a position of power in the University.'

Lichet scowled when a servant interrupted his performance to announce visitors. He started to refuse Bartholomew and Michael permission to enter, but the Lady's eyes snapped open, and she overrode him by beckoning them forward.

'Well?' she demanded. 'Who killed Margery? I am sure you have been exploring the murders, given that a scholar died as well.'

'I ordered them to do it,' put in Lichet quickly. 'I would have solved the mystery myself, but I decided to apply my superior abilities to being Acting Steward instead. I shall shoulder Marishal's responsibilities for as long as he is . . . indisposed.'

'Drugged senseless, you mean,' put in Bartholomew disapprovingly. 'Which is a dangerous thing to do and—'

'When do you expect him to wake?' interrupted Michael, aware that such an accusatory discussion was likely to do more harm than good. 'There are questions that only he can answer.'

'Not today,' replied Lichet stiffly. 'Tomorrow, perhaps. I shall see how he feels.'

'He will *feel* inclined to help them, and you will tell him so, Master Lichet,' said the Lady sharply, and turned back to the scholars. 'Now tell me what you have learned. Albon gave me his report earlier, but it was disappointingly sparse.'

Michael hastened to oblige, finishing with the fact that Margery had written to invite Roos to a secret meeting in the cistern 'at the usual time'.

'My goodness,' said the Lady flatly. 'You have been busy.'

'Now just one moment,' snapped Lichet, still blinking his astonishment as he raised his hand for clarification. 'You claim that *Roos* was on the council?'

'He called himself Jevan while he was here,' replied Michael. 'But yes. Were you not included in the secret? Dear me!'

'No one was, other than my steward, Margery and a few guards,' said the Lady. 'I recruited him fourteen years ago – offered him a lucrative post in exchange for spying on Badew. After all, only a fool does not monitor her enemies. And it worked. Why do you think Badew has never managed to do me any harm?'

Lichet was stunned. 'Roos deceived his friends – and everyone here – for *fourteen years?*'

The Lady shrugged. 'He was a clever man. Of course, he was never included in any sensitive castle business – one can never trust a man who betrays his friends. Yet he served me well enough, although he was coming to the end of his usefulness – Badew is getting too old for mischief.'

'I beg to differ, madam,' argued Lichet. 'Why do you think Badew is here now? It is *not* to tell Marishal that his twins dispatched Talmach – Marishal already knows those rumours.'

'Badew thought I was dead, and he came to dance on my grave,' replied the Lady. 'While Michaelhouse and Clare Hall came to see what I had left them in my will.' She smiled haughtily at the scholars. 'As I said, Roos served me well.'

'He was kin to Margery,' interjected Michael hastily, eager to move away from the awkward subject of their reason for visiting Clare. 'Is that why you invited him to play Judas?'

The lady inclined her head. 'The family connection meant he was more willing to listen to my proposal than he might otherwise have been. They were cousins and he loved her – perhaps more than he should have done, given that she was another man's wife.'

'His affection may have been reciprocated,' said Michael, and produced the onyx rings. 'He wore his around his neck, while hers was on her finger.'

The Lady frowned as she took them. 'I remember hers. It is tawdry, and I once asked why she did not don a nicer one – she had plenty. She told me that it repre-sented a penance. She confided no more and I did not press her, sensing it was something she was reluctant to divulge.'

'I do not think they were fond of each other,' said Lichet. His expression was sullen, and it was clear that he bitterly resented being left in the dark. 'Whenever I saw them together, they were quarrelling.'

'They did argue,' acknowledged the Lady. 'Indeed, Roos was the one person who could shake her from her gentle equanimity – something not even the twins could do, even at their worst.'

'Do you know why Margery wanted him to come to

Clare this time?' asked Michael. 'It was not for a council meeting – the next one is not until June, as you know.'

'I have no idea,' replied the Lady. 'Perhaps Marishal can tell you, although you will have to wait until tomorrow, when Master Lichet's potion has worn off. I imagine Roos was glad that you decided to accompany him here, though – he met Simon Freburn on the way home last time.'

'And lost an ear,' put in Lichet with a smirk.

The Lady was silent for a while, thinking. 'I dislike what is happening in Clare,' she said eventually. 'Not just the murders of Margery and Roos, but the other deaths, too. You two have shown yourselves adept at unearthing secrets, so you will investigate those as well as Roos's.'

'I shall see they do,' vowed Lichet. Then he glared at the two scholars. 'Of course, when I told them to investigate Roos's death, I also ordered them to report any findings directly to me, so as to spare you the unpleasantness of this sort of audience. I am sorry they chose to disobey me.'

'Thank you for your concern, Lichet,' said the Lady briskly. 'However, from now on, I want Michaelhouse, Albon *and* you searching for answers. They are coming far too slowly for my liking, and I want this matter solved and settled before the Queen arrives.'

'You want three investigations to run concurrently?' asked Lichet uneasily. 'That is not a good idea, madam. We will fall over each other in—'

'Nonsense! A little competition is healthy. And to make matters more interesting, I shall offer a reward to the successful party. One hundred marks.'

It was a fortune, and Lichet's eyes lit greedily. 'Then I shall have it,' he declared. 'I am the one with the best mind.'

'I am not sure it is wise to offer that sort of incentive,

My Lady,' objected Michael. 'It may encourage a false solution from someone who just wants the money.'

'Then you must ensure that yours is the right one, and that it is presented to me first,' retorted the Lady. 'However, no one will have anything until I am fully satisfied. And speaking of satisfaction, what is happening with my paroquets, Doctor? You promised to cure them, if you recall.'

'Lichet refused to let him see them,' replied Michael, before Bartholomew could tell her that he had done nothing of the kind.

The Lady scowled at the Red Devil, whose face was tight with fury at the revelation. 'I shall thank you not to countermand my orders, Lichet. I do not tolerate insubordination. Do you hear?'

Her voice was loud, and several courtiers near the door grinned their delight at his discomfiture. He bowed stiffly and took his leave, evidently deciding that it was more prudent to retreat than stay and risk another. The Lady's gimlet eye swivelled around to Bartholomew, and she flapped an impatient hand for him to help her to her feet.

'As I cannot trust anyone to do what I ask, I suppose I must take you to see the birds myself,' she grumbled. 'I want them mended, and you may have five marks if you succeed.'

'And *you* may have two marks for getting Lichet into trouble,' whispered Ereswell to Michael, as he passed. 'To go with the pig money that you have already won.'

Michael accepted the coins with a grin. 'But keep your purse handy. I have not finished with your Red Devil yet. Not by a long way.'

The Oxford Tower was the shortest and oldest of the four turrets, and possessed the smallest, meanest rooms. Bartholomew recalled Ella saying that it was where the least important guests were usually housed – which had included the men from Clare Hall before they had decanted to the Swan. Its stairs were worn, and the doors to its chambers were so thick and sturdy that he found himself thinking that it would serve as a very good prison.

'You forgot to ask the Lady if Lichet was with her at the time of the murders,' he murmured as they followed her up the stairs.

'I did not forget,' Michael whispered back. 'I just decided it would be better if Lichet was not there when I did it – prompting her into saying what he wants.'

'I do not think there is much chance of that. She knows her own mind.'

'Regardless, I shall ask her when we are alone – and when the occasion is right.'

The paroquets were on the top floor, so it took a while to reach them, as the Lady moved at a very stately pace. This suited Michael, who also disliked racing up steep and narrow staircases, and it gave Bartholomew time to dredge his memory for what little he knew about paroquets.

Fortunately, one of his teachers in Paris had owned one, so while no expert, he was not a complete stranger to the species. He recalled that the bird had been an unruly creature, which had learned bad habits far more quickly than good ones. It and its owner had been devoted to each other, and when he had last heard of them, both were living happily together, with the paroquet dictating their social life and terrorising the students.

'What is wrong with your birds?' he asked, during one of their several lengthy breathers. The Lady used these to gaze out of the windows, watching her retainers scurry about with a critical eye. The shirkers would no doubt receive a dressing-down later.

'They eat vast quantities of food – more than is natural,' she replied. 'I am worried that it will adversely affect their health, and they are sweet creatures. I do not want them to sicken.'

'There is nothing wrong with a healthy appetite,' declared Michael. 'And if Matt recommends putting the poor things on a dietary regime devised by that maniac Galen, ignore him. Galen might have been a great physician in ancient Greece, but his ideas have no place in a modern society.'

'I see,' said the Lady, amusement flashing in her eyes. 'However, the paroquets are costing me a fortune in expensive delicacies, and they have a taste for fine wines, too. I want them cured of their gluttony, because it would be a great pity if they grew too fat to fly.'

'I do not envy you this task, Matt,' murmured Michael, as the Lady turned to climb the final flight of steps. 'It is cruel to deprive a living being of its preferred victuals.'

Before Bartholomew could think of a suitably diplomatic reply, the Lady opened the door to a spacious chamber with windows on all sides. In the middle was a T-shaped structure, on which perched three birds. They had long tails, grey faces and crafty eyes. The largest screeched its excitement when it saw the Lady, and flew to her outstretched arm. It bobbed up and down until she gave it a nut, which it snatched and began to gnaw greedily with its sharp black bill.

'Grisel loves almonds,' said the Lady, watching it fondly. 'And meat, of course.'

'Meat?' echoed Bartholomew warily. 'I am not sure that is—'

'God save the Queen,' declared Grisel nasally, then added something that sounded like 'Bring van the hold down.'

'It talks?' blurted Michael. 'My goodness!'

'My goodness, my goodness,' croaked Grisel, casting a pale eye in the monk's direction. 'Hold the van down bring.'

'Grisel used to live on a ship,' explained the Lady. 'Hence the nautical terminology.'

'I do not like the look of its beak,' said Michael uncomfortably. 'It could relieve a man of fingers, noses, ears and even eyes.'

'It could,' agreed the Lady with a smile that was not entirely pleasant. 'So you had better be on your best behaviour. His companions are named Blanche and Morel. All three were Margery's originally. She gave them to Anne, to keep her company in her cell, but they kept escaping through the squint to fly around the church.'

'How were they enticed back inside the anchorhold again?' asked Bartholomew curiously.

'With almonds,' replied the Lady, returning Grisel to his perch and offering him a second nut. There was something of a rumpus when the other two tried to relieve him of it. 'A few weeks later, Anne sent them to me – a bribe, in the hope that I would reinstate her as castle nurse.'

'Is that an option?' asked Michael. 'I suspect she is far more suited to tending youngsters than pretending to be holy.'

'The Church condemned what she did to Suzanne de Nekton,' said the Lady, looking away, 'and I must uphold its strictures, regardless of my own private thoughts on the matter. I am afraid Anne will be an anchoress for the rest of her life.'

'But you kept the bribe,' noted Bartholomew, thinking it should have been refused if the Lady aimed to occupy the moral high ground.

She regarded him coolly. 'A church is no place for paroquets, and they are happier here. Besides, Anne could not give them what they need – namely a lot of very costly treats and a proper keeper to mind them. Katrina de Haliwell used to raise peacocks for me.'

Bartholomew and Michael had not noticed the woman

standing by the door. Katrina was pretty, dark-haired and freckled, and wore a black bodice of the kind that had recently come to denote widowhood. She had intelligent green eyes and a mischievous smile.

'At last,' she said, when the Lady introduced Bartholomew. 'I expected you days ago. Did Master Lichet spin you a tale about the birds being his responsibility?'

'Well, physician?' demanded the Lady, sparing Bartholomew the need to reply. 'What are you waiting for? Payment in advance? I am afraid that is not an option. You may only have the five marks when you have diagnosed the cause of their overeating.'

'Nuts,' said Grisel, nodding sagely. 'Queen God save. Down the van bring hold.'

'Matt will calculate their horoscopes,' said Michael gravely, although Bartholomew could tell he itched to laugh. 'Although inspecting their urine is likely to prove more of a challenge.'

'Then we shall leave him to it,' said the Lady. 'Come, monk. Accompany me back down the stairs. You have a killer to catch and I have estate business to attend, so neither of us can dally here.'

Bartholomew was not entirely sure where to begin. The paroquets regarded him with distrust, and he stared back, ready to duck if one flew at him. He knew from his teacher's bird that they could move fast, and he still had a scar on one knuckle to prove it, dating from a time when he had been eating a piece of bread that the creature had decided was going down the wrong throat.

'They do not look overfed,' he said, and glanced surreptitiously at Katrina. It would not be the first time a keeper had requisitioned stores that her charges never saw.

'They eat what they need,' she replied loftily. 'However, it is not their diet that worries me, but the fact that they fight. Yet when I separate them, they pine.'

'Van the down hold bring,' confided Grisel.

'Of course they fight,' said Bartholomew. 'You have two males and one female.'

Katrina regarded him coolly. 'So what do you suggest we do? Buy another female? But what happens if Morel and Grisel still prefer Blanche? Then we will still have two sparring cocks, but will have added an offended hen to the equation.'

Bartholomew wondered how he had let himself be manoeuvred into a position where he was obliged to act as a counsellor for a love triangle between birds. 'Have you tried distracting them from their amours by giving them interesting things to do?'

She frowned her bemusement. 'Such as what?'

He raised his hands in a shrug. 'Teach them tricks, give them toys to play with, provide things for them to chew – although preferably not meat.'

'I would never give them meat,' replied Katrina crossly, then flushed when she realised this was probably not what he had been told. 'Other than when it is necessary.'

Her arrangements with the kitchens were none of his concern, and he was about to say so when Grisel flew to his shoulder, precipitating a sudden memory of his student days. Life had been so simple then, when all he had to do was absorb as much knowledge as he could. Now he was a teacher himself, although that part of his life would be over when he married Matilde. He experienced a sudden sense of misgiving. Was she worth it? To take his mind off such uncomfortable questions, he went to the window and looked out, the bird still on his shoulder.

'You have a good view of the Cistern Tower,' he remarked.

'Yes, but I did not see who murdered Margery, if that is where this discussion is going. Yet I might have done, because I was up at the time. The squires woke me with

236

their racket at midnight, and I could not go back to sleep again. I read for a while, then went to nocturns in the chapel.'

Bartholomew frowned. 'You cannot have done – Heselbech rang the bell, but then decided he was incapable of doing his duty.'

'Then his memory is flawed, because he *did* do it. He was behind the rood screen, of course, so I could not see him, but I certainly heard him reciting the words.'

'And it was definitely Heselbech?'

'Well, he is our chaplain, so who else could it have been?' Katrina gave a sudden chuckle. 'Your friend Master Langelee? He came out as I went in, but he reeked of ale and was just as drunk as Heselbech. It is a pity he is a scholar, as he is a very attractive man.'

'Langelee is?' blurted Bartholomew, then decided that he did not want to know the answer. 'Was anyone else in the chapel when you arrived?'

'Just Albon, although he was at the front, as near to the chancel as he could get, whereas I kept to the back. He was already kneeling there when I went in, and he stayed after I left. He spends a lot of time praying – probably asking God for an excuse to get him out of going to war.'

'Then God has given him one,' said Bartholomew, going to put the paroquet back with its companions. 'He has vowed not to leave Clare until Margery's killer is caught.'

'The Lady will not allow him to wriggle out of his obligations that easily – she wants the squires out of her hair.' Katrina sighed. 'Yet I wish I did have something useful to tell you. Margery was my friend, and I should like to help you catch her killer.'

'Perhaps you can,' said Bartholomew, and told her about Roos's double life. 'We do not know why she summoned him, but it must have been important, as she told a terrible lie to get him here.'

Katrina frowned thoughtfully. 'Margery liked him to bring her things when he came. I assumed they were from London, but perhaps they were from Cambridge . . .'

'What sort of things?'

'She never said, but you might want to look into it – it could be important.'

She changed the subject then, and told him how she had been invited to work at the castle after being widowed. She had accepted with alacrity, because her husband had left her penniless, and it was an opportunity to secure a suitable replacement.

'Have you found one?' Bartholomew hoped she would not set her sights on Langelee, because the Master was likely to take what was offered, then trot home without a backward glance.

Katrina sighed ruefully. 'Originally, I thought one of the squires would do. They are young, vigorous and have good prospects. But it transpires that they are scum – they grab what they want, then move on, leaving broken hearts behind them. Nuport was *my* nemesis: once he had added me to his tally, he went after the baker's sister.'

'I see.'

'Thomas is all right, though – he has a sense of humour and I like men who laugh. But he is too much in his sister's sway, and I do not want to wed twins. So I have decided to make a play for Albon – I think I can secure him before he goes to war. He will treat me well, although he is as dull as ditch-water and a coward into the bargain.'

Bartholomew blinked. 'You would pay that price for a secure future?'

'You would never ask that question unless you had experienced real love yourself. Well, I wish you joy of your paragon, but *I* must take what I can get. Albon will suit me well enough.'

'Suzanne de Nekton. Was *she* one of the squires' victims?'

Katrina shook her head slowly. 'They may be callous, but they are not rapists. It was another man who destroyed Suzanne. She had to ask Anne for help, but there were problems . . .'

'*Were* there problems? Anne told me that Suzanne just screamed a lot.'

Katrina winced. 'She whimpered. However, Anne told Suzanne to stay up here and rest when she had finished, and Grisel sensed her distress – it was him who screamed, not Suzanne. Unfortunately, the noise attracted attention, with the result that Anne is walled up in the church, and there is no one left to help needy girls.'

'Perhaps it is just as well. Scraping inside them with a hook is dangerous.'

'Giving birth is dangerous,' countered Katrina. 'I have lost several friends to childbed fevers. Anne provided a valuable service, and it is a wicked shame that she was punished for it.'

It was an uncomfortable conversation for Bartholomew, and although he had always been able to see both sides of this particular argument, it was not something he was about to discuss with a stranger. He hastened to move on.

'Anne said Suzanne was sent to a nunnery.'

'A place where she is safe from ruthless men – including her loathsome father, who claims she shamed him. He is a tanner, but you would think he was a lord from the way he acts.'

Bartholomew left the Oxford Tower full of dark thoughts. Matilde wanted children, but she was old for first-time motherhood. What would he do if there was a choice between losing her and wielding a hook? He sincerely hoped he would never have to find out.

# CHAPTER 9

The next morning was Sunday, and the scholars were woken by the joyful jangle of Sabbath bells. Langelee was heavy-eyed and weary, having spent another evening with his warrior friends. Michael had also stayed up late, reviewing what he had learned about the murder of Roos, but Bartholomew had gone to bed early and slept like a log, so he rose refreshed and alert. He set about washing and shaving, full of vigour and high spirits, the black thoughts of the previous night forgotten. For now, at least.

'Do not splash,' snapped Langelee, flinching from the flying droplets. 'And do not inflict that dreadful singing on us either. It is unkind.'

'We have a lot to do today,' said Michael, primping in front of a mirror, 'because the Lady's hundred marks should go to Michaelhouse – not to Albon, and certainly not to Lichet. Will you be available to help, Matt, or are you more concerned with the Lady's birds? Or is it their keeper who has caught your eye?'

'I do not blame you,' said Langelee before Bartholomew could reply. 'That Katrina de Haliwell is a handsome lass, although she has the appetite of a horse if the tales in the kitchens are true. But watch yourself – you do not want tales getting back to Matilde. Women can be touchy about that sort of thing.'

'What tales?' objected Bartholomew. 'All I did was examine her paroquets.'

'Of course you did,' said Langelee with a man-of-the-world leer. 'But tread with care. She wants a husband to replace the one who died, and will accept anyone who can provide her with a decent standard of living.'

'Well, that eliminates Matt then,' quipped Michael. 'Because he will not earn enough to keep himself once he leaves Michaelhouse. He will be almost entirely reliant on Matilde.'

'What did you two do while I was busy earning five marks for Michaelhouse?' asked Bartholomew archly, electing to overlook the fact that the money would not be theirs until the Lady was satisfied that he had actually done something useful.

'Quite a lot, actually,' replied the monk. 'We contrived to slip into the Constable Tower behind Lichet's back, but Marishal was slumbering so deeply that neither of us could get any sense out of him. Then we visited all the taverns in Clare, asking after Bonde and the hermit.'

'Oh,' said Bartholomew, conceding that they had achieved rather more than he had. 'What did you learn?'

'That everyone is worried about Jan, because they like having a holy man in their town, but they are glad to be rid of Bonde, who they think is dangerous.'

'He *is* dangerous,' said Langelee soberly. 'You can tell just by looking that he is violent. He could well be our culprit, lying low until the fuss dies down, at which point he will strut back and resume his role as the Lady's favourite henchman. Of course, the hermit was also wandering around the castle at the time of the murders . . .'

'He was,' acknowledged Michael. 'But I discovered last night that he has a deep-rooted terror of underground places, and could no more enter the cistern than fly. Moreover, he adored Margery, as she not only built his cottage but gave him money for his weekly shopping. The townsfolk believe that he witnessed the killer emerge bloody-handed from his crime, and fled in terror.'

'Perhaps he saw Bonde,' suggested Langelee, 'who then set off after him. That would explain why both have gone.'

241

'I agree that Jan knows the killer's identity,' said Michael. 'Or rather *knew*, given that I doubt he is still alive. But I am not sure the culprit is Bonde. There are still others to consider.'

'Who?' asked Langelee tiredly. 'I keep losing track, because they are on and off the list like jumping fleas.'

Michael began to list them. 'First, Nicholas. I know you are all admiration for him, Master, because he is hearty, strong and decisive, but I cannot take to him at all. There is something sinister beneath that bluff exterior.'

'You doubtless say the same about me,' retorted Langelee. 'But you would be wrong.'

'You are not artful enough to be sinister,' said Michael, and hurried on before Langelee realised that was no great compliment. 'Then there are Marishal, his twins, Lichet, Bonde, Albon and Grym. Not Badew and Harweden, though – they could never have gained access to the castle.'

He did not mention that Prior John was also a suspect, for the simple reason that Langelee would disagree, and he did not want to waste time arguing about it.

'I thought we had decided that Grym was too fat to squeeze down the cistern steps,' said Langelee. 'You only just made it, and he is much stouter than you.'

Michael eyed him beadily. 'He is a suspect for killing Godeston, on the grounds that he likes to dispense hemlock for medicinal purposes, which Matt says is a risky thing to do. Of course, Lichet uses it, too . . .'

'He does,' agreed Bartholomew, rather eagerly. 'And perhaps there is a good reason why he has kept Marishal asleep for two days – namely that *he* killed the man's wife.'

Langelee frowned. 'Are we looking into Mayor Godeston's murder now as well? I thought John told us to leave that to him.'

'He did,' said Michael, 'but the Lady wants *all* the suspicious deaths investigated and she charged us to do it. I have no objection, though. Godeston's curious death follows five others, and it is possible that we may only have answers when we look at the whole picture.'

'How will we do that?' asked Langelee helplessly.

'By re-questioning witnesses, starting with you. You were in the castle when Roos and Margery were killed. You must remember *something* to help.'

Langelee looked pained. 'All I recall is lugging Heselbech to the chapel for nocturns – which he never celebrated because he was too drunk.'

'But he *did* celebrate it,' said Bartholomew. 'Katrina was there, and she heard him.'

Langelee shrugged. 'Then he must have managed to rouse himself after I left. I did not notice her, though. Did she see me?'

Bartholomew nodded. 'She said you were coming out as she was going in.'

'You must be losing your touch, Master,' said Michael wryly. 'You do not usually neglect to notice pretty women. Or shall we just put it down to how much you had had to drink?'

Langelee regarded him archly. 'The strain of running a foundering College must be depriving me of the ability to enjoy life.' He was silent for a while, thinking. 'Perhaps *Roos* killed Margery because he was irked with her for dragging him to Clare under false pretences.'

'And then what?' asked Michael. 'Stabbed himself and threw his own body in the water?'

'I suppose it is unlikely. But he was a vile man. Only vermin betray their friends – Badew and Harweden trusted him, and he repaid them with treachery. You should find out when he was last in Clare – see if his presence corresponds to the other suspicious deaths.'

'I did,' said Michael. 'And it did not.'

Langelee looked disappointed. 'Then the culprit must be Lichet. He is not a good man either.'

'No,' agreed Bartholomew keenly.

'The Lady's courtiers certainly do not like him,' said Michael. 'They told me that he does sit with her while she sleeps, but he comes and goes at will. Thus he cannot prove where he was at the time of the murders – which took place in the tower where *he* lives.'

'Albon believes Lichet's alibi, though,' mused Langelee. 'Of course, *he* suspects that the killer is a squire, and thinks that quiet, godly patience will shame the culprit into a confession. He was still sitting in the bailey when I left last night. What an ass!'

At that moment, the priory bell began to ring, summoning the friars to prime in their chapel. Michael became businesslike, standing and rubbing his hands together purposefully.

'Right,' he said, glancing one last time in the mirror to ensure that every hair was in its proper place. 'As soon as we have fulfilled our religious obligations, we will talk to Marishal.'

'What if Lichet has dosed him with more soporific?' asked Langelee.

'We must prevent that if we can,' said Bartholomew. 'Keeping healthy patients asleep for days on end will do them no good whatsoever.'

'When we have finished with Marishal,' Michael went on, 'we shall set about finding the mysterious priest who entered the castle after Langelee and Heselbech.'

'*If* it was a priest,' cautioned Bartholomew. 'It was too dark to see properly, and while you are prepared to accept the watchman's testimony, I think that his claim about religious men gliding to their offices is preposterous. You are a monk, but you cannot glide.'

'Of course I can,' objected Michael, stung. 'I just choose not to.'

\* \* \*

Michael attended Mass in the priory, but Bartholomew and Langelee went to the parish church instead. Langelee thought the office there would be shorter, and he hated being inactive for too long, while the physician wanted another opportunity to study the fan vaulting. Unfortunately, much of the scaffolding still remained in place, so its true glory was yet to be revealed.

'It will never be ready in time for the Queen,' predicted Langelee. 'Nicholas was too ambitious, and should have given himself another week.'

'I am looking forward to meeting Cambrug,' said Bartholomew, but then sighed ruefully. 'Although he will probably be far too busy to bother with the likes of me.'

'Well, if he does deign to acknowledge you, ask about those cracks,' said Langelee, peering upwards. 'I do not want to be crushed by falling masonry during this ceremony, and it would be good to know if we should stand in the south aisle instead. That has a much more sensible ceiling.'

At that point, Nicholas jangled his handbell and the service began. It was not well attended, and Anne could be heard throughout, issuing instructions to him through the squint. At one point, Bartholomew and Langelee exchanged an amused grin, but soon wished they had not.

'It is unbecoming to smirk during Mass,' came her admonishing voice. 'You should be heartily ashamed of yourselves.'

'It was one quick smile,' objected Langelee, moving towards her cell so she would not be obliged to yell. A few of the sparse congregation were men he had approached for donations, and he did not want them to think him impious. 'And what gives you the right to berate us anyway? You are more interested in telling the vicar his job than saying your own prayers.'

'I would be a poor anchoress if I did not involve

myself in religious affairs,' retorted Anne. 'And advising Nicholas is how I choose to do it. But never mind that. Do you have any interesting news? It is frustrating, being shut in here with no way to find out what is going on outside.'

Langelee considered carefully. 'Well, we are worried about the hermit – that he saw the killer, and has been dispatched in his turn.'

'Then I shall pray for his soul,' said Anne. 'Although he was a worthless fellow, and Clare will be much nicer without him. He did not wash, you know. Margery was always good to him, but I do not know how she stood the stench.'

'Have *you* heard any rumours about who the killer may be?'

'The town says he is from the castle, and the castle says he is from the town. However, I can tell you that Margery's family would never have hurt her, no matter what you might have heard about the lack of affection between them. Ella and Thomas are scamps, but there is no real harm in them, while Marishal loved her, even if he was always too busy to show it.'

'Michael thinks that Nicholas might be the culprit,' confided Langelee in a low voice. 'It is outrageous, I know, but—'

'Nicholas?' interrupted Anne, shocked. 'Do not be ridiculous! He is a priest. The villain is more likely to be one of you scholarly types. We never had any trouble before you lot arrived.'

'Yes, you did,' countered Bartholomew, unwilling to let her get away with that one. 'Starting with Roger, and followed by Talmach, Charer, Wisbech and Skynere.'

'Oh, yes,' said Anne. 'I had forgotten about them. Do you want me to keep an ear out for pertinent confessions then? I will do it in exchange for a seed cake and a bottle of lavender water.'

'Speaking of confessions,' began Bartholomew, 'I met Katrina de Haliwell yesterday. She told me that Suzanne—'

'I provided a valuable service,' interrupted Anne angrily. 'As I told you before. And my skills are badly missed. Take Isabel Morley, for example. She is carrying Quintone's child, but he refuses to marry her. I could have helped, but now she is condemned to bear a bastard and be shunned for the rest of her life. What a waste!'

'I was going to say that Katrina claims it was the paroquets who screamed, not Suzanne,' said Bartholomew. 'She only whimpered.'

There was a short silence as this information was digested.

'Then I am sorry for all the bad things I said about her,' conceded Anne eventually. 'Still, life in here has its advantages. I am warm, dry, well fed and people revere me. I cannot complain.'

They met Nicholas as they were leaving the church. He was bringing his breakfast to share with Anne – a pan of coddled eggs, good white bread, dried fruit and a dish of stewed onions. It was a good deal better than what was usually served in Michaelhouse on a Sunday, and Bartholomew saw that Anne was right to claim she was well looked after.

'Two warriors together,' said the vicar with an approving smile when he saw Bartholomew and Langelee. 'A veteran of Poitiers and a soldier from York. How are you this fine morning?'

'I am not a warrior,' objected Bartholomew. 'I am a physician.'

Nicholas patted his arm. 'You can be both, and there is no need to be modest on my account. I am all admiration for the number of Frenchmen you slaughtered single-handed.'

'There are *three* enquiries into the murders of Roos

247

and Margery now,' said Langelee, changing the subject quickly before Bartholomew could berate him again for telling lies. 'Run by Michael, Lichet and Albon. The last two are unlikely to succeed, but our Senior Proctor is a remarkable man, and no killer has bested him yet. I should warn you that he has you in his sights.'

'Me?' blurted Nicholas, startled. 'But I have not killed anyone! Well, not in Clare, at least. And I try to stay away from the castle, on the grounds that it is full of folk who I do not like.'

'Well, do not tell him *that* when he questions you, or he will assume that you took the opportunity to dispatch a couple,' advised Langelee. 'Apparently, two Austins entered the castle at the salient time – Heselbech and one other. He thinks the mystery priest might have been you.'

'Then he is wrong,' said Nicholas firmly, 'as Anne will attest. Brother Michael cannot doubt the word of a holy anchoress.'

Bartholomew knew he could.

'Well, just be on your guard,' said Langelee, and glanced at Bartholomew. 'Do not look so disapproving. You remember what I was telling you about loyalty earlier? Well, that extends to telling fellow ex-warriors that they may be unjustly accused of a nasty crime.'

'Michael will have a job to waylay me today anyway,' said Nicholas, 'as I shall be very busy. Not only do I have all my usual Sunday offices, but there is the scaffolding to dismantle, and Margery is due to be buried later.'

'Buried here?' asked Bartholomew. 'Not in the castle?'

'The chapel is reserved for the Lady and her kin, so yes, Margery will come to me. I shall put her in the chancel – the best spot in the whole church, right in front of the altar.'

'That is good of you,' said Langelee. 'But why? Because you are an Austin, dedicated to keeping the peace? Your strategy may well work: the town will be glad to see Margery in such an auspicious place, while the castle will be grateful to you for treating her remains with such respect.'

Nicholas regarded him stonily. 'I do it because I liked her. If it had been any other castle resident, they would have gone on the boggy side of the churchyard. Prior John does not approve of my partiality, but it is the town that pays my stipend . . .'

'Will there be trouble at the funeral?' asked Langelee. 'The town objecting to a lot of the enemy pouring into their parish church?'

'They will overlook the outrage for Margery's sake,' said Nicholas. 'She was loved by all.'


Bartholomew and Langelee returned to the priory just as Michael and the friars were emerging from their more extensive devotions in the conventual chapel. The monk's fine voice had far outshone the manly rumbles of the Austins, and he was modestly accepting the praise they were lavishing on him for his exquisite rendition of the *Gloria*.

'They should hire someone to sing for them if they cannot do it themselves,' Michael muttered, as they traipsed towards the refectory to break their fast. 'Because they sound like what they are – a lot of old soldiers more used to bawling tavern songs than psalms.'

'God will not mind,' said Langelee. 'He likes ex-soldiers. It says so in the Bible.'

'I am sure it does not,' countered Michael, 'and besides, I am not sure they are *ex*-soldiers. They are all wearing some form of armour under their habits, while Weste has a cudgel and Heselbech would chop off his fingers if he tried paring fruit with that great big knife in his belt.'

'Of course they are armed,' said Langelee impatiently. 'Keeping the peace here is dangerous.'

249

'I do not equip *myself* with weapons when I patrol Cambridge,' argued Michael. 'Their precautions are excessive. Besides, I have never been comfortable with men who take holy orders to atone for violent pasts. You never know when they might revert to type.'

Langelee glared. 'In other words, you think that one of the Austins killed Margery and Roos, just because some watchman *thinks* a second friar followed Heselbech and me into the castle.'

'I do. John, Heselbech, Weste – all look as though they would be happier in mail than a habit, and their priory is more like a barracks than a House of God. I wish I had suggested staying somewhere else.'

But he revised his opinion when he saw the Sabbath breakfast table. There was bread, plenty of meat, a whole cheese and butter – the kind of spread he loved. As a sop to health, there was a tiny dish of dried figs, although Bartholomew was the only one who ate one. It was old and stale, leading him to conclude that they had probably been making an appearance every Sunday for months, and as the friars shunned them, would continue to do so for many more to come.

As conversation was permitted that day, it was not long before the subject turned to murder. John asked for an update on the investigation, and Langelee provided him with one, ignoring the warning kicks that Michael aimed at his ankles under the table. The monk did not want to share everything they had learned.

'I immortalised *Roos* in my Book of Hours?' breathed Weste, stunned. 'I had no idea! All I can tell you is that "Jevan" had nasty glittering eyes that belied his avuncular white hairs. I sensed at once that there was something distasteful about him.'

'And you were right,' said John, lips pursed in disapproval at Langelee's revelations. 'The only crime worse than the breaking of sacred oaths is betraying one's friends. You were perceptive to have depicted him as Satan.'

'I agree,' said Heselbech, baring his terrifying teeth in a grimace, while there were fervent nods from all around the refectory. 'It is despicable, and the Devil will certainly have his soul now.'

'So you think Roos got his just deserts?' fished Michael.

Heselbech regarded him evenly. 'Yes, if you want the truth. However, *we* did not kill him. I was asleep in my chapel, and everyone else was here, celebrating nocturns.'

'You were not asleep,' Bartholomew told him. 'Katrina de Haliwell heard you praying.'

Heselbech blinked. 'Did she? Goodness! I have no recollection of it at all.'

'I am not surprised, given the state of you,' smirked Langelee. 'You did not really *ring* the bell either – you clutched the rope for support. Then your hands slid down it and you fell over.'

'It was *I* who recited nocturns in the castle,' announced Weste, and raised his hands apologetically when everyone looked at him in surprise. 'I knew Heselbech would be incapable, and I did not want him in trouble with the Lady, who attends that ceremony on occasion. So I followed him and Langelee to the chapel, and *I* did the honours at the altar, while he snored in the corner.'

Heselbech clapped him on the shoulder. 'You are a good friend, Weste! The Lady would have docked my stipend if she had caught me napping, so I appreciate you looking out for me.'

'Well, I do not,' said Michael sourly. 'Why did you not mention this sooner? You must see it is important. We wasted hours pondering over the mysterious second priest.'

Weste was unrepentant. 'It is *not* important, because I neither saw nor heard anything to help your investigation. And I did not tell you, because I did not want

251

Heselbech's condition to become a subject for gossip. Of course, he has made no effort to conceal his shortcomings himself . . .'

Heselbech grinned. 'And rightly so, because it has done my popularity the power of good. Castle folk like me more now they realise that I am just like them.'

'So who else was in the chapel?' asked Michael angrily, glaring at Weste. 'Or will you lie about that as well?'

Weste made a placatory gesture. 'Just two people – which is why the office *had* to be said. Katrina de Haliwell and Sir William Albon.'

'I cannot believe this,' said Michael in disgust. 'Lies and deceit from fellow clerics! How am I supposed to solve these murders when even friars regale me with falsehoods?'

'You should have confessed sooner, Weste,' said John admonishingly. 'But what is done is done, and we are not in the business of recrimination. Judgement is for the Lord to dispense, not us, so we shall say no more about it. Agreed, Brother?'

Michael looked as though he had a very great deal more to say, but confined himself to an angry sniff, and for a while there was silence, the only sounds being the clank of knives on pewter plates and the occasional murmur of thanks as platters were passed. Eventually, Langelee spoke.

'I do not like Anne. She is not very religious, and I am surprised the Church does not pull her anchorhold down and send her on her way. Why do you tolerate her, John?'

'Guilt,' explained the Prior sheepishly. 'When I first learned that she poked about inside pregnant girls with hooks, I was appalled, and it was my horror that compelled the Lady to punish her. Anne's crimes might have been overlooked otherwise, as there is an unspoken but widely held belief that she did a lot of good.'

'So why did you not order the sentence commuted?' asked Bartholomew.

'Only a physician with a reputation for heterodoxy could pose such a question,' said Heselbech before John could speak for himself. He eyed Bartholomew coolly. 'Because it is *wrong*. A life is a life, and it is not for Anne to decide who should live and who should perish on a hook.'

There was a second uncomfortable silence, which again was broken by Langelee, who tended to be immune to chilly atmospheres.

'I have been thinking about the hermit, Brother. You believe he is dead, but you may be wrong, and if you are, we should hear what he has to say. So I will hunt for him today.'

'I will keep you company,' offered Weste, his one eye gleaming at the prospect of an adventure. 'I am sure Father Prior can spare me for a few hours.'

'Perhaps we can all go,' suggested Heselbech, surging to his feet with a grin of happy anticipation. 'I would not mind an excursion and—'

'No,' interrupted John, raising his hand with a tolerant smile. 'The Queen will arrive the day after tomorrow, and we do not have time for jaunts. If you want exercise, Heselbech, help Nicholas. He still has a lot of scaffolding to remove, and I am sure he would be glad of another pair of hands.'

Heselbech walked away, shoulders slumped dejectedly, as did most of the others, although Weste and Langelee set off towards the stables with a spring in their step.

'Watch out for Simon Freburn,' John called after them. 'We do not want you to come back *sans* ears.'

'No fear of that,' declared Langelee, clearly delighted by an opportunity to gallop around the countryside with a sword at his side. 'No mere outlaw will get the better of us.'

'I hope his confidence is not misplaced,' said Michael worriedly.

It was raining, so Bartholomew and Michael returned to their lodgings to collect cloaks. Bartholomew picked up his shabby, burned academic one and regarded it with regret.

'You will have to wear Albon's,' said Michael. 'Of course, it is far too good for the likes of you – you will ruin it within a week. If it was black, I would take it for myself.'

'Then I am glad it is red,' said Bartholomew, making a vow to look after it. Once he left the University, and was no longer obliged to wear Michaelhouse's uniform, he would need a new one, and Albon's gift would fit the bill perfectly. Moreover, he was sure Matilde would like to see him wearing more becoming colours.

'With the exception of a dry afternoon here and there, it has been raining for weeks,' grumbled Michael, sitting on the bed to exchange shoes for boots. 'We are lucky Roos and Margery were found – that cistern must be full to overflowing by now.' He shuddered. 'What if someone was trapped down there, with the water steadily rising?'

'I imagine most people know to stay out of it. And the well needs to be deep to serve hundreds of people in the event of a blockade. Lack of fresh water is one of the main reasons for the fall of fortresses in—'

'Those rough Austins have brought out the warrior in you,' interrupted Michael accusingly. 'Because I never expected to hear *you* waxing lyrical on the intricacies of siege warfare.'

'It is the mechanics of the cistern that intrigue me,' explained Bartholomew. 'Not the purpose for which it might be used.'

But Michael was not listening, his mind back on the investigation. 'We had better find out what Marishal has to say about the death of his wife first, and when we have finished, we will re-interview Thomas, Ella, Lichet, Albon and Nicholas. That should keep us busy for the morning.'

'And beyond,' muttered Bartholomew. 'I should visit the paroquets, too. The Lady will not give us five marks if she finds out that I only examined them once.'

'I cannot see the Queen taking to the roads in this weather,' remarked Michael, wincing as they stepped outside and rain blew straight into their faces. 'Not even to watch a fan-vaulted ceiling dedicated. She will send word that she is unavoidably detained, and postpone the visit until summer. You mark my words.'

'Good,' said Bartholomew. 'The town and the Lady might be friends again by then.'

A thick, drenching drizzle fell as they walked from the priory to the castle, and the River Stour was an ugly brown torrent. People scurried along with their heads down and their hoods up, and Bartholomew felt his hopes rise: the rain would dissuade folk from taking to the streets to protest about the murders, which could only help the cause of peace. Then he heard the hiss of angry conversation drifting from the alehouses they passed, and realised that the malcontents had just taken their complaints indoors.

He and Michael entered the inner bailey and were greeted by a curious sight. Albon had erected the pavilion that he intended to take on campaign with him – a glorious affair of red and gold stripes, with frills around the edges and a large pennant flying from the roof. It was wholly unsuitable for the conditions he was likely to encounter, and the squires, who had been given the task of erecting it, were hot, cross and fractious.

'Look what they have done to themselves now!' exclaimed Michael. 'They have shaved off all their hair except the fringe at the front. What are they thinking? They look absurd!'

'It is the latest Court fashion, apparently,' explained Quintone, overhearing. 'Thomas had a letter about it from London, and he said the Queen would consider them peasants unless they did the same. He declines to do it himself, though, on the grounds that he is only a steward's brat, whereas the squires are the sons of nobles.'

Bartholomew shook his head wonderingly. 'Were they born gullible, or did they learn it?'

'I am glad *I* am not going to war with Thomas,' confided Quintone. 'If he cannot be trusted not to make his friends a laughing-stock, how can he be trusted to watch their backs in battle?'

'Why has Albon pitched his tent?' asked Bartholomew. 'To make sure that he has all the right pieces before he leaves for France?'

'No – because he does not want to sit out in the rain while he waits for the killer to confess.' Quintone smirked. 'It took the squires most of the night to get the thing up.'

'So Langelee wins the wager,' murmured Michael. 'We gave Albon until yesterday to persist with this nonsense, whereas Langelee predicted it would last until tonight. Of course, now he has somewhere comfortable, Albon might confound us all by staying put for the next month.'

'Well, he does look magnificent in there,' said Bartholomew, glancing through the entrance to see Albon on his throne, another fine cloak cascading artistically around him and his gold-grey mane brushed until it shone. His expression was one of pious fortitude, and the physician wondered if he might stay that way not just for a month, but for as long as the army was needed in France.

He stepped towards him, intending to thank him again for the cloak, but found his way barred by the squires. Close up, their heads looked sore, covered in small cuts and grazes, which suggested they had shorn themselves rather than entrusting the task to a professional barber.

'Your master will not thank you for keeping folk out,' remarked Bartholomew. 'He wants the culprit to go in and confess, which will not happen with you lot loitering outside.'

'You mean *you* are the killer?' asked Nuport, blinking stupidly.

'Not *him*,' said Thomas, regarding the physician with an expression that was difficult to gauge. 'He is a veteran of Poitiers, and they do not kill women and old men.'

Bartholomew was not so sure about that, but the squires stepped aside to let him pass anyway.

The inside of the pavilion was very luxuriously appointed. Clearly, Albon had an eye for his creature comforts. The knight waved a dismissive hand when Bartholomew indicated his new cloak with a grateful smile, although it was clear that he was pleased his largesse should be appreciated.

'It is just a trifle,' he declared. 'And valour should be rewarded. It was brave of you to put yourself in danger to save a minion. True knightly behaviour.'

'Speaking of true knightly behaviour, your squires could do with learning some.'

'I am aware of that,' said Albon with a pained expression. 'And I shall teach them, with God's help. They are not bad lads – just ones in need of a gentle guiding hand.'

'A guiding hand, certainly,' agreed Bartholomew. 'Although a gentle one will be of scant use. I speak from experience – I have students just like them.'

'I know what I am doing,' said Albon, although Bartholomew begged to differ, and wondered how long it would be before the knight conceded that his ruffianly charges were beyond him.

As he and Albon were alone, Bartholomew decided it was a good opportunity to ask about the night of the murder, although not with much hope of learning anything useful. Albon was too self-absorbed to be an observant witness. Even so, the knight listened carefully to his questions, and considered each one thoroughly before venturing a reply. At first, Bartholomew assumed he was being conscientious, but then realised that Albon was desperately bored, and an interview represented a welcome distraction.

'I went to nocturns in the chapel,' the knight began. 'I had hoped to be alone, but a woman stood at the back and fidgeted the whole way through, which was very annoying. She left as soon as the rite was over, which allowed me to pray without the distraction of rustling kirtles.'

'Were you aware that it was Weste, not Heselbech, who recited the office?'

'No, but what difference does it make? Both are priests. I appreciate that there are some who would prefer the castle chaplain to a friar from the town, but I am not one of them.'

'Did you see anyone else out and about that night?'

Albon grimaced. 'I hesitate to mention it, out of loyalty to a fellow warrior, but Langelee was with Heselbech. They made a dreadful racket with the bell ropes, then staggered behind the rood screen, where I heard one of them fall over. It was most unedifying. Then Langelee left, and I saw another shadow glide into the chancel – Weste, according to you.'

'Will you really stay here until the culprit confesses?' asked Bartholomew, sorry that Albon was able to tell him nothing he and Michael did not already know.

Albon smiled serenely. 'Yes, but it will not be for much longer. Today is Sunday, that most holy of days, when everyone attends church. The killer's wicked heart will be touched by God, so I anticipate collecting a hundred marks before sunset.'

'And then you will go to France?'

'I am afraid I cannot, because the Queen will be here. The Lady will need a strong arm during such an eventful time, and I cannot abandon her in her hour of need.'

'But Her Majesty might stay in Clare for weeks, or even months.'

'She might,' acknowledged Albon, not at all dismayed by the possibility. 'But France will still be there when she has gone. Of course, her husband may have signed a peace treaty by then . . .'

'Your squires will be disappointed to miss the slaughter.'

'It cannot be helped, and I must do as my conscience dictates. I hope the culprit comes to me soon, though, as I fear Lichet might otherwise accuse an innocent person, just to get the reward. It is a pity the Lady offered such an enormous sum.'

'What will you do with it, if you win?'

'Why, give it to the parish church, of course,' replied Albon, so promptly it was clear that he had already given the matter exhaustive consideration. 'The ceiling is magnificent, but it would look better still with a picture of *me* on it.'

Bartholomew left him contemplating the kind of image that would best do him justice, and went in search of Michael. He found the monk listening to a very testy debate between Nuport and the freckled squire named Mull about a guy rope that had no obvious purpose. Apparently, the tent had not been erected as per the manufacturers' instructions, and Mull thought they should take it down and start again, when the function of the stray rope might become apparent. Nuport was of the opinion that they had struggled with the pavilion quite long enough, and that the offending line should be snipped off and forgotten.

'I hope Nuport wins,' said Michael to Bartholomew. 'Because it would give me great pleasure to see the thing topple down with that lot inside it. And that includes the sanctimonious Albon.'

The two scholars had not taken many steps towards the Constable Tower when they were intercepted by Lichet. The Red Devil's hair hung in soggy rats' tails around his face, while his cloak was saturated, suggesting he had been up and about for hours.

'I have been interviewing witnesses all night,' he informed them importantly. 'And I am almost ready to announce my conclusions. The killer will be in custody today, and I shall have the hundred marks while you two continue to flounder.'

'Perhaps,' cautioned Michael. 'But just naming the killer will not do – the Lady wants proof of his guilt. Otherwise I could just say that you are the culprit, and march off with the money.'

Lichet sneered. 'Oh, I shall have proof, do not worry about that.'

'Good,' said Michael briskly. 'But we want to talk to Marishal now. Is he awake, or have you dosed him with more soporific that will see him sleep the day away?'

'I offered him another draught, but he refused,' sniffed Lichet, apparently having forgotten that the Lady had forbidden him to dispense more. 'He is a fool to reject the medicine that will spare him the agony of grief, but it is not my place to insist. I shall reserve my expertise for people who actually appreciate my help.'

He turned and stalked away, full of arrogant pride. Seeing such a tempting target, Nuport scooped up a handful of mud and lobbed it, hitting Lichet square in the back. The Red Devil whipped around, and the fury on his face was such that the laughter died in the young man's throat.

'Do that again, and I will turn you into a pig,' Lichet

260

snarled. 'And serve you to your cronies, roasted with an apple shoved in your mouth.'

'*Turn* him into a pig?' murmured Ereswell, as he ambled past with his arms full of clean white linen for the Queen's private chamber. 'How, when he already is one? I do not know which of that pair I detest more – Lichet or Nuport. I live in hope that they will dispatch each other.'

'Nuport might dispatch Lichet,' remarked Bartholomew. 'His expression is murderous – he did not appreciate being threatened in front of his friends.'

'And Lichet did not appreciate being humiliated with a fistful of filth,' said Ereswell. 'He will not forget such an insult, and Nuport should watch himself.'

As befitted a man who ran a great household, Marishal lived in considerable comfort, and his quarters were almost as luxurious as the Lady's. The walls were covered with tapestries, the mixture of which suggested they had been chosen because he liked them, not because they went with the rest of the décor. Yet Margery's hand was also everywhere, from the bright cushions that were scattered along the benches to the light, airy nature of the family solar.

Marishal was standing by the hearth when the scholars were shown in. He wore an exquisite gipon with tight sleeves and flowing skirts, which had been embroidered with silver thread. His belt was silver, too, and on his feet were soft slippers that looked as though they had been imported from the east. His hair had been oiled and he was freshly shaved. All he needed, thought Bartholomew, was a circlet of gold on his head, and he might be mistaken for a prince. He was pale, but the numb shock had gone, and he seemed in control of himself once again.

'Lichet left me a potion,' he said, gesturing to a brimming cup on the table. 'But I have slept enough, and it is time to confront my anguish. Indeed, I would have

261

done it yesterday, but he slipped his "remedy" into my breakfast pottage without my knowledge.'

'Did he indeed?' murmured Bartholomew. 'That was unethical.'

'We appreciate that this is a difficult time for you, Master Marishal,' said Michael kindly. 'Yet I imagine your children must be a great comfort to you.'

Marishal sniffed and did not acknowledge the last remark. 'Margery will be buried today. Nicholas has offered her the best spot in the entire church, which is good of him. Of course, it is no less than she deserves, sweet saint that she was.'

He talked a little longer about Margery and her life, but told them little they did not already know, other than the fact that he had been devoted to her and now deeply regretted not giving her the attention she deserved. His occupation was a demanding one, but she had always been patiently understanding of the long hours he worked. Eventually, Michael steered the subject around to Roos and his double life as a member of the Lady's council. Marishal smiled wanly, and remarked that he was surprised it had taken them so long to uncover the truth.

'Were you aware that Margery sent him a message,' asked Michael, electing to ignore the criticism of his talents, 'urging him to come with all possible haste? Indeed, she was so determined that he should answer her summons that she claimed the Lady was dead, and told him to hurry if he wanted to make the funeral.'

Marishal blinked. 'Well, that would certainly have brought him running! The Lady promised to leave him a little something in her will, and he would have wanted to be on hand to claim it. But why would Margery invent such a terrible lie?'

'We were hoping you could tell us,' said Michael.

Marishal raised his hands in a helpless shrug. 'I cannot

imagine what prompted her to do such a thing. Are you sure it was her?'

Michael showed him the two letters from Roos's room, and explained how they had come by them. Marishal clutched them to his breast while tears brimmed in his eyes.

'She wrote these, without question. She nearly always corresponded with the council for me, confirming our Quarter Day gatherings. She hoped that it would allow me to spend more time with her, although it rarely worked out that way.'

'So there was no extraordinary session,' pressed Michael, 'organised to deal with some urgent and unexpected problem?'

Marishal wiped his eyes. 'If there were, Roos would not have been included. A few minor matters are aired on Quarter Days, and there is always a nice feast afterwards, but all the important decisions are made by the Lady and me alone, as and when necessary. The Quarter Days are essentially a sop to the likes of Roos, Albon and Lichet, who like to feel valued.'

'And they are unaware of this?' asked Michael, who would have seen the truth in a trice.

Marishal gave another weary smile. 'It is easy to deceive self-absorbed men. But to return to Roos: he was *not* here on council business, and I know of no reason why Margery should have wanted to see him. I wish I did, because then her death might make sense to me.'

'We know they were kin,' said Michael. 'Could it have been some family concern?'

'Their ties were distant, so no. Of course, it was their relationship that made him the perfect choice to monitor the University on our behalf. It was my idea to recruit him, although the Lady will remember it as her own. I invented the name "Philip de Jevan" as well. It has a nice ring about it, and Roos approved.'

'To monitor the *University*?' echoed Michael, narrowing his eyes. 'Are you saying that Roos spied on us all, not just Badew?'

Marishal spread his hands. 'Information is power, and your *studium generale* takes my Lady's money, so yes, we expected his reports to be wide-ranging. You do it for the Bishop of Ely, and Master Heltisle of Bene't College does it for the King, so there are precedents.'

To conceal his consternation that his arrangement with the Bishop should be common knowledge, Michael showed Marishal the onyx rings. 'Have you seen these before?'

Marishal nodded. 'They are family heirlooms. Roos gave one to Margery, and she wore it to please him, although she never liked it very much.'

'We have been told that Roos and Margery were once . . . close,' said Michael. 'Is it true?'

'What gossips people are!' exclaimed Marishal angrily. 'Do they have nothing better to do? And yes, he *did* once pay suit to her, but then she met me. He was disappointed, but could see she was in love with a younger, brighter man. However, their brief and ancient amour had nothing to do with their deaths. Margery and I have been married for twenty-four years, and his infatuation died a long time ago, along with any resentment he might have harboured.'

'I am sorry, but I must ask: where were you between nocturns and dawn on Friday?'

'In here mostly, with my three clerks. We are frantically busy with the royal visit, and Thursday night was particularly hectic, because letters had arrived from Court detailing certain demands that must be met. The Clare Hall men offered to help . . .'

'They mentioned working all night,' said Bartholomew, recalling that they had been far from pleased about it.

'I heard the bell chime for nocturns, but we had no

264

time to attend. Later, I went to the Oxford Tower, to collect any documents that Donwich and Pulham might have finished, and on the way, I heard Adam the baker race screaming from the cistern . . . then everything is a blur.'

He could tell them no more, so Bartholomew and Michael left him in peace.

'He works so hard that he has missed the most important thing in his life,' said Bartholomew soberly. 'Time with his beloved wife. And now she is gone, so he will never have it. Therein lies a lesson for us all.'

Which meant, he thought, that he *should* marry Matilde as soon as he could. Marishal would spend the rest of his life lamenting the choices he had made, so Bartholomew should make sure he did not do the same. Or would he then regret abandoning the teaching he loved so much?

'He was too busy to notice what she was doing, as well,' mused Michael. 'Perhaps a constantly absent husband made her lonely, but her old flame Roos was there to step into the breach.'

'Regardless, Marishal did not kill them, not if he has three clerks to provide his alibi.'

'Clerks who work for him, and who will say anything to keep his favour. And he did not mention taking them with him when he went to collect documents from the Oxford Tower. However, remember that we were also told how Thomas was quickly on the scene once the alarm was raised. Perhaps it was *he* who disapproved of his mother cavorting with another man.'

'I suppose we can try speaking to him again,' said Bartholomew without enthusiasm. 'Although I suspect it will be a waste of time.'

The twins were near the chapel, laughing helplessly, and it was obvious to anyone watching that yet another prank was in the offing, suggesting that they had learned nothing from the near-incineration of Adam. That day, Ella had donned a plain blue kirtle that matched her eyes, while Thomas wore shoes with points so long that they were fastened to his knees with ribbons.

'You will trip,' warned Bartholomew, then wished he had kept his thoughts to himself, as it would be rather satisfying to see the odious young man fall flat on his face.

'Not me,' declared Thomas confidently, 'although Nuport will take a tumble when he orders the cobbler to make him footwear to match mine – which he will, because he is a stupid oaf, who copies everything I do, even when it is obviously a joke.'

'I thought you were friends,' said Bartholomew, bemused by his malice.

'Companions,' corrected Thomas shortly. 'It is not the same.'

'Even so, you would be wise not to alienate him. You might need him in France.'

'Need him?' scoffed Thomas. 'I would sooner trust a gnat, which would have a good deal more sense and be more likeable into the bargain. Besides, what do you know of France and war?'

'More than you ever will – *he* fought in the Battle of Poitiers,' retorted Michael, and seeing this failed to impress, added, 'The Prince of Wales himself praised his valour.'

The last part was pure fabrication, but Thomas regarded Bartholomew with new interest. 'Then perhaps you should join us when we leave. A physician might come in useful.'

'You are not going anywhere as long as your mother's killer is at large,' Michael pointed out. 'Albon has sworn not to leave Clare until the culprit is caught.'

'Yes,' acknowledged Thomas with a grimace. 'Which

266

was reckless, because not every crime has a solution, and he might be here for ever.'

Which would suit Albon perfectly, thought Bartholomew wryly.

At that moment, a cluster of kitchen maids walked past, and one darted forward to press something into Thomas's hand. It was a cake, warm from the oven. He accepted it with a gracious bow that made her blush prettily before scampering away to rejoin her fellows. Recalling what Katrina had said about the squires' morals, Bartholomew wondered how long it would be before she was used and tossed aside with a broken heart.

'So what other questions do you have?' asked Thomas, tearing his eyes away from the jauntily swaying hips. 'To ask yet again where we were on the night of our mother's murder? Very well: we were in Ella's room playing board games.'

'But you arrived very quickly after Adam raised the alarm,' said Bartholomew.

'Yes, because we live close to the Cistern Tower. I was still dressed, so all I had to do was run down one flight of stairs and trot across the bailey.'

'And Adam's screeches were not very loud at first,' put in Ella. 'He began with a few whimpers, which we heard because my window was open. Thomas jumped up at once to see what was wrong, so he had a head start when Adam really began to howl.'

'What did *you* do?' Bartholomew asked her.

'Unlike Thomas, I was *not* dressed. By the time I was, he and the others had been down into the cistern, found our mother and Roos, and climbed back up to the bailey again.'

Michael nodded to the pink pearls around Ella's neck. 'Those belonged to Margery. Could you not have waited until after her funeral before raiding her jewellery box?'

Ella regarded him steadily. 'She told me I could have them when she died.'

'Did she? Why? The pair of you were not close, by your own admission.'

'So what? I am still her daughter – her *only* daughter. But if I am a thief, then so are you. I know you stole the onyx ring from her corpse, because I watched you show it to the Lady.' She held out her hand. 'And I want it back.'

'Your father has it,' replied Michael, unmoved by the accusation. 'Along with the matching one owned by Roos. Ask him for them.'

Ella's eyes flashed angrily, and it was clear that she would never dare. She went on an offensive to disguise her annoyance. 'Although why she agreed to wear an heirloom from that disgusting old lecher is beyond me. He was all pawing hands and will not be missed.'

'What about Talmach?' asked Michael innocently. 'Is he missed?'

'Terribly,' replied Ella coldly. 'His death turned me into a widow. I know there is a rumour that Thomas and I made an end of him, but it is a lie. We never touched him or his saddle.'

'Ask Anne the anchoress,' put in Thomas. 'She knows us better than anyone, and will tell you that we are no killers.'

'I miss Anne,' sighed Ella, sadness replacing her ire at Michael and his questions. 'She was more fun than everyone else put together, and the castle is dull without her. It is a pity the Austins made such a fuss about Suzanne. If they had controlled themselves, Anne would still be here.'

'They did not make nearly as much a fuss as that wretched tanner, though,' said Thomas, and glanced at the scholars before explaining. 'Suzanne's father. The Austins were all righteous indignation, but Nekton was

268

poisonous, and it was he who really forced the Lady's hand. That vicious-tongued hypocrite has a lot to answer for.'

'We have not met Nekton yet,' said Bartholomew, wondering if the aggrieved tanner was responsible for some of the murders – Margery, Roos, Talmach, Charer and Wisbech had associations with the castle, where Anne had done her work. 'Where does he live?'

'Not in Clare,' smirked Thomas vengefully. 'After all, who wants to reside in a house that is always infested with rats and fleas? And who wants to tan hides that no one will buy? He took himself off to London in the end, where I hope he will be miserable.'

'But what father would not object when he discovered that the castle's nurse had carried out an illegal and dangerous procedure on his daughter?' asked Michael reasonably. 'He could hardly pretend it did not happen and look the other way.'

'Why not?' asked Ella coolly. 'Other fathers did – lots of them. And because of Nekton's mean spirit, *we* lost our beloved nurse and Clare lost a woman with a very useful skill.'

'It is difficult to know what to make of them,' remarked Michael, as he and Bartholomew walked away a few moments later. 'They care for no one but themselves, and they are certainly callous enough to dispatch their mother and a kinsman to suit themselves. And yet what would be their motive? Not a string of pink pearls, surely?'

Bartholomew shrugged. 'Who knows? I do not understand them either.'

'It is hard to blame Margery and Marishal for declining to dote on them,' the monk went on. 'I imagine their stupid japes and arrogance were a cause of shame and embarrassment to two such respectable, hardworking people. Did you notice Marishal's reaction when I remarked that the twins must be a comfort to him? He does not love them, and I suspect Margery found it difficult, too.'

'So what now? A word with the squires? I know Adam told us that they went to bed at midnight and did not stir again until morning, but he cannot have watched *all* their doors and windows. One may have slipped out quietly on his own.'

'You mean Nuport,' surmised Michael. 'The most loathsome and vicious of the pack. But does he have the wits to commit such a serious crime and leave no clues or witnesses?'

'No, but there is always an element of luck involved. And perhaps there *was* a witness anyway – the hermit, who you think has been dispatched in his turn.'

The squires were struggling to stabilise Albon's pavilion. The wind was no more than a whisper that day, but even that was enough to make it billow alarmingly, and Bartholomew was under the impression that it might take to the skies at any moment. As they passed, Ereswell whispered that it leaked as well, so its owner would be in for a wretched time if, God forbid, he should ever be compelled to use it on a military campaign.

Like Thomas, the squires wore shoes with ridiculously long toes, although theirs were so extreme that they were able to tie the ends to their belts. Combined with their harlequin hose, flowing sleeves, oiled beards and part-shaven heads, they looked worse than absurd, and Bartholomew wondered how much more preposterous they would make themselves before Albon put an end to it. However, while Nuport strutted about proudly, clearly delighted with himself and the way he looked, his friends were now aware that they were a laughing-stock, and were obviously uncomfortable.

'What, again?' groaned Nuport, when Michael ordered

them to recount their movements on the night of the murder. 'We have already told you, Brother – we spent the evening in the Bell Inn, and came back here at midnight.'

'After which we all flopped into our beds and went to sleep,' finished Mull. 'Except Thomas, who went to visit his sister.'

'Flopped into your beds alone?' asked Michael. 'Or did you have company?'

'Alone, unfortunately,' sighed Mull. 'Sir William made us promise to remain chaste until we reach France, lest God punishes us for lechery. It is very hard, which is why we are forced to drink so much ale and wine – to suppress our natural appetites.'

'I must remember that excuse for the next time *I* have a drop too much claret,' murmured Michael, fighting down the urge to laugh.

'I shall not deny myself for much longer, though,' warned Nuport, and leered at a passing milkmaid; she dropped the pail she was carrying and fled. 'It was fine when it was only going to be for a few days, but now he says we might be delayed for weeks. Well, bugger that for a lark!'

'But we took a *vow* to abstain until we touch French soil,' Mull pointed out. 'You cannot break it – not if you do not want dire things to happen to you. But I agree with one thing, though: we cannot deny ourselves for much longer, so unless Sir William takes us away soon, we might have to make our own way there.'

'Lord! That would be dangerous,' said another lad worriedly. 'We need a knight to guide us or we are likely to be dispatched by the first Frenchmen we meet.'

The squires exchanged anxious glances – all except Nuport, who scoffed his disdain for their faint-heartedness, and then informed them that if they felt the urge to take a girl they should do it and the consequences be damned.

271

'Did you know Roos, who called himself Jevan?' asked Bartholomew, changing the subject abruptly, much to Nuport's annoyance and the others' relief.

'The white-haired ancient from London?' asked Mull. 'Yes, we heard he and the scholar were one and the same, although none of us knew it before today. He was on the Lady's council, but he was an unfriendly devil, and the only person he liked was Mistress Marishal.'

'You saw them together often?'

'Just at the Quarter Day meetings,' replied Mull. 'They were kin, which explains why she did not send him packing when he pawed at her with his sweaty old hands. If it had been me, I would have punched him in the face. But she was a lady.'

'I learned a lot from observing him,' grinned Nuport. 'How to corner lasses without them realising until it is too late; how to lure them to my bed; how to snatch a grope as they pass without anyone else seeing . . . He was a master.'

'I am sure he was,' said Bartholomew to Michael, recalling Roos's unsavoury antics when they had first arrived in Clare – his near-assault of the woman sweeping the church, and then his brazen ogling of Margery. 'There was a—'

He stopped abruptly when he heard an urgent shout. It was Langelee, striding towards them with an expression that told them something was badly amiss.

'I hope he has not found the hermit dead,' said Michael uneasily.

At that moment, there was a sudden commotion in the outer bailey, which caused servants and courtiers alike to abandon their duties and hurry towards the hubbub to see what was happening. The squires were among them, leaving Bartholomew and Michael to look questioningly at Langelee.

'Weste and I had to turn back early, because his horse

went lame,' gasped the Master. 'I was just coming to tell you that I was home, when I heard Lichet and Quintone quarrelling. I joined the crowd that clustered around to find out why—'

'And?' demanded Michael sharply, as an angry roar exploded from the gathering hordes. 'What is going on? Tell us, quickly!'

'Lichet has accused Quintone of murdering Margery, and is going to hang him for it. We have to stop him, Brother, because I doubt he has proof. And once Quintone is dead . . . well, no apology will make up for such a terrible mistake.'

# CHAPTER 10

There was pandemonium in the outer bailey. Nuport was clamouring for Lichet to hurry, on the grounds that every breath Quintone drew was an affront to God and justice, and some courtiers were in obvious agreement. The servants were shocked and uneasy – Margery might have been popular, but Quintone was one of them, and they disliked the precedent that a summary execution would set.

Lichet was wearing his best cloak and a tall hat that accentuated his height, no doubt hoping to quell any objections by virtue of cutting an imposing figure. He ordered Richard the watchman to fetch a rope.

'This is my fault,' said Langelee wretchedly, as he, Bartholomew and Michael watched in horror from the back of the gathering crowd.

'Is it?' gulped Michael in alarm. 'How?'

'Weste and I met Lichet as we rode out earlier. He asked where we were going, so I said we were off to hunt for Jan the hermit – that he had probably witnessed the murders, and so will be able to identify the culprit.'

'He might, if he is still alive. But I fail to understand why—'

'Lichet now claims that the hermit *told* him Quintone killed Margery – which is a lie, because Jan is still missing. In other words, Lichet took my words and twisted them to suit himself.' Langelee's expression was anguished. '*I* put the idea of a conveniently absent eyewitness into his greedy head.'

'Hardly,' argued Bartholomew. 'He put it there all by himself.'

274

Quintone was screaming at the top of his voice, calling on God, His saints, the Lady and Albon to stop him from being murdered by the Red Devil. His choice of words did nothing to encourage Lichet to stay his hand, and the noose was around his neck by the time Bartholomew, Michael and Langelee had managed to push their way to the front of the onlookers.

'Stop!' commanded Michael with all the authority he could muster. 'You cannot hang someone without a fair trial. It is a—'

'We know how to deal with killers in Clare.' Lichet's face was flushed with excitement, and his eyes glittered vengefully as he adjusted the rope. 'We dispatch them fast, so their vile breath does not taint the air we breathe.'

'Hear, hear,' bellowed Nuport. 'He killed a gentle lady and must pay with his life.'

'No!' wailed Quintone. 'I was with Isabel Morley all that night. Ask her – she will tell you.'

He had to indicate the lady in question with his chin, because his hands were tied behind his back. She paled as heads turned towards her and opened her mouth to speak, but no sound emerged. Then she turned and fled, sobbing her distress. Quintone's face fell in dismay.

'Isabel! Come back! They will kill me unless you tell the truth. Please! I—'

His words were cut off abruptly as Lichet hauled on the rope. The Red Devil was stronger than he looked, and within moments, Quintone was kicking empty air.

'Wait!' shouted Michael, while Langelee jumped forward to tear the noose from Lichet's hands. Quintone dropped back to the ground, choking and gagging. 'The Lady wants convincing evidence before—'

'I do have convincing evidence,' snarled Lichet furiously, trying to grab the rope back from Langelee. 'But it is for her eyes only.'

Nuport powered forward with the clear intention of

275

finishing what the Red Devil had started, but Ereswell's foot shot out and he went sprawling on the ground, unable to keep his balance in his silly shoes. The squires were about to surge to his assistance when there was an almighty bellow from behind them, so loud and masterful that it brought them to an instant standstill.

'*STOP! AT ONCE!*'

It was Albon, who possessed an impressive voice to go with his impressive physique. With him were the Lady and Marishal. They processed forward, Albon clearing a path through the onlookers by dint of his haughty gaze alone – anyone in the way, courtier or servant, was treated to a pointed look until they moved. The Lady followed, leaning heavily on Marishal's arm.

'There will be no executions until *I* am certain of the culprit's guilt,' she said firmly, when she was close enough to speak without the indignity of hollering. 'After all, an apology will hardly suffice, should a mistake have been made.'

'There is no mistake,' declared Lichet, eyes ablaze with the strength of his convictions. 'Quintone slaughtered Margery and Roos, and he was seen doing it by Jan – a holy hermit, whose integrity is beyond question.'

'How do you know what Jan saw?' demanded Langelee. 'He is missing. Ergo, he cannot have spoken to you or anyone else.'

Lichet's expression was sly. 'I did not need to speak to him, because I have this instead.'

He presented a document with a jubilant flourish. It was covered in close-spaced writing.

'What is it?' asked the Lady warily.

'Something I found in the hermitage,' replied Lichet, all smug triumph. 'A detailed account of exactly what Jan saw: namely Quintone committing murder.'

'How very convenient,' murmured Michael, stunned by the transparency of the claim.

A few of the crowd, including Nuport, began to clamour for Quintone's death again, although they were a minority. Most remained silent – unsettled and uncertain.

'I doubt Jan is literate,' called Bartholomew, once the commotion had died down again. 'And even if he is, his cottage had obviously been abandoned in a great hurry. I do not see him sitting down to produce a document of that length first.'

'Of course Jan is literate,' snarled Lichet, although alarm flashed across his face that his scheme might have a fatal flaw. 'He is a religious man. How else would he read his scriptures every day?'

'I have never seen him reading,' shouted Ereswell. 'Your claims are a nonsense, Lichet, and Jan will prove it when he returns.'

'He will not return,' stated Lichet archly. 'Because Quintone has killed him as well, to prevent him from speaking the truth.' He whipped around to appeal to his supporters. 'Are you happy to let Quintone live, knowing what he has done?'

Nuport led the howl that said they were not, so the Red Devil made a third lunge for the rope. Langelee fended him off handily enough, although that would change if Lichet's allies joined the tussle. Quintone knew it, and began to sob his terror.

'Give that document to me, Lichet,' ordered Ereswell, shoving his way forward. 'I will compare the writing to yours, because I have a sample of it here.'

But Lichet was not entirely stupid, and his grin was exultant as he handed the letter over. Ereswell pursed his lips in annoyance when he saw that the two styles were different.

'He has done Quintone a serious disservice by under-estimating Lichet,' muttered Michael. 'Now the Red Devil will persist with his claims until Quintone is hanged.'

'While the real killer goes free,' Bartholomew

whispered back, 'because I suspect Quintone *was* with Isabel. Katrina told me that she carries his child but he declines to marry her. What better way to avenge herself than by refusing to provide his alibi?'

'Give me the rope, Langelee,' ordered Lichet imperiously. 'We have wasted enough time on this murderous villain.'

'Wait!' ordered the Lady irritably. 'And be quiet, while I confer with my steward.'

There followed an obedient silence, broken only by the occasional rustle of clothes as some of the senior courtiers eased forward in the hope of catching what was being said. At first, Albon was able to drive them back with his basilisk glare, but as time ticked past this grew less effective, obliging him to draw his sword. He was openly relieved when Marishal eventually stepped away from the Lady and addressed the crowd in a clear, ringing voice.

'Jan's claim must be verified before Quintone is executed,' he announced. 'My Lady is wise. God knows, I want my wife's killer dead, but we must ensure that the right culprit pays the price.'

'But Jan's claim *is* verified,' objected Lichet indignantly, and brandished the document again. 'He left written testimony of Quintone's guilt. What more do you need?'

'Execution is not a matter to be rushed,' said the Lady curtly, clearly annoyed at having her decision questioned. 'Besides, I have seen Quintone and Isabel making moon eyes at each other, so perhaps they did lie together that night. Where is she?'

There followed a brief hunt, after which Isabel was propelled forward, dragging her feet with every step, and her face streaked with tears of shame.

'Now tell the truth,' ordered the Lady harshly. 'Or you will join your lover on the scaffold.'

'He is not my lover,' gulped Isabel in a feeble attempt

at injured defiance. She swallowed hard when the Lady scowled. 'Although he *was* with me that night. But we were not lying in sin.' She flailed around for an alternative explanation when the Lady's eyes narrowed, and relief lit her face as one occurred to her. 'We were reading your new Book of Hours.'

'Of course you were,' said the Lady flatly, her acid voice cutting through the titter of amusement that rippled through the onlookers. 'And I am a fairy.'

'You "read" all night?' demanded Lichet, all open incredulity. He came to loom over Isabel in an obvious attempt to intimidate her. 'You did not part even for a moment?'

'Well, he went to fetch some ale,' conceded Isabel, her face scarlet with mortification. 'We were hot and thirsty after . . . He was gone longer than he should have been.'

'The jug was empty, so I had to broach a new cask,' squawked Quintone, pale with fright. 'But it only took a few moments. Please, Isabel! I will marry you if you tell the truth.'

Albon stepped forward, his noble visage troubled. 'You did not mention fetching ale when I interviewed you on Friday, Quintone. Why not?'

'Because I knew what you would think,' whispered Quintone, slumping in defeat as his world crumbled around him. 'But I was not gone long enough to kill anyone – just the time it takes to go to the cellar, grab a cask, roll it up to the kitchen, find a hammer to knock out the bung . . .'

He trailed off miserably when he saw what everyone was thinking – that there would have been ample opportunity to slip to the cistern and plant a dagger in the chests of two victims.

'Lock him in the dungeon,' ordered Marishal briskly. 'Lichet, Albon and Michael will continue their enquiries, and we shall assess their findings when they are all complete.'

'Mine are complete now,' declared Lichet haughtily. 'Quintone is the guilty party, and I do not need to explore the matter further. The only reason these scholars challenged my conclusions is because *they* want the reward.'

'The day after tomorrow,' said the Lady to Michael. 'Before the Queen arrives. That is when I shall decide Quintone's fate. So, if you really think he is innocent, you had better have another culprit ready or I shall have to accept Master Lichet's testimony.'

Quintone howled his innocence until he and his captors entered the Oxford Tower, and were out of earshot. Then Marishal clapped his hands, ordering everyone back to work. They went reluctantly, disquieted by what had happened and not sure what to believe. Lichet was on the receiving end of angry glowers from Quintone's friends, and there were more tears shed for Margery.

'Lichet should watch himself,' muttered Langelee. 'The servants do not appreciate outsiders accusing one of their own, and he has made many enemies today. In fact, perhaps we should go home. Clare has grown far too dangerous.'

'It is unlike you to run from trouble,' said Bartholomew, taking in the Master's wan face and unsteady hands. 'Has something happened to unnerve you?'

'Other than watching a man almost executed for a crime he did not commit?' asked Langelee archly. 'No, nothing at all.'

'And what makes you so sure that Quintone is innocent?' demanded Michael, narrowing his eyes suspiciously. 'He lied to me as well as Albon – said he spent the night with friends in the stables. Moreover, he was one of the first to arrive when Adam raised the alarm. I do not approve of Lichet's tactics, but it is entirely possible that he does have the right culprit.'

'Quintone has no *reason* to kill Margery,' argued Langelee. 'No motive.'

'How do you know?' pressed Bartholomew. 'Perhaps she tried to force him to marry Isabel. She was a good woman, and would not have condoned ungentlemanly conduct towards a vulnerable girl. Roos might have supported his kinswoman, so Quintone killed them both.'

'No one commits murder for so paltry a reason,' snapped Langelee.

'Marriage is not paltry,' averred Bartholomew fervently. 'Believe me.'

'Perhaps not,' conceded Langelee, 'but I still do not see Quintone dispatching Margery and Roos. It does not *feel* like the right solution. And you two agree, or you would not have helped me to prevent his execution.'

'I do agree,' said Bartholomew, although Michael made no reply. 'However, if Quintone is hanged, the crime will be declared solved, and all the other suspects will be deemed innocent. *That* is why Lichet wants him executed without delay – so that no one will ever accuse him, even though he is likely to be the real culprit.'

'I suppose we can continue our enquiries,' said Michael wearily, 'although I sense we will not have the hundred marks anyway. If you want the truth, I think we should spend the remaining time recruiting more benefactors. We have a few, but not nearly enough.'

'I will do that,' said Langelee briskly. 'While you see what you can find out about the murders. And at first light tomorrow, I shall resume the hunt for Jan.'

When the Master had gone, Bartholomew saw Isabel slinking past. She was older than he had first thought, and had disguised the fact with a careful application of face paints. Her clothes were too big, clearly handed down from someone else, and there was a bitterness in her expression that suggested she knew there was no good future for her, regardless of whether or not her erstwhile lover was hanged. Michael intercepted her.

'You and I have spoken twice now,' he said sternly. 'You informed me both times that you were with the Lady's other maids at the time of the murders. You lied.'

'So did Quintone,' she snapped back, unrepentant. 'He claimed he was in the stables.'

'And look where such dishonesty has taken you both – him accused of murder and you shamed in front of everyone. If you had told the truth, I might have been able to protect you.'

Isabel sneered at him. 'Oh, yes! I should have confessed that I was lying with a man. What does my reputation matter?'

'Well, nothing now,' Michael pointed out drily. 'But why him? Surely you could do better?'

'You mean one of the squires? They bed us happily enough, but they do not want marriage. And now I am in trouble, which was never a problem when Anne was here to . . . offer advice.'

'So what will you do?' asked Bartholomew, his voice more kindly than Michael's.

Isabel looked away. 'I do not know. Visit kin in the country for a few months, I suppose. Perhaps the Lady will take me back afterwards. She has overlooked these mishaps in the past.'

'Tell us what happened on the night of the murders,' ordered Michael. 'Truthfully this time, if you please.'

Isabel glared at him. 'There is no more to tell: Quintone and I were together most of the night, then he left to fetch us some ale. He *was* longer than he should have been, and he told me that he had had to broach another keg. I believed him at the time.'

'And now?'

Malice flashed in Isabel's eyes, and it was clear that more untruths were in the offing, but then she looked at Michael and thought better of it. 'He did not kill anyone. Why would he? We both liked Margery, and neither of us knew the scholar.'

'I suspect you did – it transpires that Roos donned a beard and called himself Philip de Jevan.'

Isabel gaped her astonishment. 'Truly? But they are so different – one smart with a white mane, the other scruffy and unshaven. Are you sure?'

Michael inclined his head. 'So tell us what you know about Roos.'

'He was always panting after Margery when he came for council meetings. Me and the other girls took bets on how long it would be before he cornered her alone. She hated it, so we often contrived to rescue her.'

Michael regarded her coolly. 'You did not tell me this before, either.'

'Why would I? As far as I was aware, "Jevan" was miles away, lurking in whatever hole he lives in when he is not here. I had no idea that he was a factor in Margery's death.'

'So his attentions were definitely unwanted?' pressed Bartholomew.

'Yes – she was a married woman and respectable.' Isabel gave a bitter smile. 'Not like me. But Roos was annoyingly persistent. He fawned and simpered, and would not leave her alone.'

'But she loved her husband?'

'She did. Master Marishal neglected her shamefully, but she loved him all the same.'

Armed with the new information, Michael descended on others who might have known about Roos's unhealthy obsession with another man's wife. Bartholomew helped for a while, then slipped away when he saw Katrina emerge from the hall, where she had just dined. She was carrying a basket, which he offered to carry. As they approached

283

the Oxford Tower, they heard Grisel screeching furiously on the top floor, while Quintone howled piteously in the basement.

'I hope Quintone does not carry on too long,' said Katrina. 'Grisel does not like it.'

Bartholomew felt like pointing out that Quintone would be none too happy with the situation either, but he held his tongue. Her basket was heavy, and when he tweaked aside the cover, he was astonished at what lay within: cakes, fruit, a platter of meat, bread and a flask of wine.

'I hope this is not all for the birds,' he said as he followed her up the stairs. 'It is unsuitable—'

'You think I would feed them wine? No, that is for me, although it is not something I shall ever admit to the kitchen staff. You see, I cannot always abandon my charges when meals are served in the hall, and only a fool does not take precautions to protect her stomach.'

She and Michael had a lot in common, thought Bartholomew.

'God the save Queen,' declared Grisel when they arrived, then added hopefully, 'Nuts?'

'Margery's funeral is today,' said Katrina, paring an apple into thin slices, while three pairs of eyes watched in greedy anticipation. 'I hope there is no trouble – she would not have liked it.'

'Nicholas thinks it will pass off peacefully, out of respect for her.'

'Yes, but that was probably before the Lady decreed that it should be the castle chaplain who conducts the ceremony, not Nicholas. The town will be affronted on their priest's behalf.'

'Van the bolt bring down,' declared Grisel, accepting a piece of apple. 'Queen the save God.'

'They are fellow Austins,' said Bartholomew. 'Nicholas will not mind.'

'Oh, yes, he will, and he will bray his indignation in

no uncertain terms. Heselbech will decline the "honour", but the Lady will insist, and Prior John will tell Heselbech to obey her – he has no choice, unless he wants to risk the money she gives his convent.'

Slighting Nicholas was a bad move on the Lady's part, and appeared to be deliberately provocative. 'Why would she do such a thing?' asked Bartholomew, bemused.

'Because I think she aims to end the feud by forcing it to a head,' explained Katrina. 'It will result in a skirmish, which she will win, because she has armed troops at her disposal. Once the town is defeated, she can sue for peace on her own terms, and the conflict will end.'

'But the townsfolk outnumber her soldiers by a considerable margin. She might lose.'

Katrina grimaced. 'Lichet told her she would not, and no one was there to challenge him – Marishal was drugged, Albon was investigating murder, and Lichet had given everyone else jobs to do. Prior John came to talk sense to her, but the Red Devil refused to let him in.'

'Well, Marishal is back now. Lichet's reign of ineptitude is over.'

'But the damage is done. Worse, she ordered Heselbech to preside over the rededication ceremony, too. If Margery's funeral does not ignite a riot, that insult certainly will. Still, at least she stopped Lichet from executing Quintone. I do not like Quintone, but he should not hang on evidence fabricated by the Red Devil. Besides, I am sure the murderer is Bonde.'

'Why? Have you learned something new since we last spoke?'

'No, but everyone knows that he has killed before. Besides, he is a monster and I hate him.'

She spoke with such passion that Bartholomew regarded her askance. 'Why do—'

But Katrina raised a hand to stop him. 'I have said too much already, and I can see Brother Michael down in the bailey, looking around for you. You had better go.'

Bartholomew glanced out of the window, and saw she was right. 'Please tell me what you know about Bonde,' he said quietly. 'It may help us catch Margery's killer.'

'I do not believe it will. However, I know one thing that might. It regards the priest who chanted the office of nocturns on the night of the murders . . .'

'That was Weste. Heselbech was too drunk, so Weste did it for him.'

Katrina nodded impatiently. 'Yes, I know. I heard them discussing it while the trouble with Quintone was raging – it is what set me thinking. Weste recited nocturns, Langelee had gone, Albon knelt by the rood screen and I was at the back of the chapel. But what was Heselbech doing?'

'Sleeping – Weste heard him snoring in a corner.'

'But not for long, or Albon would have complained. Our noble knight is a pious man, and would not have tolerated a lot of snoring while holy words were being uttered. Which means that Heselbech spent part of the time doing something else.'

'Or he shifted into a different position, where his throat did not vibrate so much.'

'Maybe. But there was something about Heselbech's eyes during his discussion with Weste . . . I cannot explain exactly, but you could do worse than speak to him again.'

'God the Queen save,' cawed Grisel, bobbing up and down. 'Down bring the van hold.'

Bartholomew and Michael found Heselbech in the castle chapel, kneeling by Margery's coffin. It was draped in rose-coloured velvet, and surrounded by pots of wild flowers. The muddy footprints that trailed to it from the door suggested that a large number of people had already been in to pay their respects.

286

'Her funeral is in an hour,' said Heselbech shortly, glancing up at the two scholars, but declining to rise. 'And I am ordered to conduct it, so I cannot talk now. I must prepare.'

'Do you mind taking Nicholas's place?' asked Bartholomew. 'Knowing it will cause resentment among the townsfolk?'

'Of course I mind,' snapped Heselbech. 'It is a stupid decision. Lichet's no doubt, as the Lady seems to listen to every damn fool word that spills from the fellow's mouth.'

'Perform the rite together,' suggested Bartholomew. 'Then you cannot be accused of disobeying orders, and Nicholas's pride will remain intact. It might ease the situation.'

'Or make it worse,' grumbled Heselbech. 'The town will complain that he had an inferior role, while the castle will think that he refused to let me do my duty. But it is worth a try, I suppose. If we can put on a show of unity . . .'

'It *is* worth a try,' insisted Michael. 'Or you may find yourself officiating over a brawl.'

'Very well.' Heselbech turned back to the coffin. 'Now please leave me alone.'

'Just one quick question: why did you lie about sleeping all through nocturns on the night of the murder? We know you did nothing of the kind.'

It was not quite what Katrina had reported, or what Bartholomew had told Michael, but the bluff made Heselbech's eyes widen in alarm.

'Says who?' he demanded.

'This castle is home to three hundred people,' Michael told him sternly. 'It is impossible to do anything without being seen. So what happened? You slept while Weste prayed, but then something woke you and you went outside. What was it?'

'A call of nature,' replied Heselbech shortly. 'We rarely drink to excess nowadays, so I am out of practice. *That* is what roused me. Then I came back in and nodded off again. Your witness will confirm that I was out only for the time it took me to relieve myself.'

Michael glanced at Bartholomew, who shrugged to say it was possible – Heselbech might have snored to begin with, but had fallen silent after he had made himself comfortable.

'So what did you see out there?' pressed Michael. 'Or rather, *who*?'

'A shadow,' replied Heselbech reluctantly. 'By the Cistern Tower, although I thought nothing of it at the time. Why would I? As you said, there are three hundred souls here, and there is always someone wandering about, even in the dead of night.'

'But you recognised the person, of course,' said Bartholomew, watching him closely. 'As chaplain, you know everyone here. So who was it?'

'I could not tell – just someone in a cloak. His hood was up, because it was raining, so I did not see his face. All that I can tell you is that he ran away from the cistern.'

'In other words,' said Michael harshly, 'you saw the killer and decided not to mention it. Why would you do such a thing?'

'We cannot know it was the killer,' said Heselbech defensively. 'Not for certain.'

'Of course we can.' Michael was angry and exasperated. 'Who else would be racing away from the scene of the crime at the salient time? So what more can you tell us about the villain, other than that he wore a cloak?'

'Nothing. It was only a fleeting glimpse, and I was drunk.'

'But it was definitely a man?' pressed Bartholomew.

Heselbech nodded. 'It was too large for a woman, and the gait was masculine. But he was too far away for me to notice anything else – and it was very dark.'

'But you *must* remember something useful!' cried Michael. 'This is the man who slaughtered Margery and an innocent scholar, and *you* saw him. Surely you want him brought to justice?'

'Of course I do,' snapped Heselbech crossly. 'But there is nothing more I can tell you. I wish there were – Margery was a good woman, and the castle will be poorer without her – but all I had was a quick glimpse of a cloaked figure haring away into the night.'

'Was it Quintone?' asked Bartholomew, unwilling to give up. 'Or Bonde?'

'Not Quintone – someone bigger. But I cannot talk now. I have a saint to bury.'

'He knows more than he is saying,' growled Michael, as he and Bartholomew left the chapel. 'He is holding something back.'

'Holding *what* back, though? The identity of the killer?'

'I think he is telling the truth about not seeing the man's face, but it is patently obvious that he has his suspicions about the culprit's identity – he saw enough to be sure it was not Quintone, which means he witnessed more than he is prepared to admit. I shall tackle him again later. Perhaps the funeral of one of the victims will prompt him to do the right thing.'

'There is another possibility,' said Bartholomew. 'Namely that *he* is the culprit.'

'Yes,' said Michael softly. 'It had crossed my mind.'

The parish church was packed to overflowing and the atmosphere was tense, particularly at the front of the nave, where wealthy merchants jockeyed with courtiers for the best places. There was a buzz of agitated conversation, most of it revolving around the fact that the Lady had slighted Nicholas by refusing to let him conduct a ceremony in his own domain. The townsfolk were livid,

289

and the castle people were smugly delighted, an attitude that promised to cause yet more bad feeling.

But Clare's feuding factions flew from Bartholomew's mind when he entered the church. The scaffolding had been removed from the chancel – although the nave was still full of it – allowing him his first real glimpse of the finished ceiling. It was even more glorious than he had anticipated, and all he could do was gaze upwards in admiration, until Michael brought him back to Earth with an irritable pinch.

'You are supposed to be watching our suspects and witnesses, not gawping like a halfwit,' he hissed. 'Or do you want to return home and tell our colleagues that Michaelhouse will close at the end of the year, because we failed to win that hundred marks?'

Bartholomew dragged his eyes from the splendours of Cambrug's creation, and fixed them on those who were assembling below it instead.

Albon had arrived with the squires. He removed his beautiful hat with an elegant flourish, and strode to the rood screen, his bearing regal. Paycock stepped forward with the obvious intention of preventing him from taking a place so near the front, but the squires were quick to form a protective cordon around their hero. Thomas was with them, and Bartholomew could not help but notice that the others stood closer to him than to Nuport, who alone had refused to exchange his outlandish clothes for ones that were more suitable for the sombre occasion.

Ella was with her father, whose face was pale and waxy. He was clutching her arm almost desperately, but she was more interested in nodding greetings to the people she knew. Clearly, providing filial comfort was not high on her list of priorities that day. The Lady was behind them, leaning on Lichet's shoulder for support. When Ereswell tried to speak to her, the Red Devil shoved him back, which drew smirks from the watching townsfolk, particularly Grym, who was resplendent in robes of pale green and gold that gave him the appearance of a large pear.

'The Queen will be impressed by that ceiling,' muttered Langelee, joining Bartholomew and Michael because all the wealthy merchants he wanted to target for donations were currently jostling for space in the nave, leaving him with nothing to do. 'But there are some huge cracks. You could not see them when the scaffolding was up, but you can now.'

'I asked Nicholas about those when I went to ask if he minded being barred from taking the leading role at a ceremony in his own church,' said Michael. 'He told me that they will all be filled with glue soon, so will not show.'

'*Does* he mind being publicly slighted?'

'Oh, he is furious. However, in the interests of peace, he has agreed to work with Heselbech, so let us hope his parishioners are equally magnanimous.'

Heselbech's opening speech was a masterpiece of conciliation and forgiveness, which he claimed was what Margery would have wanted. He gave it in Latin, French and the vernacular, to ensure that everyone understood, after which he and Nicholas began the funeral rite. Even so, there were angry murmurs from the castle contingent whenever they heard Nicholas's voice, and grumbles from the town whenever Heselbech spoke.

It was over eventually, and the more important members of the congregation traipsed to the chancel to see Margery interred. It was then that the brewing trouble erupted.

'Wait a moment!' cried Paycock in angry disbelief. 'That spot is where *I* am going to be buried when I die. I paid for it in advance, and I have a letter from the Bishop to prove it.'

'Lord, so it is!' muttered Nicholas, flushing red with embarrassment. 'It slipped my mind in all the turmoil of the last few days. But there is nothing we can do about it now, Paycock. Margery is here and the vault is open so—'

'But it is the best place in the entire church,' protested Paycock, livid. 'Which is why I want it for myself. I am sorry, Nicholas, but you will have to make other arrangements for Margery.'

'He will not,' said Marishal dangerously. 'She goes in the place that was promised.'

'You can have the porch instead, Paycock,' called Thomas provocatively.

'Stop it!' snapped Albon with stately authority when Paycock took an angry step forward, fists at the ready. 'This is a church, not a tavern. Behave yourselves – all of you.'

Paycock lowered his hands, but his protest was far from finished. 'You cannot allow this, Nicholas! First, they foist their chaplain on us, and now they steal our best vault. Be a man, and tell them where to—'

'Leave Nicholas alone, you,' came a waspish voice from the squint. 'And if your tomb is so important, why did you not come here earlier, to protect it?'

'Because I did not think it was necessary,' yelled Paycock. 'How was I to know that the rats in the castle would stoop so low as to steal a man's private burial space?'

'No one stole anything,' declared the Lady curtly. 'Now step aside, Paycock. Your behaviour at the funeral of a good woman is disgraceful, and you should be ashamed of yourself.'

It was one insult too many. Paycock's friends objected heatedly and the chancel was suddenly full of clamouring voices, which Heselbech tried in vain to quell. Nicholas made no attempt to help his colleague, and instead went to stand near the squint, where Anne regaled him with her opinions about the situation.

Hot words soon turned to shoves. Albon immediately whisked the Lady away, shielding her from buffets with his own body, although there was definite fear in his eyes as he did so. Most of the squires hastened to help, although Thomas was more concerned with protecting his sister. By contrast, Nuport was in the thick of the fracas and enjoying every moment of it.

Then the Austins appeared, smoothly and professionally insinuating themselves between the warring factions. John nodded to Heselbech, who hastened to resume his prayers and lower Margery into the vault. The ceremony was over quickly then, and the friars ensured that the two sides dispersed in opposite directions. Even so, it was a tense business, and they heaved a collective sigh of relief when the last of the mourners shuffled out and peace reigned once more.

'I am going to close my doors now,' sniffed Nicholas, looking around at the aftermath of the scuffle in disapproval. The floor was strewn with items that had been dropped, including gloves, hats and the occasional weapon. It was also filthy from the mud that had been tracked in from the street. 'It will take me ages to clean all this up.'

'I will help,' offered Heselbech generously. 'It will take half the time with two of us at work.'

Nicholas thanked him with a smile. 'But once we have finished, the church will not reopen until the rededication. I do not want any more mess *or* fighting in here. Besides, I still have the nave scaffolding to pull down, which can be done more safely if the place is empty.'

'I hope everyone will refrain from skirmishing when the Queen is here,' remarked Michael. 'Her ministers impose heavy penalties on those who break the King's peace.'

Then Grym waddled up, his amiable face creased with worry.

'You must come at once, Prior John. Albon has made an announcement in the market square, accusing the hermit of killing Margery and Roos. The townsfolk are outraged.'

'*Jan* is the culprit?' came Anne's voice. 'I might have known! He always was a rogue.'

'Are you sure, Grym?' asked Michael, ignoring her. 'Albon said nothing about having solved the case when he was here for the funeral, and that was only a few moments ago.'

'Probably because he did not know then what he *thinks* he knows now,' explained Grym. 'Namely that Jan's dagger was discovered in the cistern, next to the bodies. Lichet just told him.'

'But that is untrue,' objected Bartholomew. 'We never found the murder weapon.'

'I know that,' said Grym impatiently. 'But Albon swallowed the tale and acted on it, just as Lichet predicted he would. That Red Devil really is a poisonous snake, because when the story is proven to be false, no one will take any investigation conducted by Albon seriously again.'

Prior John called his weary friars to order, and although they lined up gamely enough, it was obvious that most of them had hoped to repair to the priory for a much-deserved cup of ale and a warm supper. Ex-warriors they might be, but none were in their prime, and they had reached the age where they appreciated their creature comforts.

'Some of you had better look for Jan as well,' Grym told them. 'Because Albon has just ridden off on his great white destrier with the avowed intention of hunting him down. *He* will not lynch anyone, but the squires are with him and they might. Moreover, they intend to start their search in Mayor Godeston's woods – which is another insult to the town, as they have not secured the permission of his heirs.'

294

John began to issue orders, sounding more like a military commander than a prior. 'Langelee – will you take a patrol westwards? Heselbech can ride north, Weste will search south and Nicholas must take the east. Your remit is to find Jan – do *not* engage with Albon's troops. I will stay here with a dozen men and keep the peace. And God have mercy on us all.'

There followed a flurry of activity, with some friars racing away to saddle horses, and others forming themselves into the units that would impose order on the town. When the church was empty, Nicholas locked it, then hurried to the priory stables to collect a horse himself. Within moments, Bartholomew and Michael were alone in the graveyard.

'It is a pity Nicholas decided to "improve" this place,' sighed Michael, looking up at the gleaming new stone-work. 'I have been told countless times that the town and castle were the best of friends before the restoration began.'

'Do not blame him,' called Anne from her window, and Michael grimaced. He had forgotten that she could eavesdrop on discussions outside the church as well as through the squint. 'And all was *not* peace and light anyway. The two sides have been sniping at each other for years, and anyone who tells you otherwise is a liar.'

'Do you really think Jan is the culprit?' Bartholomew asked her, although with not much hope of a sensible answer.

He did not get one. 'Yes, because he is a rogue, as I have told you before. And Quintone is innocent – he is not very nice, but he is no killer.'

Bartholomew was about to ask more when a dirty lad hurried up to him with a message from Grym. He opened it, and learned that before galloping off to hunt hermits with Albon, Nuport had trounced Adam the baker, as a punishment for making such a fuss about the prank that had seen him set alight. Grym wanted Bartholomew's help to repair the damage. To encourage him to go, Grym offered a free demonstration of how hemlock could be used to dull pain.

Bartholomew set off at once, leaving Michael to help the Austins. He was glad to be thinking of medical matters – he was a lot more comfortable with those than with murder and mayhem.

The boy conducted him to Grym's house on Rutten Row, which was like no other home he had ever visited. It had been built to accommodate a very large man. The front door was twice as wide as all the others on the street, and the furniture had been reinforced to take the additional weight. Bars had been fitted to the walls next to each chair, so that the occupant could use them to heave himself upright, and every pot, platter and bowl in the kitchen was large enough to feed ten.

'No!' gulped Bartholomew, when he saw how much hemlock Grym was about to give Adam. He did not want yet another death to aggravate the trouble that was brewing – and the dose Grym had prepared for the baker was perilously close to the amount that might prove fatal. 'We shall use poppy juice, lettuce and bryony instead.'

He expected Grym to argue, but the barber shrugged amiably and they set to work. Grym transpired to be an indifferent practitioner, but was happy to let Bartholomew do what was needed, so the baker was spared too much discomfort. When they had finished, four more patients were waiting for their services – men who had evaded the friars' patrols, and had managed to engage in fisticuffs with hotheads from the castle.

It was dark by the time they had mended everyone as best they could. Wearily, they retired to Grym's solar, where there was a roaring fire and a gargantuan feast waiting. Bartholomew accepted an invitation to dine gratefully, although he felt like an elf in the lair of a giant, dwarfed as he was by everything in the room.

It was not long before Michael arrived, ostensibly to ask after Adam, although Bartholomew was sure some innate sense had told him that good food was on offer. Yet even the monk could not match what Grym packed away, and the two of them watched in awe as four ducks, a haunch of venison, three loaves and a whole turbot disappeared into the barber's churning maw.

'And a dried apricot,' he said with a smile, holding it in the air before popping it into his mouth. 'Because all good *medici* know the importance of a balanced diet.'

'I suppose you refer to Galen,' said Michael sourly. 'The bane of my existence. Matt is always braying to me about his nasty theories. Personally, I think there was something wrong with the fellow, because it is not natural for red-blooded men to fuss about with vegetables.'

'I quite agree,' said Grym, much to the monk's delight. 'But you must eat one dried apricot every week, because it keeps the blood rich.'

Bartholomew was about to remark that he had never heard such arrant nonsense when there was a clatter of footsteps, followed by Thomas's distinctive voice, barking at Grym's servants to let him in.

'Oh,' he said curtly, when he saw Bartholomew and Michael. 'What are you doing here?'

'They are my guests,' replied Grym pleasantly before they could speak for themselves. 'Why? Is there a medical emergency?'

'An accident,' replied Thomas. 'Sir William has fallen off his horse and cracked his head.'

# CHAPTER 11

The next day was cold, wet and windy, and Bartholomew woke long before dawn, dragged from sleep by rain pounding on the roof. Langelee and Michael were already up – it was only when the downpour reached Biblical proportions that it had penetrated the physician's consciousness – and were sitting by the hearth, talking in low voices.

'You would never make a soldier, Bartholomew,' remarked Langelee. 'You would drowse right through an attack, and only stir when it was over and you had missed all the fun.'

Bartholomew yawned. 'What are you doing?'

'Discussing Lichet's claim that Albon flung himself from his horse deliberately, because he realised he had made a mistake about the hermit and could not face the disgrace of being wrong.' Michael shook his head in disgust. 'I fail to understand why the Lady does not send him packing. She is an intelligent woman, and must see he is a charlatan.'

'More warlock than charlatan,' countered Langelee. 'Word is that he has bewitched her.'

Bartholomew rubbed the sleep from his eyes. 'You did not tell us how you fared last night in your search for Jan and Bonde.'

'Because there was nothing to report,' said Langelee with a grimace. 'We found neither hide or hair of them. But I was not here when you outlined your conclusions regarding Albon. Obviously, we can rule out suicide, so was it an accident or murder?'

'He died of a wound to his head,' replied Bartholomew.

'It might have been caused by him falling from his horse, but it is equally possible that someone hit him.'

'In other words,' said Michael acidly to Langelee, 'our trusty Corpse Examiner refuses to commit himself.'

Bartholomew shrugged. 'I am no Lichet, inventing evidence that is not there.'

'When I got back, I inspected Albon's saddle,' said Langelee, 'bearing in mind what happened to poor old Talmach. But there were no suspiciously "frayed" straps. Then I assessed his destrier. It is a solid beast, trained for battle, so unlikely to shy for no reason – and even if it had, Albon was a knight who should have been able to manage.'

'Really?' asked Bartholomew. 'I thought his martial skills left a lot to be desired.'

'He was a poor warrior, but a respectable horseman,' explained Langelee. 'Which suggests to me that his death is definitely suspicious. After all, what are the chances that he should die in exactly the same manner as Talmach?'

'But Talmach's saddle had been sabotaged,' Bartholomew pointed out. 'Whereas you have just told us that Albon's was not.'

'There are more ways to make a rider fall than tampering with his tack,' said Langelee. 'And the killer is not a fool. He will know not to go a-sawing through leather a second time.'

'Murder, then,' concluded Michael. 'So who did it? The hermit, to avoid being arrested?'

Langelee grimaced. 'Even Albon should have been able to fend off that feeble specimen.'

'Bonde?' suggested Bartholomew. 'Perhaps Albon happened across *his* hiding place.'

'Or a townsman,' countered Langelee. 'They were furious when Albon invaded Godeston's woods without asking his heirs first.'

'Or a squire,' put in Bartholomew. 'Because they know

Albon's ineptitude would have got them killed in France. They admired him outwardly, but they may have harboured secret misgivings. Especially Thomas and Mull, who are no fools.'

'Albon certainly had reservations about them,' mused Michael. 'I am sure that is why he offered to find Margery's killer – he was frightened of travelling to France with a murderer in his train. He wanted his squires to be pretty angels, all adhering to his own chivalric ideals.'

'Then there is Lichet,' said Bartholomew, 'who is determined to have a hundred marks, and perhaps decided to reduce the competition to one other investigation.'

Langelee sighed. 'You two are making this very complicated, and some philosopher or other once said that the simplest answer is usually the right one. I cannot recall who he was offhand . . .'

'Occam,' supplied Bartholomew, unimpressed that the Master could not remember something so basic. 'His "razor" contends that in competing hypotheses, the one with the fewest assumptions should always be chosen first.'

Langelee snapped his fingers. 'Occam! There is the fellow! Well, in this case, I suggest that someone from the town made an end of Albon for daring to trespass in Godeston's woods. And you know what that means.'

'Not really,' said Michael, ever wary of the Master's idea of logical analysis.

'That we will never solve the crime, because we are strangers here and we do not know the people involved. I think we should cut our losses and leave. I know we want the Lady's money, but it is not worth our lives, and the town and the castle will stage a pitched battle soon. I sense it with every fibre of my being.'

'So do I, but the Austins will stop it,' said Michael. 'And if they cannot, we have faced pitched battles between opposing factions in the past.'

'But you two are my responsibility,' argued Langelee.

'And the University cannot manage without its Senior Proctor, while Matilde will be irked if anything happens to Bartholomew. Moreover, unmanly though it is to admit it, you two are my friends and I do not want you dead. Ergo, we go home today.'

'We cannot leave empty-handed,' objected Michael, dismayed. 'Michaelhouse will founder without money, and it will break my heart to see it closed down.'

'Besides, if we disappear all of a sudden, people may assume that *we* are the culprits,' Bartholomew pointed out. 'That we are fleeing the scene of our crimes because we feel the net tightening around us. It is Monday today, and the rededication is tomorrow evening. I suggest we wait until then before going – it is what we told everyone we would do.'

'Very well,' agreed Langelee, although he was clearly unhappy. 'But we must be on our guard. And we are *not* going to the ceremony. It would be too dangerous. We shall slip away the moment it starts, so that if anyone does accuse us of anything untoward, we shall have a head start. We will not be missed until it is over.'

'Now that really would look furtive,' said Bartholomew, raising his eyebrows. 'And what about Simon Freburn? Is it not asking for trouble for the three of us to travel at night?'

'I will beg a couple of sturdy friars from John,' determined Langelee. 'And Pulham, Donwich, Badew and Harweden will come with us, as they will not want to be left behind.'

'I suppose we can do that,' conceded Michael, 'if it makes you happy. So, it means we have roughly thirty-six hours to expose the killer and save Michaelhouse from an ignominious end.'

'Is that feasible, Brother?' asked Langelee tiredly. 'You had only just finished telling me how you have no proper leads to follow.'

'Perhaps not, but I still have my list of suspects, which is much more manageable now I have decided that Marishal is innocent. I know genuine grief when I see it – he did not kill his wife. That means we are down to Nicholas, the twins, Lichet, Bonde and Heselbech.'

'And John,' murmured Bartholomew, although not loud enough for Langelee to hear.

'How can it be Heselbech?' demanded Langelee impatiently. 'He saw the killer sneaking around the castle. He cannot have done that if it was himself.'

'Because he is a proven liar,' replied Michael, 'which means we cannot believe a word he says. He probably invented this hooded figure to mislead us.'

'Well, you are wrong,' said Langelee firmly. 'And the culprit is not Nicholas either. He and Heselbech are old soldiers, for God's sake.'

'Quite,' said Michael. 'So I recommend we begin our day by seeing what we can learn about the pair of them.'

'Not me,' declared Langelee in distaste. 'If you want to indulge in that sort of thing, you can do it yourself.'

'So how will you spend the rest of our time here?' asked Bartholomew. 'Convincing the good people of Clare that Michaelhouse is deserving of all their spare money?'

'No, I shall hunt for the hermit again. He is in danger as long as Albon's accusation hangs over him, because someone may decide to avenge Margery without waiting for a trial.'

'I am not sure that anyone took Albon's claims seriously,' said Michael. 'Other than a couple of squires, perhaps. But you are right. If Jan is still alive, he must be protected.'

'John will lend me a horse.' Langelee stood and began to don clothes suitable for a jaunt in the rain. 'If Jan is out there, I will bring him back.'

'Do not forget to look for Bonde as well,' Michael reminded him. 'He disappeared with suspicious haste when it became clear that the murders of Margery and Roos would be investigated properly. And of all our suspects, he is the one who has committed murder before.'

'I know,' said Langelee. 'But unless he is a complete fool, he will be long gone by now.'

Rain fell steadily as the scholars walked to the Prior's House, Langelee to beg for help in finding Jan and Bonde, and Michael and Bartholomew to ask if John had learned any more about the murders – including Albon's – while he and his friars had patrolled the town the previous night. Langelee and Michael had heard them come home at midnight, cold, wet and weary, when the inclement weather had finally driven the last of the troublemakers indoors, although Bartholomew had slept through the commotion their return had generated.

Everything dripped, and the sky was a dull, sullen grey. It was not far from the guesthouse to John's quarters, but water was trickling down the back of Bartholomew's neck before he reached it anyway. He had decided against wearing Albon's cloak that day, lest someone accused him of callousness, and his old one was wholly incapable of keeping him dry in such a deluge, especially with so many holes burned in it.

'Not a word about Heselbech and Nicholas being on your list,' warned Langelee before he knocked on the door. 'John will not let us stay here tonight if he knows you entertain suspicions about two of his friars.'

Bartholomew and Michael readily agreed. It was no time for sleeping under hedges, and they were unlikely to find accommodation anywhere else in Clare that night – not on the eve of a royal visit, when any free rooms would be waiting to receive far more important guests than mere scholars from the University at Cambridge.

They were conducted to John's solar by a servant, and arrived to find him in conference with his senior officers, including Weste and Heselbech. All looked tired and anxious. John's bald head was beaded with sweat, Weste's face was pale against his black eyepatch, while Heselbech gnawed nervously at his lower lip; his filed teeth had made it bleed, but he was too agitated to notice.

'Albon's accident is a bad business,' said the Prior unhappily. 'It will aggravate the trouble between castle and town for certain.'

'How do you know it was an accident?' asked Michael shortly.

John regarded him stonily. 'Because a murder will result in a full-blown riot. It was an accident, Brother, and you had better tell everyone so or face the consequences.'

'No,' said Michael firmly. 'You tried that with Godeston, and it did not work. Of course Albon was murdered. Two knights dead in almost identical circumstances within a few weeks of each other? How could it be anything else? And everyone in Clare will know it.'

'No, they will not,' insisted John. 'And it *did* work with Godeston. We created enough uncertainty to make some folk stay their hands. We can do the same with Albon.'

'It will fail, John,' Langelee told him kindly. 'And may even make matters worse – people will assume you are concealing the truth for sinister reasons of your own. We know your intentions are honourable, but can you be sure that others will think the same?'

John rubbed a hand over his shiny pate. 'Then how do *you* suggest we avert trouble? Because you must see that if any more people die, it will create rifts that may never heal.'

'We avert it by exposing the killer,' said Langelee, making it sound simple. 'Michael and Bartholomew will continue their enquiries here, while I hunt for Bonde and the hermit again.'

'Albon died in Godeston's woods,' said Bartholomew, aware that the friars were not as friendly as they had been a few days before. He supposed they had been discussing the murders, too, and had mooted the possibility that the more recent ones were down to strangers. 'Some of you were nearby when it happened, looking for Jan. Did you see anything that might help?'

'I am afraid not,' replied John, 'because I ordered all the patrols to stay well away from that particular area, lest it annoyed Godeston's heirs. Is that not so, men?'

Everyone nodded except Weste, who frowned. 'I thought *you* were over in that direction, Heselbech. Not *in* the woods, but skirting around the edge.'

Heselbech bared his pointed teeth in an uneasy smile. 'Yes, but all I saw was the squires bringing Albon out, slung over his horse like a sack of flour. It was unkind – he would have hated the indignity of being toted through the town with his arse in the air. I imagine it was Thomas's idea: the others would have fetched a bier.'

'Do you think one of them brained him?' probed Michael.

'Thomas might have,' replied Heselbech promptly. 'He is a sly devil, and it is a pity he did not inherit his mother's goodness. Then Nuport is a vicious brute, not above biting the hand that feeds him. The others are decent lads, though.'

'With your permission, Father Prior, I would like to help Langelee,' said Weste, changing the subject abruptly. 'I enjoyed myself yesterday. It was good to be in the saddle again.'

'You may go, but not until we have discussed our final arrangements for the Queen's visit,' said John. 'It will not take long. Lord! I hope we can impose some order on the town before she arrives. It would be a great pity for her to see us at each other's throats.'

Everyone trooped out so that John and Weste could get on with it, and once in the yard, Heselbech began to organise the brethren into peace-keeping patrols.

Judging by the number of volunteers, this duty was a lot more desirable than staying behind to pray, cook and clean.

'They may have taken holy vows,' remarked Langelee, watching Heselbech's arrangements approvingly, 'but they will always be warriors at heart.'

'And that is what worries me,' said Michael unhappily. 'Especially in Heselbech, who would have kept quiet about being near the spot where Albon was killed if Weste had not spoken up. I imagine Weste will be biting his tongue now.'

'Rightly so,' said Langelee harshly. 'He should have kept his mouth shut.'

Michael's eyes narrowed. 'Why do all ex-soldiers possess this reckless need to protect each other? It is a dangerous game, Langelee, because while you and John may once have been comrades-in-arms, you do not know these others. You may be defending killers.'

'They are good men whose aim is to prevent a blood-bath,' argued Langelee stoutly. 'God's teeth! This place is worse than Cambridge. I cannot imagine why you were so keen to visit it, Bartholomew. Matilde was wrong when she claimed it to be a lovely town.'

'Perhaps it was different when she was here,' said Bartholomew. 'She had a—'

'I will escort you to the castle,' interrupted Langelee briskly. 'And when you have finished, get the watchmen to bring you back. Do *not* wander about on your own. Is that clear? I cannot have Fellows slaughtered on my watch. It would be acutely embarrassing.'

Langelee was right to be cautious, as the town felt distinctly uneasy that day. Michael declared a pressing need to attend to his devotions, so they went to the church first, only to find that prayers were being held in the graveyard, as Nicholas had declared the building off limits until the rededication. The vicar's performance – a startlingly brief one – was indifferent, and all the way through, Anne could be heard waylaying passers-by with demands for gossip and treats.

'I should become an anchorite,' muttered Langelee. 'It is a very comfortable existence.'

'You would hate it,' predicted Bartholomew. 'And I suspect she does, too. She may claim she is content, but she is a gregarious soul who misses the bustle of castle life. It was a cruel punishment to inflict on such a person. Almost worse than death.'

Nicholas came to pass the time of day with them when he had finished officiating at his makeshift altar, although his eyes strayed constantly to the door, where workmen emerged with planks and coils of rope. Bartholomew wanted to peep inside, to see more of the nave without the scaffolding, but Nicholas informed him curtly that it was out of bounds to everyone, with no exceptions.

A combination of unease, exasperation and concern for his College's future turned Michael brusque, and he addressed the vicar curtly.

'You are still on our list of suspects for Roos and Margery's murders,' he said, ignoring Langelee's irritable sigh for having ignored his opinion on the matter. 'Your alibi is Anne, but she was almost certainly asleep at the time, so we are disinclined to accept it.'

'She *was* awake!' cried Nicholas. 'And I did not kill anyone. Why would I? And more to the point, *how* could I? I would have had to get past the castle guards, and I never did. Ask them.'

It was a good point, but Michael pressed on anyway. 'You dislike the Lady for interfering with church business – not only trying to oust you from your spacious home to a poky cottage, but telling you which services you may or may not conduct.'

'It *is* irksome,' conceded Nicholas, 'but I would not

resolve the matter by murdering her steward's wife and a scholar who was a stranger to me.'

'Roos was not a stranger – you knew him as Philip de Jevan.'

Nicholas blinked. 'It is true, then? A rumour to that effect is currently racing through the town, but I assumed it was nonsense. However, it is irrelevant to me, as I had nothing to do with his death, regardless of who he happened to be. Anne! Tell Brother Michael that I was saying nocturns when Margery Marishal and Roos were killed.'

'I have already told you that he was,' came the anchoress's irritable voice. 'No doubt you think I was dozing. Well, for your information I would *love* to sleep all night, but my cell is right next to the chancel, and I challenge *you* to slumber through the racket priests make when they are about their holy business. I was awake, and Nicholas was here.'

Michael's troubled expression suggested that he did not know what to believe. When there was no reply, Anne changed the subject to one she considered more interesting.

'Isabel Morley came to me last night, begging for my help. It is a pity that I am stuck in here, because the stars are favourable for my hook today. A few scrapes would solve all her problems.'

'Or compound them,' countered Bartholomew.

Uncomfortable with such a discussion, Michael and Langelee went to corner Paycock, to see if he might be persuaded to donate funds to a College in exchange for Masses for his loved ones, while Nicholas hurried to oversee the work in the nave. Bartholomew was left to talk to Anne alone.

'Now Isabel will have to swallow herbs to save herself from the perils of childbirth,' the anchoress went on grimly. 'Tansy and pennyroyal. And those are dangerous.'

'Yes, they are,' agreed Bartholomew, hoping it was not a hint for him to wield a hook in her stead. He thought about Mistress Starre in Cambridge, and her potions for desperate women. Then he recalled the many times he had been summoned when things had gone catastrophically wrong.

'Although not nearly as dangerous as having a baby,' Anne flashed back.

'Isabel is not worried about giving birth,' Bartholomew countered, although even as he spoke, he was aware that Isabel's reasons for wanting a way out of her predicament were really none of his business. 'She just wants to end an inconvenient pregnancy.'

Anne snorted her disdain. 'Spoken like a true man! It should be *our* decision what happens inside our own bodies, and all I can say is that if I had to choose between childbirth and a hook, I know which I would pick.'

'Fortunately for you, it is not a decision you will ever have to make.'

'I hope you are not implying that I am too old for motherhood,' said Anne frostily.

'I am implying that you are unlikely to conceive when you are walled up in a cell. Unless you happen to know some very unusual manoeuvres.'

The moment the words were out, Bartholomew wished he could retract them, sure she would not appreciate risqué remarks. She had proclaimed herself to be a holy woman, after all. Thus he was relieved when there came a peal of extremely lewd laughter.

'I must remember to tell Nicholas that one!' she crowed. 'It will amuse him greatly, and he needs to smile, as he is altogether too anxious about the ceremony tomorrow.'

When Bartholomew had finished with the anchoress, he found Michael and Langelee waiting for him by the porch door. They left the churchyard, Bartholomew

309

acutely aware that Langelee kept his hand on the hilt of his sword as they went. The atmosphere along Rutten Row was fraught, with clots of townsfolk gathered on every corner, muttering darkly. Any castle inhabitant rash enough to venture out was subject to torrents of abuse, although the three scholars received nods and even the occasional smile.

'It is because Bartholomew helped Adam,' explained Grym, who was emerging from his house as they passed. 'I told everyone that Adam would have died without our cooperative efforts, so you University men are in favour. Of course, it may mean trouble for you at the castle. They have taken against Adam now he refuses to bake for them again.'

Bartholomew, Langelee and Michael hurried on, and when they reached the barbican, it was to find that the number of guards on duty had been doubled, while archers lined the walkways and battlements. Langelee inspected the precautions with an approving eye.

'You must still be on the lookout for treachery from within, though,' he warned Richard the watchman. 'There must be any number of servants with links to the town, and you can never be sure of their loyalty.'

'Marishal ordered all those expelled,' sighed Richard. 'Which was ill-advised, as they will swell the enemy's ranks, and might mean the difference between victory and defeat for us. I do not know how we reached this pass – not when relations between us have been cordial for centuries.'

'The Austins will prevent a battle,' said Langelee soothingly, although Richard's worried expression suggested that he did not think they would succeed. 'But I am going to hunt for Bonde and the hermit today. Do you have any advice about where to look?'

'The hermit could be anywhere, but Bonde has kin in Stoke by Clare, which is three miles east along the river. Do not go alone, though. He is dangerous.'

'So am I,' declared Langelee with a grin. 'But I take your point. Weste has offered to come.'

'A good warrior,' acknowledged Richard. 'But Bonde is low and crafty, so watch yourself.'

Langelee inclined his head and strode away. Michael sketched a benediction after him, and muttered a prayer that over-confidence would not see him hurt.

'I seriously doubt that anyone will attack a fortress,' Michael told Marishal crossly a short while later. He was irked because the portcullis had been down and the guards were under orders to lift it no more than a fraction, compelling any visitors to crawl inside on their hands and knees. The squires had been watching, and there had been a good deal of merriment at the monk's expense. 'Your precautions are excessive.'

'Are they?' Marishal had declined Lichet's sleeping potion for the second day running, and was the Lady's steward once more, radiating confidence and efficiency, although his eyes were sunken and his face drawn. 'The town hates us, and now they have murdered Albon.'

'How do you know it was them?' asked Michael. 'Do you have evidence that—'

'I do not need evidence to confirm what any rational man can see,' interrupted Marishal shortly. 'Albon was our mightiest warrior, and his execution is a direct challenge to our authority.'

'But the townsfolk *liked* Albon because he was taking the castle's rowdy young men away to France,' argued Bartholomew. 'None of them wanted him dead.'

'Have you found out what happened to him yet?' asked Michael, when Marishal made no reply. 'We tried to question his squires last night, but Lichet ordered them to pray in the chapel instead.'

'Then speak to them now,' said Marishal briskly. 'Come.'

He led the way to the knight's frilly pavilion, which now had a distinctly lopsided appearance. The squires stood rigidly to attention at intervals around it. Each wore a peculiar black cloak shorn off just below the shoulders, which meant the rest of their finery was sodden and all were shivering – except Thomas, who had opted for a sensible oiled garment that covered him to the knees.

'I cannot credit that they *still* believe what Thomas says about courtly fashion,' murmured Michael, shaking his head in disgust. 'I have encountered some dim-witted lads in my time, but none as stupid as this horde.'

The squires did not respond when he informed them that he wanted their accounts of what had happened to their hero, and only stared blankly and annoyingly ahead. Bartholomew wondered if that was Thomas's doing as well, or if the mute guard of honour had been their own idea.

Before the monk could repeat himself, Marishal intervened, his voice tight with anger. 'Answer him, you silly young fools,' he snarled. 'And when he has finished, you can divest yourselves of these absurd clothes, don sensible ones, and report to me in the hall. There is much to do before the Queen arrives, and I will not have idlers in my castle.'

'Our duty lies here,' replied Nuport defiantly. 'It is what Sir William would have wanted.'

'But he is not in a position to say so, is he,' snapped Marishal. 'So you now have a choice: make yourselves useful or get out of Clare. And that includes you, Thomas.'

'Me?' blurted Thomas, startled. 'But I am a—'

'Your days of indolence are over,' interrupted Marishal harshly. 'As from today, you will either work or starve. It is your choice: I do not care one way or another.'

And with that, he turned on his heel and strode away. The slight spring in his step suggested that he had enjoyed the confrontation, perhaps because he thought that

Margery would have approved of his taking a firm hand at last. The squires gazed after him in dismay, although several folk who had overheard the exchange nodded their approval. They included Ereswell, who evidently thought it was the scholars' influence, as he touched his purse in a way that indicated another donation would be coming Michaelhouse's way.

'Right,' said Michael, rubbing his hands together as he turned to the shivering young men. 'To business. You were with Albon when he fell: tell us exactly what occurred.'

'A townsman threw a stone that killed him,' said Nuport sullenly, resentful at the unpleasant direction his life was about to take. 'In other words, he was murdered. And we plan to avenge him.'

'Did you see a missile lobbed?' asked Bartholomew.

'No,' replied Nuport shortly.

'Then did you see a townsman running away shortly afterwards?'

'No,' said Nuport a second time, and scowled. 'The culprit kept himself hidden. But it does not matter if we spotted him or not, because it is obvious what happened.'

'Really,' said Michael flatly. He addressed the others. 'Now tell us what you *know* to be true, not what your lurid imaginations suggest.'

'Sir William ordered us into a fan formation, so as to cover more ground,' obliged Mull. He looked miserable – what little hair he had left was plastered to his head, while water dripped from his gaudy clothes. 'Which meant that we grew further apart with every step we took, so none of us were with him when he . . . But Thomas was the closest. Tell him, Tom.'

Thomas spoke reluctantly. 'I heard him yell, and I assumed he had caught the hermit – he was an excellent tracker. But I arrived to find his horse grazing and him lying senseless next to it.'

313

'So he might have fallen off by accident,' said Bartholomew, who was a dismal rider, and quite often toppled out of his saddle for no reason apparent to those who were good at it.

'It is possible,' replied Thomas. 'But highly unlikely. He was a knight.'

'What did he shout, exactly?'

'It sounded like "you", but I cannot be certain. However, I can tell you that none of us knocked him from his seat, because the offender would have galloped away afterwards, and I would have heard the hoofs. But there was just the yell and the thump of him hitting the ground. It means the killer was on foot, whereas we were all mounted.'

'Did you meet anyone else in the woods?'

All the young men shook their heads.

'They were deserted,' said Mull. 'Probably because it was raining, and they are not a very nice place to be at the best of times. They are terribly boggy and full of brambles.'

'My father can go to the Devil,' announced Thomas suddenly and angrily. 'I am not scrubbing floors – I am going to find that damned hermit. He stabbed my mother, and I bet he killed Sir William, too, thus destroying our one chance to escape this hellhole and do something interesting.'

'Jan did not kill your mother, no matter what Albon thought,' said Michael quietly. 'Indeed, I suspect he is also dead – dispatched to prevent him from revealing what he saw as he prowled the castle that night.'

At that point, they were joined by Ella. She had been inside the pavilion with Albon's body, listening to the discussion secretly, but now she emerged to stand with her brother.

'The monk is right, Tom,' she said softly, squeezing his arm to make him look at her. 'We have known Jan all our lives and he has never hurt a fly. Besides, he is terrified of horses – he would have gone nowhere near Sir William's great destrier.'

'Well, Matt?' asked Michael, when the twins and the squires had trooped away. Most went willingly, more than happy to exchange their outlandish clothes for dry ones, although resentment was in Thomas's every step and Nuport was patently livid. 'What do you think?'

'They did not kill Albon,' replied Bartholomew. 'He represented a life of adventure and they wanted him alive. Of course, Nuport does have an unpredictable temper . . .'

The rest of the day was taken up with interviewing as many castle residents as would speak to them. It was a frenzied business. Not only was Michael acutely aware that he only had until the following evening to earn the hundred marks, but everyone was frantically busy with preparations for the royal visit. Lichet had failed to implement Marishal's meticulously planned timetable while he had been in charge, which had lost them three full days. Marishal was determined to make up for lost time, and drove everyone relentlessly. No one had time to talk, and their answers were necessarily terse. Bartholomew grew increasingly frustrated with their lack of progress, and, desperate to achieve something useful, he went to re-examine the cistern.

It had been eerie the first time he had visited, when others had been with him, but it was far more so on his own. It was full of echoing drips, and the lamp he carried did not penetrate very far into the darkness. Splashes and ripples came from every direction, and the near-constant rain of the last few days had caused the water to rise dramatically, so that the pavement where he had examined the bodies of Margery and Roos was now at least six feet below the surface.

He did not stay long, and escaped outside with relief.

315

He met Richard at the top of the stairs, and used him to conduct one or two experiments regarding how far sound carried from the bailey to the cistern and vice versa, although it told him nothing to help with the murders.

Dusk came, but there was no let-up in Marishal's preparations, even though it was clear that everyone was exhausted. He seemed to be everywhere, issuing directions in a non-stop torrent. He was an exacting taskmaster, and if a job was not done to his satisfaction, the culprit could expect a dressing-down and an order to do it again. Whether it was a genuine desire for perfection, or an attempt to distract himself from his grief, Bartholomew did not know.

The squires and Ella suffered most under his blistering tongue, and there was a general consensus among servants and courtiers alike that this should have happened years ago. As an act of petty retaliation, the twins managed to stage one or two small pranks, but people were too busy to be amused at their victims' discomfiture, so they soon desisted.

Bartholomew was about to return to Michael, when there was a commotion outside the Oxford Tower. Marishal emerged from it with Quintone, who was grinning triumphantly. People stopped what they were doing to stare.

'I am releasing him,' Marishal announced in ringing tones. 'I have been reflecting on Lichet's claims all day, and I have decided that he is wrong. He is so determined to have the reward that he has overlooked certain basic facts.'

'Are you sure?' asked Thomas, dangerously bold. 'Because if you are mistaken, you are freeing the bastard who murdered our mother and your wife.'

'I am sure,' replied Marishal. 'For two reasons. First, the ale barrel *was* empty when the servants retired to

316

bed, and a new one *had* been brought from the cellars during the night. And second, Isabel *did* entertain Quintone in her bed, because three witnesses now attest to it – witnesses who told the truth once threatened with dismissal if they did not.'

'Perhaps you are right, but you still cannot let him go,' persisted Thomas stubbornly. 'Not until the Lady gives her permission. She may not agree with your assessment of the situation.'

'And Lichet certainly won't,' murmured Ella.

The look Marishal shot them was enough to make both flinch. 'Do you think I would make this sort of decision without consulting her? We discussed it at length, and she concurs with me.'

A murmur of satisfaction rippled through the onlookers. All were delighted that Lichet's investigation had been assessed and found lacking – and relieved that their Lady had finally started to question his opinions.

'So who did kill Margery?' called Ereswell.

Before Marishal could reply, there was a groan, and the pavilion suddenly collapsed in on itself, the sodden material too heavy for the inexpertly assembled poles. The squires regarded the mess in dismay, although the smirk exchanged between Thomas and Ella suggested that they had seen it coming, and may even have helped it along.

'I want that cleared away at once,' Marishal told them shortly. 'And Albon taken to the chapel. Can you manage it alone, or shall I send a scullion to supervise?'

'You should,' said Quintone, revelling in the role of a man who has been publicly acquitted. 'Because they are useless.'

Not surprisingly, one man was particularly outraged by Quintone's release. Within moments, Lichet hurtled from his quarters in the Cistern Tower, where Ereswell had taken great pleasure in breaking the news to him, and stormed across the bailey towards the steward.

'Are you mad?' he demanded. 'To release the villain who slaughtered your wife?'

'Quintone is not the culprit,' replied Marishal, eyeing him in rank disdain. 'I should have known that the only way to find the truth was to investigate for myself.'

'Quintone is guilty,' said Lichet between gritted teeth. 'And you will look a fool when you are forced to recant.'

The argument swayed back and forth, and Quintone prudently took the opportunity to slink away, no doubt afraid that Lichet would win, and he would find himself with a noose around his neck again. Bartholomew went in search of Michael and found him in the hall, grazing on the cakes that had been set out for the few retainers who had time to eat one.

'Did you learn anything helpful today, Brother?' Bartholomew asked. 'I did not, other than that Margery and Roos could have screamed at the tops of their voices from inside the cistern, and no one would have heard them, not even if they were right by the door.'

Michael shuddered. 'That is an unpleasant thought – that they howled for rescue as the killer attacked them in that terrible place. And I am afraid the only new thing I discovered came from Isabel Morley, whose father was a soldier.'

'Not an old comrade of Prior John and his cronies?'

Michael nodded. 'Apparently, something happened to make the whole lot of them decide to end their brutish lifestyles, although he never told her what. Unfortunately, he is dead now, so we cannot ask him.'

Bartholomew frowned. 'So this is useful how, exactly?'

'It proves that the Austins are men with dubious pasts, and three of them – John, Nicholas and Heselbech – are on our list of suspects. When we know what they did to necessitate them taking holy orders, we may have answers about the murders.'

Bartholomew regarded the monk uncertainly. 'I am not sure that follows. And besides, how can we find out, if the source of the information is dead? By asking the friars themselves? I do not see that taking us very far.'

'It will not. However, according to Isabel, John kept documents about it, so we shall engage in a little burglary tonight. Or rather, you will. I shall stand outside and keep watch.'

'No,' said Bartholomew, unwilling to employ that sort of tactic against ex-warriors with deadly pasts. 'You can do it while *I* keep watch.'

Michael shot him a sour look, but his reply was drowned out by the burgeoning quarrel between Marishal and Lichet.

'You will *not* have the Lady's hundred marks,' Marishal was informing him sharply. 'Not for Quintone. If you want the money, you must produce a credible suspect and proper evidence – not the brazen forgery you presented yesterday.'

'It was not a forgery,' declared Lichet, outraged. 'It was genuine. But I would not expect a man of your low intellect to—'

He stopped speaking abruptly when Marishal took a threatening step towards him. Realising that he had gone too far, he bowed curtly and stalked away. Several courtiers gave a spontaneous cheer, but it petered out when Marishal glared at them as well, and they hastened back to their duties before he could load them with more.

'So who is the killer?' asked Michael, catching the steward's arm as he strode past. 'Have you solved the case, and I am wasting my time by persisting with my questions?'

Marishal smiled thinly. 'I have my suspicions. All I need is the evidence to prove them.'

'We have suspicions, too,' said Michael. 'And I am afraid they include your son and daughter, who cannot prove where they were at the time of the murders. Are they on your list, too?'

Marishal regarded him steadily. 'If Thomas and Ella conspired to murder Margery, I will hang them myself. You seem shocked, Brother. Why? Margery was my wife, and I loved her more than life itself. The twins . . . well, she gave birth to them, but neither looks like me.'

Michael raised his eyebrows in surprise. 'Is this a new thought, or one that has been festering for a while?'

Marishal glanced around to ensure that no one else could hear. 'Ever since they were born, which was roughly nine months after Roos had been especially persistent with his attentions. She never said anything, but I knew my wife . . .'

Bartholomew regarded him askance. 'Are you saying that Roos was their father?'

Marishal shrugged and looked away. 'It would explain why they have yellow hair, just like his when he was younger. Mine was – and still is – black.'

'Margery had gold hair,' Bartholomew pointed out gently. 'Perhaps they got it from her.'

Marishal's face was impossible to read. 'Well, we shall never know, now that both of them have gone. The Lady wants to see you, by the way. She is in the Oxford Tower with her birds. Do not keep her waiting.'

'He *does* think they killed Margery,' murmured Michael as they hurried across the bailey. 'Lord! I should not like to be in his shoes. He must be a soul in torment.'

'Is he? There is no love lost between him and the twins, and he told us himself that he was too busy to bother with their upbringing. Now we know why: the sight of them was a constant reminder of the suspicion that his beloved had been with another man.'

The Lady was disappointed when Michael confessed that he had made scant progress with his enquiries that day, although it was difficult to converse, as Grisel was flying between his perch and her head, which she found far more entertaining than anything the monk had to say. Katrina was laughing, a sound that the bird mimicked with disconcerting accuracy. Bartholomew found himself wondering why no one had offered to marry her. She was pretty, intelligent and had a sense of humour, which were advantages that far outweighed her lack of money, in his opinion.

'I had high hopes when Master Donwich bragged to me about the Senior Proctor's superior investigative talents,' the Lady scolded. 'And I was sure Michaelhouse was going to have my hundred marks. Indeed, it was why I offered such an enormous sum – so it would go to a worthy cause. You have let me and your College down, Brother.'

'Do not give up on me just yet,' said Michael stiffly, disliking the censure. 'These matters cannot be rushed. And if you do not believe me, then look at Lichet: he made a precipitous announcement, and now he must live with the ignominy of being wrong.'

'Yes and no,' said the Lady. 'He continues to swear that the document he found is genuine, and has promised to bring additional proof of Quintone's guilt tomorrow. So you must hurry, Brother, because I do not want him to have my money.'

'Why not?' asked Bartholomew, bemused. 'I thought you liked him.'

'Of course I do not like him,' barked the Lady impatiently. 'I keep him at my side because my courtiers had started to take my largesse for granted, and I wanted to shake them out of their complacency by feigning fondness for a grasping stranger. It worked – my people have never been more attentive. I shall be able to dismiss the Red Devil soon, and good riddance.'

Bartholomew stared at her, stunned that she should be so calculating. Then he reconsidered. She had ruled a large estate for decades, which she could not have done without a certain degree of ruthlessness. Old and ailing she might be, but there was still a core of steel in the Lady of Clare.

'Bring the hold down van,' suggested Grisel. 'God save the Queen.'

'So what will you do now?' asked the Lady. 'Other than wait to see if Master Langelee can bring the hermit and Bonde home to answer your questions?'

'We have a number of leads to follow tonight,' lied Michael, ducking as Grisel swooped past his tonsure. 'And a wealth of information to sift through. Be assured, madam, we are a long way from being defeated yet.'

'Then let us hope your hubris is not misplaced, because I want this killer caught before the Queen comes. I intend to enjoy her arrival and the rededication ceremony without worrying about murderers popping out of the woodwork to spoil everything.'

'Down the van bring hold,' said Grisel. 'Ha ha ha.'

The Lady stroked the bird's soft feathers. 'Perhaps we should have let you investigate instead, Grisel. You have more sense than all the rest of them put together.'

It was pitch dark by the time Bartholomew and Michael ran out of people to interview, and with a sense of bitter frustration, they began to make their way back to the priory. Lights spilled from the houses they passed, and as many owners were wealthy enough to afford glass, the two scholars could see inside to where families and servants were settling down for evening meals and entertainment. Paycock was holding forth to a table of nodding men in one, his fierce expression suggesting that whatever he was saying, it was nothing temperate.

Bartholomew was uneasy, wishing they had done what Langelee had ordered and asked the watchmen to escort them back to the priory. Michael had demurred, wanting to use the time to discuss what they had learned without interested ears flapping.

'And what *have* we learned?' Bartholomew demanded, weariness turning him curt. 'Nothing, despite our best efforts. And now time has run out, because we leave tomorrow. We have failed – failed Michaelhouse, failed the Lady, and failed Margery and Roos.'

'Not yet,' said Michael stubbornly, although exhaustion edged his voice, too. 'There are a few hours left to us, and I am not giving up until every last one of them has expired. Besides, we might strike gold tonight, when you search John's house for these documents. I hope he does not keep a servant, because we cannot afford to have you caught.'

'I will not be caught,' replied Bartholomew firmly. 'For the simple reason that I am not going. *You* can do it. Do not worry – I will distract John while you are inside.'

'But I do not trust you to keep him busy,' objected Michael, alarmed. 'And what if it entails squeezing through a window? I might get stuck, and where will that leave us?'

'In a very embarrassing position,' acknowledged Bartholomew. 'So you had better stick to using doors instead.'

The monk did his best to persuade him to change his mind, but Bartholomew was adamant, so in the end it was Michael who crept through the shadows to the Prior's House. The physician went to the refectory, where he gave the Austins an account of the investigation to date.

Unfortunately, as he had little new to report, it was difficult to keep their attention, and he lost count of the times that John stood to leave, obliging him to gabble like a lunatic to make him sit down again. By the time a lamp went on in the guesthouse – the sign that Michael was back – Bartholomew was ready to weep with relief.

'You are no raconteur,' said John, eyeing him balefully. 'I could have summarised your discoveries in a few short sentences, and your loquaciousness does not say much for the University's rules on brevity.'

Bartholomew aimed for the door, eager to be away from him, but bumped into Heselbech on the threshold. The chaplain was returning from the castle, where he had just recited evening prayers.

'Weste and Langelee are still out,' he reported worriedly. 'I hope they have not run into difficulties. They should have been home by now.'

'If they are not back by morning, we shall send out a search party,' determined John. 'There is no point in doing it now, not in the dark. Shall we pray for their safety?'

He led the way to the chapel, leaving Bartholomew to return to the guesthouse alone. The physician's head ached from tension and his hands shook. He opened the door to their room, where he saw that Michael had washed, shaved, changed into a nightgown, and set his damp clothes by the fire to dry.

'Oh, I see,' he said heavily. 'You finished your search ages ago, but did not light the lamp until you felt like it. That was unkind.'

'I forgot,' lied Michael airily. 'But we both wasted our time, I am afraid. I did find the documents, and they *were* about past misdeeds, but they pertain to illicit relationships with married women – it seems the Austins sired half the children in the county before swearing their vows of chastity.'

Bartholomew was disgusted that he had put himself through such an ordeal for nothing. 'I suppose it explains why they are so keen to redeem themselves with pious behaviour, but you are right – the discovery does not help us.'

'I did find one thing of note, though,' the monk went on. 'A recent letter from Margery, in which she expressed a wish to leave a large manor to the priory and promising to amend her will accordingly. Unfortunately, she died before she could do it, which makes it unlikely that the Austins killed her – including Nicholas, who was to have been paid a princely sum for drafting the deed of transfer.'

'Then why did they not tell us?' demanded Bartholomew, exasperated.

'Probably because none of them realise how close they are to the top of the list,' sighed Michael. 'I imagine they would have done, if they had.'

'Nicholas did,' argued Bartholomew. 'You told him.'

'Yes,' acknowledged Michael. 'But I have a feeling that he dislikes me as much as I dislike him, so he is perfectly happy for me to waste my time barking up the wrong tree. He is the kind of man to care more about spiteful vengeance than catching a killer.'

'Well, look on the bright side,' sighed Bartholomew. 'Our suspects are now down to four: Bonde, Lichet, Thomas and Ella. We shall concentrate on them tomorrow. Or were you telling the truth when you informed the Lady that you had plenty of leads to follow tonight?'

'We had one,' said Michael gloomily. 'The documents in John's house. So let us pray that one of us has inspiration about how to proceed before morning, or your earlier gloom about us letting everyone down may transpire to be prophetic.'

# CHAPTER 12

It was still raining the next day – their last in Clare – although not as hard. It was, however, falling on already sodden ground, so there were muddy puddles everywhere, while the river was a swift brown torrent. Bartholomew had neglected to put his clothes to dry the previous night, so had to force his feet into wet boots, while his cloak was cold and damp around his neck. He looked longingly at Albon's, but decided it was not worth the risk.

He and Michael ate a hasty breakfast, both anxious about the fact that Langelee and Weste were still missing. Michael eyed the Master's empty bed anxiously.

'I hope no harm has come to him. I imagine Talmach and Albon thought they could look after themselves, but look at what happened to them.'

Bartholomew agreed. 'He is an experienced soldier, but that is no defence against slyly slashed saddle straps and devious ambushes. Let us hope that he and Weste just lost track of time, so were forced to camp. Regardless, I think we should go and look for them.'

'I do, too.' Michael stood purposefully. 'So pack our belongings: we leave as soon as we have tracked them down. I shall be sorry to miss tonight's ceremony, not to mention the last chance to win a few more benefactors, but Langelee is right – none of this is worth our lives.'

'And the killer? Or have you given up on solving the case?'

'I fear we must, much as it pains me to say it. There is no time to work on that *and* ride out to look for the Master.'

326

They shoved their belongings into saddlebags, then hurried to the stables to ready their nags. Prior John saw what they were doing, and came to voice his own concerns about the missing men.

'It would be better if we went to look,' he said, nodding at Heselbech to make the necessary arrangements. 'We will bring them back – and hunt for Bonde and the hermit at the same time.'

'We can manage, thank you,' said Michael shortly. 'We are—'

'We know the area, you do not,' interrupted John. 'I shall lead the search myself, while Heselbech minds the priory. We will find Langelee, I promise. And if he and Weste are in trouble, then we are far better equipped to deal with it than you two. No offence intended.'

'Stay here and hunt killers instead,' suggested Heselbech slyly. 'I am sure you would like one last chance to win the hundred marks.'

'It is kind of you to offer,' said Bartholomew coolly. 'But we would rather go ourselves.'

'Please,' said John, reaching out to pull the reins from the physician's hands. 'I know you were at the Battle of Poitiers, and that you are a highly accomplished warrior, but hacking down an enemy in hand-to-hand combat is not the same as following their scent through unknown territory. Let us do it. It will be safer for all concerned.'

There was a brief tussle over the bridle, but Bartholomew yielded in the end, knowing that John spoke the truth: the friars *were* better equipped to mount the kind of hunt it would take to find two men who might be anywhere. However, that did not mean he was happy about abrogating the responsibility to comparative strangers, and it was with a sense of deep unease that he watched John begin to choose the horses he wanted to take.

'Why did you not tell us that Margery planned to leave

327

you a manor in her will?' asked Michael, whose expression was equally troubled. 'It would have been helpful to know.'

'Because she died before she could make her wishes legal,' explained John, his eyes and most of his attention on the stables and their equine counterparts. 'So now it will never happen – it is irrelevant.'

'It is not irrelevant,' countered Michael. 'For two reasons. First, it means that you are unlikely to have killed her, on the grounds that you would have waited until the affidavit had been signed—'

'I hope you did not have any of *us* on your list of suspects,' said John indignantly, horses forgotten as he glared at the monk. 'We might have gone to war in the past, but we are in holy orders now, and we take our vows seriously. If I had any inkling that you thought otherwise, I would not have extended our hospitality to you these last few days.'

'And second,' Michael went on, unfazed, 'it may be a motive for Margery's murder – that someone did not want the manor to come to you, so killed her to prevent her wishes from being implemented. Thomas and Ella, for example, who may want the property for themselves.'

'But they did not know what she intended,' argued John. 'No one did, other than her and us. Indeed, I cannot imagine how *you* found out. She did not even confide in her husband, lest he tried to persuade her to leave it to the twins instead.'

'He would not have done that,' averred Michael. 'He does not like them very much.'

'No one does, but they are his flesh and blood.' John's eyes widened in sudden alarm. 'Or does he fear they are cuckoos in the nest? Lord! I hope he does not remember that I had a mop of golden curls as a youth – much like Thomas's, in fact. I never went anywhere near Margery, but . . .'

'No,' said Michael flatly. 'He does not think the twins are your doing.'

'Thank God for that! It would have been difficult to disprove after all these years.'

John turned back to his duties without further ado. Once the horses were saddled, he picked the roughest and meanest-looking friars to ride out with him, while the remainder were instructed to prevent trouble in the town or guard the priory against attack.

'We have done our utmost to remain aloof from this feud,' he told them soberly, 'but mobs are fickle, and one side may decide to assault us instead. You must all be on your guard.'

And then he and his ruffians were gone in a business-like rattle of hoofs on cobbles. All were armed with knives and cudgels, and as their functional oiled cloaks covered their religious habits, they looked more like a military fighting unit than a group of clerics.

'He is right, Matt,' said Michael, seeing the physician was still far from happy about leaving Langelee's safety in their hands. 'They are better at this than us, and I know they will do their best for him. Besides, I cannot say I am averse to having one final crack at catching the killer.'

'I suppose we can corner Lichet, Thomas and Ella again,' said Bartholomew without enthusiasm. 'Bonde is unavailable, so they are the only suspects left.'

'To the castle, then,' said Michael.

They had grown so used to the town's rancorous atmosphere that they barely noticed it as they hurried towards the fortress. They heard snippets of conversation as they went, chief of which was outrage that it was to be Heselbech, not Nicholas, who would preside over the rededication ceremony that evening. There was also anger that the church was to remain closed until then, even though the last of the scaffolding had now been taken down. Bartholomew stopped to exchange brief greetings with Grym, but then wished he had not when he saw Paycock was with him.

'The castle has no right to prevent us from seeing the fan vaulting *we* paid for,' Paycock snarled. 'All *they* bought was a south aisle that no one wants.'

'But closing the church was Nicholas's idea,' Grym pointed out reasonably. 'The castle had nothing to do with it.'

'Oh, yes it does,' argued Paycock. 'Anne told me that Nicholas made that decision purely because he is so hurt about being barred from his own ceremony. And his disappointment is understandable. He has been planning the affair for months, and all of a sudden, the *castle* chaplain is named priest in charge.'

'Cambrug should arrive this morning,' said Grym in a transparent effort to change the subject to something less contentious. 'He will be delighted by all we have achieved since he left – his lovely fan vaulting covered in beautiful geometrical artwork. He will jump for joy.'

'Then he will have to do it in the graveyard,' muttered Paycock venomously. 'Because *he* will not be allowed inside the church either.'

Bartholomew left Grym trying to placate him, and hurried to catch up with Michael. They reached the castle, and found it on full alert once again, although the monk was spared from crawling under the portcullis a second time, as their arrival coincided with a delivery of fish, so they were able to walk in behind the cart.

'What time do you expect the Queen, Richard?' asked Bartholomew as they passed through the gate. The watchman wore his Sunday best, and had shaved for the occasion.

'Probably this afternoon,' replied Richard, his eyes bright with excitement. 'She will want to be here well before the ceremony, so she can change into finery that reflects the importance of the occasion. Her coronation robes, perhaps. They would be suitable.'

'What if she is late?'

'Heselbech will wait until she is ready.'

'That will not please the town,' warned Michael. 'Indeed, it is asking for trouble.'

Richard smiled. 'They will not mind delaying for her. She is the Queen.'

'Yes, but she will stay in the castle,' Michael pointed out. 'Not in the town. Ergo, you may find they are less accommodating than you expect.'

Richard frowned his concern, and they left him pondering the matter, for which Bartholomew was grateful. Complacency was the last thing they needed while Clare was in such turmoil.

The first person they met inside was Quintone, who had also dressed with care. He held himself with lofty dignity, clearly intending to make the most of the fact that he had been unjustly accused. He obeyed orders slowly, and brayed about claiming compensation for the suffering he had endured. A few servants nodded support, but most were unsettled by his defiance and contrived to keep their distance. Nuport watched him with a dark and brooding expression.

'You court danger with this rash display of mutiny, Quintone,' cautioned Michael. 'It would be wiser to chalk it down to experience and forget about it.'

'I was innocent and the Lady freed me,' declared Quintone haughtily, then sneered in Nuport's direction. 'So *he* can sod off. He cannot touch me now, and nor can that stupid Lichet.'

'Are you willing to bet your life on it?' asked Bartholomew. 'Because that is effectively what you are doing with your imprudent swaggering.'

Quintone spat his disdain for the advice. 'They dare

not come anywhere near me! They will have to stay in Clare now that Albon cannot take them to France, but they will bully *me* no longer. I shall stand up to them, just like Master Marishal did yesterday. And I will win.'

Bartholomew was far from sure he would. 'It is not—'

'And while we are talking, let me take this opportunity to inform you that *Bonde* is the killer,' announced Quintone with great confidence. 'I was too frightened to mention it before, but my brush with death has made me a stronger, bolder man. Bonde is a lout, and I know it was him who killed Mistress Marishal and the scholar.'

'You do?' asked Michael warily. 'How? What is your evidence?'

'I do not have any – not as such. But talk to Katrina de Haliwell if you do not believe me. She will tell you what kind of man Bonde is, because she knows him better than any of us. She was all for taking him as a husband at one point, but then she changed her mind. Ask her why.'

'You do it, Matt,' ordered Michael, once the servant had strutted away. 'I shall see what Ella and Thomas have to say, although I doubt either of us will learn much of value. Meet me here as soon as you have finished. And hurry – we do not have a moment to lose.'

Bartholomew was not averse to seeing Katrina again, although he was aware that time was of the essence. He hurried to the Oxford Tower, and began to climb the steps, taking them two at a time. He arrived to find Grisel contentedly chewing the head off a wooden soldier, while Blanche and Morel ripped a doll to shreds between them.

'God save the Queen,' muttered Grisel. 'Hold the bring van down.'

'I decided to do what you suggested and keep them amused,' said Katrina, smiling delightedly. 'It worked!

There has not been a fight all morning. The Lady will have to give you the five marks she promised now, because you *have* cured them.'

'Unfortunately, she is also concerned about the amount of expensive food they eat,' said Bartholomew wryly. 'And I have done nothing to reduce that. I imagine they will consume just as much wine, fruit, cakes and meat as they have always done.'

Amusement sparkled in Katrina's eyes. 'Perhaps they will. My charges have always had healthy appetites, and I would not see them go hungry.'

Bartholomew was reluctant to waste valuable time discussing what she did with the supplies she claimed from the kitchens, so he turned the subject to Bonde instead. 'You said he was your chief suspect for the murders at one point, but you never did explain why. Will you tell me now?'

Katrina's face darkened. 'I would rather not.'

Bartholomew pressed on anyway. 'Quintone mentioned that you considered marrying Bonde at one point, but then you thought better of it. Please tell me what you learned about him, Katrina. If you are right, and he did kill Margery, it may help us see that justice is served.'

Katrina raised her eyebrows. 'I did not need to "learn" about Bonde, because I knew what kind of man he was the moment I set eyes on him. And I never – not once – entertained the notion of making him my husband. Quintone is wrong.'

'So what kind of man is Bonde?'

Katrina's face hardened. 'He expects women to fall at his feet because he is a favourite of the Lady. When they resist his so-called charms, he forces them to give him what he wants.'

'Did he force you?'

She smiled rather vengefully. 'He came up here once to try, but he reckoned without Grisel, who bit off part

333

of his nose – you may have noticed the scar.' She stroked the parquet fondly.

'Nuts,' said Grisel immediately, and Katrina obliged.

'Did you tell the Lady?'

Katrina shook her head. 'She will hear no bad word against Bonde, because he is useful to her – more so than his victims. And I like living here.'

Bartholomew was thoughtful. 'Is he one of the reasons why Anne's services were in such high demand? For Suzanne de Nekton, for example?'

Katrina met his gaze levelly. 'Yes – he raped her. Then he slashed her face and threatened to kill her if she told anyone what he had done. *That* is why she did not want to bear that particular child, and why Anne agreed to relieve her of it.'

'But Suzanne confided in you anyway? Or in Anne?'

'She did not "confide" anything – the ordeal drove her out of her wits for several hours, during which she babbled uncontrollably. Stupid Bonde underestimated the impact his vicious assault would have on his victim.'

'Then why was he not called to account for it?'

Katrina's expression was bitter. 'Because the Lady did not believe it of him. Thomas did, though. He cornered Bonde and issued a warning – not justice in the courts, but meted out quietly in the dark one night. Bonde has behaved since, but we all worry about what will happen when Thomas leaves.'

Bartholomew had difficulty seeing Thomas in the role of gallant protector, but supposed it explained why so many women seemed to like him. Moreover, Thomas – with Ella – claimed to have driven Suzanne's unsympathetic father from Clare, so perhaps he *had* taken it upon himself to wreak revenge upon the people who had most hurt the girl.

'Everyone thinks Suzanne was sent to a nunnery,' he said reflectively. 'But you told me that she is in "a place where she is safe from ruthless men" which is not quite the same. Where is she?'

'I do not know what you are talking about,' declared Katrina, holding his eyes in a way that made it obvious that she was lying.

'The paroquets cannot possibly eat everything you take from the kitchens,' he said patiently, 'while you usually dine in the hall, so have no need for additional food. These baskets of meat, wine and fruit are for Suzanne – you are hiding her. So I repeat: where is she?'

There was a moment when he thought Katrina would deny it again, but then she sagged in resignation. 'Very well, then. Come with me and inspect Bonde's pretty handiwork.'

Although Bartholomew knew he should spend every moment of his last few hours in Clare helping Michael, he still followed Katrina down the stairs. One part of his mind told him that his 'discovery' regarding Suzanne might allow him to name Bonde as the killer for certain, but the saner part told him that all it would actually do was underscore what he already knew – that Bonde was a vicious and unlikeable tyrant who abused his position of power.

Katrina had been clever in her choice of hiding place, and had selected a tiny chamber built into the thickness of the Oxford Tower wall. Its entrance was concealed by a heavy tapestry, and there was no reason for anyone to know of its existence, although when she unlocked the door and pushed it open, he saw a window that would be visible from the outside: a keen observer would know a room was there. It was very dark inside, as the shutter was closed, although he could make out plenty of cushions and rugs.

'What are you doing?' came a shocked voice, making Bartholomew and Katrina turn quickly. Ella was behind them. 'We swore to keep this a secret, and you bring a *stranger* here?'

'A physician,' said Katrina. 'He wants to know about Bonde – what kind of monster he is.'

'You could have just told him,' snapped Ella. 'You did not have to show—'

'We need help, Ella,' interrupted Katrina quietly. 'The Lady was ill last month, and we all thought she would die. What will happen to Suzanne when she does? Her heirs will be all over the castle, and Suzanne will be found. We *must* plan for the future.'

Before Ella could reply, footfalls sounded on the stairs below. It was Quintone, bringing treats for 'the birds'. Quickly, Katrina bundled Bartholomew and Ella into the room and locked the door behind them. In the darkness, they heard her thank Quintone politely and send him on his way. His footsteps receded.

A moment later, Katrina unfastened the door and joined them inside, while Ella strode to the window and opened it, allowing daylight to flood into the room. It illuminated a young woman, huddled in one corner like a frightened rabbit. She had long silky hair and her skin was as soft as peaches. The scar across her cheek was not as terrible as Bartholomew had anticipated, although it had still been an unconscionably cruel thing to do. Unsurprisingly, Suzanne was very fat – Katrina stole her vast quantities of food, while proper exercise would be all but impossible in the cramped little chamber.

'This is Doctor Bartholomew,' Katrina told her brusquely. 'One of the scholars who has been exploring what happened to Margery. You must tell him about Bonde. I am fairly sure that her murder can be laid at *his* feet, and it is time to end his reign of terror.'

'Bonde did not kill her – Quintone did,' countered Ella, clearly furious with Katrina for breaking their trust. 'My father and the Lady were wrong to pronounce him

336

innocent, because he has always been an arrogant pig. Just look at the way he seduced poor Isabel.'

'It was "poor Isabel" who did the seducing there,' said Katrina wryly. 'And Master Marishal has now established that three separate people saw Quintone lugging ale from the cellars. Ergo, he has an alibi. But Bonde does not. Go on, Suzanne. Repeat what you told me just an hour ago.'

Suzanne spoke with obvious reluctance, all the while casting petrified eyes in Bartholomew's direction. 'Bonde was lurking by the Cistern Tower just after nocturns that night. I saw him through my window. It was dark, but I would know his silhouette anywhere.'

Bartholomew went to the window. It afforded an excellent view of the cistern door, much better than the one from the birds' room above, because that window was glazed – theirs was distorted by imperfections in the glass, while Suzanne's view was clear and unimpeded.

'Why were you awake at such an hour?' he asked.

'Because I have slept badly ever since . . . I saw Bonde just a few moments after Katrina and Sir William Albon went into the chapel for nocturns.'

'Albon,' muttered Katrina in disgust. 'What a wicked waste of an eligible bachelor! Now I shall have to start looking all over again.'

'What was Bonde doing?' Bartholomew asked Suzanne.

'He went to the cistern door, and then I lost him in the shadows. A short while later, I saw him creeping away.'

'Was this "short while" long enough for him to have gone down the stairs, killed two people, and climbed back up again?'

'Yes,' whispered Suzanne. 'I believe it was.'

'Then why did you not mention it sooner?' demanded Bartholomew, exasperated. 'If you were afraid to speak to Michael, Lichet or Albon, why could you not have

337

told Katrina or Ella? They would have ensured it reached the right ears.'

'Because any investigator worth his salt would have demanded words with me directly,' replied Suzanne miserably. 'And rightly so, when a man's life depends on it. But people here hate me – they think it is *my* fault that Anne is in an anchorhold. I cannot face them.'

'Did you see anyone other than Bonde, Albon and Katrina?' asked Bartholomew.

'Lots of folk. Margery, who took refreshments to those who worked all night; Roos, who we all called Jevan – I saw him go through the cistern door; Quintone and Isabel frolicking together; two Austins and a scholar, who entered the chapel; Jan the hermit, who was following Bonde; Richard the watchman, who did a few laps around the bailey to stretch his legs as is his wont . . .'

Which explained why Richard had not mentioned Bonde disappearing at the salient time, thought Bartholomew – he had been wandering about alone himself. Had Richard been afraid that *he* might be accused of the murders if he could not prove his whereabouts for every moment of that fateful night? Or had he kept quiet out of loyalty to a man who stood watch with him? Or was it simple expediency, as Bonde was not only the Lady's favourite henchman, but a violent criminal who had already evaded charges of rape, murder and assault?

'. . . Ereswell went to the Constable Tower for some early business with Marishal,' Suzanne continued. 'And I think Lichet left his quarters at one point, although I cannot be sure. It was too dark to see him properly.'

Bartholomew rubbed his eyes tiredly, feeling the solution to the crime slip further away with every name that fell from her lips. He and Michael would never identify the killer in the allotted time left now, and he was sorry that Michaelhouse was going to lose its last chance of survival.

Katrina was more interested in solving a different problem. 'We need help, Ella. You and Thomas cannot keep everyone distracted with pranks indefinitely. It has been eighteen months now, and it is obvious that you are running out of ideas, because your japes are becoming increasingly stupid, annoying or dangerous.'

'Yes, I know,' acknowledged Ella ruefully. 'We *have* resorted to desperate measures of late – such as encouraging the squires to wear silly clothes.' She glanced at Bartholomew. 'And setting Adam the baker alight when he was ordered to clean all the rooms on this floor. Thank God he was a thief, and we were able to divert him with a silver box filled with hot embers.'

'It will be more difficult than ever now that no one is going to France,' Katrina went on. 'And it is only a matter of time before bored squires come up here to poke about in a tower that we have so far managed to keep them out of.'

Ella was silent for a moment, then became decisive. 'Then he must mend Suzanne's face,' she said, nodding at Bartholomew. 'And when she is whole again, we will find her a nice husband in some remote village. My mother's pearls will be her dowry.'

'I cannot repair her now,' said Bartholomew, aware of Suzanne's growing alarm at the plan. 'It is eighteen months too late. But I can take her to someone who will teach her how to disguise the mark.'

Matilde championed their town's prostitutes, where disfiguring injuries were not unusual from vengeful or drunken customers, so she had no small experience with women like Suzanne. Moreover, she would offer far more sensible advice than the girl was getting from her well-meaning but misguided friends.

'Good,' said Katrina in relief, before Suzanne could voice her reservations. 'It is settled then. She will go to the University with the scholars when they leave.'

'*Your* future is bright,' Ella informed Suzanne bitterly. 'Unlike ours. Katrina will wither away up here with her birds, while I will be married off to another elderly suitor. It is a wretched shame that Albon is dead, because I was looking forward to Paris. So was Thomas. He does not want to be the Lady's steward when our father dies.'

'Then go anyway,' suggested Katrina, as though it was nothing to pack up and decant to another country. 'What do you have to lose? However, I most certainly will not "wither away" up here – Master Grym smiled at me the other day, and he is a kindly soul.'

'And too fat to make a nuisance of himself by demanding his conjugal rights at every turn,' mused Ella. 'Yes, you could do worse than an amiable and wealthy barber.'

His mind churning, Bartholomew ran to find Michael, although he had been far longer than they had planned, and the monk was not waiting at the agreed rendezvous. Unfortunately, no one was able to tell him where his friend might have gone.

'Try the kitchens,' suggested Nuport snidely. 'Where the food is kept.'

His cronies sniggered. They had been put to work toting blankets to the palace from the laundry, and their revenge for being forced into such menial work was to drop their loads 'accidentally' in the mud. Then Nuport's pugilistic face darkened, and Bartholomew turned to see Quintone strutting towards the gate. The servant was still in his finery, and there was defiance in his every step. Marishal was behind him, his face dark with anger.

'Come back!' the steward roared. 'How dare you walk away while I am talking to you!'

Quintone turned slowly and with deliberate insolence. 'Things are going to be different from now on, Marishal,' he called back challengingly, 'because I am not taking orders from anyone in here – the place where I was very nearly murdered.'

'Then you are dismissed,' retorted Marishal shortly. 'Now get out of my sight.'

'I was going anyway,' declared Quintone insolently. 'I will fare far better in the town than in a castle ruled by an old woman and her monkey.'

Marishal did not dignify the insult with a reply, and only turned on his heel and stalked inside the Constable Tower, slamming the door shut behind him.

'Quintone goes too far,' remarked Mull, watching the servant swagger away. 'I have no great love for Marishal, but no minion should cheek the steward.'

'He stole my hat last night,' growled Nuport, his brutish face harsh with anger. 'I tried to grab it back, but he danced away with it, laughing. And *I* do not believe he is innocent of murder, so he had better stay out of my way, or I shall give him something to remember.'

The other squires murmured their approval, and Bartholomew hoped Quintone would have the sense to moderate his behaviour before he burned too many bridges. He resumed his hunt for Michael, and eventually learned – from Thomas, who was sweeping the stables, resentment in every stroke of the broom – that Lichet had taken the monk to the cistern not long before.

'Doubtless to view some clue that everyone else has missed,' sneered Thomas. 'But I went down there with Ella on Saturday, and there was nothing to see. Ergo, whatever Lichet has "discovered" will be something he has planted himself.'

'I just met Suzanne de Nekton,' said Bartholomew. 'You have been—'

'So what?' demanded Thomas, immediately defensive. 'Is it a crime to keep someone safe in a room that no one else is using?'

'I was about to commend your courage and compassion,' said Bartholomew quietly. 'And to ask if your mother knew what you had done?'

Some of the bristling rage drained out of Thomas, and he shook his head. 'She would have told my father, who would have ousted Suzanne on the grounds that her accusations reflect badly on Bonde. The Lady thinks Bonde can do no wrong, you see, so her faithful steward must share her opinion. My father has always been her creature.'

Bartholomew disagreed. The steward might be loyal, but he was his own man, and it was a pity the twins disliked him, because he was sure they could have worked together to devise a solution that did not entail Suzanne being locked in a tiny cell, living in constant fear of discovery and eating herself into an early grave.

'My mother was a fool,' Thomas went on bitterly. 'She knew what Bonde was like, but insisted on being nice to him, thinking to repair his bad nature with gentleness. What she should have done was use her influence to get him banished. It was ultimately *his* fault that we lost Anne.'

'I suppose it was,' acknowledged Bartholomew, thinking of the chain of events that had led to the nurse becoming an anchoress. 'Combined with the shocked reactions of Suzanne's father and the Austin friars.'

'Yes, their sanctimonious outrage did not help.' Thomas sighed. 'My mother did her best with herbs and practical advice for the girls that fell into trouble after Suzanne, but she could never match the service that Anne provided.'

Bartholomew thought it was just as well, but it was not the time for such a discussion, so he hurried to the cistern instead. Thomas followed, although to escape his sweeping duties, rather than from a desire to be helpful. Bartholomew reached the door and tried to open it, but it was shut fast. He turned to scowl at Thomas, wondering

342

if the twin had lied about Michael and Lichet as part of some new prank.

'They are unlikely to have locked themselves inside. What are—'

'Well, they must have done,' interrupted Thomas shortly. 'Because I saw them go in, but I did not see them come out again – which I *would* have noticed.'

'Would you? Why?'

Thomas shrugged slyly. 'Because they are two men who annoy me, and so would benefit from being the butt of a jape.' He rolled his eyes with exaggerated weariness when he saw the expression on Bartholomew's face. 'A harmless one, so do not look so worried.'

But Bartholomew's concern was not for Thomas's petty plans to settle scores, but because he was suddenly assailed by the conviction that all was not well. He kicked the door, then charged at it with his shoulder, but it did not budge and all he did was bruise himself. He glared at Thomas, who was watching with folded arms and an irritating smile.

'Will you help me?' he demanded testily. 'Michael might be in danger down there.'

'From Lichet?' Thomas laughed derisively. 'If your friend can be bested by a low specimen like that, then shame on him. But wait here. I will send my father to you with the key.'

He sauntered away whistling. Agitated, Bartholomew kicked the door again, but the wood was unusually thick, and all he did was add stubbed toes to his sore shoulder. He persisted, though, until he heard an angry voice a few moments later.

'There is no need to damage castle property,' snapped Marishal, shoving him out of the way, key in his hand. 'This door was freshly painted last week.'

'The Queen will not notice a few scuffs,' retorted Bartholomew, and squinted up at the sky, trying to gauge the time. 'I suppose she will arrive at any moment now . . .'

'She is not coming,' said Marishal sourly. 'A messenger arrived an hour ago, to say that she has been delayed by floods. Tonight's ceremony will have to proceed without her.'

'Then the squires have not yet heard the news,' remarked Bartholomew, glancing to where Nuport and his friends had finished lugging blankets, and were trailing to the outer bailey with shovels; they dragged their feet, clearly hating the humiliation.

A vengeful expression flitted across Marishal's face. 'I must have forgotten to mention it to them.' He inserted the key and made a moue of annoyance. 'It is *not* locked. Whose idea was it to haul me from more important duties on a fool's errand? Yours, or my idiot son's?'

'If it is not locked, then open it,' ordered Bartholomew curtly.

Marishal obliged, and Bartholomew saw that the door had been fitted with a mechanism that allowed it to be firmly secured from the outside – a tiny lever that slotted discreetly into a groove in the wall, which could be released by a quick twist of the handle.

'There,' said Marishal. 'Although I do not know why you could not have done it yourself.'

'Because I did not know how,' retorted Bartholomew, feeling he could come to dislike the steward. 'And why would you install such a thing anyway? It is simply begging for someone to be shut inside – especially with pranksters like your twins around.'

'Lichet put it in, after a leak saw us ankle-deep in mud for months,' explained Marishal. 'It prevents the door from bursting open when the water in the cistern reaches bailey height. The ground here is boggy now, so you can imagine what it is like when the cistern overflows.'

344

Bartholomew was growing angrier with every word the steward spoke. 'Then why did no one tell us about this sooner?' he cried. 'It is possible that the killer trapped your wife and Roos inside by deploying the thing. And now Lichet – a suspect for the murders – is down there with Michael.'

Marishal's eyes narrowed. 'Then I suggest we go and make sure all is well. And if the Red Devil does transpire to be the beast who stabbed Margery . . .'

With mounting trepidation, Bartholomew began to follow him down the steps, but they had not gone far when he heard the door slam shut. He scrambled back up again, only to discover that Lichet's device had slipped into place. The door was closed, and no amount of shoving and kicking would make it budge. They were trapped.

'Damn!' muttered Marishal. 'The wind must have caught it. Thank God the Queen is not coming today. It would have been very inconvenient – not to mention embarrassing – to be stuck down here when she arrived.'

'*Did* the wind catch it?' asked Bartholomew uneasily. 'Or did someone shut it on purpose?'

'Well, it was not Lichet – not if he is already down here. But I suspect it was the wind. If the door slams hard enough, the mechanism does drop into place of its own volition. I have seen it happen before. I told Lichet to fix it, but it seems he forgot.'

'Hey!' bellowed Bartholomew, thumping the door with both fists for good measure. '*Help!*'

'Save your breath. The only folk working in the inner bailey today are the cooks, and they are too far away to hear you.'

Bartholomew knew, from the experiments he had conducted with Richard the previous afternoon, that this was true. The door was unusually thick – understandably so, given that it was intended to keep the bailey from flooding – and he had not heard the watchman yell from inside, even when he had pressed his ear to the wood.

'But there *must* be a way of opening it from within,' he said agitatedly. 'Otherwise, the system would be fundamentally flawed – not to mention dangerous.'

'Well, it was Lichet's design, so what do you expect?' shrugged Marishal. 'I did suggest he include a way for someone to escape, should they inadvertently be locked in, but he said no one would be that stupid. Shall we see what he has to say about it now?'

It was not an easy descent for two reasons. First, because Marishal held the only lamp, and he was not very good at shining it in such a way that both of them could see. And second, because Bartholomew felt his apprehension grow with every step he took. On the upside, they did not have far to go, as the water had risen so much that it had reached the uppermost of the eight doors.

'Michael?' he shouted, taking the lantern and ducking through it. 'Where are you?'

'Matt!' came the monk's voice warningly. 'Go back! Lichet is here.'

Lichet was indeed there, standing a few feet away holding a crossbow. The sight was too much for Marishal, who surged forward with a howl of rage, clearly of the opinion that Lichet with a weapon proved that he was Margery's killer. He barrelled past Bartholomew, and had almost reached his target when he skidded in the wet. He fell, and his momentum carried him clean across the slick pavement and into the water beyond. He disappeared with a splash and was gone.

There was a shocked silence. Then Bartholomew ran to look for him, almost losing his own footing in the process, but the water was black and empty. A sinister ripple on the surface showed that a strong current was

346

running, and he could only suppose it had dragged the hapless steward away.

'Forget him and stand with your friend,' ordered Lichet, brandishing the crossbow.

It was then that Bartholomew saw Michael. The monk had been forced to walk further around the inside of the cistern, to the point where the pavement tapered abruptly from a wide viewing platform to a narrow service ledge. It was too thin for his princely bulk, so he held himself rigid, terrified that he would slip and share the steward's fate.

'Do it, Bartholomew,' hissed Lichet, taking aim. 'I will not tell you again.'

But the physician baulked, knowing that once he was there, he and Michael would be doomed for certain – Lichet would shoot one of them, and have plenty of time to reload before the other could counter-attack. Their only hope was to remain apart, forcing Lichet to divide his attention. He stood carefully, but made no attempt to do as he was told.

'So you are the culprit,' he said heavily, talking in the hope of gaining a few moments to devise a way out of their predicament. '*You* stabbed Margery and Roos.'

'No!' shouted Lichet agitatedly. 'As I have been explaining to this stupid monk, I have killed no one. Charer the coachman was an accident – he was drunk when he came down here, and he fell. You saw for yourselves how easily it can happen when Marishal did it. It was over in a flash.'

'So you carried his body to the river,' surmised Michael. His voice was unsteady. Of all the ways there were to die, drowning was the one that held the greatest fear for him. 'Why?'

'Why do you think?' snapped Lichet. 'Because I live upstairs, and I did not want to be accused of his murder. Too many people resent the favour the Lady shows me, and they would have used Charer's death to do me harm. So I took him to a place where he would be found quickly, and then decently laid to rest. It did no harm.'

'On the contrary – it did a very great deal of harm,' argued Bartholomew, assessing the distance between him and Lichet with a view to launching an assault. He might have managed on a dry floor, but not on one that was so treacherous. 'It led castle folk to assume that Charer was murdered by townsmen.'

'I know,' acknowledged Lichet sullenly. 'But it is not my fault that they are ignoramuses. Now stop blathering and walk towards Michael. At once!'

'If you are innocent, why are you threatening us?' asked Bartholomew, standing his ground.

'Because *he* asked the Lady what she was doing on the night of the murders.' Lichet glared at Michael. 'And she told him that she read all night – alone. So I had no choice but to entice him down here with the promise of answers. I did not want to kill anyone, but now I have no choice.'

'In other words, he lied,' called Michael. 'He has no alibi.'

'Yes, I lied, but that does not make me the killer,' Lichet shot back. 'Yet you would have accused me any-way, and I have no way to prove my innocence.'

'So why *did* you lie?' asked Bartholomew.

'Because no one would have believed the truth,' replied Lichet wretchedly. 'Which is that I was sound asleep all night, and only woke when Adam raised the alarm. And of course I was one of the first on the scene – I had the least distance to travel.'

'Then we shall help you prove it,' coaxed Bartholomew. 'We can—'

'It is too late,' cried Lichet desperately. 'Because now I have threatened to kill you, and there is the small matter of Marishal's death to explain.'

'But that was not your fault,' persisted Bartholomew. 'He fell – we all saw it.'

'It does not matter – folk will claim it is murder because I failed to fish him out.' Lichet's expression turned haunted. 'Unlike Charer – I splashed about for an age in the hope of saving him.'

'Why were you down here together at all?' asked Bartholomew, more to keep him talking than for information.

'I saw him totter through the upstairs door, so I followed him to make sure he came to no harm.' Lichet shook his head bitterly. 'It was an act of compassion – simple, honest concern for a fellow human being. I asked what he was doing, and he said he had come to fish! The man was a drunken sot, and his friends should have minded him better.'

'There is still hope for Marishal,' said Bartholomew quickly, as Lichet raised the bow again, his eyes full of fear and despair. 'He—'

'There is not! Besides, if he dies, the Lady will appoint me as her permanent steward. The post is hereditary, but I cannot see her wanting Thomas.'

'No,' conceded Bartholomew. 'But you have not killed anyone yet, so—'

'I saw Margery and Jevan . . . I mean *Roos* together the night they died,' blurted Lichet, and ran a trembling hand over his face. 'I have mentioned it to no one else, because *I* wanted to be the one to solve the mystery. Roos was angry with her, and she was trying to calm him down. I imagine she invited him here to make peace.'

'Probably over the letter she sent to Cambridge,' surmised Bartholomew. He glanced around. 'Although it is a curious place for an assignation—'

'He liked it here,' said Lichet hoarsely. 'God knows why. She probably chose it to appease him.' He took a firmer grip on the bow. 'But I must go. I cannot miss the Queen's arrival.'

'Wait!' cried Michael, as Lichet aimed at Bartholomew. 'We can help—'

'No!' barked Lichet. His voice shook – he was not a natural killer, and was clearly appalled by the situation in which he had found himself. 'You will betray me. You already know my qualifications from Bordeaux are bogus. You will tell the Lady, and she will send me packing.'

'We will not,' promised Michael desperately. 'And I can award you a degree from Cambridge if you like. It is easily done – a few strokes of a pen and a stamp of the Chancellor's seal.'

'You will renege on the offer the moment you are free. Besides, I have it all worked out. I shall blame Quintone when your bodies are found – and earn another hundred marks for solving the mystery of *your* deaths.'

Bartholomew forced himself not to flinch as Lichet's finger tightened on the trigger. Then there was a sudden splash, and a hand shot from the water to grab the Red Devil's ankle. It was Marishal. The crossbow bolt went wide, although Bartholomew was sure he felt it whip past his ear. Lichet lost his balance on the slippery pavement, and fell heavily, landing close to the steward – who reached out to plunge a dagger into his chest. Lichet twitched briefly and died. It all happened so fast that Bartholomew and Michael could do nothing but gape.

'Do not just stand there, man,' shouted Marishal angrily, hauling himself out of the water with the agility of a much younger man. 'Help the monk off that ledge.'

Bartholomew hastened to obey. Once on safer ground, Michael dropped to his knees in relief, drawing in huge unsteady breaths.

'I heard it all,' said Marishal, water streaming from his clothes as he looked dispassionately at the man he had killed. 'He may not have stabbed Margery and Roos, but he was about to dispatch you. He deserved to die. He is—'

He stopped. A peculiar sound was coming from deeper in the cistern, a rumbling that started softly, but that grew steadily louder. The surface of the water began to shiver more violently.

'What is that?' gulped Michael, clambering quickly to his feet and looking around in alarm.

'Someone has opened the valves on the roof tanks,' explained Marishal in a shocked whisper. 'Water is pouring down the pipes – and as the cistern is almost full already, it will soon reach the ceiling. I am sorry, Brother, but it seems you are destined to drown today after all.'

# CHAPTER 13

The rumbling grew ever louder, and within moments, water swirled over the lip of the pavement and flowed towards them, foaming from the force of the deluge.

'The steps!' yelled Michael. 'Quick! Climb up—'

'The door is secured from the outside,' shouted Marishal, and in the flickering lamplight, he was almost as wan as the monk. 'The stairwell will flood as quickly as the cistern, and no one will hear us shout for help. We will die there for certain.'

'Thomas,' said Bartholomew with desperate hope. 'He knows we are down here – he came to ask you for the key.'

'I sent him to spread word about the Queen being delayed.' Marishal staggered as water surged around his knees. 'He will not know anything is amiss until it is far too late.'

And he might have been the one to open the valves anyway, thought Bartholomew – to rid himself of Lichet, two annoyingly persistent investigators and an unloved father in one fell swoop.

'But the cistern is a clever piece of engineering,' he said urgently. 'Lichet installed the silly device on the door, but the original architects were much more sensible. They will have predicted that someone might be trapped one day and catered for such an eventuality. We just need to find—'

'Yes!' Relief blazed in Marishal's eyes. 'There *is* a special chamber. It is almost directly above where Michael was just standing – I remember being shown it as a child. Access is via a ladder, assuming it has not rotted over the years . . .'

The ladder was still there, although by the time they reached it, water was bubbling around their thighs. Bartholomew went up it first, alarmed when the ancient rungs flexed under his weight, sure they would not take Michael's. He climbed quickly, the lamp in one hand. Eventually, he reached an irregularly shaped chamber, which he predicted would be above the cistern's ceiling, so would form an air pocket.

Marishal followed, but Michael was heavy and not particularly agile. Rungs snapped when he trod on them, and twice he fell back into the churning water, saved from being swept away only by the fact that he was strong – and terrified – enough to keep a powerful grip on the uprights. It felt like an age before Bartholomew and Marishal finally managed to pull him to safety.

Then the water rose higher than the opening to their refuge, effectively cutting them off. The sound of rushing water faded to a muted rumble, and the loudest sound was their own breathing.

'We will not suffocate just yet,' Bartholomew assured Michael, aware that the monk was trying not to pant. 'There is air enough to last a while.'

'Thank God for small mercies,' gulped Michael. 'Of course, we shall starve instead, because it might be weeks before we are found, especially if the cistern is kept full.'

'*I* cannot stay here!' cried Marishal, horrified. 'The Lady needs me. The Queen may not come today, but she will arrive sooner or later, and I must be there to ensure that all runs smoothly.'

'While I have a University to manage and a College to close,' said the monk, and glanced sadly at Bartholomew. 'We cannot save Michaelhouse now. Even if we do survive this terrible experience, we have not secured enough money to make a difference.'

'It was not the wind that shut the door,' said Bartholomew to the steward, his mind running in a different direction entirely. 'It was the killer. He trapped Michael and Lichet first, then decided to add you and me to his tally of victims – doubtless to ensure that no one is left alive to investigate.'

Marishal regarded him with haunted eyes. 'Then he must have been very close to hand, given that the door slammed so soon after we began our descent.'

'Yes,' agreed Bartholomew. 'So *think*. Who else was nearby?'

'Someone who hid himself well, because I did not see a soul. Did you?'

Bartholomew shook his head, although he could not escape the conviction that Thomas might have ignored his father's order to tell everyone about the Queen's change of plan, and followed him back to the cistern instead.

'I did not either,' confessed Michael. 'All my attention was on Lichet. He said important evidence was down here, and I was so frantic for answers that I rashly believed him.'

While they talked, Bartholomew took the lamp and explored the chamber in the hope of finding something that would allow them to escape. There was nothing, but . . .

'Do you recognise these?' he asked, holding up a white wig and a matching beard.

'Roos's,' replied Marishal. 'He must have come here to don his disguises.'

'Lichet said that Roos liked the cistern,' recalled Bartholomew. 'Now we know why – and why Margery suggested it as a place to meet. It is somewhere he felt safe and comfortable.'

Marishal covered his face with his hands. 'And she *did* know about this room, because I showed it to her years ago. I had forgotten about it, but clearly she never did, and she shared the secret with him – as a place he could use without fear of discovery. It is my fault that—'

'What is this?' interrupted Michael suddenly, leaning down to pluck something from the floor. He grimaced irritably. 'That is a stupid question! I know what it is – it is Langelee's letter-opener. What I should ask is: what is it doing here? We know he lost it after a night of drunken debauchery at the priory . . .'

'Which was the same night as Margery's murder,' said Bartholomew, taking the little implement from him and peering at it in the dim light.

Marishal was looking from one to the other in bemusement. 'What are you saying? That *Langelee* is the killer?'

'No, of course not,' said Michael irritably. 'However, he lost his letter-opener that fateful evening, and for it to be here . . . *Is* it the murder weapon, Matt?'

'No – the wounds on both victims were too large to have been made with this.'

Michael was thoughtful. 'Nicholas coveted that blade, and I suspected straight away that he was the one who stole it. So what does this tell us? That he is involved somehow?'

'He is a lout, who had no business taking holy orders,' said Marishal. 'Why do you think I chose Heselbech to bury Margery and preside over the rededication ceremony tonight? However, I know for a fact that Nicholas had nothing to do with killing Margery and Roos. He has an alibi.'

'Yes, in Anne,' acknowledged Michael. 'But we suspect she was fast asleep in her cell at the salient time.'

'Of course she was,' said Marishal impatiently. 'She would not disturb her precious slumbers for mere holy offices. No, Nicholas's alibi is Barber Grym and two artists, who were in the church from nocturns to dawn. The work is behind schedule, you see, so they met there to see what could be done to hurry it along. All swear that Nicholas recited his office, then stayed on to pray.'

Michael stared at him. 'Then why did Grym not mention this to me?'

'Did you ask him about Nicholas?'

'Well, no,' conceded the monk. 'I have concentrated on witnesses from the castle, because it was here that the crimes were committed.' He glanced at Bartholomew. 'So how did the letter-opener end up in this place? I suppose Nicholas might have stolen it later, but Langelee is sure he lost it during the night – around the time when he was helping Heselbech to the chapel.'

'He must have dropped it, after which someone else picked it up and brought it here,' said Bartholomew, although his words sounded unconvincing, even to his own ears, and he could think of no reason why anyone would do such a thing.

'He told us that after leaving Heselbech, he went straight back to the priory,' said Michael in a low voice. 'But it was a lie, because I heard him come in much later. He claimed he had to stop to vomit, but . . .'

'So Langelee *did* kill my wife?' demanded Marishal, looking from one to the other. 'Christ God! No wonder you two have failed to solve the crime!'

'I suspect *Heselbech* thinks Langelee is the guilty party,' Bartholomew told Michael unhappily. 'He came to after Langelee had deposited him on the chapel floor, and while Weste was reciting nocturns on his behalf, he went outside to relieve himself . . .'

'Where he saw a "shadow" by the cistern,' finished Michael. 'He assured us that it was too dark to allow identification, but we both had a feeling that he knew who it was anyway.'

'But he would never admit it, because of the vows that the Austins have sworn to protect fellow ex-warriors.' Bartholomew felt sick, especially when he recalled the Master's reaction as he realised the letter-opener had gone. It was not the loss of a much-loved possession that had caused his distress, but the knowledge that it might later surface to incriminate him.

'Langelee has been different since the murders,' Michael went on shakily. 'He did not drink as heavily the following night, and he has been uncharacteristically subdued and morose.'

Bartholomew was thinking fast. 'Margery and Roos: we have assumed that because they were killed with the same weapon, it was wielded by the same hand. But what if it was different?'

'Go on,' said Michael warily.

'Langelee suggested several times that Roos killed Margery, but we dismissed it. What if he is right, and Roos stabbed her in a fit of rage? We know they quarrelled that night, because Lichet just said so, and he had no reason to lie. Langelee is not a man to stand idly by while a woman is harmed . . .'

'So he fought Roos, and it is obvious who would win that encounter,' finished Michael. 'Roos was knifed, after which he fell in the water to drown. But why did Langelee not—'

'The water!' shouted Marishal suddenly. 'It is going down! Thank God! Someone must have opened the sluices in the kitchen. We are saved!'

He grabbed the ladder, fretting impatiently for the water to subside enough for him to leave. He was down it sooner than was safe, although Bartholomew and Michael were more cautious – partly because of the missing and fragile rungs, but mostly because they were afraid of what would inevitably have to happen once they were outside. Moving with care, as the water was still calf high, the two scholars eased around the ledge.

'Where is Marishal?' asked Bartholomew worriedly, when they reached the wider part of the pavement and there was no sign of the steward. 'I hope his impatience has not seen him swept away. It would be a pity for—'

He faltered when he heard voices coming towards them. One was Thomas's and the other . . .

'Oh Lord,' gulped Michael. 'It is Langelee!'

Bartholomew and Michael hurried towards the stairwell, but what they saw as they approached stopped them dead in their tracks. Marishal lay senseless on the ground at Langelee's feet, while Thomas hovered uncertainly behind him. Langelee was wet and muddy, and bore the signs of having spent a night in the open. Yet he was rosy-cheeked and his eyes were bright, suggesting that he had recently enjoyed reverting to the warrior he had once been.

'Marishal lunged at me with a blade,' he explained, as Bartholomew eased forward cautiously to inspect the fallen man. 'God knows why. Regardless, I reacted instinctively, and he will wish he had been less belligerent when he wakes up.'

'He did lunge,' said Thomas, his face creased with confusion. 'And it took *me* by surprise, too. He is not usually given to brawling.'

'Well?' asked Langelee of Bartholomew. 'Will he live?'

Bartholomew nodded, and scrambled quickly to his feet, feeling vulnerable on his knees with the Master looming over him.

'You were lucky,' Thomas told him and Michael. 'I happened to hear the roar of water as it was released from the tanks on the roof. Knowing you were down here, I raced to open the kitchen sluices, praying that I was not too late.'

'You *were* too late,' said Michael shortly, while Bartholomew pondered the length of time it had taken, and wondered if Thomas had "raced" or strolled. 'But we found a refuge. Did you see who went to the roof to open the taps? Or who shut the cistern door behind Matt and your father?'

'No,' replied Thomas, 'because I was busy doing what I was told – spreading the word about the Queen. Everyone is milling around the gatehouse, gossiping about it, and as far as I could tell, the inner bailey was deserted.'

'It was,' agreed Langelee. 'Indeed, I only came up here because I was looking for you two. Heselbech said you were worried about me, so I came to report that I am safe.'

'Well, clearly someone was about,' persisted Michael. 'Someone who wants Matt, Lichet, Marishal and me dead, and who went to considerable trouble to do it. We almost drowned.'

'Well, thank God you did not,' said Langelee, and his eyes strayed to Marishal's prostate form. 'I wonder why he assaulted me. All I did was come to save his miserable life.'

'He thinks you know more than you should about Margery's death,' explained Michael, and held up the letter-opener.

Langelee stared at it and the blood drained from his face. 'Where was it?' he breathed in a strangled whisper. 'Not in that horrible secret chamber?'

Michael rubbed his eyes tiredly, while Bartholomew's stomach churned, and all he wanted to do was to run up the steps as fast as he could, to avoid the revelations that were coming.

'Start at the beginning, Master,' said Michael in a low, flat voice. 'We know you left Heselbech in the chapel and went back outside. What happened next?'

There was a moment when it looked as though Langelee would attempt to bluster his way out of his predicament, but one glance at Michael convinced him not to try. He raised his hands in a shrug of resignation, his face ashen, and spoke in a voice that shook.

'I saw Roos and Margery creep into the cistern, and I was drunk enough to indulge my curiosity. If only I had been sober! Then I would have known to mind my own business.'

'So you trailed after them,' surmised Michael.

Langelee nodded. 'And heard a violent quarrel over the letter she had sent him – the one where she lied about the Lady being dead. I followed their voices to that nasty chamber, and was about to ask what was going on, when Roos whipped out a knife and stabbed her. It was so fast – over before I realised what was happening.'

'So you killed him in return,' said Michael hoarsely.

'Of course not! I tried to go to her, to see if she could be helped, but Roos was insane with rage. He kept flailing at me with his dagger, screeching that it was her own fault for "using" him. He was armed and I was not, but it was easy to keep him at bay even so, by pushing him back.'

'Which explains the marks on his chest and arms,' muttered Bartholomew.

'I had to dodge and duck around a bit, which is probably when I lost my letter-opener. I reached Margery, but his antics made it impossible for me to examine her, so I gave him a harder shove to knock him away. I heard him stumble, but all my attention was on Margery . . .'

'And?' demanded Michael. 'What then?'

'There was nothing to be done for her, so I turned back to him – at which point, I saw that he had fallen on to his own knife. He was lying on his front, unmoving.'

'Dead?'

'I thought so. As they were both beyond earthly help, I decided to carry their bodies to the foot of the stairwell, then summon help to lug them up it. I took Margery first, then went back for Roos. Imagine my horror to discover him gone!'

'Gone?'

'He was not where I had left him. I did my utmost to find the wretch, and eventually I spotted him face-down

360

in the water some distance away. He must have regained his wits, tried to stand up, but lost his balance and toppled in to drown. Worse, he had managed to knock Margery into a place where I could not reach her either. I did not know about the sill below the surface then, obviously . . .'

'Because if you had, you would have been able to retrieve both bodies, and fetch help to carry them outside, as you had originally planned,' surmised Bartholomew.

Langelee nodded. 'But now I had two corpses that I thought were beyond my grasp. So I decided to beat a hasty retreat, and let folk make of the situation what they would.'

Michael was exasperated. 'Why could you not have told us? We have been chasing our tails for the last five days, searching for a killer who does not exist.'

Langelee winced. 'I was afraid it would bring Michaelhouse into disrepute, and then we would never win the Lady's favour. How *could* I confess – to you or anyone else?'

'Your secret is safe with me,' said Thomas softly.

The three scholars turned to look at him. Bartholomew had certainly forgotten the young man was there in the strain of hearing Langelee's confession, and he suspected the others had, too.

'What are you saying?' demanded Langelee sharply. 'This had better not be a prelude to blackmail or I will—'

'It is not,' Thomas assured him quickly. 'However, I hated Roos for the way he pestered my mother, so I am grateful to you for pushing him on to his own blade. He deserved it, as payment for fourteen years of harassment and then stabbing her in cold blood.'

'I did not do it on purpose,' objected Langelee indignantly.

'It does not matter – the outcome is the same,' said Thomas. 'Here. Shake my hand.'

'No,' said Michael, stepping forward to prevent it. 'That

is not the way justice works. There must be a proper enquiry.' He scowled at Langelee. 'It will be much harder to persuade people that you are innocent now. Staying silent was a foolish decision.'

'Yes,' acknowledged Langelee tiredly. 'But I was drunk at the time. Have *you* never made a bad choice when you were silly with ale?'

'Not on this scale,' retorted Michael tartly. 'You do realise that you will have to resign as Master? We cannot have a killer at our helm.'

'It has never bothered you before,' said Langelee, bemused.

'Right,' said Michael, becoming businesslike before Thomas could ask Langelee to explain his intriguing remark. 'We shall take Marishal to a place where he can recover, then I must tell the Lady what has happened.'

'I will do it,' offered Langelee. 'You might forget to ask for the hundred marks – which we should have, because we can name Margery's killer.'

'I hardly think a demand for money will make her favourably disposed to accepting our story,' said Michael coldly. 'So you had better wait outside. When we have finished, we shall leave Clare. Assuming she lets us go, of course, and does not order our arrest.'

'Then be careful,' warned Langelee. 'You may have found out what happened to Margery and Roos, but there remains another killer at large – the one who claimed Talmach, Godeston and the others. He has you in his sights and will be deeply disappointed to see you still alive.'

'That is true,' said Bartholomew to Michael. 'Whoever it is must think that we are on the verge of unmasking him, although nothing could be further from the truth.'

'If we had time, we might be able to identify him by applying logic to all we have learned,' said Michael tiredly. 'But it is too late. We will tell the Lady what happened to Margery and Roos, and then we must escape this violent little town while we can.'

It was not easy to assist the dazed Marishal up the steep spiral stairs, but they managed eventually. Then they took him to the Constable Tower, where Langelee and Michael stood guard outside while Bartholomew and Thomas settled him in a chair to recover. All three scholars were acutely aware that they were probably being watched by someone who was prepared to go to extraordinary lengths to see them dead.

'He bears some of the blame for what happened to her,' said Thomas, regarding his father dispassionately. The steward was regaining his senses fast, and Bartholomew anticipated that it would not be long before he was on his feet again. 'He knew Roos pestered her, but he did nothing to stop it, because Roos was useful to the Lady.'

'Yes,' sighed Bartholomew. 'A lot of people made poor judgements in this sorry affair.'

Leaving Marishal and Thomas to resolve their differences in private, Bartholomew rejoined Michael and Langelee, and then led the way to the palace. Langelee dragged his heels, desperately trying to think of ways to explain what had happened without it reflecting badly on the College.

'There is something I forgot to mention in the cistern,' he said, stopping abruptly for at least the fourth time. 'Namely the cause of the argument between Margery and Roos.'

'You did not forget,' said Michael curtly, continuing to stride on. 'You told us it was over the letter she sent. Roos objected to being told lies, and I know the feeling.'

'Wait!' snapped Langelee, grabbing his arm. 'Yes, he was angry with her for enticing him here under false pretences, but you have not asked the most important question of all: *why* she went to such lengths to get him to come.'

'Well, we know it was not for the pleasure of his company,' said Bartholomew, his interest piqued, even if Michael was too irked to acknowledge that Langelee might still have something important to contribute. He frowned, his mind working fast. 'He brought her gifts when he came, and Katrina thought they might be important in understanding why she died. Are they?'

Langelee nodded. 'I heard her say that her previous pleas for him to visit had gone unheeded, and she was desperate. He snarled that he had been disinclined to make another journey after losing an ear. Then she told him that she had had no choice but to lie, because the situation was urgent.'

'So what did he give her?' asked Michael waspishly. 'Do you know or must we guess?'

'Medicinal herbs,' replied Langelee triumphantly. 'At least, that is what she kept asking him to hand over. He informed her that he had not brought any, but she did not believe him, and accused him of withholding them out of spite.'

'Of course!' exclaimed Bartholomew in understanding. 'Mistress Starre in Cambridge sells a concoction of tansy and pennyroyal to end unwanted pregnancies. Thomas mentioned that his mother supplied "herbs and practical advice" to women in trouble, while Anne said that Margery had tried to take over where she had left off – not with a hook, but with potions.'

'But that is illegal,' said Michael shortly. 'And dangerous.'

'Very,' agreed Bartholomew. 'Which is why Margery wanted them brewed by someone who knows what she is doing. But it is not something you can send a servant to buy: Mistress Starre is choosy over customers, as she could hang if someone reported her to the authorities.

But she will know Roos. We shall ask her when we get home, but I imagine she sold him some.'

'Then it will have been for Isabel Morley,' determined Langelee, 'as she is with child but Quintone declines to wed her. Poor Margery was just trying to save some hapless girl from ruin.'

'Perhaps Isabel's case was urgent, but I suspect these "remedies" are needed on a fairly regular basis,' said Bartholomew. 'The squires make promises of marriage that they have no intention of honouring, while Bonde is a rapist.'

Michael was unconvinced. 'But Roos could have sent a pot of the stuff with a messenger. He did not have to deliver it in person.'

'Would *you* entrust someone else with that sort of task?' asked Bartholomew. 'As you pointed out, it is illegal, and there would have been no end of trouble for everyone concerned if it was intercepted by the wrong people. Besides, I imagine Roos liked the power it gave him over her – knowing he was the only one who could provide what she needed.'

Michael made a moue of distaste. 'What a vile individual he transpired to be.' Then he glanced at Langelee, as if the mention of one such person had brought another to mind. 'You have not told us where you were all last night. We were worried, although we should have known that you can look after yourself.'

'Weste and I rode further afield than we intended while looking for Jan,' explained Langelee, 'and it seemed reckless to continue in the dark, so we camped.'

'Jan,' mused Michael bitterly. 'Now I understand why you so "bravely" offered to hunt for him. It was to find out what he had seen while he crept about the castle in the dark. What will you do if he identifies you as the killer?'

'That will not be a problem,' replied Langelee airily,

'because we *did* find him, but the only soul he saw that night was Bonde. Incidentally, we found Bonde as well. Unfortunately, you cannot question him, because he is dead.'

'How did he die?' asked Michael acidly. 'By falling on his own dagger, like Roos?'

Langelee shot him a reproachful look. 'I do not know what happened to him – there are no marks on his body. Jan knows, but refuses to say. Weste and I took him to the priory, in the hope that John can coax the truth out of him. He is there as we speak.'

'Then go and find out if he has,' instructed Michael, 'while Matt and I talk to the Lady. Once you have spoken to John, stay in the priory until we are ready to leave. Do you understand?'

'Of course,' replied Langelee stiffly. 'I am not stupid.'

'I am not so sure about that,' muttered Michael venomously.

'What a wretched mess,' spat the monk, once Langelee was striding purposefully towards the gate, although it was clear that he resented being in a position where he was obliged to take orders from one of his Fellows. 'Damn Langelee and his soldierly ways!'

'But *we* would have been curious, if we had seen Margery and Roos sneaking around in the dark together,' said Bartholomew reasonably. 'We also would have followed them, and tried to help Margery after she had been stabbed. *And* we might have shoved Roos away if he had attempted to stop us. Do not be too hard on him.'

'But we would not have lied about it afterwards,' snapped Michael.

'He did not lie. He just did not tell the truth.'

'Sophistry! His misguided antics have done us immeasurable harm. We should never have allowed him to drink with a lot of ex-warriors. Of course, I do not know how

366

we could have stopped him. He has always been a man to follow his own inclinations.'

'Shall we see the Lady now?' Bartholomew did not want to discuss it any longer, torn as he was between sympathy for a friend who had made a bad decision, and concern for how it would impact on Michaelhouse. 'It will not be a pleasant interview, and I want it over.'

But they entered the palace to find it empty, except for one or two servants and Ereswell.

'She has gone to dine with a friend, who lives to the north of the town,' the courtier explained. 'Then she will attend the rededication ceremony in the church. The Queen may not be coming, but my Lady knows where her duty lies.'

'Lichet is dead,' Michael informed him shortly. 'An accident in the cistern. Will you arrange for his body to be retrieved? I am not sure Marishal is well enough to think of it.'

'Lichet dead?' breathed Ereswell, before a delighted grin spread across his face. He winked. 'Then see me before you leave. I always pay for services rendered.'

'We did not kill him,' said Michael in alarm. 'It was—'

'Of course you did not, Brother,' interrupted Ereswell with another wink.

'This is turning into a nightmare,' grumbled Michael, as they hurried through the gate, which they were able to do as the portcullis had been raised to let the Lady out, and the guards had not yet closed it again. 'Clare will think that Michaelhouse is full of assassins and— What are *they* doing?'

A crowd of townsmen was marching towards the castle. They were led by Grym, who was being forced to waddle faster than was comfortable for him, and his plump face was scarlet and sweaty. Paycock was at his side, urging him on. Bartholomew grabbed Michael's arm and hauled him back through the gate, thinking it would be safer than standing outside at the mercy of an unpredictable mob. The moment they were through it, a deafening rattle sounded as the portcullis slammed down behind them.

'Please ask Marishal to come out,' called Grym breathlessly to the castle guards who were busily nocking arrows into their bows. 'He needs to take control of your squires.'

'They have accused Quintone of theft,' elaborated Paycock, thrusting forward belligerently. 'So he claimed sanctuary in the church. But they are threatening to break it.'

'No one breaks sanctuary,' called Richard the watchman from the wall-walk above. 'Not even them. They know that if they do, they will be damned for all eternity.'

'Then Marishal must come and remind them of it,' snarled Paycock. 'Because Quintone has renounced his ties with the castle, and is now one of us. So if those louts lay one finger on him—'

The rest of his sentence was lost in a roar of fury from the crowd – Marishal had appeared, roused by the sound of the portcullis being dropped with such urgency. The steward was pale and unsteady on his feet. Thomas tried to offer a supportive arm, but Marishal knocked it away with a snarl. Thomas shot him a glower of his own, and came to talk to Bartholomew and Michael instead.

'I told him everything,' he said softly. 'About Roos killing my mother and Langelee trying to help her. He believes me, but it has opened a painful wound and he is deeply angry . . .'

Bartholomew could see it was true: the steward's rage was apparent in the way he was glaring at the assembled townsfolk – as if he itched to vent his spleen on them for the hurt he had suffered.

'Disperse,' he ordered contemptuously. 'Or I shall order my archers to shoot. Besides, you should be in the church. You will have to stand at the back unless you get there early.'

'Not so – the ceremony is postponed until your bloody Lady finishes chatting to her friends,' shouted Paycock. 'It is outrageous and an insult! It is *our* church, so what right does *she* have to keep us hanging about?'

'That is high-handed,' murmured Michael to Bartholomew. 'And foolish, too, given the unsettled mood of the town. It is begging for trouble.'

'And now her squires threaten a man who has taken refuge in our church,' Paycock raged on. 'So what are you going to do about it, steward?'

'The squires will not break sanctuary laws,' declared Marishal scornfully. 'However, I shall fetch them back – not because you tell me I must, but because I choose to do so.'

His scathing tone did nothing to soothe ruffled feathers, and the mob surged forward indignantly. Then the portcullis clanked up and soldiers poured out, Marishal in the vanguard. The crowd's advance stuttered to a standstill at the sight of so much naked steel, and for a moment, there was an uncomfortable and silent impasse. Grym broke it.

'We shall walk to the church together, Marishal,' he said, holding out his hand in a gesture of reconciliation. 'Side by side. And while we go, I shall explain the nub of the problem. You see, Quintone was wearing a hat that your boys claim is stolen—'

'Because it *is* stolen,' interrupted Thomas, while his father only stared at the proffered hand until Grym lowered it. 'It belongs to Nuport.'

The barber gave a pained smile. 'Regardless, he has been inflaming the situation by taunting them with it. They have never learned to rise above an affront, and there will be a brawl unless you take them home.'

'Quintone thinks that being cleared of murder gives

369

him licence to behave as he likes,' said Thomas to his father. 'And I am afraid Grym is right – there *will* be a spat unless we intervene.'

Marishal began to issue orders to his soldiers. Some were instructed to remain at the castle, while others were told to form a protective phalanx around him. The towns-folk resented arms being toted openly through their streets, so there was a lot of angry muttering as he and his men set off along the road called Nethergate. Grym waddled along at his side, desperately trying to soothe the situation with appeasing remarks, but Marishal's face was cold and hard, and he gave no indication that he was listening.

'When trouble does erupt,' murmured Michael, as he and Bartholomew trailed along behind them, 'it will be his fault. Grym is trying his best, but Marishal is deter-mined to be truculent.'

'A fight may be what he wants,' said Bartholomew, recalling what Katrina had told him. 'It will allow the castle to defeat the town, after which the Lady's authority can be stamped on Clare once and for all. And Marishal *will* win – he may have fewer men, but they carry real weapons. Of course, his victory will come at a terrible price. For both sides.'

They arrived to find the church and its environs thronged with people, because the promised presence of the Queen had attracted visitors from the surrounding villages, as well as the town. There was a good deal of disappointment that she would not now be making an appearance, which Paycock and other malcontents were quick to turn into open disgruntlement.

Then there was a terrible scream. The door was ripped open and Quintone stood there, howling in pain and disbelief. Blood streamed down both sides of his face.

'Lord!' muttered Michael, shocked. 'Someone has chopped off his ears.'

370

# CHAPTER 14

The townsfolk were outraged. Not only had the squires committed an act of violence against a man who had renounced his ties to the castle and declared himself to be one of them, but they had broken one of the country's oldest and most inviolate laws. Paycock led the way in demanding that they answer for the crime at once, over-riding Grym's meek suggestion that they wait until tempers had cooled.

'There they are!' screeched Paycock, stabbing his finger towards the opposite end of the churchyard, where the squires could be seen climbing over the wall. 'After them!'

Nuport released a jeering laugh as he and his cronies bounded away. One or two of his fellows paused just long enough to make obscene gestures to their pursuers, then they all disappeared across the nearby fields. Their obvious high spirits suggested that they had no idea of the seriousness of the situation they were in. Bartholomew wondered why, and then realised that the answer lay with the wineskins each was clutching.

'They are drunk,' he said in disgust. 'That is why they have thrown good sense to the wind.'

'It is Anne's fault,' said Grym, who had come to stand next to him. 'Many of the visitors from the villages brought her gifts of food and wine today, and she had so much that she offered to share. I think she was overly generous to the squires . . .'

'Then let us hope they are not too inebriated to run fast,' said Michael drily. 'Because I doubt they will survive if they are caught.'

'Thomas!' exclaimed Bartholomew, suddenly aware that

the young man was on the receiving end of some very venomous glares. He had not been involved in violating Quintone's sanctuary, but the townsfolk were unlikely to make such a distinction, and there would be a fight for certain if he was attacked – his father might not think much of him, but the castle guards would not overlook an assault on their steward's heir.

Michael strode towards the twin. 'Go and fetch the Austins. Tell them they are needed here.'

'I cannot,' replied Thomas, either careless or oblivious of the danger he was in. 'Most of them rode off to search for Langelee and Weste, and they have not come back yet. The few who remain will not abandon their priory, lest it is sacked by—'

'Heselbech and Weste are there,' interrupted Michael. 'Tell them what is happening, and urge them to bring as many friars as they can spare. Go! Hurry!'

But Thomas ambled away with such insouciance that Bartholomew knew he was going to be of scant help in the brewing crisis. Michael turned to Marishal next.

'Send your men to find the squires before the towns-folk tear them to pieces. Tell them to box Nuport's ears while they do it – that may appease the mob. For now, at least.'

Marishal inclined his head and went to issue a series of low-voiced commands to his men. They saluted and left, although, like Thomas, not very fast. Bartholomew watched them go with some concern. Had Marishal told them to take their time in the hope that the squires *would* be caught by the townsmen, giving him a pretext to attack in revenge? The steward had scant regard for the young men, so might well consider them expendable. Or had his orders been unintentionally half-hearted, because he was still groggy from Langelee's punch?

'Take Quintone inside the church, Matt,' Michael was saying, 'and give him something to stop that howling – it is making the situation worse. I expected Grym to do it, but he is just standing there like a great lump of lard.'

Bartholomew fumbled for the poppy juice he carried in his bag. 'I can help him, but not inside the church – the door is shut again.'

'Nicholas?' bellowed Michael authoritatively. 'Open up.'

'Never!' came the priest's indignant voice. 'I did it once for Quintone, who promptly claimed sanctuary and all the trouble *that* entails. Then I let the squires in to pray, and they repaid my kindness by committing a terrible crime. Well, I have had enough. My church stays closed until the Queen arrives.'

'She is not coming,' called Grym. 'Have you not heard? Please let us in, Nicholas. Quintone needs to lie down, and it cannot be out here in all this dirt. And do not suggest taking him home, because he does not have one – he has not yet had time to secure lodgings in the town.'

There was an indecisive pause. 'Let me consult with Anne. She will know what to do.'

Bartholomew was glad so many of the mob had hared off in pursuit of the squires, because he felt exposed and vulnerable crouching next to Quintone. He was relieved when there was a clank a few moments later, and the church door opened.

'Anne says a *few* of you may come in, as long as you behave,' said Nicholas. 'No pushing, no swearing and no fighting. Oh, and wipe your feet, please. I spent all night cleaning the floor, and I will not have it marred with filthy boot prints.'

Together, Bartholomew and Grym carried the swooning Quintone inside, and laid him on Roger's tomb. Bartholomew sewed up the gaping wound where Quinstone's ears had been, while Grym swabbed away the blood, although the physician could not help glancing up from time to time. Now all the scaffolding was down, the ceiling was revealed in its full glory. It was magnificent, and he hoped there would be a moment to admire it properly before he left.

Yet even the fan vaulting could not distract him from the growing conviction that Clare was about to suffer a calamity that would change it for ever, and which he was powerless to prevent. The streets would run with blood, and the murders that had gone before would be a mere drop in the ocean compared to the carnage that would follow. He felt his stomach churn as he desperately tried to think of a way to stop it.

'Fasten his ears back on,' came a voice from the anchorhold, and Bartholomew turned to see beady eyes watching with unabashed interest. 'I would.'

'They would fester,' replied Grym. 'And we do not have them anyway.'

'Nuport probably ate them,' declared Anne, loud enough to be heard by the crowd that milled around outside her other window; they gave a collective growl of anger and revulsion. 'He can be a dreadful brute on occasion.'

Bartholomew moved to block her view of what he was doing in the hope of avoiding more such remarks, and while he stitched, he listened to the discussion taking place between the others who had managed to slip inside when Nicholas had opened the door. They included Michael, Marishal, a handful of courtiers and several town worthies, the ubiquitous Paycock among them.

'I understand why you let Quintone in,' Marishal was saying irritably to the vicar, 'but why did you then admit the squires? It was a stupid—'

'Oh, so it is my fault, is it?' interrupted Nicholas archly. 'The castle louts come here and commit a dreadful sin, but *I* am to blame?'

'Yes, in part,' Marishal snapped back. 'Anyone can see they are drunk, so will be more asinine than usual.'

'They told me they wanted to pray,' said Nicholas defensively. 'I assumed they were sincere.'

'Then you are a fool, too,' spat Marishal in disgust. 'Pray indeed!'

'They had better not show their faces in my town again,' declared Paycock, bristling with indignation. 'Because if they do, I shall smash them in – personally.'

He waved his fist to show that he meant it. Then there was an imperious hammering at the door, followed by an angry order for it to be opened at once.

'It is Cambrug!' exclaimed Nicholas in startled delight, irritation evaporating like mist in the sun. He beamed happily and ran to let the famous architect in, ushering him over the threshold with the kind of deference usually reserved for royalty.

Cambrug was of middle height with squat, ugly features, travel-stained clothes and a sulky scowl. He ignored the vicar's gushing welcome, and stood with his hands on his hips, gazing up at his creation with professional detachment. Grym was among the many – townsfolk *and* castle men – who immediately hurried to fawn over him, so there was an unseemly scrum that resulted in him being very roughly jostled.

'Get away!' he snarled, and glowered at Nicholas. 'I have just been informed by some peasant outside that the Queen is not coming. Could you not have written to tell me? I have ridden all the way from Hereford for nothing.'

'Hardly nothing,' objected Nicholas, stung. 'We still have a lovely evening planned.'

'Besides, we only had word ourselves this morning,' added Marishal. 'By which time it was too late to inform anyone. But we shall make your stay a memorable one, never fear. We have prepared a nice suite of rooms in the castle with—'

'No, he will stay with me,' stated Paycock firmly. 'My

375

house is a lot more comfortable. The company will be better, too.'

'We took all the scaffolding down,' said Nicholas unctuously, before Cambrug could accept either offer. 'As you can see. Her Majesty will miss the rededication ceremony, but that is her loss, and at least her haughty priests will not try to make unnecessary adjustments to it.'

'So you will preside, Nicholas?' asked Paycock. 'Good! The castle can piss off home then, because now the Queen is not coming, neither will they. It will be our ceremony and ours alone.'

'We certainly will attend,' countered Marishal sharply. 'The Lady is looking forward to it, and she will be here as soon as she has completed her business in the north of the town.'

'Her *business*?' echoed Paycock scathingly. 'Her gossiping with friends, you mean. Well, she can stand in the south aisle, because *we* paid for the nave, and it is our right to use it.'

'But the ceiling is not yet finished,' objected Cambrug, who had continued to peer upwards critically. 'There are several unpainted sections that—'

'Nonsense,' stated Grym, and lowered his voice. 'It is either a ceremony or a battle, Cambrug. You choose – but remember that any blood spilled will be on your hands.'

Cambrug sniffed. 'I suppose the finishing touches can be added later.'

Grym nodded to Paycock and his cronies, and anything else the architect might have said was lost as the townsfolk hurried away to begin their preparations. Lamps were lit, candles set out, and flower displays lifted on to windowsills. But Marishal and his courtiers had their own opinions about what should be done to beautify the church, and arguments soon broke out. Anne listened from her cell, and Bartholomew was unimpressed that

376

every time she spoke, she invariably made matters worse.

'Not long now,' said Nicholas, nodding approvingly as an elaborate arrangement of dried flowers was plonked on the font. 'Then my ceremony will begin. Heselbech may steal the leading role, but everyone will know that he recites the words I wrote.'

'Well, *I* shall not stay for it,' declared Cambrug unpleasantly. 'You dragged me here with the promise of a royal audience, but now you—'

'Go back to Hereford, then,' called Anne crossly. 'We are tired of your bleating. If you cannot be genteel, then there is no place for you in Clare.'

Cambrug blinked his astonishment that anyone should dare address him with such brazen disrespect. 'I am not—'

'We do not want you here anyway,' she forged on, getting into her stride. 'You are a vile old misery – even worse than Roger, and *he* could not open his mouth without moaning. The ceremony will be much nicer without you.'

'And it will take place today, because our holy anchoress says that is when the stars are most favourable for it,' put in Nicholas. 'Her opinion is good enough for me.'

'Your holy anchoress is not an architect,' flashed Cambrug, bristling with outrage at the insults that had been heaped upon him. 'So do not blame me if the place tumbles about your ears in the middle of your stupid celebrations. You should have let me examine the roof before you ripped the scaffolding down. You did promise that you would wait.'

'What is this?' cried Marishal, listening to the exchange in alarm. 'Are you saying that it is unsafe? That the roof might fall on the Lady?'

Cambrug eyed him loftily. 'I cannot answer that until I inspect the quality of the work that was done after I left. However, I decline to do it now you have offended me. Not unless you beg.'

'Please, dear Cambrug, will you kindly help us to—' began Grym obligingly.

'No!' barked Marishal. 'There will be no begging here. Cambrug will do the job for which he was paid, and inspect the roof with good grace.'

'Shan't,' said Cambrug, folding his arms and putting his nose in the air.

'Because he knows there is nothing wrong with it,' called Anne provocatively. 'And he cannot stand the fact that we have achieved so much without him. It is jealousy speaking.'

The architect bristled anew. 'I am not staying here to be abused. I am going back to Hereford this very moment – and I wish a plague on Clare and everyone in it!'

When Quintone had been sewn up, bandaged and carried to Grym's house to recover – much to the barber's obvious reluctance – Bartholomew gave the fan vaulting his full attention, although it was difficult to see it in detail, as dusk was falling. He wondered why Nicholas had elected to hold the ceremony at night, when even a thousand lamps would be unequal to showing it at its best. Then he reconsidered. Or had the vicar actually been rather wise, as the dark would hide any small imperfections?

'Perhaps Cambrug was right to say that the scaffolding should not have come down until he had inspected the work,' he said to Michael. 'Because those unpainted sections have lots of small cracks, and it will be difficult to fill them with glue now they cannot be reached so easily.'

Michael glanced around uncomfortably. 'I have a bad feeling about this ceremony. Why must it still go ahead, even though the Queen will not be here, and it will throw together a lot of people who hate each other? There is something not quite right about the whole affair.'

Bartholomew stared at him. 'I have been thinking the same. All the murders – not just Margery and Roos, but

Roger, Skynere, Albon and the others – have resulted in one thing: widening the rift between town and castle.'

Michael agreed. 'The deaths of Roos, Margery and Charer were random events, with no malice aforethought, but someone has been quick to make folk believe otherwise. Something unpleasant *is* in the offing, and I sense it will happen tonight.'

'Do you think the ceremony should be cancelled?'

'Of course, but that will never happen. Nicholas will refuse, and if the Lady or Marishal try to insist, we shall have a riot for certain. The best course of action is to let it proceed, and hope there are enough Austins to prevent too much bloodshed. But who would want the town in an uproar? Paycock? He loves discord.'

Bartholomew grabbed Michael's arm and hauled him to the south aisle, a place shunned by both town and castle, and so somewhere he and the monk could confer without being overheard.

'Not Paycock, but someone who has a grievance against both sides and wants revenge. Someone who exacerbates the feud with bad advice and loud opinions. Someone who gave wine to the squires, knowing it would prompt them to reckless behaviour. Someone who provided a valued service to troubled girls for years, but was punished for it by being walled up in a cell. Someone—'

'You are insane, Matt!' cried Michael, shocked. He lowered his voice when Marishal glanced towards them. 'I know Anne is no more holy than we are, but she is still a—'

'Someone who insists that tonight's ceremony goes ahead, because "the stars are auspicious",' Bartholomew went on. 'Someone who told Nicholas to let the squires into the church, even though it was obviously the wrong thing to do. Perhaps she even encouraged them to violate sanctuary – she would have seen what was happening through her squint, and I am sure she did not stay silent.'

379

'You are wrong,' hissed Michael. 'Anne cannot possibly have known what really happened to Roos and Margery, but the culprit used their—'

'She did not need to know the truth – she just had to twist it to suit herself.' Bartholomew grew more certain with every word he spoke. 'But let us consider each death in turn, Brother – the logical analysis that we both know will provide answers.'

'We do not have time,' objected Michael agitatedly. 'We have to tell the Lady what happened down in the cistern, and then—'

'We must *make* time. First, Roger. He died here, in the church where Anne lives.'

'But she is walled in. She cannot have—'

'Next, Talmach, the unwanted husband of Ella, who loves Anne like a mother. How convenient! Anne did not kill Charer, because Lichet told us what happened to him, but she certainly accused the castle of the crime.'

'Well, someone from the castle *was* involved in—'

'Wisbech was killed next, clearly as a ploy to drag the Austins into the feud, although John declined to be manipulated. Wisbech, Skynere and Godeston were poisoned with hemlock, a herb familiar to all those who dabble in dubious medicine – which Anne does.'

'And *non*-dubious medicine,' Michael pointed out. 'You and Grym use it as well.'

That was true, but Bartholomew ignored it. 'And when Godeston died, Anne was quick to claim that he was poisoned by a townsman in revenge for Margery.'

'You read too much into her idle musings, Matt. She also accused the Austins at one point.'

'Exactly! Which is evidence that she wants them involved in the dispute, so there will be no peace-keepers. Her remarks are *not* idle musings, but carefully contrived rumour-mongering. Think about what she has said in the last hour alone – a claim that Nuport

380

ate Quintone's ears, and comments that set town and castle against each other as they prepared the church for the ceremony.'

'You argue your case well,' acknowledged Michael. 'But there is one big problem: Anne is walled inside her anchorhold and cannot get out. Or are you suggesting that she persuaded someone else to kill on her behalf?'

'Why not? Nicholas does everything she wants, and you heard him call her "sweetest love". She is obviously popular with people from both sides of the feud, as her cell is always full of gifts. Perhaps some of them repay her in other ways – not food and wine, but deeds.'

Michael shook his head. 'I cannot see—'

'The Lady said Anne is clever and resourceful. And I am not sure she *is* walled in anyway.'

'Of course she is,' said Michael impatiently. 'The only openings are the two windows, which are far too small for anyone to squeeze through.'

'She keeps one section of her cell covered by a screen—'

'Yes, and the wall beyond it is solid stone. I checked it myself.'

'Then what about the floor? It is always covered in straw, so how do you know there is not a trapdoor beneath? For a start, how did she get all that nice furniture in there?'

'Put in as the cell was built, probably – which was fairly recently, as Nicholas told us that Cambrug designed it specially for her.'

But Bartholomew shook his head. 'I have seen anchorholds before. They reek, because their occupants never get out. But Anne's always smells clean and fresh.'

Michael was becoming exasperated. 'Perhaps she is just more particular about hygiene.'

'Do you remember Margery telling Lichet about a dream she had – of Anne and Nicholas walking hand in hand in the bailey? What if it was not a dream? What if she actually saw them?'

Michael opened his mouth to tell the physician that he had lost his grip on reality when he saw someone hurrying towards them. 'Oh, Lord! Here comes Langelee. Now what?'

The Master had changed his muddy clothes at the priory, but as he had no spare cloak, he had borrowed the one that Albon had given Bartholomew. Aware that it might be recognised by someone who would take umbrage, he had turned it inside out, so that the black silk was on the outside and the red wool was on the inside. He was sombre-faced, subdued and pale – the revelations in the cistern had taken their toll on his customary jauntiness.

'I know you ordered me to stay put,' he began before Michael could berate him, 'but I have important information. When I arrived at the friary, Jan was demanding to return to his hermitage. Weste asked me to escort him there, because he could spare no one else. I did not like to refuse, not when the Austins have been so hospitable . . .'

'*Too* hospitable,' muttered Michael tartly. 'If they had been less free with their ale . . .'

Langelee went on hurriedly. 'It was the first time that I had been alone with Jan, and I found him eager to talk. He confided that he had dared not speak while Weste was with me, because of the oaths of loyalty the friars have sworn to each other.'

Michael regarded him anxiously. 'Are you about to tell us that one of them is the killer?'

'He is,' predicted Bartholomew. 'And it will be Nicholas – Anne's good friend.'

Langelee gaped at him. 'How did you guess?'

'Later,' said Michael tersely, before Bartholomew could embark on a lengthy explanation. 'What else did Jan tell you?'

'That the reason he left Clare in such terror was because

he had watched Anne poison Mayor Godeston – her and Nicholas together. They are lovers, apparently.'

'So we were both right,' said Michael, acknowledging Bartholomew's look of triumph with a nod. 'I thought from the start that there was something amiss with that vicar, although neither of you believed me. But is Jan sure about what he saw?'

Langelee nodded. 'He also spotted Anne and Nicholas out on the nights that Wisbech and Skynere were poisoned, as well as shortly before Talmach and Albon came to grief. They had no idea he was watching them then, but they saw him when Godeston died – hence his abrupt flight.'

'He could not have confided in someone first?' asked Michael crossly. 'To protect the town that feeds him? He might have saved lives if he had. So much for the selfless holy man!'

'He did not think anyone would believe him. Anne is supposed to be walled up, and the whole town is convinced of her sanctity.'

'Suzanne de Nekton saw Jan trail Bonde to the Cistern Tower on the night that Roos and Margery were murdered,' recalled Bartholomew. 'Did he tell you about that?'

Langelee nodded again. 'But he assured me that it was just coincidence – neither of them saw or heard anything pertaining to the murders. However, Bonde's first interviews with Michael and Lichet convinced him that he might be blamed anyway, so he decided to disappear until the fuss had died down – at Anne's instigation, of course.'

'But he did not go far,' said Bartholomew. 'Just to the woods . . .'

'Where Jan watched Anne feed him hemlock,' finished Langelee. 'Afterwards, Nicholas hid the body, although not very well, as Weste and I unearthed it without too much trouble.'

'But why would she kill Bonde?' asked Michael, still sceptical. 'He liked her well enough to wish he had married her.'

'He ran all manner of errands for her apparently, including tampering with saddle straps. As he lay dying, she calmly informed him that his death was to ensure that he did not interfere with the plan that will swing into action tonight.'

'What plan?' gulped Michael in alarm.

'Jan did not hear that bit. However, remember that Bonde's first loyalty was to the Lady, which means he would have baulked at any plot to harm her—'

At that moment, Grym waddled up, his plump face creased in agitation. 'Quintone has just informed me that *Anne* told the squires to cut off his ears,' he announced. 'Pain must have driven him out of his wits, because no anchoress would do such a terrible thing. Do you have any medicine to calm him, Matthew? I dare not dose him with hemlock, as—'

He stopped at the sound of angry footsteps, and turned to see who was coming. It was Cambrug, saddlebags slung over his shoulder. The architect addressed him with sneering contempt.

'Nicholas does not have the good manners to spare me a moment of his time before I leave, so I am forced to deal with you, Acting Mayor. The cracks in the ceiling are ugly. Roger should have reported them to me, so I could tell him how to mend them. Where is he?'

'Dead,' replied Grym, and raised his eyebrows at Cambrug's start of surprise. 'You did not know? Nicholas promised to write and tell you. Roger was killed by a piece of falling scaffolding back in April.'

Cambrug regarded him in disgust. 'Then of course there will be unsightly gaps in the stone. Only experi-enced masons – like Roger – know how to join blocks seamlessly. You should have—'

384

'The anchorhold,' interjected Bartholomew urgently.
'You built it for Anne. Were you given any particular
instructions?'

Cambrug scowled his indignation at being interrupted.
'Just to make it comfortable,' he replied shortly. 'Which
I did not need to be told, given that someone will spend
the rest of her life in it. I included a stone floor for
hygiene, two windows with—'

'Did you include an emergency exit?'

'I did, as a matter of fact, and it is a very sensible precau-
tion. Churches catch fire, condemning their anchorites to terrible deaths. So I installed a tunnel that leads
to the vicarage. It is a very clever solution on my part:
Anne can escape in the event of a disaster, but only her
priest can open the trapdoor. It means she cannot abandon
her vocation for paltry reasons.'

'No wonder Nicholas does not want to move house,'
muttered Michael.

The church was now dark and full of shadows, as the
lamps had been very cleverly placed so that most of their
light shone upwards. Their beams were not strong enough
to reveal the cracks or unpainted sections, but they
certainly illuminated the intricate stone lace of the fan
vaulting. Once Cambrug had stamped away, full of hubris
and foul temper, Michael turned to Grym.

'There will be trouble for certain if the ceremony goes
ahead tonight. As Acting Mayor, do you have the authority
to cancel it and impose a curfew?'

'Yes, in theory,' replied Grym unhappily. 'But no one
will obey it. Go and look out of the window, and you will
see why the situation has gone well beyond my control.'

The three scholars did as he suggested, and saw that
an enormous crowd had gathered in the churchyard, lit
by dozens of flickering torches. It comprised not just the
residents of Clare, but folk from the surrounding villages

as well. And its mood was ugly. Most were armed with sticks or knives, and were yelling abuse at a contingent of soldiers from the castle, all of whom had drawn their swords and were bawling back.

'They are quarrelling over Quintone's ears,' explained Grym. 'And there are twice as many of them now as there were when I came in, with more flocking to join them as we speak.'

'Then do your duty and order them to disperse,' said Michael curtly. 'They are your people.'

'They are not! I do not know most of them, so why would they listen to me? Look – you can see Paycock over by the gate, and even he senses the situation is out of control. You can tell by the anguished expression on his face.'

It was true. The feisty bailiff was watching the howling crowd with an expression of open horror, and it was clear that he had not anticipated such a vigorous reaction to his rabble-rousing.

'It is very convenient for Anne that Paycock has been agitating,' mused Michael. 'And making sure that no slight to the town is overlooked. Are they friends?'

'Not friends exactly,' replied Grym, 'but she saved his daughter from an embarrassing pregnancy, so he has always been in her debt.'

At that moment, there was an especially angry roar from the crowd, which made the barber turn a sickly green colour. He turned abruptly and aimed for the back door.

'Where are you going?' demanded Langelee, moving to block him.

'Kedyngton,' replied Grym shortly. 'Clare is too dangerous for a man who is not very quick on his feet, and I shall be an obvious target if the castle attacks. You must excuse me.'

'You will stay and shoulder your responsibilities,' countered Langelee sternly. 'Or your town will be ablaze before the night is out. You cannot abandon it now.'

'Oh, yes, I can,' declared Grym, lowering his head and charging for the door again; his bulk was such that even Langelee was unequal to preventing his escape. He called over his shoulder as he went, 'It is every man for himself tonight. I shall return when all this nonsense is over.'

'In that case, we should leave, too,' determined Langelee, staggering in the barber's wake. 'I do not see why we should risk our lives when Clare's leaders are unwilling to do so. I have seen some serious disturbances in my time, but none involving quite so many people.'

'But the castle will win,' predicted Michael. 'Its warriors have proper weapons.'

'They do,' acknowledged Langelee, 'but the town has the benefit of reinforcements from the villages. I should not like to hazard a guess as to who will emerge the victor. Neither, probably – both will have lost too much.'

'Anne,' said Bartholomew urgently. 'She started all this, so she can stop it. People listen to her. If we can force her to tell everyone to desist . . .'

He hurried to her cell and peered through the squint. He could not see her, but the screen covered the far side of the chamber. A carefully aimed stone thrown by Langelee knocked it over. Behind it was a very comfortable bed, but no one was in it. The cell was empty.

'Do you see what lies on her pillow?' asked Bartholomew. 'A length of purple silk.'

'Mayor Godeston's,' breathed Michael, watching Langelee hook it towards them with a broom. 'Discovered missing when his body was found. Give it to me. It will serve as evidence against her – assuming we live to produce it, of course.' He shoved the filmy material into his scrip.

'You will not need it,' predicted Bartholomew, 'because she will not be here. You can see for yourself that most of her things have gone, and she was quite open about the fact that she sells all the gifts she cannot use. She has plenty of money to start a new life somewhere else, once her evil work here is done.'

'With Nicholas,' surmised Michael. 'Or without him, depending on whether her affection for him is sincere. I know we have no authority to meddle here, but I could not live with myself if I did not at least try to prevent a massacre. Will you help me?'

'I will,' said Langelee keenly. 'What do you want me to do?'

'Fetch the Austins. Thomas was supposed to do it, but I have a bad feeling that he is under Anne's influence, too, and the message may not have reached them. I know some of the friars are still out looking for you and Weste, but bring as many as you can.'

'Very well.' Langelee raised the hood on Albon's cloak to hide his face. 'What will you do?'

'Find Anne and Nicholas,' replied Michael grimly, 'and see if we can put an end to what they have ignited. Nicholas's house is as good a place as any to begin our search.'

The atmosphere outside was poisonous, and a steadily strengthening wind did nothing to help. It made the trees roar, and it whistled through the gravestones, an agitated, unsettling sound that made the crowd more jittery. Bartholomew and Michael were jostled and shoved mercilessly as they hurried to the vicarage, careful to keep their heads down lest even a wrong look should encourage someone to swing a punch. When they arrived at the vicarage, Marishal was just coming out.

'If you want Nicholas, you are out of luck,' he reported tersely. 'He has abandoned us, taking most of his belongings and all the church's silver with him. I suppose he is offended, because Heselbech was chosen to take tonight's ceremony.'

'What are you doing here?' demanded Michael. 'You are meant to be looking for the squires.'

'We found them – they are safely back inside the castle. And I am here because Ereswell could not find the church silver in the vestry, and it is needed for tonight's ceremony. I came to ask Nicholas where he had stored it.'

Bartholomew pushed past him and gazed around the handsome room in which he and his colleagues had been entertained only a few nights before. It had been stripped of anything portable, and because the floor was devoid of rugs, he saw the trapdoor near the hearth. He pulled it up to reveal the tunnel. A closer inspection revealed fresh boot prints – Anne had donned footwear suitable for travel. He hurried back outside, where Michael was trying to reason with the steward.

'Take your people home. You may lose the confrontation that—'

'Why should *we* withdraw?' demanded Marishal angrily. 'Anne is right: it is time the townsfolk learned their place, and if I do not teach them, no one will.'

'Anne?' groaned Michael. 'You have been listening to her? Can you not see what she is doing? She *wants* you to tear each other apart. And you are playing right into her hands.'

'She would never hurt us,' stated Marishal stubbornly. 'She raised my children and she was born in the town. The Lady treated her harshly it is true, but—'

'The Lady,' interrupted Michael urgently. 'Where is she? She will listen to sense, even if you are too obstinate to—'

'It is too late,' gulped Bartholomew. 'Look!'

Near the church's north porch, several hundred townsfolk were facing a thin line of heavily armed guards. The soldiers would almost certainly be killed, but not before giving a good account of themselves with their wickedly honed blades. With sickening inevitability, the two sides

389

began to close in on each other amid a frenzy of howled insults and abuse.

'For God's sake, Marishal!' cried Michael. '*Stop* it!'

But Marishal could only stand in open-mouthed shock at the scale of the trouble, and then the opportunity to intervene was gone. The two factions clashed. Horrified, Bartholomew watched as several men fell and were trampled. He raced towards the mêlée, and managed to drag one to safety before he was crushed to death. It was Paycock.

'Christ God!' the bailiff gulped. 'Anne said the castle would never dare fight us if we turned out in force. If I had known that we would come to actual blows, I would never have . . .'

Bartholomew ducked into the fray a second time, and managed to retrieve a second casualty. It was someone small and light, although it was not until Michael appeared with a lamp that he was able to recognise the victim as Badew. The elderly scholar was dying, bleeding from a dozen wounds, all in his back – he had been trying to run away when he had been cut down.

'I only went out for a moment . . . to see what was happening,' Badew whispered, white with shock. 'But I was caught by the mob . . . swept forward . . .'

Bartholomew did what he could, but to no avail. Badew's last words were characteristic of the man he had become since losing University Hall.

'The Lady . . . a whore,' he whispered, gripping Bartholomew's wrist with hard, bony fingers. 'Her name cannot . . . be associated . . . with a College . . . it must be . . . *Badew* Hall.'

'Hush,' chided Bartholomew in distaste. 'This is not the time to—'

'She is . . . a harlot.' Badew's grip tightened. 'I hid in her chamber . . . saw her relieved of . . . an unwanted child . . . with my *own* eyes . . .'

390

Bartholomew struggled to mask his revulsion for the old man's malevolence. 'Enough! If you really did witness such an incident, you would have made it public years ago, so do not—'

'She would have . . . denied it.' Badew's fingers were like hooks in Bartholomew's arm. 'Or sent . . . Bonde to kill . . . had to wait . . . until her tongue . . . stilled by death. My tale is true . . . swear on my soul.'

'What did he say?' asked Michael, hurrying forward a few moments later with the accoutrements needed to give last rites, although he would be anointing a corpse with his chrism.

'Nothing,' replied Bartholomew, thinking it was best to let such poisonous words die with their speaker. 'Where is Langelee? He should have fetched the Austins by now.'

'I hope he has come to no harm,' said Michael worriedly. 'He was wearing— Matt!'

The last was delivered in a gulp of alarm. The skirmish had expanded quickly, as more people had raced to join in, and it was now converging on them from two different directions. The combatants were so intent on trouncing each other that they cared nothing for the scholars caught in between. Michael hauled Bartholomew roughly to his feet.

'Stand tall, Matt. If we are to die tonight, then we shall do it with dignity.'

# CHAPTER 15

The two raging battles edged ever closer, and just as Bartholomew was bracing himself for the impact, there came the shrill bray of a trumpet, followed by the thundering beat of drums. Both were loud enough to rise above the screams and clash of weapons, and most participants broke off the engagement in alarm, looking around wildly for the source of the racket.

'The Queen!' gulped Ereswell. 'She has come after all, and will fine us for breaking the King's peace.'

A ripple of consternation went through the ranks of castle and town alike. However, it was not a royal procession that marched towards them in neat, military formation, but the Austins. Each wore a helmet and a breastplate painted with a bright white Crusader's cross, and was armed with a sword or an axe. Their religious habits were kirtled around their knees.

Bartholomew looked for Langelee, and saw him in the middle of the platoon, similarly attired, but with Albon's cloak wrapped around his body in lieu of a breastplate, black side out. It served to make him appear bigger and more powerful than ever, a Goliath compared to those around him.

'By my mark . . . *halt!*' bellowed Weste, who looked particularly warlike with his eyepatch. The column came to a neatly executed standstill. 'Prepare *arms!*'

There was a businesslike clatter as weapons were brought into a position where they could be deployed. Then there was silence. The Austins stood like stone, a human wall bristling with sharp points, strategically placed to prevent the different skirmishes from uniting into one massive brawl.

'We are warriors of Christ,' declared Prior John in a ringing voice. 'Ready to defend God's peace against sinners who would break it.'

'You are old men,' someone sneered. 'You cannot tell us what to do.'

The speaker was Nuport, his cronies at his heels. All were red-faced and unsteady on their feet, suggesting they were still under the influence of Anne's wine – and they had to be very drunk, thought Bartholomew, or they would have had the sense to stay in the castle after Marishal had rescued them. There was a furious growl from the townsfolk when they were recognised, to which Nuport responded by brandishing his sword.

'Anyone who raises a hand in violence will lose it,' announced Prior John loudly. 'After which I shall excommunicate him.'

'Who cares about the Church?' spat Nuport. 'We are not afraid of you, John. We are squires, trained in the art of war and—'

Weste moved so fast that Nuport had no idea he was in trouble until he was seized by the scruff of the neck, neatly flipped head over heels, and deposited in a muddy puddle. The unruly squire spent the next few moments spitting dirt from his mouth and trying to rub it from his eyes. There was a collective gasp of astonishment, after which a few townsfolk began to laugh. So did one or two courtiers, although not quite so openly.

Feeling castle honour was at stake, Mull lurched forward, but there was a blur of flying habit and multi-coloured hose, and the lad found himself flat on his face with John's boot planted on his rump to keep him there.

'Would anyone else like to try?' the Prior asked, looking

around archly. 'You can see we are just old men, and who cares about the Church?'

There was absolute stillness from both sides, as no one dared move lest they were singled out for attention. All except for one person.

'They broke sanctuary,' Paycock screeched, stabbing an accusing finger at the squires. 'They dragged Quintone out from under the altar and chopped off his ears.'

'Is this true, Nuport?' asked John, very coldly.

'He taunted us,' said Mull in a small, defensive voice when Nuport declined to respond. 'He stole Nuport's hat and waved it at us, laughing that there was nothing we could do about it. Then Anne shouted that such insolence was an insult to the castle, so . . .'

'You are all excommunicated,' pronounced Prior John, jabbing a finger at each of the shocked squires in turn. 'Unless you come to me tomorrow with contrite hearts and beg me to reconsider. I urge you to think very carefully about what you do next.'

'Yes, do,' jeered Paycock gleefully. 'And we shall be there to witness your humiliation.'

'You are excommunicated, too,' snapped John, rounding on him. He raised a warning hand as a stunned Paycock opened his mouth to object. 'Say no more! You will only make matters worse for yourself.'

The bailiff gazed at him in dismay, but wisely elected to hold his tongue. There was some agitated muttering among the assembled masses, but it stopped when John's gimlet eye turned towards the culprits. Again, there was silence.

'Now, we shall all go to church,' said John, once he was sure that everyone was suitably cowed, 'where we will make our peace with God and each other. Anyone who wants to fight can stay out here – excommunicated and excluded from our Lord's grace. And bear in mind that

He can read minds, so I recommend you abandon any thoughts of crafty vengeance once you are inside.'

'I am not going in there,' declared Paycock defiantly. His cronies inched away from him, lest it should be assumed that he spoke for them as well. 'Not to hear the *castle* chaplain preach.'

'You *cannot* go in,' said Ereswell. 'Not now you are excommunicated. You are not allowed.'

'He may join us,' countered John graciously. 'But the castle chaplain will not perform the ceremony, and nor will the parish priest. *I* shall do it. Does anyone object?'

No one did.

Despite the church's impressive size, it was still a crush to fit everyone inside, especially as no one wanted to use the south aisle. The Austins managed to persuade a few folk from the outlying villages to stand in it, but only because they did not understand the politics involved. Most of the congregation were crammed uncomfortably into the nave. There was a lot of jostling, which was not easy to prevent, and it was clear, despite John's dire warnings of what would happen to those who broke the peace, that trouble was not far below the surface.

The tension ratcheted up even further when the Lady deigned to arrive, still brushing cake crumbs from her clothes after spending a pleasant afternoon with friends. There was no hint of apology for keeping everyone waiting, and when her knights began to shove people out of the way so she could stand at the front, the town's resentment bubbled even more fiercely. It was a struggle for the Austins to keep the hotheads from both sides in line.

'I should help the wounded,' murmured Bartholomew, aware that there was a distressingly large number of them lying on the recently abandoned battlefield, and that Grym had last been seen driving a cart towards Kedyngton as fast as his horses could pull it.

'No,' hissed Michael, grabbing his arm. 'It is too dangerous for you to wander off alone – I sense this business is far from over. For a start, Marishal is muttering to the Lady, doubtless telling her that a Michaelhouse man killed Roos. We must stay together.'

Bartholomew was unhappy about neglecting what he considered to be his moral duty, but he followed Michael to the vestry, where John was donning vestments, assisted by Langelee.

'What took you so long?' demanded the monk accusingly, closing the door so that their conversation would not be overheard by the milling crowd outside. 'God only knows how many people died or were wounded in that fracas. We expected you a lot sooner.'

'Because John has only just returned after spending the day looking for me and Weste,' explained Langelee defensively. 'Then more time was lost as we decided how best to stage an impressive entry.'

Michael gaped at him. 'I hardly think—'

'It was necessary, Brother,' interrupted John curtly. 'If we had just trotted up all muddy and ordinary, no one would have taken a blind bit of notice of us. Then the carnage would have been truly terrible.'

'Have either of you seen Anne?' asked Bartholomew, still far from certain that going ahead with the ceremony was the right thing to do. 'Or Nicholas? They have questions to answer.'

'I met Anne not long ago,' replied John. 'She was talking to Cambrug. He declared himself astonished to see her out of her cell, but his shock was not nearly as great as mine. I had rashly assumed that, as an anchorite, she was walled in permanently.'

'Cambrug will have mentioned that we asked him about the tunnel,' predicted Michael. 'So she will know the game is up. She will be halfway to London by now.'

'I shall go after her tomorrow,' promised Langelee.

'She will not escape, never fear. But you had better start this rite, John – your audience is growing restive.'

John brushed himself down, adjusted his stole, and opened the door. He nodded to four waiting friars, who lit enormous torches and began to sing at the tops of their voices. Heads promptly turned towards the little procession, and Bartholomew hoped the Austins would manage to produce enough of a spectacle to keep their congregation's attention long enough for tempers to cool.

'I cannot stop thinking about Roger,' he told Michael worriedly. 'He was Anne's first victim – the man who should have overseen the safe completion of the ceiling. But there are cracks, and I had the feeling that Cambrug was concerned about them, although he was not about to admit that there might be flaws in his design, of course . . .'

Michael regarded him in alarm. 'You think Anne killed Roger so that no one would know the thing is unstable? That she *wants* it to tumble down?'

'Why not? It will kill everyone who did not die in the battle she provoked. Including the Lady – the woman who devised the singularly cruel punishment for her old nurse.'

'But it will only kill everyone if it comes down tonight,' reasoned Langelee. 'Which is unlikely, or there would have been warning signs when the scaffolding was dismantled.'

'Perhaps there were,' said Bartholomew quietly. 'But Nicholas closed the church, so who would have seen them, other than a few labourers who can be bribed to keep their mouths shut?'

'Even if that is true,' countered Langelee, 'there is nothing to say that it will fall today. It might be years before—'

'No,' interrupted Bartholomew. 'It *will* be tonight, because I have a bad feeling that Anne is still here, so that she can make sure of it. Do you remember Grisel, the talking paroquet that Anne gave the Lady? It must have overheard her plotting and remembered certain words—'

'Words like *nuts*?' scoffed Michael. 'Really, Matt! We do not have time for—'

'It means that specific phrases were used often enough for Grisel to remember and mimic them,' Bartholomew forged on. 'They are not nautical expressions, as the Lady believes. We did not understand them, because Grisel does not recite the words in the same order every time.'

'I have no idea what you are talking about,' said Langelee impatiently.

'Anne did not say "down the van bring hold" or "hold the bring van down" in Grisel's hearing. She said "bring down the fan vault". She *does* mean to collapse the ceiling – presumably at the point in the ceremony where everyone shouts God save the Queen. Although as Her Majesty is not here, she will have to devise an alternative—'

'And you base all this on the testimony of a bird?' cried Langelee in disbelief.

'And what Anne said herself. Days ago, she told me that she was looking forward to tonight, as it would be "the culmination of all my labours". I thought she was taking the credit for the rebuilding, but that is not what she meant at all. She referred to her work in igniting a feud between two factions that have been friends for centuries.'

'I am not sure, Matt,' said Michael, shaking his head doubtfully. 'And what can we do about it anyway? If we try to clear the church, the fragile truce that John has established will be shattered, and we shall have a blood-bath for certain.'

'I know what we can do,' said Langelee suddenly. 'Stop Anne.'

'Yes,' said Bartholomew tightly. 'But how?'

'I know where she will be. Do you remember Nicholas taking us to the roof space when we first arrived? There was more scaffolding up there, which he said was no longer needed, as the fan vaulting was finished. But perhaps there was another reason why it was left.'

'Namely that the vaulting will not stay up without it,' finished Bartholomew. 'And that a few strategically knocked-out sections is all it will take to see the whole thing collapse.'

'So we had better hurry if we want to prevent a massacre,' said Langelee grimly.

It was not easy to reach the door to the roof, as the church was so tightly packed with folk. John was doing his best to put on an entertaining display, which included plenty of singing, abruptly clanging bells and forays into the nave with holy water, but the rite was necessarily in Latin, which few people understood, so it was difficult to keep their attention. The atmosphere was tense, and the dim lighting in the church encouraged nasty little skirmishes to break out.

'I hope your plan will not necessitate a lot of leaping over rafters,' whispered Michael worriedly, as they eased carefully through the throng. 'I am not very good at that sort of thing.'

They reached the door with relief, glad it was in the south aisle, which was empty except for a handful of bemused villagers and two children playing hopscotch on the flagstones.

The door was locked from the inside, but this was no problem for Langelee, who shattered the wood with a single kick. Michael and Bartholomew jerked away in alarm, sure the resulting crash would bring people running to see what was going on. Luckily, it coincided with a sudden swell of sound from the chancel, as John and his helpers broke into a noisy anthem. The children glanced towards the scholars, but their attention soon returned to their game.

'Albon?' came a querulous voice, and they turned to see the hermit emerge from the shadows. 'Is that you, back from the dead? To haunt us for not catching your killer?'

'No, it is just me, Jan,' said Langelee, hastily adjusting the cloak so that more black lining and less red wool showed. 'Listen – lives are at risk. Go home and pray that we can save them.'

Jan's face lit up. 'You want me to provide a miracle? Then I shall see what I can do – on condition that if I succeed, you will tell everyone about it. I am sick of being second best to Anne.'

'You will not be second best after tonight,' muttered Langelee. 'Whether you provide a miracle or not.'

He pulled out his letter-opener – the only weapon he had left from the arsenal he usually carried – and led the way up the stairs. Bartholomew followed, heart pounding, and Michael brought up the rear. The monk was soon breathing hard, and Bartholomew was glad that the Austins were singing a gusty *Gloria*, because otherwise all of Clare would have heard him panting. Then they reached the door at the top, and Bartholomew started forward urgently, afraid that Langelee would kick that open, too, thus warning Anne that they were coming. But it was unlocked, and they only had to push it to get inside.

The roof looked much the same as it had when Nicholas had showed it to them a few days before – a complex mesh of beams and struts. The only difference was that the scaffolding supporting the ceiling had since been dismantled. Or mostly dismantled. The few sections that were left were badly buckled, suggesting that they alone were supporting the immense weight of the stone domes below – something they were never intended to do.

'Filling the cracks with glue would have been be a waste of time,' whispered Langelee. 'There is a serious structural weakness here.'

'And Anne and Nicholas *do* mean to bring the whole thing down,' Bartholomew whispered back. 'Because there they are.'

He nodded to where a lamp glowed dimly some distance away. It was roughly where the nave met the chancel, and the stone rood screen would be directly beneath. Two shapes were hunched over it, one large and the other small: Nicholas and Anne, watching the ceremony through one of the larger fissures.

'Wait here,' ordered Langelee. 'I will see if I can get a better look.'

He began to clamber across the timbers towards them, moving with impressive agility for a man his size. Bartholomew held his breath, partly from fear that Langelee would be seen by the huddling pair, but also that he might dislodge some critical joist and the ceiling would fall anyway.

'Anne is holding a mallet,' the Master reported a few moments later, arriving back as silently as he had left. 'I think she aims to clout that big central truss with it when the time is right.'

Bartholomew peered forward, and saw that the strut in question had been dislodged from its moorings, so that one sharp blow would knock it away completely. Then its weight would be added to the already vulnerable ceiling, and a major collapse would be all but inevitable.

'What shall we do?' he gulped, struggling to quell his rising horror. 'Try to reason with them? I doubt Anne will listen, but Nicholas might.'

'He will not,' predicted Michael. 'Not as long as she

is there to tell him what to think – just as she has been doing all along.'

'What, then? We cannot just crawl over there and lay hold of them. We might reach one undetected, but then the other will belt the truss and that will be that.'

Langelee brandished his letter-opener. 'I can disarm one by lobbing this, but not both. Do either of you have a weapon? A surgical blade will do.'

But Bartholomew had left his medical bag in the vestry, thinking it would be in the way when he was in the roof, while Michael rarely carried knives of any description. Langelee scowled his disbelief that the two of them should have set out on such a venture without arming themselves first, conveniently overlooking the fact that he too had failed in that respect.

'Then I shall immobilise one with a flying dagger, while you two leap on the other,' he determined. 'Agreed?'

'No,' hissed Bartholomew, knowing the monk was physically incapable of the stealth required for such a mission. 'I will go. Michael can stay here and relay a message: if I can come within grabbing distance of Anne, I will raise my left hand, and he will signal that you are to aim at Nicholas; if I raise my right hand—'

'I am to stab Anne,' finished Langelee. 'Fair enough. What can possibly go wrong?'

To Bartholomew, the rafter along which he inched seemed far too thin to bear his weight. Worse, the cracks in the stone domes seemed much bigger now – large enough for him to see into the nave below. He stopped for a moment and peered down. He was directly above the rood screen. On one side, John strove valiantly to entertain his restless congregation, while on the other was a heaving mass of heads. He thought he could see the Lady's among them, surrounded by her courtiers. He dragged his eyes away from the dizzying sight, and resumed his journey.

Halfway along the beam was a thick post, supporting the roof above. Unfortunately, there was no way around it – other than stepping out on to one of the domes, which might then collapse under his weight. He shot Michael a stricken glance. The monk understood his dilemma at once, and made a vigorous pointing movement with his finger, indicating that Bartholomew was to look above his head.

He saw immediately what Michael wanted him to do – jump up to a convenient strut and swing himself around the post by his arms. It would be a dangerous manoeuvre at the best of times, let alone when failure would mean him landing hard on the ceiling, precipitating him and tons of stone down on to the people below. Moreover, the rood screen had a lot of pinnacles. He would almost certainly end up impaled on one, which would be a terrible way to die.

He glanced at Michael again, and saw the monk urging him to hurry. He supposed Langelee was in place, waiting for the signal to attack. He looked at Anne and Nicholas just a few feet away from him, and felt his resolve strengthen. Perhaps he would fall, but at least he could die in the knowledge that he had done his best to thwart their horrible plot. He jumped.

The strut creaked ominously, and there was a moment when he thought his fingers would not hold him. But he managed to shift his grip, and felt himself secure enough to throw one hand forward. It worked, so he did the same with the other. And then he was past the obstruction. He let himself drop, landing with a soft thump on the other side of the beam, going down on one knee for better balance. It put him closer to one of the cracks, allowing him to see more of the nave below – and the folk who had no idea of the danger they were in.

He stood on unsteady legs, and saw with horror that Nicholas was no longer there. He looked around wildly.

Where had the vicar gone? Had Langelee already deployed his blade? But he could not see the Master either – only Michael, who was no more than an unmoving shadow by the door. But Anne had not hit the scaffolding yet, and if he could just wrest the mallet from her . . .

She glanced up as he stepped forward, and her hand tightened around the mallet, warning him against coming any closer.

'Oh, it is you,' she said flatly. She wore a kirtle and cloak that Margery must have given her, as both were rose-coloured. 'I was hoping for Marishal or one of the Austins. I was looking forward to showing them that they were beaten.'

'Where is Nicholas?'

Anne smiled nastily. 'There are *two* weak points in this ceiling – Roger was kind enough to identify them for me when he caught me up here one day – and I am not a woman to leave anything to chance. Nicholas is at the other, waiting to act on my command.'

Bartholomew raised his left hand, then pushed Nicholas from his mind, trusting that Langelee would do what he had promised. He turned all his attention to Anne, ready for the moment when her defences were lowered, so that he could dart forward and rip the mallet away from her.

'Do not think you can stop me,' she told him smugly. 'When I wave to Nicholas, two fan vaults will collapse simultaneously. The chances are that they will bring down the rest of the ceiling as well, after which we shall clamber to safety. You, of course, will fall with the stone.'

It was then that Bartholomew saw she wore a harness, which would prevent her from toppling into the abyss, should she lose her footing.

'It will not work,' lied Bartholomew. 'You can hit the scaffolding all you like, but nothing will happen.'

'Roger said it would, and I trust his opinion more than

404

yours. No, do not inch towards me! Stay back, or I shall do it now.'

Bartholomew could see she meant it. He took a step away, hoping that Langelee had already dealt with Nicholas, and would be able to sneak up behind Anne and disable her as well. All he had to do was keep her talking until the Master could oblige. Slowly and deliberately, so there could be no misunderstanding, he raised his right hand, hoping that Michael would understand.

'But you killed Roger,' he said, to prevent her from asking what he was doing.

'Yes, when he threatened to tell everyone that the ceiling was unsafe. I wanted it kept secret, for obvious reasons.'

'But your friends are below us,' blurted Bartholomew desperately. 'Children you nursed, girls you saved from—'

'Yes! And do you know how many of them spoke up for me when I needed them? Two – Ella and Thomas. Margery tried to take up where I left off, although she was never very successful. Herbs do not work nearly as well as a hook.'

'But people love you,' persisted Bartholomew. 'They bring you gifts and seek your advice. You cannot betray their trust by crushing them all!'

'Oh, they flocked to me when I declared myself holy,' she hissed malevolently. 'But by then it was too late. I was walled up and they had earned my enmity. *All* of them.'

'Including Bonde?' Bartholomew raised his right hand again, more urgently this time. 'He did your bidding, but was repaid for his loyalty with a cup of hemlock.'

'Hemlock,' mused Anne. 'A very useful herb, although annoyingly slow to act. And before you ask – yes, I used it on Wisbech, Skynere and Godeston, too. Killing them was easy.'

'As easy as Talmach and Albon? I know you stabbed

405

Talmach after he fell from his horse, while Albon died when you lobbed a stone at him. Thomas heard him shout "you" in surprise.'

'Not me – Bonde, although on my orders. I told him to lie low after Roos died, lest your clever monk probed matters that did not concern him.' She grimaced. 'And I could have added him, you, Langelee and Marishal to my tally if Thomas had not opened the kitchen sluices. I shall have stern words with that boy before I leave.'

'It was not you who locked us in the cistern,' countered Bartholomew. 'You might leave your cell at night, but you would never risk it in broad daylight.'

Anne regarded him in disdain. 'You think I cannot move undetected in a place that was my home for thirty-seven years? Pah! What a fool you are.'

'And all to stir up hatred between the town and the castle?'

Bartholomew raised his right hand a third time, waving it frantically. He risked a glance at Michael, but the monk was nowhere to be seen. What was going on?

'It worked,' said Anne smugly, 'and after today, there will never be peace again. How dare they misuse me! I saved countless girls and their families from disgrace, but how was I rewarded? With a fate worse than death – it took me less than a week to know that life as an anchoress would be a living Hell.'

'Please,' begged Bartholomew, watching her fingers tighten around the mallet. 'It is not—'

'Do you hear?' she asked, cocking her head suddenly. 'Everyone is about to be asked to shout God save the Queen. It is time. Now, Nicholas! *Now!*'

There was nothing Bartholomew could do but watch as Anne gave the scaffolding a tremendous clout with the mallet. At the same time, there was a flicker of movement further down the roof. His stomach lurched in horror.

It was Nicholas, swinging at the second weak spot. Langelee had failed! He lunged towards Anne, but it was too late. There was a sinister creak, and a lump of ceiling simply dropped away.

Appalled, he watched it fall. It landed with a tremendous crash, and dust billowed everywhere. He glanced at Anne, and saw rage and disappointment in her face – a much smaller piece than she had anticipated had come adrift, and it had landed on the rood screen, where no one was standing. Meanwhile, nothing at all had happened to Nicholas's section.

Furiously, Anne stood and prepared to jump on the unstable dome, to collapse it with her own weight. Bartholomew sprang towards her but she jigged away, and as she did, she lost her footing. She screamed as she disappeared through the hole. The harness prevented her from falling to her death, but she had been overly generous with the amount of line she thought she would need, and she plummeted twenty feet before she was jerked savagely to a halt.

'It is Margery Marishal!' yelled Richard the watchman, seeing the rose-coloured costume and drawing his own conclusions. 'Come to haunt us for quarrelling. She hated discord.'

The harness was poorly designed, and the jolt had broken some of Anne's ribs. She was in pain, moaning pitifully for Nicholas to help her.

'She is calling for the priest,' blurted Ereswell. 'Someone fetch him, quickly! I cannot bear to hear that saintly lady wailing in such torment.'

At that point, Langelee joined Bartholomew on the beam, wiping a bloodstained blade on his sleeve: Nicholas was no longer a problem. The Master put the letter-opener away carefully, then reached down to help Bartholomew pull Anne to safety. As he did so, Albon's cloak slipped forward in all its scarlet glory.

'And *that* is the ghost of Sir William,' shouted Nuport, whipping out his sword. 'Wearing his battle gear, which means he wants us to fight.'

Even as Langelee tugged the offending garment out of sight, Michael swung into action. He pulled the piece of purple silk from his scrip and stuffed it through one of the cracks. The material was so light that it took an age to waft downwards, drawing every eye in the church towards it. It provided ample time for him to scramble towards Langelee and hiss an urgent instruction.

'I am the spirit of Godeston,' the Master boomed, in the very plausible imitation of the Mayor that had so amused Bartholomew a few days earlier. 'I command you to go home. To stay is to die.'

There was a murmur of consternation and the definite beginnings of a move towards the doors. Immediately, the Austins hastened to open them and usher folk outside. Unfortunately, Nuport had other ideas.

'No – we should fight,' he yelled. 'Death to all who—'

The words died in his throat when Anne's harness burst open, leaving Bartholomew and Langelee hauling on an empty rope. Both toppled backwards, while she dropped down to the rood screen below. There was a terrible scream, and when Bartholomew could bring himself to look, he saw she was impaled on one of the pinnacles. She hung there, her head covered by the rose-coloured hood, directly above the carving of the Blessed Virgin with Margery's face.

Anne had just enough dying strength to raise one arm and point. It was impossible to know what she was trying to convey, and it was almost certainly chance that caused her finger to wag in Nuport's direction, but the gesture achieved what words could not.

'Oh, Christ!' the squire gulped. 'She has me in her sights. Out of the way! Let me *past*!'

'Go home and lock your doors,' bellowed John, as the squire's panicky flight caused others to follow. 'And keep them locked, on peril of your souls. There are a great many restless ghosts abroad tonight.'

'Well, that is one way to clear a church,' remarked Langelee, watching as the place emptied quicker than he would have thought possible. 'Thank God for gullible minds!'

# EPILOGUE

### *Three days later*

Although it meant missing the beginning of term, Bartholomew refused to leave Grym – back from Kedyngton now the danger was over – alone to deal with the aftermath of Anne's grand plan to avenge herself on Clare. He stayed, working day and night to help those who had been wounded, both in the fight and in the stampede to escape from the church afterwards. All the while, Michael, Langelee and the Austins comforted the dying and buried the dead. Eventually, the physician felt he had done all he could, and traipsed to the priory to tell his friends that he was ready to go home.

He found them in the refectory, counting the donations that they had managed to scrape together. The largest was from Ereswell, and was a reward for ridding him of Lichet. Michael had wanted to refuse it, but it was a *very* generous sum. The second-largest was five marks from the Lady, as Katrina had deemed the paroquets cured. The total was not enough to save Michaelhouse permanently, but it would keep the wolf from the door for a few more weeks.

Bartholomew slumped on the bench next to them and accepted a cup of ale. For a while, all was silent except for the clink of coins. Then Prior John and Weste joined them, the latter wearing the cloak that denoted his new post – vicar of the parish church.

'I still cannot believe that the people of Clare were so credulous,' said Bartholomew, his thoughts returning again to the plot that had so nearly succeeded. 'How could they believe that the ghosts of Albon, Godeston and Margery had come to punish the unrighteous?'

'Because the light was poor, bits of the ceiling had just fallen down, and most were still unsettled by the skirmish,' replied John. He smiled. 'At least, that is the practical explanation. I am more inclined to thank God for a miracle.'

Bartholomew glanced at Langelee. 'What does the hermit think?'

'Oh, that there was indeed a miracle,' replied Langelee, 'and that his prayers brought it about. He claims all the credit for keeping the ceiling intact until everyone had escaped, and he is now more popular than Anne ever was. Moreover, there has been no trouble since, which is another miracle as far as I am concerned.'

'It is a pity the rest of the ceiling collapsed the following day, though,' sighed John, 'because it took the new clerestory with it. The top half of the church will have to be rebuilt – again.'

'And it will,' said Vicar Weste, 'although not with fan vaulting designed by Cambrug. The town cannot afford it, and the castle has agreed to stay out of parish affairs from now on. Of course, it was Anne who encouraged the Lady to meddle, and to build that unpopular south aisle.'

'The south aisle that will provide the town with a temporary place of worship while the nave is out of action,' said John. 'It will serve a valuable function for many months to come – much better than having to use the churchyard.'

'And peace reigns in our town again,' finished Weste happily.

'It will not last,' predicted Michael. 'You agreed not to excommunicate the squires in exchange for an abject apology, and they are suitably chastened. But their mortification will wear off, and they will soon turn bored and vicious again.'

'Nuport will not,' said Bartholomew soberly. 'He died

this morning, from wounds sustained in the stampede to escape Margery's ghost.'

'And the rest will not be here,' said John. 'Clare is too small for such an unruly horde, so Langelee has offered to take them to France.'

'I have a hankering to see the place again,' explained Langelee, 'and they will fare better with me than with poor old Albon.'

'They will,' agreed Bartholomew. 'But are you sure you want to go?'

Langelee nodded. 'I have my own penance to make, and the King's army will be a lot more enjoyable than a pilgrimage. Peace will be declared in a few weeks, but His Majesty will still need men to help him keep the concessions he has won, so there will be plenty for me to do. Besides, academia has been fun, but I am ready for a new challenge.'

'You will be missed,' said Bartholomew sincerely, watching Weste and John leave, both sensing that this was a discussion they did not need to hear.

'I know,' said Langelee. 'But it will not be for ever, and I shall come back to Michaelhouse eventually. Until then, you can put my stipend in the College coffers. It will help a little, along with these donations.'

'Not to mention the Lady's hundred marks,' said Michael smugly, and upended a heavy purse on the table. Coins spilled from it and lay in a gleaming pile.

'How in God's name did you manage that?' gasped Langelee, gazing at him in disbelief.

Michael smiled haughtily. 'By telling her who killed Margery.'

'Did you tell her who killed Roos, too?' asked Langelee uneasily. 'Marishal will not blab – he promised to keep quiet on condition that I take Thomas and Ella to France when I go. But I thought you had agreed to keep my role in the affair quiet. For Michaelhouse's sake.'

'I gave her the truth,' replied Michael. 'Namely, that Roos stabbed Margery in a fit of pique, and was mortally wounded in the struggle that followed. The Lady was so relieved to put the matter behind her that she virtually threw the money at me.'

Bartholomew was more concerned with the arrangement that Langelee had made with the steward. 'You cannot take Ella to war. *She* is not a squire.'

Langelee waved a dismissive hand. 'Neither twin will go to war. I will drop them off in Paris, along with the pregnant Isabel Morley and poor scarred Suzanne de Nekton. The four of them plan to settle there together.'

'But Thomas is not free to go off and live in another country,' said Michael. 'The stewardship of Clare is hereditary – he will have to stay here and do his duty.'

'Not if Marishal has other children,' explained Langelee. 'And he will take a new wife at the end of the year. Katrina de Haliwell offered to do the honors and he has accepted.'

Bartholomew laughed. 'Well, she did say she wanted a secure future, and she does not care who provides it. Marishal will suit her perfectly – he will be busy with the Lady's business most of the time, leaving her free to do as she pleases. She must be delighted with her good fortune.'

'Poor Margery,' sighed Michael. 'Of all the victims in this sorry tale, she is the one who grieves me most. She was a good woman, and it is just that her killer was dispatched in his turn.'

'I am glad you feel that way,' said Langelee, 'because it means you might say a few Masses for me. None for Anne, though. If we include all the people who died in the fight, she claimed twenty-three lives in the end, not to mention some serious injuries. She is doubtless perched on the Devil's shoulder as we speak, furious that she did not kill ten times that number.'

'And Nicholas will be next to her,' added Michael. 'I

knew from the moment I set eyes on him that he was a rogue, and I was right. You two should have listened to me.'

'We should,' agreed Langelee. 'Because he was a thief as well as an accomplice to murder. We found his cart in the woods today, loaded up with all the church's silver.'

Michael turned to Bartholomew. 'Please tell us what Badew whispered before he died. Was it the secret he came here to share? The one he refused to divulge as long as the Lady is alive?'

'I believe so,' replied Bartholomew. 'But it was not a secret, it was an accusation – one final, vicious attempt to hurt her when she was not in a position to defend herself. He aimed to tarnish her memory, in the hope that Clare Hall would rename itself as Badew Hall. It was shabby and sly, but it might have worked.'

'And this accusation entails what, exactly?' asked Michael keenly.

But Bartholomew shook his head. 'It cannot be true, so what is the point of making it public? It is best that such a distasteful allegation dies with him.'

'Perhaps,' said Michael, determining to wheedle it out of him later. 'Yet I cannot say I am looking forward to the journey home – not carrying all this money. Freburn will be delighted if he happens across us, but my ears will not.'

'Freburn will not bother us,' declared Langelee confidently, then made an impatient sound at the back of his throat when Michael started to ask what made him so sure. '*Think*, Brother. Who else chopped off someone's ears recently?'

'Nuport? You think he was masquerading as Freburn? I do not believe you!'

'Well, you should, because he told me so himself. Bartholomew asked me to carry him to Grym's house for medical treatment, and the rogue mistook me for Albon

415

in my nice new cloak – he bleated a confession before I could stop him.'

'No,' said Michael, shaking his head. 'This cannot be true. Roos would have recognised him when he was attacked after the last council meeting.'

'Nuport was not a total fool – he wore a mask to hide his face. Apparently, the real Simon Freburn and his sons were hanged months ago, but Nuport started a rumour that they were alive and in this area, which allowed him to terrorise travellers as he pleased. He did it for the riches, and because inflicting pain gave him pleasure.'

'Then some of his cronies helped him do it,' said Bartholomew. 'Because "Freburn" was always accompanied by his "sons". And you are about to take them to France. What if they decide they like the look of *your* ears?'

'Then they will lose their own,' shrugged Langelee, unperturbed. 'But they are different lads now they are away from Nuport's malign influence, and I should like to give them a chance to make something decent of themselves. You will see what I mean on the way to Cambridge.'

'They will escort us there?' asked Michael uneasily.

Langelee nodded. 'To make sure you and the money arrive safely, and so that Suzanne can spend a few days with Matilde, learning how to disguise scars. Besides, I must tender my resignation as Master properly, or our colleagues will speculate.'

And if they did, even their wildest imaginings would not come close to the truth, thought Bartholomew wryly. Then he groaned as an unpleasant thought occurred to him.

'Oh, Lord! There will have to be an election.'

'Will you stand, Brother?' asked Langelee.

'No, of course not,' retorted Michael. 'I shall tell the others that I am taking the post, and they will accept my offer with suitable gratitude. I should have done it years ago, because I am sure I can use my University connections to secure Michaelhouse a better future.'

'The College will thrive with you in charge,' predicted Langelee, gripping his shoulder in comradely affection. 'And Matilde will make a good wife for Bartholomew. He is a lucky man.'

'Yes, I believe I am,' said Bartholomew. He realised he was looking forward to seeing Matilde again, and perhaps Langelee had a point about it being time for something different. But he still had one term left, and the longer he stayed in Clare, the more of it would be lost. He stood abruptly.

'Where are you going?' asked Michael, who still had a full cup of wine.

'Cambridge,' replied Bartholomew. 'Where we belong.'


*Clare, seven months later (November 1360)*

The Lady was dying. She felt she had lived a godly life, and had no regrets. Except one.

She had married three times for duty, and then she had fallen in love. Unfortunately, her beau already had a wife, and their unguarded passion had almost been her undoing. Fortunately, Anne had been on hand to prevent the loss of her good name and everything she had held dear.

The Lady sighed when she thought about the old nurse. If only Anne had chosen somewhere other than Grisel's room for Suzanne de Nekton to recover. Then the scandal would never have broken, the Austins would not have been so horrified, and Suzanne's father would not have made such a fuss. Of course, once the tale was public, the Lady had had no choice but to condemn Anne, which had precipitated the whole bloody business – Anne's horrible revenge, the murders, the loss of the church's roof, and the deaths in the fighting.

She pondered the day when Anne had come with her hook. *Had* Roos been hiding behind the tapestry, as he had always claimed? She shuddered. It did not bear thinking about – that horrid, salacious little man watching Anne work her magic. She wished she had known he was there, as she would have risen up and plunged a dagger into his black heart herself.

Roos had been quick to come to her afterwards, telling her that he could be useful if she made it worth his while. And so she had. She had given him a place on her council, paid him handsomely for his continued silence, and pretended that she was interested in the reports he gave her about Badew and the University. But the truth was that every time she saw him, she itched to tear out his scheming, rapacious tongue.

She had remarked to Bonde once that Roos's presence was unwelcome, and the henchman had offered to relieve her of the problem permanently. She had accepted with relief, but Bonde had made a mistake and killed an innocent instead. Terrified that the truth would come out if the matter went to trial, she had spent a fortune on bribes for the judge – which had done nothing for her reputation as a just, God-fearing woman. And Roos had lived on, blithely oblivious of the danger he had been in.

She stared into the darkness. Yet there had always been small inconsistencies in what Roos claimed to have seen, and she had suspected for years that he had lied about being in the chamber himself – that it had actually been someone else watching. But no other blackmailer had come to demand favours from her, so she could only assume that either Roos had killed him, or they had reached an agreement to share Roos's ill-gotten gains.

She sighed. Of course, she had done poor Margery a grave disservice by condemning her to Roos's pawing hands all those years, but it could not be helped. Besides, she knew why Margery wore the cheap little ring that Roos had given her, and why the twins had Roos's golden hair. Margery had only given herself to the man once, but she had been burdened with the consequences for the rest of her unhappy life. The ring had been her penance, a constant reminder of why Roos's advances had to be tolerated – she dared not repel him too harshly, lest he then ran to her husband with the tale of her betrayal.

The Lady glanced at the man who lay next to her, sleeping peacefully and blissfully unaware that her life was slipping away. Robert Marishal – the only man she had ever truly loved. He would marry Katrina the next day, and although he swore that nothing would change, the Lady knew it would. Katrina was not kind, unsuspecting Margery, and would notice her new husband slipping away with suspicious regularity. The Lady was not about to risk her good name now – not after all the trouble she had taken to keep it pure and free from scandal.

Was it coincidence that she would die on the last night that she and Marishal would ever spend together? She closed her eyes and sighed. Probably not.

# HISTORICAL NOTE

Richard de Badew founded University Hall in 1326, but he was not a wealthy man, and his College soon fell into financial difficulties. Within two years, its scholars approached the wealthy Elizabeth de Burgh, begging for help. She responded by giving them a church and the income it would generate. It seems she was willing to do more, but only if Badew relinquished all claim on the place. The Fellows were keen for this to happen, so charters were drawn up in 1338, but Badew delayed signing the necessary quit-claim until 28 March 1346, almost certainly for no reason other than pure bloody-mindedness. Once the quit-claim was executed, University Hall became known as Clare Hall (although it is now Clare College, and a new Clare Hall was founded in 1966). Two of its first Fellows were John Donwich and John Pulham.

Most of what is known of Badew comes from mentions of him in various legal documents, which show that he was involved in several quarrels with younger colleagues – eight lawsuits simultaneously at one point, which must have eaten away at his personal finances and perhaps explain why he was unable to finance University Hall properly. He and Saer de Roos were sued by a woman named Joan de Marishal in 1316, while Henry Harweden, a crony of Badew's and Chancellor of the University himself, was deposed amid accusations of assault and corruption.

Elizabeth de Burgh liked to be called the Lady of Clare. She was widowed three times before she was thirty, then took a vow of chastity, which effectively prevented her from being married off to anyone else – and she was a good catch, given that she was a very wealthy lady. She owned several large estates, but her seat of power was the castle in Clare, the remains of which still stand in the lovely country park today.

Some of her household accounts survive, and provide a fascinating glimpse into the practical side of running a large medieval household. She lived lavishly, and her 'court' was often graced with royal and noble visitors. Her steward was Robert Marishal (or Robert the Marshal), who married Margery and had two children, Thomas and Elizabeth. Marishal is mentioned in the Lady's will, but Margery is not, suggesting that she had predeceased her mistress. It has been suggested that Marishal was related in some way to Badew. The accounts suggest that Marishal liked to go hawking, a pastime usually reserved for the nobility, indicating that he was rather more than just a retainer.

Many of the characters in *The Habit of Murder* are based on names in the Lady's will – Adam the baker, Richard the watchman, Sir William Albon, Katrina de Haliwell, Suzanne de Nekton, Isabel Morley, William Talmach, Peter de Ereswell, Philip de Jevan, Charer the coachman, Justin the forester and John the hermit (called Jan here to avoid too many Johns). Also mentioned is 'Master' Philip Lichet, who was probably a clerk or a secretary, and Anne de Lexham the anchorite. Anchorites were men and women who elected to withdraw from secular society, often taking up residence in small, permanently enclosed cells attached to churches. The practice was popular in the Middle Ages, and some of their anchorholds survive today, although there is no trace of Anne's.

John de Heselbech and Robert de Wisbech were castle chaplains in the 1360s. They were friars from Clare's Austin Priory, and were 'lent' to the Lady in exchange for a generous donation to the convent's coffers. The

Prior at this time may have been a man named John, and there was a cofferer named John de Weste, although he was never an illustrator of books.

Grisel, Blanchard and Morel were horses in the Lady's stables, but household accounts show that she did own exotic birds as well – perhaps parakeets or parrots – and there are entries made for the purchase of almonds for them.

Stephen Bonde was another member of the Lady's retinue. He was accused of murder, but she seems to have secured his acquittal, even though it appears that he was guilty. Simon Freburn and his sons were also criminals, notorious as robbers and thieves.

Another scandalous crime was committed in the 1380s by Sir Thomas Nuport, who with Thomas Marishal, John Mull and several others broke the sanctuary of the church and assaulted one John de Quintone. It seems that Quintone stole some of Nuport's property, then fled to the church for sanctuary. Nuport and his friends dragged him out and cut off his ears. Afterwards, under threat of excommunication, the culprits were obliged to walk barefoot through the town and beg forgiveness.

Records tell of other people who lived in Clare at this time. They include Nicholas de Lydgate, who was vicar of Sts Peter and Paul from 1350 until 1361. There was a bailiff named William Paycock, and other local worthies were Hugh de Godeston, Robert Skynere and John Grym, barber of Rutten Row.

The innovative fan vaulting in the cloisters at Gloucester Abbey (now Gloucester Cathedral) is attributed to Thomas de Cambrug (or Thomas of Cambridge), who installed it between 1351 and 1364. When he had finished, he went to Hereford Cathedral, where he built the chapter house. He never worked in Clare, although the parish church was rebuilt in the fourteenth century. A mason named Roger is mentioned in the Lady's will.

And finally, Ralph de Langelee was Master of Michaelhouse until 1361, after which Michael de Causton appears in the records.